PRAISE FOR THE SIRANTHA JAX NOVELS

Endgame

"I strongly recommend this series to anyone who enjoys good sci-fi with strong female characters who are a little flawed and yet keep ticking out of sheer tenacity." —*Rabid Reader*

"Infusing love and war together to make a pulse-pounding, heartbreaking read, the Sirantha Jax series . . . will remain on my keeper shelf for some time."
—*Under the Covers Book Blog*

"Fast-paced and filled with action, Ann Aguirre makes it clear that war is vicious, bloody, and gory as everyone, including the ethical heroine (and readers), feels they entered hell."
—*Genre Go Round Reviews*

Aftermath

"Highly satisfying . . . *Aftermath* has all of the heart, soul, adventure, and sense of wonder that you could ask for in a character-driven series like this." —*SF Site*

"Chock-full of adventure . . . It's tautly written with a surprise around every corner." —*All About Romance*

"Aguirre's writing is tight, and the characters have plenty of depth . . . [She] is quickly becoming one of my favorite writers, and *Aftermath* is a big reason why." —*ScienceFiction.com*

"Ann Aguirre is an amazing storyteller." —*Smexy Books*

"Aguirre has created a fleshed-out futuristic world and, yes, a strong heroine to lead us through it." —*Giraffe Days*

"This is a great science fiction tale in a strong series . . . Anyone who visits the Ann Aguirre universe knows [it] is an entertaining, exciting realm." —*Midwest Book Review*

continued . . .

Killbox

"Fraught with action, farewells, and sorrow, fans of this series won't be able to put *Killbox* down . . . Ms. Aguirre has left the reader hanging with a finish that guarantees the reader will be on pins and needles waiting for the next installment."

—*Fresh Fiction*

"Rife with huge, tender emotions, rough anguish that makes me cry, and moments, snatches of joy, that make all of that anguish worthwhile . . . This is the kind of story that makes the emotional roller coaster of reading so appealing."

—*Lurv a la Mode*

"Oh wow! I literally inhaled this book, and I could not put it down . . . An epic space opera . . . Five out of five stars!"

—*The Book Pushers*

Doubleblind

"The world-building was not only tight but excellent. Ms. Aguirre weaves some amazing cultural, environmental, and physical details into the Ithtorian world that I found fascinating, and it is what made this book stand out for me."

—*Impressions of a Reader*

"One of my favorite aspects of this series is Jax. I love her as a heroine, and this book really allows Jax to shine."

—*Smexy Books*

"What marks this series as excellent is the complexity of character . . . Plus, there's the fact that Ann Aguirre tells a good story, plain and simple . . . *Doubleblind* was a fantastic installment in the series, and, while being immensely satisfying, it still left me wanting more in the best possible way."

—*Tempting Persephone*

Wanderlust

Grimspace

PERDITION

THE DRED CHRONICLES

ANN AGUIRRE

ACE BOOKS, NEW YORK

THE BERKLEY PUBLISHING GROUP
Published by the Penguin Group
Penguin Group (USA)
375 Hudson Street, New York, New York 10014, USA

USA | Canada | UK | Ireland | Australia | New Zealand | India | South Africa | China

Penguin Books Ltd., Registered Offices: 80 Strand, London WC2R 0RL, England
For more information about the Penguin Group, visit penguin.com.

PERDITION

An Ace Book / published by arrangement with the author

Ace Books are published by The Berkley Publishing Group.
ACE and the "A" design are trademarks of Penguin Group (USA).

For information, address: The Berkley Publishing Group,
a division of Penguin Group (USA),
375 Hudson Street, New York, New York 10014.

ISBN: 978-0-425-25811-8

PUBLISHING HISTORY
Ace mass-market edition / September 2013

PRINTED IN THE UNITED STATES OF AMERICA

10 9 8 7 6 5 4 3 2

Cover art by Scott M. Fischer.
Cover design by Lesley Worrell.
Interior text design by Kelly Lipovich.

ALWAYS LEARNING   **PEARSON**

To those who know why the caged bird sings

Acknowledgments

The person who helped most with this book is Bree Bridges. I mention her a lot because she's the first person I turn to when I have a plot problem or I can't figure something out. She's so smart that she can usually tell me in seconds where I went wrong or what would fix the book. So thanks, Bree. Thanks to Lauren Dane for always listening to me, no matter what I'm saying. And thanks to Donna Herren for always being willing to cackle maniacally with me. Thanks to Megan Hart for making me laugh and understanding . . . everything. Thanks to Viv Arend for all the love.

Next I thank Laura Bradford, who sells all my books and is a wonderful agent and friend. Anne Sowards has been a joy to work with, so I appreciate her as well. I can't believe it's been six years! Thanks also to the team at Penguin for creating such wonderful books.

Thanks to the Loop That Shall Not Be Named. You're like the Sisterhood of the Traveling Pants times five, except it's a different *P* word. I cherish and appreciate your boldness and bravery, your humor, your innovation and creativity, and your indomitable spirits. Just knowing you all makes me better.

Much love to my family, who never complains, no matter how busy I am. You make it possible for me to live my dreams, and I adore you.

Finally, thank you to my readers. You humble and gladden me when you write, so keep in touch. I'm at ann .aguirre@gmail.com.

◁ 1 ▷

The Dread Queen

Pain was a flower.

It began with crimson petals, threaded white, and ended with a black, black heart. *Like mine.* Since she'd taken Queensland half a turn ago, she had perfected the art of how much a captive could take before he broke. Some men ate agony like candy, while others were fragile as a bird's bones.

Dred watched as her men carved lines into the intruder's skin. "It doesn't have to go down like this, Eli. Tell me why you're really here. Then defect from Grigor, swear to me, and I'll let you serve."

That was bullshit. Since they were all liars, murderers, and thieves, it wasn't as if she could trust Eli's word should he give it. She might convince him of her sincerity, however, and learn something about her enemies' intentions. The deception didn't trouble her. For all she knew, this man's mission was to stick a silent knife in her kidney.

"Never," Eli gasped, red-tinged sweat dripping down his arms. "You don't understand. Grigor will kill me. He'll hunt me down."

Fear wins over self-preservation.

"Not inside my territory," Dred said.

She leapt down from the throne cobbled together from scrap metal and rusty chains. It was an affectation, but one that amused her. Between the braids, the tattoos, and the leather rumored to be human skin, men found it hard to meet her gaze. Eli was no exception; Tameron had sold her legend completely. Some of it was bullshit, of course.

"You can't keep me safe," he whispered. "Grigor has eyes everywhere."

"That's impressive cowardice." When she got within kicking distance, Eli flinched and shielded his face. Dred laughed softly. "You think I can't break your teeth through those arms?"

"I know you can," he whispered.

"Good. Now tell me why you're inside my border."

"I was scavenging on Grigor's orders. I didn't know I'd crossed!"

Since there were checkpoints and sentries posted anywhere territories overlapped, that was impossible. The only way Eli could be here was if he'd intentionally come through the ducts or sought some other secret way through her security. And there was no innocent reason he'd have done that, especially not on Grigor's orders.

"Keep lying to me, and you won't last the hour."

"Kill him," Einar advised.

The man holding the prisoner's right arm was a tall, muscular blond with hair that looked like he hacked it off with a rusty knife. Scars covered Einar from head to toe; his lip pulled sideways from a nasty slash to his face, and he was a missing an earlobe. Since he bathed, Einar was also one of the best catches in Perdition, their private name for the hellhole the Conglomerate had chosen to house its worst offenders.

Dred circled thoughtfully. Each time she gave the order, it got easier, like she lost a little more of her soul. She couldn't have him learning her defensive strategies or finding her hidden weapons caches, then reporting to Grigor. Each time there was an incursion, she had to assume the worst and react accordingly. Things had been unsettled lately, and both Grigor and Priest were daring more, pressing harder from each side.

She jerked a nod at Einar. "Do it."

"No, pl—" The giant snapped the prisoner's neck before he finished begging for his life.

"I suspect he was a spy," Tameron said. "You couldn't let him live."

Tam was a slight, dark-skinned male, younger than Dred, but it was impossible to say how much. She didn't ask people how old they were, where they were from, or what they'd done to get tossed in here. None of that mattered inside Perdition. It only mattered how hard you'd fight to stay alive. He was also invaluable in keeping her regime on track; he supplied insights about her enemies and quiet information about the mood in Queensland, which was what the men called her territory.

The prison ship was the brainchild of some bright-eyed Conglomerate drone. *Take one of the old deep-space asteroid refinery ships and retrofit it for incarceration. We clean out overcrowded prisoners, and we can focus on those offenders who have a legitimate chance at rehabilitation.* Back when they first commissioned the prison ship, she'd heard the rationale on the bounce, like everyone else. Turns later, they had a floating city full of criminals, its orbit fixed in the middle of nowhere.

Never dreamed I'd end up here. But then, who does?

"Send the body for processing," she told Einar.

With a nod, the giant hoisted the corpse to his shoulder and headed for the chute where they deposited all organic waste. It would be processed and converted into fertilizer for use in the hydroponics gardens, which didn't work as well as they were supposed to. Half the lights had burned out, and it wasn't like they could requisition new ones. Occasionally, supplies came in with a load of prisoners and a unit of new Peacemakers. None of the fish ever went after a one-ton machine armed with laser cannons, disruptors, and shredders, fortified with heavy armor. Plus, it was impossible to get to the docking bay. Every emergency door on Perdition went into lockdown, and energy fields came up when a ship arrived, sealing off the area completely. Only after the ship departed did the fail-safe kick off, leaving the fish to make their own way and avoid agitating the droids.

Usually that meant joining with whatever territory you found yourself in. Sometimes, when numbers got low, due to violent death or illness, sectors sent recruiters to wait outside the first set of emergency doors. Though Perdition had four would-be kings, it only had two queens, and Dred was the only one they called so. The other female leader, Silence, didn't seem to be looking to build an empire; she just enjoyed the art of death. Dred had been around enough to know that Silence had a gift because the other woman did it so quietly, so cleanly, you'd almost fail to note she'd garroted clean through your throat. She didn't often mess with Silence, who killed for pleasure, not defense, not to keep people out of her territory. And there was no predicting the behavior of someone like that.

She felt cold eyes on her. Spinning, she saw Lecass watching with a small group of his followers. He had been part of Artan's regime, but so far, he hadn't made a move. The man's inaction troubled her as much as a challenge would. Deliberately, Lecass stared until she gave him her back, a calculated insult. One of these days, he would tire of the quiet drama and step things up. Dred would be ready.

Up until half a turn ago, Artan ran Queensland, though it was called Artania, then. He had been a raving narcissist with periodic fits of utter egomania, and from what Dred had been able to tell, he'd suffered from delusions of grandeur, which complemented his persecution complex. Consequently, his favorites didn't usually last more than a few months. *Until me.* She didn't know if that spoke well of her survival instincts or if it branded her a masochist.

Tam turned as the lights flickered. "That means a ship's coming in."

Because the machinery was so old, it stressed the circuits. The ship couldn't efficiently light the whole vessel as well as go into lockdown. It had been a while since she'd headed toward the docking area to assess the new fish. She wasn't greedy for bodies, like Grigor and Priest were. Grigor fed on fear, sometimes literally, she thought, and Priest brainwashed his recruits into thinking he was the living incarnation of some god. They worshipped him over in Abaddon, which was what he called his section of Perdition.

She cocked her head, knowing it was a scary look. "Want to go see what the universe has thrown away today?"

Tam nodded. "We lost a few guys in the skirmish with Grigor."

Most of their daily conflicts occurred with Grigor or Priest, the two greatest threats to Queensland. Grigor had been here longest, and he was constantly pressing to see what new areas he could claim. Dred had the bad luck to be his neighbor. With Priest on one side and Grigor on the other, she was fighting constantly to maintain her territory.

Sometimes, however, Mungo came out in search of blood; and you had to fight hard against his people. They were the hungriest in the ship. He was a short, red-haired man with a bushy beard, pale blue eyes, and rosy cheeks. By his appearance, one could be forgiven for guessing he was harmless . . . right before he ripped out your throat with his bare hands and tried to eat your face. She'd heard that Mungo liked children best . . . for all kinds of things, and those preferences had gotten him thrown into Perdition early on.

They prey on weakness. Uncertainty.

She had little of either left in her. Whether her decisions were right hardly signified. Nothing mattered in this hole. The smart ones gave up and died; maybe they found the afterlife the priests and holy women had promised, shortly after her arrest. At first, during the trial, she had missionaries in her cell every day, trying to save her soul, trying to sell her on Mary's grace, but after everything she'd seen, everything she'd done, she couldn't believe.

Could. Not.

The awful cast of her ability had burned anything like faith out of her. Over the years, she'd learned to block it out—to read darker emotions only of her own volition. Otherwise, she lived with a barrage of other people's violence drumming in her skull. That was probably why she'd snapped. Maybe her sentence would've been lighter, at a different facility, if she could have brought herself to whisper those words of remorse the judge so badly wanted to hear.

But she couldn't. Because she wasn't sorry for a single murderer she'd put down. From the tone of her trial, it was clear they thought she was insane—and it would've only made her case worse if she'd admitted to being an unregistered Psi, using illegal gifts to hunt down psychopaths. Though Dred had heard that less than 3 percent of humanity possessed talents like her own, Psi Corp required all Psi-positives to be delivered to the nearest training facility, where the company oversaw their upbringing. As a kid, Dred hadn't realized she had any particular ability, and when she left home, the die was cast.

Besides, what that ancient Old Terran philosopher had written so many turns ago was true, after all. *He who fights with monsters might take care lest he thereby become a monster. And if you gaze for long into an abyss, the abyss gazes also into you.* She had become what she despised most . . . and she *belonged* here.

I am the Dread Queen.

"Come," she called to Einar, who caught up to them at a jog.

"How long until docking?" he asked.

"Half an hour," Tam guessed. "When everything goes dark, we'll know they're here."

She scanned the dingy, rusted-metal corridor walls. "Let's see how far we can get."

During docking, recruiters didn't interfere with each other, even if they crossed borders. This one time, it was allowed, because otherwise it would be impossible for any group to augment its numbers, save the one in closest proximity. On this side, that would be Priest. He cared only for adding worshippers, but it often took longer for convicts to succumb to his brand of brainwashing. It wasn't the sort of thing that made for a quick pitch. Still, she didn't linger in Priest's territory. Since they moved fast, they reached the second set of doors before the lights went down, and the barricades came up, along with the energy fields that would fry anyone who tried to cross. A few distant screams told her that some convicts had a timing problem.

Uneasily, they shared the space with Silence's people, unusual, because the quiet killer didn't often take an interest. But it had been a while for her, too. Silence must have advisors who let her know that if she killed too many of her own people out of sport, then she wouldn't have the numbers to drive off anyone intent on taking her territory. There were six in all . . . and Dred's was among the largest, with space on all decks. The lifts didn't work, but she had shaft access, which meant her people could sneak around the ship unseen. Tam was particularly good at it.

The neutral zone lay just past the docking bay, a shanty-town inside the prison ship, where fish often huddled until they realized it was worse there than when they affiliated. Townships had rules, at least, enforced by the leader's people. The neutral zone had only one—take what you can. It was impossible to sleep there without being robbed, raped, or shanked, sometimes all in the same night. And so she'd tell anyone she deemed worthy of a second look.

That was the extent of Dred's pitch: *Come with me, and you may not die.* There was no reason to be more persuasive. The smart ones listened.

In the dark, it was eerie, with only the red glow from the nearby shock field and the crackle of electricity. Silence's people didn't talk, even among themselves, and their behavior made for an uneasy truce. Tam kept a hand on his shiv, eyeing them with wary attention. On her other side, Einar played the role of gentle giant, but he wasn't gentle. Nobody inside Perdition was. If they'd been sent up on a wrongful conviction, then they learned to fight, or they died.

Einar had been inside longer than Dred, and she'd been here for five turns before she got tired of etching hash marks into a sheet of metal to mark the days. Forever wasn't a number anyway. It just was. At her best guess, she had thirty turns beneath her belt, give or take. She'd been killing for three years before she got caught. Before she got cocky. At the height of her career, she'd thought they'd never figure it out.

Ah, hubris.

At last, the vigil ended. The lights came back up, and the security measures died, which meant it was safe to proceed. Pushing to her feet, Dred signaled her two men and jogged past the two sets of security doors, through Shantytown, and toward the reception area, where fish always milled around, as if expecting to be greeted by guards, someone to tell them where to go, what to do, how to get food and water. Poor, stupid fish.

This crop looked particularly sad. A few of them were crying, faces wedged between their knees. They all wore prison-issue gray, numbers and chips in the backs of their necks. Most of them had been shorn and deloused though a few looked as though they had been dragged from the darkest hole in the system, then set on fire. The weak and wounded wouldn't last long; she ignored them.

Then her gaze lit on a man near the back. At first glance, he looked young, but his eyes refuted the initial assessment. Though he was slim and clean, with a crown of shining blond hair, his summer-sky eyes held a hardness that came only from turns of fighting, violence, and despair. He might well be the most dangerous man on the ship. *Time to find out if he's stable.* Giving Tam and Einar the order to guard her, she closed her eyes and let slip the dogs of war.

The Pale Knight

She's a beautiful killer, this princess in chains.

Her swagger amused him, especially the way she'd gone still and quiet, eyes closed, as if in some medium's trance. But it gave Jael the opportunity to study her, even with the bodyguards to either side. They didn't know it yet, but if he meant her harm, the two most dangerous men in Perdition stood no chance of keeping him from doing as he willed. The rest of the bodies belonged to human flotsam, no more important than refuse washed up on a lonely shore.

But this woman shone.

It wasn't just her long, lean form, tautly muscled and sinuous. Nor was it the gleam of her skin, artfully embellished with tattoos that curved around the graceful slope of her shoulder, played peekaboo where the strips of rough fabric gaped across her rib cage. Chains wrapped around her forearms, both weapon and adornment. They weren't merely for show, either. In an instant, he assessed how much weight they would add to a blow and judged it significant. Steel links also wrapped her boots, which hit her at midthigh. They were thin and worn, as though she never took them off. Her brown hair fell in a multiplicity of braids, trinkets woven carefully here and there, so that when she tilted her head in response to something she saw with senses other than her eyes, they clacked.

Nobody else would've heard it beneath the din. That was part of his unique heritage.

Heh. Heritage.

All told, she presented an interesting package, but it didn't explain her behavior. Jael took a step toward her, and the blond hulk at her side growled deep in his throat. Scars covered him like a map of roads he shouldn't have traveled, and the implicit threat moved Jael not at all. He'd faced worse. Killed worse. Even if this was allegedly the worst place in the galaxy, at least it was full of humans and not wretched, chattering Bugs.

"You will not approach until bidden."

"I'll do whatever I damned well like," he said softly. "And I'd like to see you stop me."

The giant took offense to his tone. Maybe they would've danced then, but the woman opened her eyes; they were green, like the rolling hills on a world where he'd killed . . . a lot of people. Funny, he could recall the exact shade of the treetops with the veined leaves glimmering in the sun but not the name of the planet.

She raised her hand, shielding him. It entertained him, that show of power. "This one could be of use. He's not mad . . . yet . . . for what it's worth."

"How do you know?" he asked, not much caring.

In a place like this, there would be petty despots. Factions. This was a sunless world where madness and depravity reigned. At least he knew not to expect order, which was a leg up from the idiots with whom he'd been forced to share transport. A few of them had found interesting ways to hurt each other, so that the ship stank of sweat and blood and urine by the time it docked. A look from Jael had been enough to deter any but those truly determined to die.

And he obliged. He had artistic hands, made for killing.

"I read you," she said.

He eyed her in surprise. "I don't come with a manual."

Though she was closer than she knew with that statement. Unease prickled on his skin. Her henchman would prove no threat, but this woman bothered him. As he stared, someone jostled him from behind. In reflex, he spun, drove an elbow into the fool's throat and ended him with a closed fist to the temple. Precision work. Perhaps he should feel some flicker of regret, but the man wouldn't be here if he wasn't a bastard. *It doesn't pay to crowd me.*

"You'll do," she said, as if that had been an audition.

"Unlikely. I have issues with authority." He turned away. The whole ship was a danger zone, but instinct told him to get the hell away from this one.

"Do you have issues with going hungry and living in filth?"

Ah. Bribery.

"Usually," she went on coolly, "I'd say, 'come with me and you may not die' but I can see you're fierce enough to protect yourself, even in Shantytown. But it's a disgusting cesspool compared to what I can offer you."

The slight, dark man on her left spoke up. "It's clean in Queensland. Plenty to eat, comparatively."

Jael cocked his head. "Bed and board? You must ken I'm a cut above. Is that the best you can do?"

"You'll never know. Good luck in Shantytown. Mind you, don't let Silence's people haul you off. They're a bit odd. And Mungo's folk are worse. But if you wind up in Abaddon with Priest . . . well." Her words trailed off, and he was meant to wonder what she knew.

It was blatant bait. Obviously, she knew the lay of the land. And she intended him to sink the barbed hook deep into his mouth like a good, curious fish. Ripping free might hurt like hell later, but he healed fast. That was the beauty and the horror of it. Not a single wound he'd ever taken in his life showed on his skin. Instead, he carried the scars elsewhere, damage so deep that he'd become a human-shaped thing. Ironic, because that was what they'd wanted him to be, so many turns ago, the fate he'd fought so hard to avoid.

"Queensland," he repeated mockingly. "How precious."

The giant stirred and growled again, taking another step toward him. *Don't,* Jael thought. *I'll have to kill you.* There was a macabre serenity about knowing even a severed spine couldn't end him, but the horror and pain lingered. The period afterward was most horrendous, where he lay paralyzed and helpless, feeling what his enemy did to him yet there could be no release; he was tied to his broken meat like a cursed devil from the old stories. So he feared no violence. Not anymore. The universe was an infinite sea of blood in which he could swim but never drown.

"I'm bored," the woman said then. "Best of luck, pretty lad. You'll need it."

She spun on her heels, threading toward the dark corridor beyond. The lights flickered, yielding an intermittent burst that made it look as if she glided, taking only one step for every meter. Despite her leather and chains, she was graceful. Quiet. And he could hear so many things. *Too many.* This place would drive him mad in short order, and it wasn't as though he had far to travel.

He expected her to pause to give him a chance to reconsider, but she didn't. In fact, she'd already written him off. That tore it. With inhuman speed, he closed the distance between them and leapt over their heads, dropping down into a fighting crouch before them.

"Maybe I was hasty," he said. "It's a curse."

"Come on then. We can't linger."

Her two minions fell back, talking softly. Jael heard every word though they were trying to be subtle. This was a skill he didn't advertise, but he could've told the woman at his side that she had slight arrhythmia.

"What do you think of the fish?" the blond giant asked.

"Too soon to say. He seems smart enough . . . and skilled. Not crazy."

"Do you think she took him because he's pretty?"

"What do you care?"

The giant sighed. "Because I'm not."

Hm. So the big scarred brute had a thing for the princess in chains. *I wonder if she knows.*

Before he could calculate how the information might serve him best, he stopped cold, held up a hand. Occasionally, his acute hearing proved useful in other ways. Jael could also hear the slight hitch in her breathing when the décor changed. New territory, he guessed. She was afraid, but the adrenaline kicked in. The woman beside him was ready for a fight—wanted one—and that was . . . enticing.

"Party guests on the way. Shall we show them a good time?"

She nodded. "Let's."

He had no weapon, but it didn't matter. The enemy couldn't have anything more than shivs, chains, hunks of metal forged into something equally primitive. There would be no blasters, shredders, or disruptors. Which made for a fine melee . . . for him, anyway.

Jael whirled into battle as the convicts broke from the shadows. They all wore the same colors, and they carried homemade knives. They radiated a desperate, frantic air; he'd seen the same light in the eyes of holy warriors—fools convinced they were dying for a holy cause instead of just dying.

Punch, block, roll. He came up behind his target and broke his neck cleanly from behind. The giant's surprised grunt told Jael the other man was surprised he had the brute strength to manage the maneuver. Everyone was, until they realized he wasn't normal. That he was other. Then the whispers would start, even here.

It was hard not to stop and watch her because she was beautiful like a ferocious storm. Her chains twirled and lashed. He leapt them while the henchmen held back, clearly worried about getting in her way. But he wasn't afraid of a misdirected blow. It was only pain, his old friend, his nursemaid and mother. She hit him once, and he shook it off, finished his kill.

There were ten bodies on the ground when he stopped moving.

"Priest's people," she said, not even breathing hard.

That meant less than nothing to him, but in time, he'd figure out the politics.

The trek through the ship was enlightening in other ways. Anything that could be stripped, stolen, or recycled had been. In places, whole wall panels were missing, and others showed signs of hard use, pocked with holes and rust and ominous stains. The floors showed just as much wear, to the point that it was miraculous Perdition held together at all.

"What'll happen when someone pries off the wrong piece?" he asked.

She cut him a wry, appreciative look. "We'll asphyxiate. No great loss, right?"

That might do it. A jolt of anticipation startled him. *I could die here.* And it wasn't an awful, terrifying thought. It was like the promise of sunrise at the end of the longest, darkest night. Another man might raise a fist and rail because he hadn't asked to be born. But Jael could only whisper in his own head: *I didn't ask to be created.*

But that was too pathetic. He'd grown accustomed to his status as renegade science project. Even took pleasure in killing the people responsible from time to time. Not all of them, of course. Some had to live because otherwise, how could they enjoy turns of tortured fear?

He smiled.

"What did you mean when you said you read me?"

"I'm Psi," she said flatly.

He actually stumbled. "Oh, shit. You're not a mind reader, are you? I hate those fookers. Always poking about, looking for your darkest secrets."

She surprised him with a husky laugh. "No, though I'd keep busy for a thousand turns in here if I were. You can't go five steps without stumbling over some ass with a dark secret."

"I don't have any. So what then?"

"I find killers . . . and I feel how they go about it. If it's rage or pleasure-driven." She was holding back, he could tell. The way she bit her lip to prevent another round of explanation.

But it was enough for now. He'd charm the rest out of her later. Women liked him; or they always had, right up until it was too late to reconsider. When you got right down to it, there was a monstrous face beneath his smooth skin.

"And me? What did you see?"

"You've taken pleasure in killing but not in a psychotic way. Your pattern felt . . . organized. Like you were righting a wrong, real or imagined. You don't kill in anger. In fact, you're mostly cold, pretty lad, like a field of endless snow."

How right she was. It shook him a bit, so he summoned a caustic smile. "Look, I'm properly undone. Watch now, you'll have me weeping. Do you think you could fix me, queenie?"

"No," she said. "I can't fix anything. I can only break it. Or kill it. But you're welcome to come sleep in my boneyard."

"Now there's an offer I can't refuse."

◄3►

Bad Omens

Dred had told him the truth, as far as it went.

Reading him had been instructive . . . and unique. She'd never encountered anyone with so much pale energy, limned in darkness. Otherwise, there was little color to him at all, as if emotion had rarely touched him. In fact, he only offered curls of cobalt blue, like a dark sea one could drown in, the color of sorrow. So he had been sad . . . and he'd frozen thereafter. His past became a mystery wrapped in that context, but it would remain unquestioned. She didn't need to know his secrets.

As she'd said, everyone had them inside Perdition, crimes for which they'd never been charged or convicted, sins that had driven them to darker deeds. There was some solace in the bottom of the abyss; this was where people rolled to a stop after an interminable fall.

After the fight, they didn't speak again. She led the way quickly through the other borders, and she didn't stop until they reached the dubious safety of Queensland. The sentries snapped to attention as she crossed with the three men behind her.

"Anything to report?" she asked.

"Nil."

Sometimes it was a colossal pain in the ass to guard so much ground. On bad days, it felt futile, like conflict they invented to keep themselves from going mad from the realization that their lives were pointless. Such nihilism would destroy her if she let it.

Dred nodded at the guards and led the way past into the heart of Queensland. She tried to imagine what it looked like to the fish—tawdry, she supposed, and full of delusions of grandeur, relics of Artan's rule. This had been a fitness room at some point, where the workers could train on the machines or run laps if they preferred. It was a good-sized space, and she'd divided it up in sections for various functions. Everyone had a job to do, as work kept her men from killing one another. Well, most days. If the tensions ran too high, she ran death matches to settle grievances. The betting distracted the convicts. Most of them were simple souls with rotten teeth and low aspirations.

"Get something to eat," she told Einar and Tam.

It was a dismissal; they left without a second look.

"You've carved out quite a kingdom here," the man beside her said.

"Not me. I only stole it."

"Possession is nine-tenths of the law. Isn't that what they say?"

"It is, but that doesn't mean I built this." After listening to Tam's advice, she'd made some improvements, though. Artan's idea of organization had been somewhat lacking.

He shrugged. "In here, keeping it seems like a fair achievement."

"Don't pretend to be kind. Don't flatter me. I brought you here because I recruit the best of the dregs, which is why my territory doesn't lose a single centimeter."

"Oh, I *like* you," he purred. "What's your name?"

"Dred."

"That must be a prison handle. No mother would name her daughter Dread."

"It's a nickname. D-R-E-D."

"Must be short for something." He cocked an inquiring brow at her.

Dresdemona Devos, she thought. But she didn't confide such things in her fish.

"Must be," she agreed aloud. "What should I call you?"

"I'm Jael," he answered.

"JL? What does that stand for?" The moment she asked, she recognized the tactical error, as she'd done the thing she just chided him over.

"Whenever you feel like exchanging stories, queenie, we can brew a nice cuppa, share our deepest feelings, and give each other matching tattoos."

She offered her sweetest smile. "The hydroponics lab *does* keep us in sweetleaf tea. It's not the finest blend, but the plants are hardy. Even gross mismanagement can't kill them."

"Splendid," he muttered. "And it's J-A-E-L since you were kind enough to share a spelling lesson with me."

"Excellent. Now I know how to write your name when it comes time to draw lots for the worst missions."

He suppressed a smile, as if her acerbic nature delighted him. Dred didn't want him to approve of her; she only needed him strong and willing to fight. Yet she sensed this man did as he pleased and only pretended to obey. She couldn't claim he hadn't warned her.

Back in Shantytown he'd said, *I have issues with author-ity.* In Perdition, however, that was like saying, *I kill people.* Other convicts would just shrug because it was a given. They didn't send people to a whitefish lockdown like this one for stealing baubles.

"Does this place have a still?"

"In fact, it does. But you'll have to earn your ration cards. I can't have all my men drunk at once. Bad for business."

"Death *is* your business."

Her smile widened. "And business is good."

"I knew you were going to say that." Dred saw how he choked his response, buried the flare in his blue eyes that looked like a tiny spark, flickering within the purest heart of flame.

"So you're Psi as well," she said, deadpan. "Precog, I suppose? Tell me, how does my story end?"

"Not with a bang but with a whimper."

"That's how everyone goes out, I reckon. Unless they're gurgling."

"I never whimper. Or gurgle."

"What's your specialty?" she asked, sobering.

It wouldn't do to like him, or to encourage teasing. She'd learned not to get attached. People died all the time in border battles, invasions . . . sometimes by their own hands. Over time, she'd discovered it was easier to go numb. The convicts who chose to live in Queensland weren't her people. They were pawns to be used or sacrificed according to her convenience. She'd do well to remember that.

"Unarmed combat."

"That's convenient, as we're fresh out of guns."

Before Dred formulated her next move, walleyed Wills broke from the curious onlookers; it was hard to talk to him because she never knew where to look. His head offered a plethora of unfortunate features from the carbuncle on his neck to the nose that sat nearly sideways on his face from so many untreated breaks. And there were his eyes . . .

Of course, he held his bag of bones. And he wouldn't go away until she let him read what they presaged about this new arrival.

"Is this a good time, ma'am?"

Not really. It never was, but Wills got downright irrational if she refused to let him exercise his gift. As psychoses went, this one was relatively harmless . . . and preferable to his setting things on fire. Wills made up for the annoyance by being able to fix damn near anything.

"Never better," she said, humoring him.

Jael fell into the spirit of the thing, leaning forward as Wills dumped the fine bones into his palms. They came from rodents that infested the ship. They'd come in with some shipment of supplies, turns ago, and multiplied like mad. She ate them when she could catch them, but the things had mutated over the turns, likely due to exposure to radiation from the aging ship. The only blessing was they could no longer fit in the ducts and panels to chew the wiring.

Muttering, Wills sliced his fingertips and handled the bones, then he spat in the bloody mess and juggled the bones and bodily fluids in his scarred palms. He whispered words in a language Dred didn't know and cast the augury. A primitive pursuit, but she didn't object.

Wills drew in a sharp breath. "Bad omens. Bad."

"What do you see?" Dred always asked. It never mattered.

The man's head came up, clarity in his muddy, miscast eyes for an instant. "Kill him now. Chaos comes. The dead will walk. And he'll cost you everything."

"Thanks for your counsel," she said, as if she hadn't heard such fire-and-doom tidings before. "I'll consider what you've said."

Wills bowed once, twice, thrice—he did everything in threes—and hurried away to cleanse his bones. The man beside her pushed out a breath, as if he hadn't realized he was holding it. Tension lingered in his shoulders, and she wanted to reassure him that Wills was full of shit. But she didn't comfort convicts.

"He's quite a character. Is it always this exciting?"

"Indeed. And sometimes we have jugglers. Want something to eat?"

"Don't be kind," he said, casting her words back like shards of ice.

"I'm not. You need nutrition to stay strong. You're no use to me if you can't fight, and I'd prefer not to cast your corpse down the chute just yet."

He *laughed* at that. Here was a man who laughed at death. And he meant it; this wasn't bravado, designed to impress her. His amusement echoed with layers, sincerity and . . . longing. Did he *want* to die, then? How . . . intriguing.

"I'd like a meal. There was nothing on the transport."

She nodded. "The system managers don't care if you starve or kill one another en route. If you do, then it's less burden on the existing resources."

"It's a business like any other with profit and loss statements. I bet they don't send much."

"No," she acknowledged. "We make do."

Besides boundaries and limited space, aggression that sometimes had nowhere else to go, townships battled for limited resources. If she lost ground, it might cost her the hydroponics lab they'd built. Not all the settlements had them. Mungo's people relied on the capricious Kitchenmates, which had to be fed a steady influx of organic matter to create food. Dred tossed corpses into the chutes for processing, which fertilized their plants, but Mungo took a different route, and his dead became something else, something hot and delicious for the table.

She quelled a shiver. It would be impossible for her to eat a steaming roast, knowing it had been a person. Even understanding how the Kitchen-mates worked didn't help. The meat might go in as human, but it would be broken down and processed and regenerated until the cellular structure matched the recipe that had been input. So unless a freakish cannibal did the programming, it wouldn't be human flesh that emerged. *And yet . . .*

"Something wrong?" Jael asked.

"No more than usual. Let's find you some food."

There was always a pot of vegetable stew bubbling away, and since it was close to the third meal of the day, she found bread cooling on the table. At her nod, Cook cut a generous slab. That was both the man's name and his job. He didn't speak or fight much, but he had a way with produce, and he knew his way around the kitchen. She'd recruited him because he was big, but as it turned out, he'd rather use his knives for chopping. Dred had often wondered how Cook ended up here, but he wasn't helpless. If you pissed him off, he'd slit your throat and go back to dicing veggies for the pot.

Once he got the food, Jael ate quickly, arms curled around the bowl to keep anyone from taking it. He used the bread to clean the dish, then handed it back. All told, it took less than five minutes.

"Been a while?" she asked.

He shrugged. "I can't remember when last I ate."

Dred didn't pursue the subject; it was too personal. She just needed to brief him and walk away. Let him find his own path.

"This is Queensland." Briefly, she outlined the size of her holding. "Once you have a chance to rest, I'll put you on the roster. You'll have shifts at various borders . . . and sometimes there will be people to kill."

"That's it?"

"More or less."

"What do you do for laughs?"

She took that to mean the men, not herself personally. Dred couldn't remember when she'd enjoyed . . . anything. Except his conversation. Which made him absolutely forbidden fruit.

Walk away. Don't go down this road. It ends in a sheer cliff with blood all over the rocky ground.

But she couldn't resist one last exchange. "Drink. Gamble. Copulate."

He flashed a white, wicked smile. "Occasional murder leavened with debauchery and vice? This sounds divine."

◁ 4 ▷

Territorial Incursion

On the second day, Jael prowled the boundaries, learning where the lines were drawn. She had guards posted on various levels to keep watch. Her top two lieutenants, Tameron and Einar, were rightfully suspicious of him; they kept an eye on him as he learned her holdings. Though it was too soon for him to factor the advantages of betrayal, he would sell her secrets in a heartbeat if it meant a more advantageous position elsewhere. But he believed her when she said it was worse elsewhere.

He breathed in deep, processing the variety of smells that carried such diverse information. Five of her men had a terminal illness; the smell of decay lingered on them, dead men walking. At least half the others wore lust like a jacket made of skins, and they watched her with covetous eyes as she strode past. Jael didn't need to read their minds to know what they wanted—and it intrigued him that she was fierce enough to keep such vile intentions in check. For despite the desire to do her harm, fear surged even stronger in her henchmen, and they wouldn't move against her.

It took him the better part of the day to patrol her territory fully. The boundaries contained some fascinating assets, but also definite defensive liabilities. If he had control of the zone, he would reorganize the deployment. Mentally, Jael reassigned the watches and distributed the personnel though it was possible she knew things about the inclinations and capabilities of her men that he didn't. There must be some reason she had managed to hold the line despite apparent missteps.

Dinner was more of the same, but he was happy enough to have hot food and human companionship that he felt fairly glad to be here. Jael suspected he was the only inmate of that mind, but they had never been incarcerated on Ithiss-Tor. Compared to the Bug prison, this place was positively luxurious. And he'd find a way out, eventually. He'd been confined more times than he could count, and they'd never managed to lock him down yet.

"Learned all my weaknesses yet?" Dred sat down opposite him, eyes watchful.

Just what do you expect from me, princess in chains?

"Not yours, though your demesne could use some work."

"Bold words for a stranger."

He flashed the smile that women seemed to find charming. "You've no idea."

"About your ideas or how strange you are?"

"Either one, queenie."

"I suspect I do," she said, surprising him. "You've killed a lot of people, and yet you don't bear a single scar. Are you *that* good, Jael, or is there more to you than meets the eye?"

People didn't usually work that out so swiftly, so that meant she was smart. He could bluff and pretend his skills were such that nobody had ever set a blade to his skin, but in the end, she'd figure it out. The first time fighting broke out, and he took a serious wound, she'd see. And he was tired of pretending, tired of lying. Her eyes would change, of course, after she learned the truth. But perhaps it was better to get it done quickly, like yanking a knife from your gut.

No. He'd be better off not sharing the truth. It always made things worse.

So he chose bullshit. "I'm that good."

She stilled, her gaze roaming over him in a way that made his skin prickle. It wasn't a look he had ever seen before, as the nature of scrutiny didn't feel judgmental, only curious. "You're lying to me. I don't like it, but I understand. You don't trust me. And you shouldn't."

"You haven't shared your life story with me either, queenie." He made his tone mocking. "What did your parents do for a living? Did you have pets?"

"My father was a scientist who fled from the Corp and took his research with him."

"So you were fugitives. But if you tell me he was attached to the Ideal Genome Project, then I have to kill you."

She actually laughed. "I don't know what he did, to be honest. He was a broken man by the time I came along, battered by desperation and constant danger."

"Do you confide in everyone like this?" If so, it might be how she maintained control over a group of vicious thugs. Make each man feel special, as if he alone enjoyed her confidence. *She could be manipulating you.*

Before she could reply, an alarm went off. "Incoming. Hope you're ready to fight, pretty lad."

"Always."

He followed her as she ran toward the incursion site. The guards she'd stationed should be sufficient—unlike a few security lapses he'd noted—but Jael never turned away from a battle. It was the one place where he needn't hide or apologize for his physical abilities. Ten men pushed against her border; he had no idea if that was a sizable party. She had four people stationed here—three male, one female—and they were holding the attackers at bay, but only just. Without blasters or disruptors, there was a limit to how effective her personnel could be. In most prisons, contraband could be smuggled in, but in Perdition, they were limited to what someone was canny enough to build from scrap parts.

In this case, some clever Queenslander had devised a rudimentary shrapnel gun, and a hard-faced woman was barraging the defenders in razor-sharp metal shards. She caught an enemy inmate in the throat; he was an idiot and pulled it out in sheer reflex. Blood sprayed from the wound.

Imbecile. I'm the only one who can survive care like that. One down. That leaves nine.

The attackers found it hard to press the charge in the face of so much jagged metal, but the barrage couldn't last forever. Apparently Dred shared his assessment.

"She'll run out of ammo soon," she said beside him. "Care to join me?"

Without waiting for his answer, she signaled for her side to cease firing, and before the enemy could react, she vaulted over the barricades and wound up with her chains. This woman was incandescent in her fearlessness—and her absolute lack of regard for her own safety spoke to him. Before Jael realized he'd made a decision, he was beside her. The invaders laughed.

It wasn't the first time he'd heard that before a killing spree. So many people judged by appearances—the last mistake they ever made. He landed an efficient kidney punch on his first target that carried enough force to leave the man pissing blood, but then Jael broke his neck cleanly. *Eight.* Beside him, Dred whipped her chain at a man's head; the resulting impact knocked him down. Dazed, the convict scrambled away, but she surged forward, relentless as the tide. The others surrounded her, but she didn't seem concerned. Instead, she whipped her chain in widening circles, injuring them all equally. The amount of pain she brought to bear was . . . impressive, even to him.

Jael stopped admiring her ferocious technique and joined the melee in earnest. He'd learned a bastard blend of martial arts from various mercs over the course of his career, and it served him well. *They might confiscate your weapons, but they can't take away your skills.* Some commander he'd served had told him that once, cautioning him never to rely on equipment or even other people. Ironically, the old man had been knifed by a prostitute, which served as a particularly eloquent culmination to his tutelage.

Four enemies broke away from Dred's chains to engage; he suspected they thought he'd be an easier fight despite the ease with which he'd dispatched their comrade. *But every man in here believes he's special, the exception to the rules.* They all rushed at once, and he took the initial hits. It wasn't that he was too slow to dodge, but sometimes it was worth the pain when they realized a killing blow wasn't sufficient to stop him. Jael ended the onslaught with three knives in him. The wounds burned, but he was used to agony; and in his darkest moments, it was better than nothing, better than numbness, because he'd never known true pleasure. Pain was the next best thing.

He offered a smile. "Is that all?"

One of them sucked in a shocked breath, but that was the last sound he ever made. Jael ended him with a closed fist to the temple. He fell heavily to the decking, and Jael guessed he'd go down the chutes Dred had mentioned the day before. The other three backed away, their shock and horror overwhelming.

Another whispered, "What *is* he?"

"Cyborg, maybe. Or augment."

Jael had heard stories about new experiments, blends of mankind and technology, but no. He was a different flavor of monster. It was odd that other creations had taken his place in the limelight. These days, it was possible for him to tell someone what he was and receive only a blank stare because the Ideal Genome Experiment was a footnote in the history of a failed corporation. The horror had lost its meaning to the general populace, but his genesis remained fresh in his mind—perfect recall of the horrors he'd endured was his cross to bear, along with his strength, speed, and ability to heal. To most, those wouldn't sound like curses, but they hadn't spent twenty years trying to die, either.

It was time to play. "The fastest of you maggots gets to live. Return to your master and tell him that Queensland has a new champion. Now *run*."

Jael laughed as a small, wiry man launched into motion. He went like lightning, leaving the rest to die. They hardly realized they'd lost the race when he killed them. There was no pleasure to be found in other people's pain, so he made it quick. Farther along the checkpoint, Dred had beaten her opponents into submission. She finished three of them with quick, efficient jabs of her knife, but the last man, she left alive.

"Take him," she ordered.

Is she talking to me?

Oddly, he didn't offer a clever reply. He'd served as a grunt before, answering to a commander's whims. When the pay had been right, he could be obedient. There was no pay here, but perhaps there would be fringe benefits if he played his cards right. He wondered if she didn't notice the blades in his side; most people reacted the first time they saw his difference. Even forewarned, they couldn't help the instinctive revulsion. Her brusque manner made for a welcome change.

Jael stepped forward and bent to lift the prisoner. Each movement sent slashes of raw anguish through him. Though he could heal the damage, he still felt all the pain. He still slung the man over his shoulder and turned to follow Dred back toward the main hall of the compound. Einar and Tameron met them at the first checkpoint; he expected some challenge from the big, scarred man, but he was waiting for a sign from his queen.

Interesting. Even the alpha males defer to her. There would be no territorial pissing here. He wondered how she managed that.

She gestured. "Bring him for questioning."

Jael obeyed, mostly because he was curious to watch her in action. From all over the compound, her men encircled the proceedings. They were silent, watchful, and it was a little unnerving from so many undisciplined killers. He didn't understand the dynamics here, and such lack of insight made him nervous. He had to figure out the hold she had, how she manipulated the rest. She didn't dominate through pure physical strength; that much was certain.

"I killed a scout recently," she told the man on the floor. "Now Grigor's sent a full hunting party. It wasn't enough to take back territory, so why don't you tell me what he's after?"

"I'll die before I talk." The prisoner spat, baring yellow teeth.

"You'll die regardless. But I get the choice of whether it's quick or slow. I can make it last days. We have medicine to heal you, just so I can start all over again."

Color leached from the captive's cheeks. "You wouldn't waste supplies on me."

"Wouldn't I?" she asked the big, scarred man beside her.

"You've done it before. Can *I* have him to play with for a bit? If you're finished."

◄5►

True Intentions

"I don't imagine you need me for this," Tam said.

Mindful of appearances, he waited for Dred's nod of dismissal. Though he didn't consider her his superior, it mattered that the men perceive his role as subordinate. He'd always preferred working behind the scenes. That way, if things went catastrophically wrong, it was somebody else's head on the chopping block.

He avoided a couple of conversations with men who wanted to press him for information on whether Dred was ready to choose a consort. They saw Einar and himself as bodyguards, not serious contenders for a place in her bed. Einar would like to change that status, but Tam's tastes ran in other directions. He slipped out of the hall with minimal fuss and negotiated the borders without the sentries seeing him. There was a certain risk in what he was doing, as Dred didn't know of his excursions. He told himself she'd approve them if he mentioned it, but it was best to maintain plausible deniability. If he was caught behind enemy lines, she could honestly claim she knew nothing of his mission and cut him loose. Tam thought well enough of his skills that he was willing to risk it.

The lights were spotty in this part of the corridor; many had been stolen, the rest burned out, and it allowed him to scramble into the ducts. Baby rodents scurried ahead of him, and he made a face as he crawled past their droppings. The adult creatures didn't fit up here, but the beasts made a nice addition to the stewpot when they caught them. Unfortunately, the things preferred the bowels of the ship, so the aliens enjoyed more fresh meat than any other sector.

Tam had long since memorized the twists and turns that would carry him above Grigor's meeting room. If he hurried, he might catch the end of the messenger's report. As he'd understood it, the new fish, Jael, had sent a runner back with a message. Grigor might reveal something of his plans, which would permit Tam to develop a counterstrategy.

Grigor, who was also known as the Great Bear, had a booming voice, audible even at a distance—and right then, he was shouting at the top of his lungs. Tam moved closer, enough that he could make out the words, even when the Bear regained some self-control.

"You dare to return to me on your knees?" he was raging. "Carrying word from some new fish who calls himself a champion?"

"I thought you'd want to know about the danger, Grigor. When I came to warn you, he had three knives in him, and he was *smiling*." Tam wouldn't have gone that route, as brutes like the Great Bear didn't appreciate any intimation that they might be bested, especially in combat.

There was a wet sound and a fleshy pop, confirming Tam's appraisal. For a few seconds, silence reigned, then Grigor's heavy boots thundered against the floor. *Pacing in a fit of rage . . . that's a good sign.* Angry men made irrational decisions, yielding the tactical advantage.

"Not a single survivor," the Great Bear snarled, "apart from this coward." The thump made Tam think Grigor had kicked the corpse. "So we learn nothing about her defenses, nothing about her numbers, nothing about her response time. That was pointless."

Grigor wasn't the smartest leader in Perdition if he thought sending ten men would yield significant insight. It would've been more productive to send one man, skilled in stealth, to prowl around and slip out without being seen. But the Great Bear did *not* specialize in subtlety; he was all boom and bluster, snarling mouth and roaring wind. He also tended to kill men who counseled him otherwise, which hamstrung him in a battle of wits. Yet he didn't lack for numbers; he conscripted all the mindless brutes and those with a yen for blood.

Tam could've pointed out that if the Bear hadn't killed his sole survivor, the man might have told him *something*, like the fact that Queensland had shrapnel guns. *Which was more than he knew before.* Tam held still, listening to the enraged pacing.

A deep voice offered, "We could send two teams next time. Strike at two points. The surprise might be enough to net some intel."

The thrill of discovery rolled through him, and Tam smiled. This was why he endured the danger and the darkness, the pleasure of unearthing information he wasn't supposed to possess. It was a comedown for the former spymaster of Tarnus, but a man must take his pleasures where he found them. In Perdition, they were few and far between.

He listened as the enemy laid out their plans, rudimentary as they were. When the celebration commenced, Tam slipped away, retracing his steps. Likely, he should mention the ducts as a potential weakness to Dred, but as long as she discussed strategy in her quarters, there should be no risk of being overheard. The ventilation in the living spaces was smaller, insufficient to hold an eavesdropper. Tam had wondered if other sectors sent men like him to watch the hall, but he'd never found anyone—and not for lack of looking.

With his customary ease, he returned to Queensland, avoiding the sentries adroitly. There was a spectacle ongoing, the sort that many convicts found irresistible. Tam didn't share their fascination with violence, but this display served a purpose. They had lashed the enemy to a metal framework, left over from Artan's day. He had often flayed his own people for imagined offenses, whispered conspiracies audible only to his own ears. The man's limbs were pinned up, spread-eagle, and he was naked apart from the covering of blood.

Einar held the title of master torturer for a reason. He knew just how to hurt a man, how to read his deepest fears. For some, sheer physical pain wasn't enough. Sometimes it required fear and tension, waiting matched with small anguish. While he had been gone, the captive's body had been transformed into a canvas, and Einar was currently creating a *chef d'oeuvre*.

Tam knew better than to interrupt. Dred moved to his side, her quiet way of showing support and solidarity. He understood that she felt beholden to him, as he'd put her on the throne the day Artan died, but Tam wasn't interested in gratitude. No, his plans for the Dread Queen were bigger and more long-ranging. Not that he'd shared them with her. Better to build, step by step, conditioning her to accept his advice. One day, the day would come when she couldn't imagine making any important decision without consulting him; and she wouldn't question when he presented his plan for the endgame, either. But in a game such as this, the final moves might be turns away. *Just as I like it.* Perdition might not possess the challenge he'd thrived on within the palace, but there were moves to be made, pawns to play, and a queen to maneuver.

THE bound prisoner radiated terror.

Once Einar finished, Dred closed her eyes to read the captive—and it was awful, a burst of necrotic color. Like biting into rancid fruit, the taste was cloying and unmistakable. This one had a pathology familiar to her, his whole being raddled with mingled lust and deviance. He thrived on domination and control, driven by darker urges to disfigure his lovers and eventually kill them when they failed to satisfy his longings. To her mind's eye, he was like a house riddled with rot, so putrescent as to teeter on the verge of collapse. Prison had not improved him. Here, he had free reign to do as he would, and the Great Bear had done nothing to quell his leanings.

When she opened her eyes, she felt dirty, as there was no way to remove his filth from inside her head. For nights to come, in dreams, she would see what he'd shown her. This connection was what started her down this road, long ago. Back then, it had gotten to the point where she couldn't know such things and take no action. At first, she'd tried telling the authorities, but they never believed her, and it was worse to have concrete surety that people committed atrocities with impunity.

As Einar stepped forward, as if to return to work, the prisoner wet himself. So many killers were cowards at the bone. It took only five seconds for him to begin babbling, "Grigor means to take the hydroponics garden. The one your champion sent back will report on your response time as well as carrying the message."

My champion. Yes, I'll need to address that at some point. But she wasn't ready yet.

"So you came at me, knowing you were expendable," she said. "How does that feel?"

A whimper escaped the man at her feet. "It's not like I had a choice."

"You pissed him off, then. What did you do?"

"Killed a girl before he was through playing with her." Horrific as that sounded, Dred had heard things were worse in Mungo's realm. Only his favorites could sleep the night through, and she pitied the fish who went unknowingly with his recruiters. He always sent reasonable-sounding men who had deceit down to a fine art.

She shook her head. "Denying Grigor his desires doesn't sound like a way to ensure longevity. Do you have a death wish?"

To her surprise, the man nodded. "It's the only way out of here. And I'm ready."

"I'm surprised he didn't execute you on the spot." The idea that Grigor was capable of restraining his urge toward carnage, capable of planning, disquieted her.

You can defeat him, hold your ground. It's nothing you haven't done before. This time, however, it felt different. She was so tired.

"Do you think there's more he could tell us?" she asked Tameron.

Tam answered, "I'd wager he's tapped out. Grigor wouldn't share the specifics of his attack strategy with a worm like this. And I have more to tell you, once he's dead."

Somehow, he always did. "At least we learned his target and can shore up defenses accordingly. So kill him," she told Einar.

He was her chosen executioner, not just because he was good at it, but because he had a terrifying aspect as well. Men knew dread and despair when they gazed on him, so she kept him close. In a place like this, those were constant companions, best tamed to hand. Einar complied, though he used a blade instead of his bare hands this time. The moment of death carried peculiar resonance, as all the decay and darkness drained away, leaving an inert form. No unholy echoes, no more wicked design.

There was a certain purity in endings.

"Circulate among the men," she said to Tameron. "Find out if they've heard anything."

"We'll have a great deal to discuss tonight," he replied.

Sometimes prison gossip offered valuable insights; she wouldn't overlook Tam's importance to keeping her boots planted firmly on top. He might look unimposing, but he had a whip-smart mind and uncanny ability to predict enemy movements. His skill at going unnoticed was excellent as well. She had sent him more than once to reconnoiter inside enemy territory, and the secrets he uncovered were always invaluable. He had told her that he'd been a spymaster on his homeworld, and that they sent him here when the

ruling lord—his former employer—was deposed in an enemy coup. She didn't know if that was true as inmates were
notorious liars, but his skill supported the story.

She nodded a thank-you to Einar. "Dispose of the body."

All around, the rest of the prisoners went back to whatever had been occupying them before. Which left her standing next to the newcomer. He seemed to be proving some
point about his toughness by leaving those knives in his side.
Any other man would be unconscious. Not that she cared.
Dred only required loyalty.

She fought the urge to offer to tend him herself, but that
wasn't how she did things. "Get patched up. The doctor's
over there."

"He doesn't have a name?"

"Not that he's willing to give. I have his prisoner identi-
fication number if it matters."

"Not at all. And I don't need medical attention." He held
her gaze as if willing her not to look away as he drew the
shivs from his flesh, one by one.

And she didn't. Dred had seen worse during her imprison-
ment. She'd seen men flayed alive, men hung on gibbets,
men burned beyond recognition. But it was somehow worse
when they sickened and died of natural ailments that could
be corrected through modern medicine. Here, though, none
of it could be mended. They had so little.

As the last knife clattered to the floor between them, Jael
pushed out a breath. Blood stained his Conglomerate-issue
shirt in three places, but not as fast as it should. His pretty
face was drawn taut, etched in the agony he'd endured in
some private ritual. It wasn't her business if he was into
self-flagellation, and yet she said, "You're fast enough to
dodge, skilled enough to destroy them. You took those
wounds on purpose. What's the point?"

"The pain is the point," he answered. "But it also established my reputation. The one who got away will tell others
that I'm unkillable. That's how places like this function."

"There *are* no places like this."

"Which makes me curious what you did to end up here."

"The same thing as everyone else. I killed a lot of people."

There were excuses she could offer, explanations, but after so long, it didn't matter. His blue gaze became piercing, as if he could look through the layers and lies down to the heart of her. She didn't like the feeling at all. Dred narrowed her eyes.

"Sometimes there are good reasons for that," he said.

"Do you want me to tell you that I was a vigilante? That I put down more rabid dogs than all the interstellar police agencies combined?" That was true, actually, but she said it in such a scathing tone that she didn't expect him to believe her.

But she'd judged him wrong. His expression lightened, gained layers of comprehension, and she loathed the stripped-bare feeling it left behind. "But when you hunt monsters, outsiders find it impossible to distinguish you from your prey."

She hated that he grasped what no one else had. It was too soon, and she wasn't an equation to be solved. "Don't. After all this time, I'm just like them."

"Are you?" he asked.

Dred strode away without answering. The newcomer got under her skin, which meant he was to be avoided. And for the next four days, she did precisely that. He didn't seem to miss her. Instead, he spent his time getting to know various factions within her territory. To her amusement, he struck the right note with each: Here he was terrifying, there charming, and in other circles, he donned yet another persona. She had to watch him as he was a chameleon, shedding his personality and becoming someone new whenever the situation required. If she let him, he would use that skill to influence her.

"You watch him a great deal," Tameron said.

Dred started. The only thing she didn't like about him was how easily he could come upon her unaware. While she trusted him—insofar as anyone in this place—he could so easily slip a knife between her ribs and take over Queensland quietly. *But he'd have to come up with a new name.* Though to be fair, the convicts had dubbed her territory after the coup. It wasn't an act of vanity, as Dred didn't care what they called the shafts and ship space that belonged to her.

"So do you." That wasn't a guess. Tam would've been observing and collecting data, as that was his habit. "Conclusions?"

"It's impossible to gauge his true nature. Too many masks."

"And does that make him less dangerous to us . . . or more?"

Tam thought for a few seconds. "More, I think. It's difficult to gauge whether a dog will bite if it doesn't growl first."

"What else have you learned? Not necessarily about the new fish."

"The word's out that Grigor means to move against the garden. And I've heard whispers that Priest may be planning a joint offensive. We could be looking at simultaneous strikes."

He'd also informed her that they could expect an assault at multiple points. If that attack came via both Grigor and Priest, it could be catastrophic for their resources. Living in a constant state of war was exhausting. Dred's temples ached, and sometimes she yearned to stand down, but she had found living underneath somebody else's aegis intolerable in here. Einar and Tameron had sided with her when she started rallying new fish to her banner. Their loyalty couldn't be rewarded with apathy.

"What do you recommend?" Few people realized just how critical Tam was to her strategies, and that was safest. If they did, they certainly would've killed him.

"It would be best if we could foment some discord in their holdings. Prevent them from coordinating the attacks."

"Is it possible that Grigor and Priest have allied?" The idea gave her chills.

They occupied space to either side of her. If they set aside their differences long enough, they could conceivably crush her, then divide up her territory and resources. Shaft access might not seem like much, but it permitted Tameron to spy on everyone else with impunity. He knew the maintenance and access ducts like the back of his hand. Her other big asset was the hydroponics garden. Tam had been warning her that things were getting too civilized here—apart from the threat of outward assault, life in her zone wasn't intolerable. But peace and prosperity made the other leaders want to wreck it.

Sometimes she felt like an empress of air and bones, but the fight never ended. She glanced at Tam, who was watching the men. Right now, the mood was quiet. He would warn her if their inclinations shifted toward aggression and bloodshed; at that point, it would be time to host another series of games. Blood sports were a way of life in her territory, not one she loved, but it was necessary. She didn't get killers to follow the rules by eliminating violence entirely. No, it had to be channeled, against the enemies, and if times were too quiet, against each other in sanctioned death matches.

Part of her, a faint and dying spark, was horrified by what she'd become, by what she permitted to happen in her holding, and what she did in the name of survival. But it wasn't in her DNA to lie down. *Perhaps that's part of my problem.* Across the main hall, a card game disintegrated into an argument, but it was settled with fists, not knives. Dred didn't intervene.

After a long silence, Tam sighed, and answered, "Yes. I don't have evidence of it yet, but I believe they're in collusion, the objective being your downfall."

"Then war is coming," she said softly. "We must prepare."

◁6▷

Blood Sport

As prisons went, this one was pretty bad. The hardest part was never seeing daylight, and he saw the results of that deficiency in the faces of those who had been confined for turns. Ostensibly, the lights compensated for the lack of sunlight, but the men were still fish-belly pale. *Not that I look any better.* When they'd dragged him out of the hole where he'd languished on Ithiss-Tor, he'd thought, *Finally. Extradition.*

But when they realized they had Jael instead of Commander March, they couldn't let him go. For crimes against humanity—an all-purpose charge—they sentenced him to life in Perdition. He guessed they didn't want to destroy Farwan's research and needed him where they could locate him should the need arise. In a political sense, his existence was a minefield, and he supposed leaders had argued as to whether he was entitled to fundamental human rights.

In the end, they decided against a death sentence. Through it all, Jael had been curious, not concerned, simply wondering how they would bring about his destruction if he was judged monstrous enough to deserve it. He had survived everything else. It would have added another layer of horror to persist through various methods of execution. In his heart, he knew his death would require primitive and barbaric measures, like taking his head.

That could happen here. The men are violent enough.

But not in Queensland. Dred had kept her promise in the sense that her territory was fairly civilized. There were no random murders, little deviance, so far as he could see. In the two weeks he'd been inside, he had explored enough of the prison ship to realize that wasn't the case elsewhere. He'd taken to marking hash tags on the wall near his pallet, so he didn't lose track of time as he had on Ithiss-Tor. There, he had descended into madness listening to the endless chittering of the Bugs echoing in the dark cavern.

Today, however, the hall bustled with activity. Men appeared to be building a perimeter in the center of the room. He watched for a moment before asking the man beside him, "What's going on?"

"That's right, you're a new fish. Those are grudge matches."

He raised an inquiring brow.

The man was clever enough to interpret it correctly as a question. "If someone does you wrong, you're not allowed to knife him. That gets you sent out of Queensland. Instead, you wait for the matches and issue a challenge. If you kill him in the ring, that's square with Dred, and there's no reprisal."

"The waiting probably helps put things in perspective, too."

"For some. There are blokes in here that live to fight in the ring, so be careful of crossing them. They can keep their urges on the chain, so long as they get to release them regular, but it don't take much to make them fix on killing somebody."

Jael nodded. "I appreciate the warning."

"No problem. Everybody was new once. I wouldn't be here if I hadn't gotten the word."

He took a second look at his benefactor. This was an old

man by any standards: weathered skin, battle scars, and thinning gray hair. If anyone was an expert on Perdition systems, he ought to be. The old-timer had probably seen regimes rise and fall, and he was still standing. That spoke of some particular savvy, which Jael intended to acquire.

"How long have you been inside?" he asked.

The man shrugged. "I don't even know. But since the place was commissioned, I reckon. How long's that been?"

"Close to twenty turns." And he'd spent them in a different prison.

Iron determination solidified in his bones. *I'm getting out of here.* Automated ships came at irregular intervals, so that meant a way out. He'd seen the defenses coming in, and they were supposed to be unbreakable. *We'll see.*

"I'm Ike," the old man said then.

"Jael. So what can you tell me about the man who ran Queensland before?"

"Artan? He was a right bastard. Back then, things weren't anything like you see now. We killed each other with as much glee as prisoners from other zones. There was no defending our borders, just chaos and bloodshed. Sometimes I think they put us inside, imagining we'll just kill each other. No need for them to dirty their hands with death sentences when they can get convicts to do the job without the moral dilemma."

"How did she take over?" he asked.

That might be too personal a question. And it revealed more interest in the Dread Queen than he wanted, but he was curious enough not to retract it. Jael waited to see what Ike said.

He didn't seem to think anything of it. "A knife in the back. She had been quietly gathering support, telling the men she had plans to make the place better. It's survival of the fittest here. And when she took down the boss man, she proved she had the guts to reign."

A simple but effective stratagem. "She must worry that somebody will try to take Queensland from her the same way."

"A bit, maybe. Most of us are happier than before she took over, so we wouldn't. But there are a few who miss the mayhem." Ike shrugged, then added, "But that's why she never sleeps alone. Tam and Einar are with her at all times."

He had no idea why he was so startled by that. Women had been using sex to manipulate men for aeons, and for Dred to use it to cement the loyalty of her two lieutenants, well, it was a canny move. At heart, males were often simple creatures—and if their base needs for food and sex were met, they could be controlled. She was clever to anticipate that and to factor it into her security plans.

"That's a good fail-safe, provided they don't turn."

"They wouldn't," Ike said. "She recruited Tam for Artan when he first got off the ship, and he's seen how it is elsewhere. As for Einar, well."

Einar's sick in love with her. He'd discerned as much the moment he saw them. *Obviously he doesn't mind sharing, however.* In a place like this, Jael supposed you got used to the constant redistribution of resources.

"Tell me—"

The old man motioned him to silence as a tall, brown-skinned woman stepped into the circle constructed of scrap metal and broken bits. Like most, she was lean, muscular, and scarred, but she'd added to her features with multiple piercings through lip and brow, shards of metal threaded through her ears. She raised both arms . . . and the rest of the talk ceased.

They have some sense of ceremony.

"Who's that?" he whispered.

"Calypso. She's the mistress of the circle."

"Are all the positions of authority held by females?"

Ike offered him an appraising glance. "Would that bother you?"

"No. I'm just wondering."

The old man shook his head. "Quiet now. Talking during the matches is a good way to get yourself challenged. I'll point out key personnel afterward."

He knew when to take a well-meant warning, so he shut

up. In her left hand, Calypso held a staff welded together from steel scraps, probably pinched from other places on the ship. She drummed it against the floor three times, and he had to admit, it made for an amazing concussive echo. At her signal, two men leapt into the circle, the first two combatants. Jael judged them relatively equal in size and strength though skill was another matter.

"State your grievance," she called.

"This bastard stole from me. I'll have his life in payment."

The other man narrowed his eyes, but he didn't deny the charge. "If I kill you, I'm acquitted."

A cheer rose up from the assembled convicts as Calypso pronounced, "Let the games begin!"

Once the woman vaulted out of the circle, the fighters rushed. Neither had any technique, but they possessed plenty of rage. Instead of watching them battle to the death, he studied the crowd. A handful of men seemed sickened rather than thrilled; others were laying bets. Then his gaze stopped on Dred—and until that moment, he didn't realize he had been searching for her.

And she was looking at him, too.

He tried, but he couldn't summon the charming smile that hid his true nature this time. So the eye contact remained somber and intense. Jael suspected she was taking his measure, appraising his reaction to the blood sport. And he wondered what his expression said. At last he lifted his chin and turned away, more unsettled than he let on.

The thief won. After that, he watched five men die in the space of an hour. Then Calypso bounded into the ring and slammed her staff into the floor, a signal that likely meant the matches were concluded. All around him, men dispersed to go about their business, such as there could be in a place like this. From the look of the furnishings, some had taken to building to stave off boredom, which led to discontent and more bloodshed. Here, however, nothing new could be created without stripping it from somewhere else. The ship was being cannibalized, piece by piece, and he wondered how long it would take before the vessel ceased functioning entirely. When life support lost enough components, it would shut down, leaving them to asphyxiate.

Not the best death.

"What did you think of the show?" Ike asked.

"I've seen better. Worse, too." Let him make of that what he would.

"I get the feeling you've seen more than I might imagine," the old man said shrewdly. "But I promised to tell you about the people in power, didn't I?"

"You did."

"Well, you already know Dred, Einar, and Tam. Now you've seen Calypso. There are really only three more people who have a say in the way Queensland runs."

"And they are?"

"Cook," Ike said, surprising him. "It's an odd thing, and the man doesn't talk much. He's pretty levelheaded, unless you interfere with his kitchen. Dred says an army marches on its belly, so we have to keep him happy."

"And that means she listens when he speaks." It was a sensible decision.

"Exactly. The other two? That's easy. There's Wills—"

"I already made his acquaintance. What's your take, Ike? Does he have any real ability?"

Ike sighed. "I believe so. She treats him like her court wizard. He's a foretelling Psi, but that gift ran him mad turns ago. I wouldn't carry his burden for a billion credits *and* my freedom."

"That's a firm refusal," he observed. "And the last man?"

A canny light entered the old man's eyes, and his thin mouth curved into a smile. "Me, of course. If we're continuing the royal metaphor, I'd be her harlequin." At Jael's raised brows, he elaborated, "I'm the old jester who tells her the key truths nobody else will speak. I'm also quietly her eyes and ears among the men. I take their measure and report any potential problems."

"You're telling me this so I don't become one?"

He shook his head. "No. You asked. Any man with the wit to wonder should have his answer."

"So she truly is the Dread Queen."

Ike met his gaze. "In our eyes, yes. She's made this place tolerable. Most of us have seen what it's like in Abaddon or—"

"I've heard that word before."

His education was spotty, though, one of the few things that gave him secret shame. Jael wished he knew more than a hundred ways to end a man's life, more than fifty ways to survive, but life hadn't taught him those things. There had been no classrooms for him or sessions with a tutor. In the eyes of most, he wasn't a person in need of education, but rather, a tool to be used, a weapon that fired on command. He wasn't even sure whether he was on the books as a sentient being, officially speaking.

Ike didn't comment. "It's a mythological place from the stories, but it means hell. And that's fairly accurate, as far as Priest's territory goes."

◄7►

The Quick and the Dead

"I'll take it from here," Dred said.

She savored the shock on the new fish's face. He had been so involved in the conversation that he hadn't noticed her approach. From his reaction, she guessed that wasn't customary. Normally, he was sharper on his feet; and in here, he needed to be. Though she wondered what Ike had been telling him, the old man wouldn't reveal anything that could be used against her.

"As you like," Ike said.

He moved off and stretched out to catch a nap. That was fairly rare. In most territories, you couldn't afford a sound sleep, as it was likely somebody would shank you for the pleasure of it. Or worse. The new fish was studying her again with those deep blue eyes, too vivid against the pallor of his skin. He had good bones, though. She didn't want to notice that. He was handsome, and he knew it, a well-made male animal.

"You said something about taking me in hand?" The question contained a mocking tone.

"Not exactly. But I prefer you address your questions to me."

"You seemed busy."

Their conversation was attracting attention, and a few men sidled closer to eavesdrop, so she beckoned him to follow. She led the way out of the main hall, which had been the primary mess, she suspected, back when the ship was used as a mining refinery. Fortunately, her zone also had facilities for the workers, which meant some privacy. Most of them were cramped, stacks of bunks one atop the other, but she had the foreman's suite, a little bigger than the rest. It was antiquated and relentlessly gray, power came with compensations for the weight she carried to keep Queensland running smooth.

Once the door swished shut behind them, she said, "I can see that you're not one to coast, so I can reckon you an asset, or you'll become a malcontent, causing problems I can't afford."

His brow went up. "You've judged me so swiftly."

"Am I wrong?"

To her surprise, he laughed. "I definitely have my own agenda."

Ah, the impossible dream. She didn't need to be a telepathic Psi to grasp his meaning. "Let me predict your path. For the next two turns, give or take, you'll devote yourself to learning the ship's systems, security measures, and routines."

"I dislike being so predictable."

A faint pang of sympathy went through her. It hadn't been so long, relatively speaking, since she went through those desperate motions, sure she would be the exception—that she could chart a path out of here and get back to what had passed for her life. But the problem was, there were no routines. The transport shuttles arrived irregularly, and everything went into lockdown. There was no way to implement a plan that required timing and preparation when you had mere minutes to get in position.

She'd tried, more than once.

Failed.

"Feel free to test my conclusions, but . . . escape is impossible."

"So," he said gently, "is my very existence. And yet here I am. Therefore, I submit to you that every problem has a solution. We simply haven't identified it yet."

Fascination sank sharp teeth into her, driving Dred to ask, "What do you mean?"

It was unprecedented; she *never* asked personal questions. From the faint flare of satisfaction in his blue gaze, he knew it, too. The bastard. But he wouldn't be drawn.

Jael merely shook his head. "I haven't known you long enough to trust you with my deep, dark secrets, queenie."

"As I recall, you said you didn't have any."

"A man who ends up in here is definitely a liar, and that's likely the least of his crimes."

"Is it yours? I thought all convicts claim to be innocent, wrongly accused."

Jael shook his head, his eyes feverish with intensity. "I'm a wicked thing, make no mistake."

"Your honesty is refreshing. And yet I think one who *admits* to being a beast cannot be so rotten as he claims."

"You'll be searching for my halo next. I'm sorry, love, but it's out for polishing."

That rejoinder, quick as it was, reminded her of an issue, one she'd left for too long. "When Grigor's men attacked, you called yourself my champion."

"You take exception to that?"

"It implies I can't fight my own battles."

"Even warrior queens have a knight who fights at their word. It doesn't mean you *can't.* Only that I will."

She'd intended to smack him down, discourage the presumption, but his words intrigued her. "So if I say kill, you'll kill?"

"Will it earn me perks and pleasures?" His look heated.

"That depends on your definition."

He lifted one shoulder in a careless, graceful half shrug. "I've been used as a weapon before."

"But you didn't like it." By the infinitesimal widening of his eyes, he was surprised she'd guessed that, but his aura gave away flashes of color, hints of old pain. Her ability used to only function on violent emotions, but she'd found her empathy to be like a muscle; the more she used it, the more she could, and the more emotions she detected. It wasn't always welcome.

He changed the subject. "If you don't mind, I'd like some answers. I had more questions for Ike, but you sent him off."

For some reason, she feared what he might ask. Personal matters were verboten, but her filters had been faintly askew with this fish since he entered Queensland. He'd gotten her talking about her father, for Mary's sake, without half trying. Who knew what he could persuade her to reveal if he applied himself?

"Give me the lay of the land. I ken there are territories, but how many, who runs them? That sort of thing."

Relief poured through her in a calming tide; her shoulders relaxed. Dred could handle inquiries about how Perdition ran. "What did Ike tell you?"

"He'd just mentioned Abaddon and Priest when you arrived."

"A religious zealot who's created a cult of sorts. Everything Priest does is for his own self-aggrandizement and to reward or punish true believers."

"He's mad, then."

"As a hatter. There are six territories, counting mine. Four are governed by men."

"And they are?"

"Mungo, who rules over Munya. Not sure if it's named after him or the word means something." She took Jael's shrug to indicate he had no idea either. "They're not too nice about their eating requirements, if you take my meaning."

"Cannibalism?" Horror drew his brows down, his lips tight.

Good to know. He apparently has limits.

"Among other things. They take prisoners in raids and

then have a barbecue. It plays hell on the ventilation system, and the smell . . ." Dred closed her eyes.

Jael swore softly. "I'm starting to reconsider this place being better than the Bug prison."

It took her a few seconds to place the reference. "You've been to Ithiss-Tor?"

Awe ran through her. Whoever he was now, he must've been important, as the Bug homeworld had been off-limits for ages, then forty or so turns ago, they opened their borders for a diplomatic envoy, and eventually allied with the Conglomerate to play a key role in the Morgut War. The galaxy was still recovering; certain outposts had fallen while others rose up. Not that she knew anything about recent interstellar affairs. Everything outside Perdition might've blown up for all she knew. But Dred felt hungry for news, and she bit down on the urge to question him further. Demonstrating eagerness would give him leverage.

"A long time ago," he said. "I stayed longer than I intended. Go on?"

She gathered he meant with the rundown of the factions. "Right. To the other side, we have Grigor's Korolévstvo. He's a bear of a man, hence the nickname." Jael raised a brow in inquiry, so she clarified, "The Great Bear. When I arrived, he was at the docking point, recruiting. He keeps the largest standing force, and I'm not entirely sure how he feeds them all. I turned him down in favor of Artan, who looked slightly less terrifying."

"No atrocities from Grigor?" Jael asked.

She shrugged. "No more than anyone else. He's a killer, of course, and a ferocious one. More to the point, he's also a conqueror. Fortunately, not a smart one."

"He wants your territory?"

Dred pushed out a sigh. Everyone knew, but it hurt to admit, "I only took over from Artan half a turn ago, and it's been tough to hold on. The Bear thinks he'll have an easy time rolling over me."

"We'll see," Jael said quietly.

To her mind, that almost sounded like a pledge of support. "Things would be grim for Queensland if space gets divvied up between Priest and Grigor. No more safety, no more hygiene. The men will lose all status, be treated worse than slaves."

"You sound like you'd mind."

For obvious reasons, she lied. "Only losing my territory. Let's see. Two domains left. Katur and the Warren are the least of my problems . . . he has the bowels of the ship and tends to collect aliens. He's a humanoid from some remote world. Don't ask me how he ended up here."

"Same as everyone else. Killed someone important or offended the wrong people."

"Probably."

"You said there were four men. That leaves two women in charge. You and who else?"

"Silence."

"An ominous name. Tell me about her."

Dred considered, trying to decide how to explain. "Her demesne lies on the other side of Grigor's from here. She and her followers devote themselves to finding new ways to kill. They're . . . incarnations of death, and they believe by being entombed here, they're already in the afterlife, so nothing that transpires matters."

"The ultimate nihilism?"

"Yes. They've all taken vows of silence except for their Speaker for the Dead, who serves as emissary on the rare occasions where communication between zones is required."

He looked thoughtful. "But if they kill one another without restraint, how does she keep up her numbers? Or defend her borders?"

"I'm unclear on how her system functions," Dred admitted. "I've heard rumors about a Festival of Death, but I don't know much about it. The wise steer clear of Silence's people. They're . . . creepy. In a place like this, that's saying something."

"They would be. There's naught more dangerous than a man with nothing left to lose."

Dred nodded, surprised at the intimate knowledge of desperation she glimpsed in him. He looked far too young to know so much. Yet she sensed his apparent age was a lie—and a riddle, like so much else about him. It took all of her self-control not to commit herself to unraveling his secrets, but her problems were far more pressing than one man ever could be, no matter how much he intrigued her.

"That ends today's lessons," she told him.

"And here I was hoping for a hands-on portion of the tutorial."

Exactly the opening I hoped for.

"Then it's your lucky day."

His brows went up. "Really? That was fast. I didn't even have to exert my natural charm."

"I suspect our definitions of the word may differ." She couldn't resist a smirk, holding the pause to see if he would break and ask.

He did. "What did you have in mind, then?"

"You're going to see Silence with me."

"After everything you said about her cult of death? Why?"

The reminder of how dire their situation had become registered anew, stealing away her mirth like a cold chill. "Because we need an alliance if we're to survive the brewing conflict. Grigor and Priest are working together, and it won't be long before they strike."

"Did you choose Silence because she's female or because she shares a border with Grigor?" he asked with keen insight.

"Both," she admitted. "I hope she realizes that if Grigor takes my zone, it won't be long before he's looking to expand his borders the other way."

"If she believes nothing matters, she may not care."

"That's a risk I have to take. He won't rest until he controls the whole ship."

"Or until he's dead."

"If you can achieve that, I'll grant any reward you like."

"Be careful what you promise," he said with a sharp smile.

"It's not a reckless offer. I said Grigor has the largest population, and he never has less than ten men at his side. Plus, you'd have to cut through multiple checkpoints to reach him."

He shrugged. "Still not impossible. It would just hurt a lot."

Who are you? she wondered. *More to the point,* what *are you?* From a few hints he'd dropped, Dred suspected he wasn't altogether human. But she didn't ask.

"Are you ready to go see Silence?"

"Do I have a choice?" By his expression, he thought the answer was no.

"Of course. If you're a sheep content to be led, then find your pallet while I handle important business." Dred spoke in a mordant tone, her gaze on his.

In response, he jerked his chin. "You've got my measure, queenie. I can't abide being left on the sidelines. You're wise to keep me close. Otherwise, it will certainly mean trouble."

Just as Wills predicted.

◀8▶

The Price of Silence

Once Dred called for her two lieutenants, they set off for Entropy, a pretentious name for Silence's zone. The princess in chains ran a tight ship, so to speak. She murmured greetings to men they passed, some roaming from the dormitories to the main hall, others heading back. From what Jael could tell, she knew their names, and they were courteous to her. It took a strong woman to earn the respect of convicts so brutal they'd been sentenced to die without ever again feeling the sun on their skin.

Me, included.

"I'll take my turn on patrol," he said then, "but I'd also like to work in the hydroponics garden if there's somebody willing to show me what to do."

Tameron aimed a surprised look at him. "Unexpected. But I can show you the ropes tomorrow."

"Thanks."

Dred was watching him, too, her expression inscrutable. But she didn't comment. Which was good because he couldn't explain the impulse. He couldn't recall ever helping anything to flower. In his life, he'd only ever rolled through like a Peacemaker unit, leaving destruction in his wake. After so many turns in solitary in the Bug prison and now this place, it seemed like time to change that.

On the way, he noted the guards who patrolled Dred's territory; they looked attentive, though he'd tighten up their passes and vary the length of time between them. If you ran things with too much precision, people learned to work around the security measures. But he'd talk to Dred in private, later. She might take exception to his critical evaluation of her system.

"The border's coming up," she said eventually. "We wouldn't be doing this if it wasn't important. But if we're spotted, fight for your lives. Grigor catches us, and we end up dead."

"Understood," Einar answered.

Tam only nodded, then she went on, "It will be safest if we go through the maintenance shafts and stay out of the main corridors. Is that a problem for anybody?"

"Not for me," Jael answered.

"I might be too loud." Einar stood quiet, waiting for her judgment.

Her strong features went thoughtful. She wasn't beautiful, but her fierceness drew the eye. Sometimes strength was better than beauty, especially in a place like this. "Head back and keep the others on point. Keep a sharp eye on our perimeters, especially all access points near the garden."

"Will do," Einar muttered.

He turned and strode away. Jael could tell he wasn't pleased, but at least the man knew his limitations. Not that Jael would mind a fight. Dred didn't realize what an asset she'd acquired, but for the moment, it was nice being treated like a person, not a weapon. That would change soon enough.

"Here," she said after they'd walked for a while. "Boost Tam so he can open the panel."

"As you command, queenie," he said with a touch of irony.

He'd never been good at taking orders unless they came with a fat payday. Yet he still cupped his hands and tossed the other man up; Tam latched onto the rungs bolted into the side high on the wall. The man fiddled with the latches, then it opened. He climbed in without waiting for the order, which made Jael think he traveled this way a lot. He tossed Dred up next, and she peered over her shoulder at him.

"Can you—"

Before she could complete the question, he took a few steps back for a running start and launched himself up. His thighs were deceptively strong, and he landed right below her, close enough to feel the heat of her body, her braids brushing against his shoulders. His whole body reacted. *It's only because it's been so long,* he told himself. With effort, he slowed his breathing and denied the response.

"Stay close," she said.

The shafts were dark and cold, coated with old mining dust. Ahead, Tam forged a certain trail, cutting left and right with no hesitation; sometimes they dropped down a level via more rungs bolted to the wall. In places the metal was unsteady, rusted, and he didn't like putting his whole weight on it. There was no way to be sure how far the drop would be should a bar tear free and send him plummeting. Jael wished being hard to kill meant immunity to fright, but he could still fear things even when he knew they couldn't end him.

"If we can sneak around like this," he whispered eventually, "so can they. Do you monitor the access points?"

She cast a scornful look over one shoulder. "Of course. I can't keep them from passing through, but if they drop out in my zone, I handle it."

Tam said nothing, likely focused on making sure they didn't get lost. He was small and quick, an excellent guide. Jael imagined that the other man had memorized where the ducts traveled and the best places to emerge. Countless moments later, he opened a panel and disappeared from sight.

Jael sighed. "He doesn't talk much."

"You could learn from him."

"It's part of my charm."

"In here, 'charm' will get you killed."

"I should be so lucky," he muttered.

"One of these days, I'll ask why you're so in love with the prospect of dying."

He cocked a half smile, knowing most women hated that look. It was the one he saved for when they realized he had no intention of promising anything other than the ferocious hour they'd spent clawing and biting. "And I might tell you if you ask me sweetly enough."

"Not going to happen."

"You should try everything once."

"Not that," she said.

Now he wasn't sure if they were talking about death or her employing wiles to get at his truths. She was an intriguing woman. As he wondered, she dropped out of sight, and he followed. This portion of the ship looked decidedly different. The walls were streaked dark, paint of some kind, making the metal look ominous and laser-scarred.

"This is the border between Grigor and Silence's territory," she said.

Jael hadn't really believed the ship could look much different from zone to zone, but double black lines were painted on the floor and walls, and primitive fencing had been erected. Four men waited on the other side, pale and quiet. On this side, the walls had red characters on them, an old alphabet he knew was called Cyrillic, though he couldn't recall where he'd learned that bit of trivia. From Surge, maybe, one of the mercs he'd served with on Nicu Tertius.

Tam stepped forward and signed to the sentries. *So Dred wasn't kidding when she said they take a vow of silence.* That would get old . . . and creepy, fast. A few minutes later, Tameron nodded and stepped back as the guards opened the gate.

Impatient, Tam beckoned them on. Once they got past the checkpoint, he explained, "They gave me today's password in case anyone stops us."

"How did you persuade them to let us see Silence?" Dred asked.

Jael was wondering the same. Though he hadn't been inside long, he understood that passing an enemy's border wasn't done lightly. According to local gossip, she'd executed one of Grigor's people for doing just that, not long before his arrival. But they had temporary clearance to be here.

"I told them it was a matter of life and death."

Dred cut Tam a look. "You realize she's much more interested in the latter?"

"It's up to you to convince her not to execute us."

Jael thought that sounded remarkably unconcerned, but maybe Tam had that much confidence in her abilities. She had rolled into Queensland and taken it over half a turn ago. That wasn't done lightly. From what he could see, the men were loyal. Well. Loyal as men like this could be.

Me, included.

Some distance from the border, the first patrol dropped down behind them. Jael had a garrote around his neck before Tam managed to signal them. The smaller man did so frantically, struggling with the assassin who held him. Jael didn't bother trying to imitate the sign; he just slammed his head back as hard as he could. He heard the crack of cartilage.

Got your nose.

Jael spun. The man didn't cry out as blood streamed down his chin. His eyes were queer, dead and empty. Despite himself, a shiver ran through him. *This place truly is hell, a mortal afterlife where they chain those too monstrous for freedom.*

Me, included.

Instead of signaling back, the sentries slipped into the darkness. Jael had preternatural senses; that wasn't a boast, but fact. He could hear Dred's heartbeat beside him, Tam's a little farther on. He heard her faint arrhythmia and Tameron's accelerated breathing. He heard the skitter of claws; the ship was infested. But from Silence's killers, he heard nothing at all.

Like they're truly dead.

Regardless, he was glad he'd been invited along so he

could see the other zone. So far, this one was grimier—
darker—than Dred's domain, and it had black paint on the
walls. Not a huge difference.

But as they approached, he breathed, "Dear Mary, what's
that smell?"

"Death," she said simply.

In his days as a merc, then from his time as a tank-thing,
born of tubes and chemicals and wires, he'd seem some horrors. They'd driven many of his pod mad. To his knowledge,
he was the only survivor of the Ideal Genome Project, and
he'd still never witnessed anything like this. The room was
full of rotting bodies, piles of bones. Obviously human, some
had been fashioned into furniture. But they hadn't been
cleaned or treated, just rawly carved, and the stench lingered.
A gaunt, sunken-eyed woman in black lounged on her grisly
throne, gray hair a wild tangle about her head. Countless
eyes fixed on them as they entered, but no one spoke.

It was silent as the tomb.

Jael thought back to Dred's casual warning about Silence's people and realized that was a massive understate-
ment. If she was seeking an alliance with this lunatic, how
bad must Grigor and Priest be? With an imperious gesture
from a skeletal arm, Silence summoned them forward.

Her eyes burned like black holes in her skull, and Jael
fought the urge to retreat. He'd never encountered anyone
who unnerved him more; he didn't like to call her a woman
because she lacked some key element of humanity. *Is that
what people see when they look at me?* The question chewed
in and burrowed deep.

Silence studied them for a few seconds, then her thin
fingers flew in complex gestures. Then a slim figure stepped
forth from the shadows behind the gruesome throne. Clad
in black, his face painted in gray and white to resemble a
skull, this had to be the Speaker for the Dead, the one soul
in Silence's domain who was permitted to speak.

All part of the spectacle, Jael decided.

The Speaker intoned, "What brings you before Death's
Handmaiden?"

It should've been a ridiculous, melodramatic question. It wasn't.

Dred held her ground. "I seek an alliance."

Jael listened while she elaborated on the coalition between Grigor and Priest and the danger it posed to Entropy should Queensland fall. In preternatural stillness, Silence listened. And then she signed to her Speaker.

Who said, "Death fears nothing. What must be, will be."

That was a load of shit. Silence was utterly demented, and no amount of logic would sway her. There was no time to check with the princess in chains as the idea came to him. He sensed stirring in the shadows, sensing that any moment, they would become the day's entertainment. Since he'd been tortured before—and he had no desire for these lunatics to learn how long he could suffer without dying—Jael stepped forward.

"Then let Death decide," he said.

Silence skewered him with a gaze made of black madness, then she signed to her Speaker. "Your words are intriguing, child."

Don't call me that. I never was one. Four turns into my creation, and I was already killing. Maybe he had no right to judge Silence.

"You said Death fears nothing, but I've heard he's a gentleman. So let your champion face me. And if I survive, you stand with the Dread Queen against Grigor and Priest."

◄9►

Bitter Bargains

The new fish was crazy.

There was no other explanation for the challenge he'd extended—without Dred's sanction. And she couldn't object without looking like she couldn't control her people. She remembered Wills's prediction about how this one would destroy everything.

Suddenly, it didn't seem so unlikely. The man was reckless beyond bearing.

Yet she let the offer stand. Worst-case scenario, he died, and she stood no closer to an alliance. Then she'd leave the corpse with Silence and follow Tam back through the shafts to Queensland and start trying to come up with a plan B before Grigor and Priest completed their battle strategies. Overall, things didn't look so bright at the moment.

"Does he speak for you?" the Speaker asked, after conferring with Silence.

Yeah, we'll be talking about that.

Tameron maintained a watchful air, but she could tell he didn't approve. There was no way to deny it without losing face and the situation deteriorating, so she nodded. Then Silence turned to Jael.

Wordless, she pointed to the center of the hall, past mounds of gray, withered bodies, beyond the bone pickets spiked into the metal flooring. Dred had been here before, carrying messages for Artan, but the horror of the place never ceased to overwhelm her. But she couldn't give any sign of that. Weakness led to teeth on your throat.

"Let the Dread Queen's champion face the Death Knight," the Speaker pronounced.

Dred found all the titles and posturing tiresome. She hadn't come up with the Dread Queen mythos, but the men ran with it, as it pleased them to have a figure around which to build a world better than the one they lived in. Without these trappings, they were all just beasts scrambling for scraps in a rusted metal cage.

An enormous male, dressed only in black leather pants, strode to the center of the hall. His arms were easily the size of Dred's head, and he stood two meters in height. Unlike Einar, he had no scars, unless you counted his expression. He wore pain like a wound, a suffering so deep it dug brackets beside his mouth, furrows etched into his brow and between his eyes. Silence's other men had eyes like hers, full of nothing, but this was a beast in chains.

Except he wasn't.

He carried no weapons, but Dred suspected he needed none.

Jael should be worried. Terrified, even. She knew he was fast—and stronger than he looked—but to beat a gladiator like this, he needed to be a hero from the ancient stories. And if he were one, he wouldn't be here. *Just as well I didn't get attached.*

Instead, the new fish strolled to the center of the hall. At some point, he'd traded his prison-issue gray for other clothing, handmade by Queenslanders. It let him blend in better, but at the moment, he looked oddly nondescript, considering what he was about to do. He raised his hands in a defensive posture, and she bit back the desire to chide him or warn him or call him names for being stupid enough, cocky enough, to toss his future down the recycling chute.

I could've used somebody like you, she thought.

The giant lashed out with a ferocious right cross, but Jael wasn't there. He danced—and it was such a graceful movement that it seemed taunting—to the side. Then he spread his arms. "I'm right here, mate. Go on, then. Show everyone how terrifying you are."

Silence's warrior rushed, head down, like an enraged beast, but Dred could tell his heart wasn't in it. Somehow, he had been forced to this role, and his body was only going through the motions. He'd killed until there was no joy in it if ever there had been. She hadn't even known that was possible, that one could rehabilitate a murderer via aversion therapy. But then again, no wonder; it required an endless number of worthless lives and the complete absence of anything like mercy or remorse. It required a certain conflation of factors.

It required Perdition.

Quick as a snake, Jael flipped the larger man in a strike so powerful, it snapped his shoulder out of socket. A normal fighter would've groaned in pain, either at the dislocation or when he hit the ground. The giant only breathed, his lungs hauling hard. She swore she saw pleading in his face as Jael kicked him in the head. In another zone, men would be cheering, taunting, placing bets. Not here.

This poor Death Knight seemed eager now. His movements became rushed, sloppy. He threw punch after punch and landed none of them. His breathing grew hoarse, which could've meant desperation, but when she closed her eyes, she read them, and saw the fluttering orange eagerness that raced through his psyche like a psychedelic.

He wants this, more than anything. Don't make him wait, Jael.

As if he heard, the new fish grew focused. The room fell to absolute stillness as Jael finished the Death Knight. He was merciful when he broke the man's neck. She'd never seen anyone fight as he did—with reckless confidence combined with such skill. It was like he could tell what his opponent would do before he did it.

Maybe he's Psi. Limited precog, applied to combat. Such a skill wouldn't surprise her, and it would explain a lot. Nobody had heard of her empathic permutation until she started trying to explain it to prison doctors, but they diagnosed her with all kinds of mental illnesses as well. They claimed the men she called killers were good family men; and she was absolutely delusional. As soon as she admitted it, then they could help her. Fix her.

Bullshit.

Dred preferred life inside to the lies they crafted and placed on her tongue in pill form. Once she spat the meds out enough, they took to feeding them to her intravenously. That kept her quiet in the planetside prison for a while. She had the dubious honor of being dubbed belatedly too dangerous for the common criminal.

As Jael stood over the Death Knight's body, she didn't move; this had to play out between Jael and Silence. He'd thrown the dice, so it was up to him to cast the winning roll. Or eat his losses. If he survived, they'd talk about his impulse-control problems.

Moving with quiet confidence, Jael presented himself to Silence, standing before the bone seat with his hands laced behind his back. Oddly, Dred thought he'd never appeared more impressive, a military cast to his stance. He actually looked like a queen's champion. While he waited, Silence conferred with the Speaker, and Dred glanced at Tam, hoping he'd offer a clue as to what was going on. He only shook his head; talking would be rude at this juncture and might screw up negotiations.

Fine. I'll wait.

"The Handmaiden will honor your bargain," the Speaker announced. "It was a good fight and a clean death. But she has terms for your agreement."

"I'm listening," Dred said.

"You are correct in that if the Great Bear swallows

Queensland, he will turn his eyes to Entropy. That one has a hunger that can never be sated even should he swallow the stars."

It was a poetic way to describe the savage, murdering conqueror, but Silence wasn't wrong about Grigor. So Dred nodded, showing they were on the same page.

Then the Speaker went on, "But the threat alone would not have been enough to push the Handmaiden to War, even though War is Death."

Weirdly, she could hear the capital letters in that sentence, as if War and Death were people. To Silence, maybe they were.

"I understand," Dred said, though she didn't, really.

This shit hole required a constant fight for survival. People who lay down, died, unless they were crazy in a sufficiently terrifying manner, so that nobody wanted to screw with them in case doing so stirred a nest of snakes so poisonous that it could end only in certain death. Silence had that down to an art, and maybe it was why she'd created the persona, ages ago. By this point, however, she believed in her own legend.

Not the sign of a stable mind. But she's my best shot.

"These are her terms. First, if this alliance results in new territory, she claims half of it as her right for aiding Queensland."

"That's fair," Tam whispered. "No need to bargain."

"Done," Dred agreed.

"But if the battle is joined and Queensland is lost, then the Handmaiden must be recompensed." The Speaker stepped forward, indicating Jael. "She will have him as the new Death Knight. The Handmaiden says while she is Death's lady, this one is his son."

"I'm nobody's son," Jael muttered.

Tam motioned him to silence, as Dred stepped closer to her self-proclaimed champion. "You had no hesitation about risking your life before. Again?"

Something like surprise flashed across his face, then he inclined his head, granting permission. It was a lightning exchange, not enough to weaken her position, but Jael seemed glad she hadn't disregarded his sovereignty. Dred wasn't even sure why she'd bothered.

She answered, "Of course, provided he's alive. If Grigor or Priest takes my territory, Jael could be killed in the fighting."

"This one always survives," the Speaker intoned. "The debt will be paid."

Dred had no idea if that was a prophecy or a prediction, but it sounded like a done deal to her. "Do we shake on it, or sign something?"

The skull face seemed affronted. "Death requires no documentation. You cannot force him to come for you, but the Handmaiden's word is good. Or do you doubt her?"

Silence stared.

"No. As far as I'm concerned, we're set. How soon can we start planning?"

The Speaker watched Silence's signs, then answered, "She will soon send me with instructions."

She wanted to protest that she was an equal partner, but if she had been able to handle Grigor and Priest on her own, she wouldn't be in Silence's boneyard. Nausea rose in her throat, suppressed all this time through sheer will, but the smell was intolerable. Somehow, she didn't flinch or weaken, kept her gaze sure and strong, until the Speaker dropped his eyes and dipped at the waist, acknowledging her dominance.

I win, you bizarre bastard. Time to go.

"Will the password hold until we reach the edge of your zone?" she asked.

"The men will see you out."

"Thank you for your time and hospitality," Tam said as he signed.

Dred guessed he was spelling out the same thing in graceful hand gestures. Silence inclined her wild mane, regal in her visceral madness. So strange, pretending she had any idea about diplomacy or courtly nonsense. *My father would've forgotten to put on pants if my mother hadn't reminded him.* But Perdition was as much asylum as prison, and when you were standing in somebody else's delusions, it was both polite and politic to play along.

As promised, the Speaker sent an escort with them all the way out to the access panel. Once they boosted up into the ducts, shivering set in. Entropy was worse than all the stories.

Jael put a hand on her arm, and it horrified her that he felt those tremors. She couldn't afford for anyone to realize how close to the surface her sensibilities ran. The Dread Queen had to be all determined iron, an ice maiden incapable of disquiet or remorse, or her enemies would eat her alive.

"Thanks for giving me a choice. I don't understand why, but—"

She substituted bravado for composure. "Step back. Or you're three seconds away from the death you seem to desire."

We don't have a connection, pretty lad. In here, people will gnaw you to the bone if you let them. It might even be me.

He narrowed his eyes. "Not even in your best dreams, love."

"Let me explain how this plays out. If you don't remove your hand, Tam has a needle full of poison that will put you to sleep. He has several in fact, so if you shake it off quickly, we'll jab you again. I'm not positive what you are, but I'm pretty sure you can't live without your heart."

A reckless laugh echoed down the ducts. "Poor, foolish queenie. I've done it for years."

Sneak Attack

Tam didn't want to kill the new fish, mostly because it would be a waste of resources. The man might be useful; certainly he'd proven he could fight. He thought Dred was overreacting, but he chose not to countermand her orders. Instead, he watched the two size each other up, then Jael stepped back.

He was smiling. "Sorry. I didn't mean to lay hands upon the queen."

"Don't let it happen again," Dred snarled.

Tam could see that she was unsettled by the visit to Silence's domain. He would be, too, if he hadn't seen—and smelled—it many times before, during his surveillance runs. Once, he'd witnessed their Festival of Death, and it had been the most grotesque and macabre spectacle imaginable, with fountains of blood and swords made of bone arming men whose sole aim was to die in a manner pleasing to Death's Handmaiden. Despite his external calm, Tam suppressed a shiver. This alliance made him uneasy, but it was necessary.

"Let's head back," he murmured, revealing none of his misgivings.

Tam knew the route with his eyes closed, but smudges in the dust and smeared palm prints made it fairly obvious, even to the other two. Maintenance tunnels riddled the ship like a honeycomb, and sometimes, he had to avoid other explorers. He motioned to Dred and Jael to step lightly as footfalls rang out in the distance. This convict must be new to the art of stealth, as he banged around, running into walls and stumbling so loud that Tam suspected they could hear him in the Warren.

"That's not normal," Dred whispered.

He only nodded. It seemed prudent to find out who this was and from what sector, so he answered in an undertone, "Wait here. Don't move."

With quiet approval, he noted how the other two hunkered down into the shadows. Their posture wasn't perfect, but Jael obviously had some experience in skullduggery. That startled Tam not at all, given the man's overall predatory air. But some predators could be trained to guard territory, and if that was the case, then Tam definitely had a use for the new fish.

He crept along the metal wall, tracking the thumps and bumps until he was right up behind the other party. At that point, he realized the man's clumsiness stemmed from injuries, not lack of care, and in the larger sense, it wasn't a man at all, but one of Katur's aliens. The creature stumbled again, reeled against the wall, and this time, its limbs wouldn't hold it. Tam weighed the risks and decided his course; he slipped back to the others without speaking.

"Who was it?" Dred asked.

He lied without compunction. "Just an oversized rodent, dying badly."

He had no way to be sure how long it took, given their relative lack of agility, but eventually, they dropped down from the access panel just inside Dred's borders. An ominous feeling stole over him when they came to the last checkpoint. Four bodies littered the ground, blood everywhere, and there was no sign of the men who had killed them.

"Grigor?" Jael asked.

Dred shook her head as she knelt. "This looks like Priest's work. See the holes punched through their palms? It's a calling card of sorts."

"A raiding party?" Tam suggested. "If so, we should look for the other incursion site. The Bear mentioned a two-pronged attack."

"Possibly. I didn't think they'd organize this quick. We need to move quietly and assess the situation." So saying, she didn't unwind the chains from her forearms.

Tam approved of that caution. If things were worse than anticipated, he could lead her away from the danger and find refuge elsewhere. He had scouted more than a dozen locations that few other men were likely to find. It was impossible to store provisions, as supplies were so scarce, but if they couldn't find Dred, then neither Priest, nor Grigor, could claim they had destroyed Queensland. Tam understood that it was a risk in setting so much power behind one woman, but he felt confident he had read her correctly. She was not a lesser metal, and she wouldn't crumple beneath the weight before the game played out.

"Follow me," he whispered to the other two.

They fell in behind him, and Jael went up in Tam's estimation. Some men saw his lack of stature and tried to shove him aside to get close to Dred. It spoke well of Jael that he was smart enough to understand that Tam's value lay in something other than battle skill or muscle mass.

The enemy had been careless, leaving bloody footprints all the way to the hall. That let Tam gauge roughly how many lay ahead. He expected a fight, but when they reached the hall, he saw a number of enemy corpses instead. Einar looked like hell, but he was organizing the cleanup. His scarred features showed immediate relief when he saw Dred returning unharmed.

"What happened?" Dred demanded.

"Skirmish." Einar indicated the damage to the main hall, along with the wounded men being tended. "Twenty-five men. It wasn't enough to seize control, so I'm not sure what Priest was thinking."

"I am," Jael said. "It's a classic guerrilla tactic. Send pawns to weaken the queen. Weaken with wave after wave of expendable forces. And once your opponent has nothing left in reserve, you send the full might of your army to crush them."

Dred turned to him. "You sound like a soldier."

"I've been one, among other things."

That surprised Tam. He wouldn't have guessed that Jael had enough discipline or self-control to accept orders on a daily basis, but as he mulled what to do with this new information, Dred said, "Good. Then you'll be in charge of tactics. Confer with Tam while I work with Einar in getting things squared away."

An admirable allocation of resources. Sometimes Tam wondered if he underestimated her. He didn't know much about her life before she had been sentenced to life—and death—in Perdition. She made it a point not to discuss her past, and she didn't ask many questions of other people, either. *Just as well. I would've lied.*

To Jael, he said, "Meet me in Dred's quarters in a couple of hours. I've something to take care of first."

Still calculating odds and scenarios, Tam hurried off to collect food and medical supplies. He hoped it wasn't too late for the creature in the ducts, as that would upset all his plans.

Astonishment colored everything for a few, brief seconds, then Jael nodded, though Tameron was already leaving. He had some time to kill, so he went to the hydroponics garden. There were a couple of workers inside, but they took no notice of him. The lights were bright, almost like the sun, and it was the most peaceful place he'd found on Perdition. Little wonder the other leaders wanted to take this oasis and burn it down. For a few seconds, he simply breathed, enjoying the way the plants scented the air. *It would be nice if I knew their names, too.*

A woman glanced at him belatedly. "Can I help you?"

He shook his head. "I'm just exploring. I'll be working here eventually, so I wanted to learn my way around."

"Let me know if you have questions," she said.

He *did* have some, and she wound up showing him how to care for some of the vegetables. Therefore, the time went fast. Eventually, Ike ambled in.

"Tam's looking for you. Just thought you should know."

Jael swore, thanked the woman for her time, and jogged toward Dred's quarters. The door swished open to reveal Tam; Jael stepped inside, and the other man indicated he should make himself comfortable. Since the room consisted of a bunk, a couple of hard chairs, and a broken entertainment console, it wasn't much, but since he was happy to be consulted on anything, he had no comment on the paltry accommodations. The merc commanders who recruited him paid him to march or kill; they didn't ask his opinion. It occurred to him that he'd only been a part of things in this way once before, and he'd thrown it away in fear the situation would sour. Fear had driven him to trade potential friendship for a payday.

Even in a place like this, he wouldn't repeat the mistake again. Lab techs had called him subhuman, but he was capable of learning from his mistakes. Of course, they'd said those things because they were rationalizing their choice to experiment on him. Jael was lucky they had never plumbed the full extent of his regenerative gifts or learned how they could be useful to other people . . . or he'd never have left the lab that last time.

They were wrong about me, he told himself. *I'm a person. I can learn. I can.*

Deep down lay the cold, curling fear that, in fact, he couldn't. That he was a broken thing, born of mechanical bits, electrical impulses, and a scientist's meddling. *Perhaps I cannot learn.* But he meant to try. He had read a story of spirits being refined in pits of fire, so that they were better and stronger when they climbed out. Back then, it had seemed likely they would only be destroyed.

But maybe not. Hope tormented him.

Jael was surprised to identify the anger he felt over the attack. Not because he was so attached to the sentries but because of what it represented. Priest and Grigor were determined to take Dred's territory. *Not on my watch.*

AFTER he sat, Tam said, "Grigor has the greater number of men whereas Priest has zealots. If he orders them to come and die, they'll do so without protest."

Jael nodded. "Priest will supply the shock troops. He'll attempt to wear us down. It will be imperative to defend, as every loss will impact morale."

"You think there's such a thing as morale in a place like this?" Tam eyed him as if he represented a question to which there was no answer.

"In Queensland, yes. It's better than Munya or Entropy or—"

"I take your point. And yes, it is. Dred tries to run this place like a city. A city where all the citizens are right bastards, but she keeps the torture and bloodshed to a minimum."

"Is it better than it was under Artan?" He didn't even know why he was asking.

Tam surprised him by answering, "Much. I was his spymaster first, but Artan was too like Grigor. No ability to plan, he only cared to take or own. There were food shortages. The hydroponics garden stopped producing, and Artan's solution was more blood sport."

"Why?" Jael asked.

"Because he knew we'd end up with less mouths to feed."

"Is that when you decided to dispose of him?"

Amusement flickered in the other man's dark eyes. "Is that what you think? I took care of Artan quietly, then deposited Dred on the throne to give the men someone prettier to serve?"

Put like that, it did sound offensive. Not only to Tameron—because it implied he couldn't lead men himself—but to Dred, as it suggested she lacked the wherewithal to seize power on her own. He suspected neither implication was true.

"Then tell me what really happened."

"I think it best that we focus on battle plans. It's too good a story for me to deprive Dred the pleasure of telling you herself."

For some reason, that sounded ominous. Jael pretended he didn't detect the faint burr of ambivalence coming from the other man. Maybe Tam thought he posed some threat to their arrangement or wanted to stretch the triangle to a quadrilateral. That couldn't be further from the truth. So few things had been his alone that he could never share a woman, even if she were his for only an hour.

"Fair enough."

For the next half hour, they discussed the probable progression of the attacks and devised strategies to counter that wouldn't end in a massive outlay of resources or in a pile of Queenslander corpses. It felt odd to play such a role, but he didn't mind. In a way, it was nice to feel like he was fighting for his home ground.

He didn't mean to stay, of course.

As soon as they dealt with this situation, he'd evaluate the ship and figure out a way to force himself back on one of the automated transports. *If I have to smash one of the Peacemaker units with my bare hands, then that's how it'll be.* He was shamed by his inability to flee the Bug planet. Mostly, that came from the absolute isolation. He hadn't left his cell in turns. The food was delivered once a day, and the bars were too strong for him to break. He'd tried tunneling out, but after he dug through the floor, he ran into a rock face so strong, it would've taken a diamond drill to cut it. If the Conglomerate hadn't extradited him, he would've died there.

However long it took.

"Those are good ideas," Tam said, seeming surprised.

"You thought I was just a pretty face?"

"No. Rather that you were conning Dred."

"Give me more credit than that," the woman said as she

entered, Einar behind. Another man followed; Jael recognized Ike, the old man with eyes that missed nothing.

"Sorry," Tam said. "I should've known you only took him up because you saw real potential."

Jael cocked a brow. "Must you make me sound like a stray pet?"

"Don't let it bruise your ego. But Tam's right; I'd have let you come to Queensland, but you wouldn't be in on the planning if you weren't a cut above." By her expression, she meant nothing against the men currently wandering her domain, handling patrols, playing cards in the hall, sleeping and taking up space.

"So it's a full council meeting," Ike said then. He dropped onto Dred's bed as if they had done this before, away from prying eyes.

"Tell me what you saw, just before the attack," Dred demanded of the old man.

Quietly, Ike summarized the assault: how Priest's hunting party came in the west corridor, fighting like madmen. There had been casualties, Jael knew, but he wasn't sure how many dead or wounded. That wasn't his purview anyway. In Perdition, it would be hard to find anyone who could be pressed to play medic. Most men inside preferred cutting people up to stitching their wounds.

"The men rallied well," Einar offered. "Considering how Priest's people are, I'm pleased with how quick we killed them."

Dred nodded at that, still looking at Ike. "Did anyone look nervous . . . or expectant? Did anyone take cover a little too soon?"

Tam copped to her line of thought at once. "You think we have a traitor?"

"I don't believe in coincidences. We set out for Entropy, and while we're gone, Priest strikes? Someone sent word, I think."

"How?" Einar asked, scowling. "The three of you were in the ducts. Comm systems have been down for years . . .

and Mungo's using half the electronics to keep his Kitchen-mates in service."

Dred tapped her fingers lightly against one thigh, just above her thin leather boots. "That is . . . an excellent question."

◀ 11 ▶

Rolling the Bones

Twenty casualties. Dred shook back her braids, trying to seem unconcerned. After the meeting, Tam had provided the preliminary head count—and they couldn't afford the losses. While Silence was a deadly killer, she didn't have the largest army. The lunatic was too fond of death, Dred supposed.

I won't lose this war in pieces. We'll regroup.

Because it needed to be done, Dred spent hours tending the wounded. Some required triage, and they had to be put down. Trying to keep them alive required resources, and she'd gotten good at knowing a lost cause when she saw one: gray skin, pale and clammy to the touch, blood gurgling in the lungs. Those were all signs that a man wouldn't last. When she found one like that, she called Einar.

He made an efficient executioner. She'd never asked him if he minded, only if he was willing. But she'd read him the first time she requested it of him, and there was only gray. He wouldn't be one of her lieutenants if he took pleasure in it, but for the big man, it was only another job. Which made her wonder about his past, but she didn't break the code to ask.

By the time she finished, all the casualties were either resting comfortably or being hauled away to the recycling chutes. Einar came back to her when the corpses were gone, looking troubled. "I've been thinking about what you said in your quarters."

"About the rat in our walls?" So had she.

Little else, too.

He glanced around, then lowered his voice. "Could Wills help us figure out who?"

"His prognostications, so far, have been just vague enough to stir up trouble without giving us any real information."

"But you think he's got a real gift."

Dred lifted a shoulder, by which she meant anything was possible. "Something drove him crazy, and he was like that when I met him. Could be a real gift."

"Or it could be the bad things he did to end up here. Or life inside." Einar sounded disappointed, as if he wanted to solve her problems with a simple suggestion.

If only it could be that straightforward—summon Wills, roll the bones, find the traitor. *Then I could make an example of him and turn my attention to defeating two dangerous enemies.*

"It couldn't hurt to ask him," she decided aloud.

Einar seemed gratified. "I'll go get him."

She sank down on her throne, wondering if her people thought she was as crazy as Silence. It wasn't a question she'd considered before, but the new fish's presence brought it to mind. Dred surveyed the scene, trying to picture it through Jael's eyes. This enormous scrap-metal monstrosity didn't exactly proclaim mental stability, and then there were the chains she wore everywhere—

"Is it true?" The speaker who had approached while she pondered was a deceptively young-looking woman: slim, tan skin, with a very pretty face. Martine also had her teeth filed to sharp points and a tendency to shove a blade through people's eyes if they annoyed her.

"What?" Dred asked.

"That we're in bed with Silence's crew?"

"Call it a working arrangement until we deal with Priest and Grigor."

Martine spat. "We should just go kill the motherfuckers."

"Feel free. If you can get past all their traps, the automated defenses Priest has co-opted—and I think he's got some of those Peacemaker units running again, too—plus all the men? Then you deserve to run all the territories."

"Those sound like excuses to me. Artan would never—"

"Artan's dead," she said icily. "So will you be if you keep questioning me."

Dred pushed slowly to her feet, unwinding her chains from her arms. She leveled her coldest look on the other woman, knowing Martine wasn't as susceptible to her legend as the men. This woman saw through the stories Tam and Einar circulated to inspire awe among the troops. Fortunately, she could perform just enough magic tricks to lend them credence.

Martine took a step back, but she didn't drop her eyes. "My man went down the chute today. What do you intend to do about it?"

I'm sorry seemed like the wrong response—insincere besides. She hadn't known Martine was shagging anyone particular and wouldn't have cared if she did. So Dred answered honestly. "I'll lay plans. And when I'm sure we'll win, we take the fight to them. I'm not Priest . . . I won't squander personnel just to test them. I didn't take Queensland by playing against long odds."

The other woman nodded. "Fine. I'll wait."

Martine stormed away as Einar approached, with Wills wriggling in his grasp. "It's not time for the spots!"

That was as normal as the man got. Dred signaled her lieutenant. "Let him go."

"Please don't let the darkness win," Wills pleaded.

Hell. That sounded almost coherent.

"I'll do my best not to," she said gently. "But I need you to roll the bones for me. Can you manage that?"

Wills stumbled toward her and clutched her hands. "He's still here."

"Who is?" The danger of dealing with crazy people was that their delusions started sounding all too plausible.

"Our enemy."

She wanted Wills to root out a traitor, and it sounded like he might already be glitching on some psychic irregularity. Pity he couldn't just point and say, *That's him.* But Dred wasn't sure she'd believe it even if the man were sane. Anyone in here might lie for his own gain or to settle a grudge. At least she could trust that Wills was a full-on nutter with moments of helpful clarity.

This just wasn't one of them.

"Can you cast for me?" she repeated.

Finally, the request penetrated. "Yes. I can."

The rodent bones came out of the sack, and the man slit his fingertips, smearing blood all over them. Once, twice, three times, then he spat and cradled the mess in his palms. He rattled the ivory, blew on it as if it were lucky dice, and cast it out so that it bounced on the ground. Dred had never seen a pattern before; to her it always looked like a random assortment, but this time, she swore she saw a pattern in the long arrangement of red-smeared bone.

"Beware the knife in the dark." For a moment, lucidity burned in Wills's eyes, and the man looked genuinely frightened.

She hid her reaction, the sickness roiling in her stomach. None of the precog's glimpses had offered a look at the past before, so this must be a coincidence. *Or history will repeat itself.*

Dred forced herself to ask, "Are you saying it's someone I trust?"

"I'm saying. Saying. Saying." Wills jerked his head to the left three times.

When he started in with the tics and the repeating random words, it was impossible to talk to him. It only came on when he was really agitated, too. "Thanks. Go . . . fix something."

Wills raked his beloved bones back into the tattered sack and hurried away; Einar watched him go, a crease between his fair brows. Then the big man shook his head.

"He makes my skin crawl. You know what he did to end up in here?" Einar's voice was a low rumble, the question soft.

"I don't ask. You know that."

"Neither did I. He was on one of his tears and wouldn't stop talking about it."

Dred knew she would regret it, but she asked anyway. "And?"

"He killed a whole building full of people. Day care, restaurants, office workers."

"Mary," she breathed. Even in here, that was saying something. "How many?"

"Over five hundred."

"Did he say why?"

Einar's gaze met hers. "He said it was going to happen anyway, and he made it quick."

"Remind me not to turn my back on him." That was the only reaction she permitted herself though a small part of her was still human enough to be horrified by madness on such a scale. The rest of her was numb, had been dead so long that the excesses and cruelties of her fellow savages no longer surprised her at all.

"I wouldn't let you. Sorry that wasn't as productive as I hoped."

She shrugged. "I didn't really expect Wills to be able to solve the problem, but there's no killing hope apparently."

"'Hope is a waking dream,'" Jael quoted softly. "And it's the last thing to go. It torments you like a bird killing itself slowly against the glass."

Dred had heard the first part of his statement before, but she couldn't recall where. At her gesture, Einar found something else to do. Prior to those words, she hadn't even noticed Jael's arrival. The new fish sank into a careless slouch at the foot of her throne, but it wasn't a subservient pose, more of a watchful one, as if he meant to kill anyone who approached. She didn't chide him. By permitting Jael to name himself her champion, she had endowed him with rights that few fish ever gained at all.

She still wasn't altogether sure why she'd done it.

"By which you mean, you still intend to escape." It was hard not to let scorn color her words, and by his expression, she'd failed.

"Given time. We have a few loose ends to tie up before I go."

At that, she laughed. "Certainly. I can't imagine why the rest of us haven't left ere now."

"You didn't have me," he answered, as if it were that simple.

Sometimes she suspected he was as mad as Wills, only prettier about it. "Then why are we bothering with Priest and Grigor? Why don't we just go?"

"I'm not a wizard. I need time to gather certain assets and learn the lay of the land. Dealing with your enemies will grant me time and opportunity to do that." He pushed to his feet and offered her a hand. "Come, I need to show you something."

She stared as if his fingers were five snakes about to strike. "I'm not interested."

Jael sighed. "Not in that, yes, I'm aware. But this? You'll want to see. I had a look around after our meeting. It was . . . most productive."

Dred was tired and hungry, but she knew a man who wouldn't be dissuaded. If he tried anything, she had her chains, and Einar was always watching. She'd lost track of Tam, but he might be around, too. With a faint mutter of annoyance, she followed the new fish.

Jael led her out of the hall and through a twist of corridors. The journey ended in a blind, a corridor ending in a blast wall. Back when it was a mining refinery, the massive ship had been outfitted with safety measures in case of a meteor shower. By pushing the button, the other end would seal, and this whole hallway was double-strength durasteel, far stronger than the bits they routinely tore free from other sections.

"I can see by your expression that you realize the purpose of this place." He seemed to be willing her to come to some other conclusion, too.

"It can be used as a bunker, or a shelter. So what?"

Jael made an impatient noise. "Look at the floor, queenie. Prove to me that you're as clever as you are pretty."

At first, she had no idea what he was talking about, but then the predator kicked in. Once, she'd been fairly good at stalking men, paying attention to the signs they left behind. This site had been used by an entrenched group. Their feet left scuffs on the metal; other gear had been set up here, resulting in a series of scratches. She bent and sniffed the ground, seeking the distinctive smell of the oil that Priest's people used in their "holy sacraments." To her horror, she found it.

"This was a campsite," she realized aloud. "Where they waited for word."

He nodded grimly. "*Inside* your borders. How, exactly, did they manage that, love?"

◀ 12 ▶

Traitors in the Hall

Jael watched as Dred scoured the area for clues, but the signs were faint enough that it was unlikely she'd find anything more. It took the combined acuity of his sharpened senses to narrow down the spot where their enemies had lain in wait. And she searched without his advantages.

Eventually he said, "I don't think you'll find anything more."

She flattened a palm on the floor, her braids tumbling over one shoulder. "It makes me sick to think of them hiding here, waiting. Secure in the knowledge that my people wouldn't report them."

"We need to plug that leak, queenie." But he understood her anger; there was nothing quite like learning people would sell you out without blinking an eye.

I was so young when I learned that lesson—that it was better to sell than be sold.

"How did you stumble onto this site?" she demanded.

Ah. Blame the messenger. This was familiar to him at least. Jael donned a mocking smile, expecting that she'd rail and drop her own failures on his head.

"There was no stumbling involved. While you were playing doctor, I searched every centimeter of the corridors." In truth, he'd gone out because he couldn't stand to watch her being kind. Even the men she judged too injured for recovery were granted a quick death. To his mind, that was better than being left to linger. He half wished somebody would offer him that release though he thrashed like a trapped animal between twin desires for oblivion and freedom.

"Nobody asked you to do that. So why did you?" By her expression, criminals didn't do extra work without threat of punishment.

"I'm guarding your flank," he said quietly. "Remember, you're all that stands between me and an interminable lifetime with Silence."

She studied him, pushing to her feet. "I can see why you'd want to avoid that." To his surprise, there were no further words of recrimination, no anger. Her manner became businesslike. The change startled him. "Did you learn anything else in your patrol?"

I'm starting to understand why men follow you, princess in chains.

"No. But I'm wondering why your guards didn't spot Priest's men. Maybe you ought to talk to the men responsible for this area. At best, they're guilty of negligence, and—"

"At worst, treason," she finished. "All right, come with me, pretty lad. Since you uncovered this lead, you get to handle the interrogation."

"And what will you be doing?"

"Standing behind you, making them afraid of worse."

Jael laughed. "You're asking me to pretend to be the nice one? I'm not sure I can sell that."

"All you have to do is refrain from hitting them."

"I might be able to do that, but the first one who lies to me—"

"I'll be watching for that," she cut in.

"That thing you do, you can tell when somebody's lying?"

How . . . awful. Jael finally understood why they called

her the Dread Queen. There was something terrible about how she read a man and sorted his truth from falsehoods. He didn't want her peering beneath his skin and seeing the monster at the bone.

"If it makes them feel . . . violent. Sometimes, when they're angry or frightened, and their story's being questioned, a killer wants to solve the problem by murdering the person making him feel that way. *That's* when I can tell. Quiet, controlled lies look the same as truth to me."

He wondered why she'd told him that and if she realized she'd given him the keys to getting away with murder in her domain. Her gaze was level on his; and if Jael didn't know better, he'd swear this was some kind of a test. He met her look with one of his own, hoping it was level and inscrutable.

"I'll bear that in mind. Let me guess—the men think you can read their minds."

"It's all part of the legend," she said. "Tam's idea, not mine. He says a little shock and awe goes a long way toward cementing their loyalty."

"Seems to be working," he observed with a touch of mockery.

She sighed but didn't rise to the bait. "Not well enough, or we wouldn't be questioning a squadron of treacherous guards."

So easily she confessed to failure, admitted her strategies weren't perfect. It made him want to help, a foreign impulse. Of course, her confidences could be a strategy, meant to bind him closer and ensure his loyalty. Some men found it impossible to resist a woman who needed them; if that was her angle, it was working better than he'd like to admit.

"Why are you telling me this?" he demanded, wondering if she would be honest. Unlike her, he wouldn't confess his tricks . . . and he'd smell a lie in her sweat, hear it in her quickened heartbeat.

Dred met his gaze levelly for a few seconds. Then she answered, "Because I *can* trust you. I've had Tam watching you since your arrival. Since you're new, you haven't had the opportunity to form any other allegiances. You've been mine since the moment you stepped off the transport."

A knife made of longing turned in his stomach. He had never belonged to anyone before. Not like this. For once, he didn't resist his better nature or pretend it didn't exist. "Point me at them, and I'll get this party started."

"I'll alert the jugglers." Her tone was wry, but she skimmed the crowd in the main hall until her attention lit on a knot of men playing cards across the way. "That's them. Looks like they've just come off patrol, and they're . . . celebrating."

Yeah, now that she'd singled the men out, he could see that their mood was quietly more euphoric than the rest of Queensland. Others were downcast or angry; those who had lost people who mattered seemed sad. But these four? None of the above. They had the relaxed body language of men who thought they'd gotten away with something.

"Just one question," he said. "Are we doing this in here?"

"Absolutely. I don't care about protecting their good names. We already know they're guilty of something. I'll throw them to the others once we're finished."

That was a cold, practical decision. Nothing angered a populace like a turncoat; these sentries would be torn to shreds. It would also give the convicts targets for their rage, making them more governable. People always responded better when they could understand the reason why a tragedy had occurred. Giving them someone to punish would also restore a sense of balance. Finally, the bloodbath should leave her in a position to take on her enemies with a focused fighting force.

Jael turned; if she wanted him to run the interrogation, he would though he'd never had a commander trust him that far before. They always kept him on a short leash, like a weapon that could explode without warning. A little voice said, *She's only trusting you because she doesn't know what you are. If she did, everything would change.* He ignored it and closed the distance to the smug-looking sentries. They stopped their card game at his approach, eyeing him.

"We're full," one of them said. He was the biggest of the

bunch, with a shock of dark hair and two deep-set eyes. A scar meandered down his left cheek. "Not dealing anybody else in."

"Downright rude, that is. But I didn't come to play," Jael said in a steely tone.

"Then what do you want?" another demanded.

Dred stepped out from behind him, then. The men froze. *That's an unfamiliar experience.* He was used to people underestimating him until they saw him fight. But these guards knew how quickly he could gut a man. And *still* they dreaded the woman behind him more. Maybe it was because they thought she could dig into their heads and pry out their secrets. Or it might be the inexorable chill of her presence; he felt it, too, now.

"You'll answer his questions," she said gently, and closed her eyes.

The reaction was immediate, so they knew what she was doing—or rather, they'd heard stories. Jael acknowledged that Tameron had a deft hand with a tall tale.

"We didn't do anything," the youngest whined.

Right. First feign innocence.

Best not to leave any doubt as to what he knew. Jael wasn't interested in excuses. "I found a campsite where Priest's people waited . . . inside your patrol route."

"No idea what you're talking about," the first one said with a cocky jerk of his chin. He was probably the leader.

"You realize I don't have to talk to you. I can just tell the rest of them"—he gestured at the men watching the exchange with narrowed eyes—"what I've learned. They'd find your bullshit compelling."

"Doubtful," Dred said softly. "He's lying. He'd like very much to slit our throats, too."

In a prison full of vicious murderers, that wasn't uncanny prognostication, but the way the sentries reacted, she'd stolen the thoughts directly from their minds. The youngest one swallowed hard, his gaze falling to his cards. He clenched his hands in his lap, and Jael realized he needed to focus on him. He switched gears.

"Why did you do it?" he asked the young one. "I just got here, and even I know Queensland is the best place inside Perdition."

"I didn't do anything," the prisoner said shakily.

Jael's tone became silky. "That's the problem. You didn't *do* anything. Your job is to report territorial incursions and summon reinforcements if your patrol isn't strong enough to drive them back. Why did you look the other way? What did Priest promise you?"

"Don't say a word," the leader warned.

When Dred focused on the kid and closed her eyes, sweat broke out on the kid's brow. It wouldn't be long now, Jael guessed. A few seconds later, the boy broke, eyes wild. "It don't matter. She knows, she always knows. She's *playing* with us."

"She can't prove anything unless you—"

But the youngest guard didn't seem to hear his cohort. He babbled to Jael, "We were so sure she'd lose, that she couldn't stand against Grigor and Priest. It seemed like a good idea to have a backup plan, you know?"

"That makes sense," he said encouragingly.

It was the sort of thing he'd do, so he couldn't judge them. But it was his job to get a confession. He'd always been loyal to his employers until he got a better offer. In this place, he wouldn't trust such a promise. From what he'd seen of Silence and heard of Grigor and Priest, Dred was the only one still clinging to sanity. That was enough to keep him in her court.

"We had *no idea* there was an alliance with Silence in the works," the boy went on. "It seemed smart to hedge our bets."

Bad luck for you. You gambled and lost.

"So what did Priest ask you to do?" he prompted.

"Just look the other way. That's all, I swear."

The man sitting beside him slammed a meaty fist into the kid's temples to shut him up. His head rocked sideways, then dropped to the table, but the damage was done. Dred opened her eyes and studied the remaining three with a gaze so cold even Jael marveled at her detachment. He also wondered if the boy had been telling the truth, but her impervious mien gave no sign.

"I find all four of you guilty," she whispered.

Before they could react, she vaulted onto the table, leaving her legs vulnerable. They could've struck out at her; though Jael would've killed them too fast for her to come to harm, she couldn't know that for certain. It was pure bravado, an absolute statement of sovereignty. Despite himself, he was impressed with her courage.

"Four traitors," she called in a ringing voice. "They gave aid to Priest's people. They overlooked the raiding party, which resulted in the death of our own. What's the payment for those who turn?"

"Death," the crowd thundered back.

"And so what is your judgment?" she demanded.

"Death!" the men shouted.

Jael dodged out of the way as the convicts stormed the table. Dred dove forward, executed a flip in midair, and landed lightly at his side. He'd never seen people pulled apart before; it was grisly, even by his standards, and he'd fought in some awful campaigns. The Dread Queen looked on with pitiless eyes, content in her ruling. For the first time, he suspected she might belong here.

As I do. But that didn't mean he'd stay. Jael had been fighting fate his whole life.

◄ 13 ►

Shopping Spree

The next day, Dred realized that Wills had said "he" instead of "they" when he'd issued his warning. Maybe the discrepancy was nothing to worry about, but it made her wonder if there was one more traitor to be rooted out. His initial reading had indicated that Jael would be the one who ruined Queensland, yet the new fish had been helpful so far. She wouldn't say she trusted him fully, but if you offered complete faith to anyone, then you were a fool. Therefore, unless he proved himself disloyal, she would use him.

It was busy in the hall today, just before mealtime. Cook was berating his helpers, a knife in one hand and a pot in the other. She didn't know what was on the menu, but it smelled decent. Probably some casserole or fricassee created from the hydroponics garden. It had been a while since they'd had protein, as the only working Kitchen-mate in her territory had shorted out a week before, and even Wills couldn't persuade it back to work. It needed parts, he said, which was part of why she was contemplating this mission.

She strode over to her throne, feeling like an idiot, but it wouldn't do for her to wait in line like everyone else. *They have to believe you're better than they are,* Tam had said. *Not so much that they become resentful, but just enough to inspire awe.* To her mind, he seemed to know an awful lot about royalty, about controlling a populace and keeping them balanced in the narrow channel between obedience and rebellion. Most days she thought Tam should be running things instead.

In due course, he brought her a bowl of a reddish, lumpy mess. She didn't ask, just dug in. He sat at the base of her throne, as if she required it of him. None of the other men dared to approach without her signal. Instead, they ate at distant tables, contenting themselves with looks from afar.

It's all so ridiculous.

"Have you heard from Silence?" she asked, after a few bites.

The spymaster shook his head. "Not so far. You know how she is. She'll wait until the last moment, then ask us for the impossible."

That sounded about right. "It's not as if we have a choice about the alliance."

"True. And we lost two more last night. They died in their sleep."

Dred bit off a curse. With the population going down, she couldn't afford a drawn-out conflict. There were two potential solutions to the problem, and since she couldn't predict a shipful of new fish arriving conveniently to bolster her numbers, she set her sights elsewhere. This might end up as a risky, pointless run, but in his last report, Tam said he thought it was doable.

"Get Wills and Einar," she snapped, once they finished their meals.

Tam hurried off, returning within moments. "Do you need me for this?"

She shook her head. "You already charted the course, and we can find our way. Keep an eye on things here, all right?"

"What's the plan?" Einar asked.

Wills merely looked perturbed, but then, he always did. His bushy hair hadn't seen a comb in turns, and it fell across his smudged brow in a tangled knot. The smell should've been horrifying, but she was used to it. So many men had given up all pretense at hygiene, and it didn't make sense to chide them when it conserved water so well.

"We're crossing the ship to the salvage bays. Some of those areas might go into lockdown at our intrusion. There's also the potential we'll run afoul of the ship's automated defenses."

Einar nodded. "The reward's worth the risk?"

"While Tam was scouting, he found a cache of broken droids. The odds are excellent that Wills can fix them."

"I can fix anything," Wills said.

Though he sounded like he was five when he talked—when he wasn't chatting up inanimate objects—he wasn't wrong. Half the salvaged tech they used only worked because of Wills. He wasn't a one-trick pony, and between the bones and his fix-it skills, he was downright irreplaceable to her crew.

"Then we use them to bolster our line," Einar surmised.

Without these droids, it would be difficult to drive Priest and Grigor away from her borders, given their injuries and losses. She had too much ground to patrol and not enough men to do it comprehensively. This would also be good for morale, another story to round out her legend. The men needed to believe she could achieve the impossible, which was why she was gearing up for danger and not sending a team to do it for her. Such deeds would keep them fighting against long odds.

"Exactly. Are you in?" she asked.

The big man folded his arms. "Just try to leave me behind."

"Am I late to the party?" Jael strolled up with his customary insouciance.

Like everyone else, he was pale, but he didn't have the same hopeless air. *Give him time.* Part of her hoped this place couldn't break him. His swagger was a large part of his charm; as she studied him, she tried to decide if they needed him. Einar was a fierce fighter, and she could hold her own, but against turrets or worse, they might need an edge.

"How do you feel about danger?"

"It makes me randy," he said promptly.

A chuckle escaped her before she could staunch it. Sometimes she truly liked the new fish. "Then come along. I'll explain on the way."

Dred signaled to Ike, indicating he should serve as her eyes and ears while she was gone. The old man lifted his chin in acknowledgment though he didn't approach. She led the others out the east corridor; she'd rather face Grigor's men than Priest's, who never surrendered. Some of them fought as suicide squads, brainwashed into believing there was more honor in dying for Priest than in returning to Abaddon. *Hard to defeat that kind of commitment.*

As they moved, she laid out the objective for Jael, who nodded. "And I'm along because you need a heavy hitter."

Einar growled at that, but she motioned him to silence. "More that we need somebody who can recover from mortal wounds."

Jael offered a puckish shrug. "At least you're honest about it."

"Tam reported seeing a scrapped industrial unit in the salvage bay. If it hasn't already been found and stripped, we could really use it." Dred was afraid to hope, given how the past week had gone. Even for Perdition, she'd lost a fair number of people, and the battle wasn't even joined in earnest; it was the death by a thousand cuts.

They walked in silence until they passed the first checkpoint. It was all quiet, and she saluted the men stationed there. They answered the gesture in kind, then her group went past. Einar wore a focused look as he scanned the dark corridors. Above, the lights flickered uncertainly, giving the halls an ominous air. It went along with the rest—with the rusted bolts and dented metal plates, the charred patches on the floor, and the vents that hung half-connected above their heads.

This whole ship is a few turns from falling apart. And nobody dirtside gives a damn.

The solid strike of boots on metal alerted her to enemies nearby—and at the first sign of trouble, Wills dodged back around the corner. As he retreated, Dred hoped he didn't go far; she didn't have time to track him all the way back to the hall, and he was mission critical. Without his mad acumen, any treasures they found in the salvage bay had to stay there. Wills had to get the droids running, ambulatory at least, if not weapons hot.

One problem at a time.

Grigor's soldiers seemed surprised to see them; they froze for a few seconds. There were six of them—two-to-one odds. They wore makeshift armor of tanned skin and scrap metal. The rusted spikes jutting from their chests and shoulders were poisoned, too. She'd learned that the hard way her first turn inside, nearly dying from a fragging scratch.

With a smile, she whipped the chains from around her wrists. Two enemies ran at her, brandishing knives. She lashed out with a sideways kick and spun the heavy metal links in a deadly figure eight around her body. If they got close enough to strike with their blades, they also had to take the hits. One tried, and she slammed the chain around his throat, pulled with all her strength. The other lunged at her, but she dove forward, carrying his cohort with her by the neck. She used all her weight when she rolled, and a snap followed. The man dropped motionless, leaving her one to deal with.

Ahead in the wall, she saw Einar slamming a man repeatedly, headfirst, into the wall, while standing on another. Jael's fight behind her was quieter, just the muffled gasp and curse followed by a dull thud. In a practiced motion, she disengaged her chain and spun it lazily.

"It's a bad day for you to have drawn this route," she observed.

The man spat a curse and ran at her. It was a bold move

if a fatal one. At the last minute, he feinted left, then slid in low, going for the hamstring. She greeted him with an elbow to the face, then a boot in the balls. That usually dropped them, but this one had more padding than most. *Smart man. Not that it'll save you.* He sliced her side before she slammed his weapon hand with the chain. His wrist popped. *Definitely broken.* And he screamed like he'd never been hurt before.

In here? Unlikely.

Dred snagged his fallen knife and opened his throat, even as he was biting at her. The survival instinct died hard. When she turned, she gave an approving nod to Einar and Jael, who also had two corpses at their feet. It was easy to read into the difference in the bodies; Einar's had been killed brutally, beaten to death, whereas Jael's victims were clean, surgical, even.

"Good work," she said, praising them equally. It didn't matter how a man went down, only that he did. "Wills!"

In answer, he loped around the corner wearing an expectant expression, like they'd stopped for a picnic. "Time to go?"

"Yeah," she said. "Let's move."

Apart from a shallow slice on her ribs and teeth marks that hadn't broken the skin, she wasn't too bad off. Of course, that was just a single patrol, and they had a long way to go. The ship was the size of a small city, with the salvage bay nestled to the far east and down several levels, not within Katur's Warren, but close enough that there might be complications. Dred had never met Katur or any of his aliens. They usually stayed close to their own territory, not prone to roaming. That made sense since there were relatively few of them, and Mungo in particular had a hate on for anybody who wasn't human.

"Injuries?" she asked.

"None," Einar said.

Jael showed her the cuts on his arm, but most were already healing. She shook her head, incredulous. "Someday, you have to show me how you do that."

"It's the power of my mind. I can also use it to order food and repair electronics." He threw her a cocky wink.

She pretended to believe him as Einar snorted. "Really? I thought you didn't use it for much of anything. Since I'm wrong, you can help Wills with the droids."

The new fish laughed. "I'll save my massive psychic displays for a more worthy cause. As it happens, though, I'm a fair tinkerer. I'd be happy to lend him a hand."

"Is there anything you can't do?" Einar muttered. "Besides shut up."

"Can't carry a tune to save my life. Most unfortunate because otherwise I'm pretty enough to be a vid star. Opine?" Jael pursed his lips in an expression so sultry that it was sure to rile Einar, and sure enough, the big man went for him.

Dred hated to step between them. But she did. "Save it for Grigor's people. Come on."

"Next time, I'll break your neck," Einar promised with a dark look.

Before the new fish showed up, there hadn't been tension. Given they hovered on the verge of an invasion, things were tense enough without adding internal conflict. *But try telling a bunch of criminals to dial it down.* Still, she couldn't let it get out of hand.

Jael shrugged. "Go ahead."

Really? You just invited him to kill you? Just when she thought she had a handle on the new fish, he demonstrated another way of being unpredictable. The big man cut his eyes to her, asking a silent question. *Yes,* she answered with a tap of a finger to the head. *He's a little crazy.* But so was everyone else in here. She'd never caught him talking to people who weren't there. *Well, not yet anyway.* Wills did that all the time, and she was still taking *him* on the mission.

Beggar queens can't be choosers.

◄ 14 ►

Pitfalls for the Unwary

Jael took two steps after the princess in chains when the first burst of not-right exploded in his veins. He stumbled, feet refusing to cooperate and it took both hands flattened on the wall to keep him upright. Dred stepped closer, but there were two of her, four green eyes peering at him. The images wavered, then warped, until nausea rushed in to accompany the heat prickling up his arms. He stared at his wounds. All but two had healed. The ones remaining were limned in black, and he felt like his arms were on fire.

"I don't feel right," he tried to say, but the words came out as gibberish.

"Mary curse it," she swore. "The wounds on your arms, did they come from knives or the spikes on their armor?"

His head was fuzzy, and he couldn't answer by this point anyway. But he was pretty sure some came from the spikes. Jael had no idea why that mattered until Einar said in disgusted tones, "The arse has gotten himself poisoned. Won't be long now."

If he could've, he would've broken the big bastard's neck, but his knees crumpled, quite beyond his volition. *It's some kind of paralytic. Wonder if it's enough to kill me.* If his lungs shut down and his brain was robbed of oxygen long enough, his body might regen, only to find his mind damaged beyond repair. The idea of living as a shambling monster sent a thrill of horror through him, but he couldn't act on it, couldn't beg her to cut out his heart or chop off his head before that happened. He had no practical experience with asphyxiation; it was one of the few tortures that various labs had chosen not to test, fearing permanent damage to the specimen.

"Let's go," the big man added. "He'll only slow us down."

Dred watched as he slid down to the floor. Jael had never felt more helpless because he couldn't move, apart from the spasms contorting his muscles. Fighting did no good. He sat where he'd fallen, head tilted back. Speculative calculation lit her green eyes, then she shook her head.

"You saw how fast he healed those cuts. I'm guessing he'll come through this, too. If I'm wrong, we have to turn back anyway because we can't breach the salvage bay without him." Her tone became brisk. "So set up a perimeter. Wills, keep watch from the south. If you see anything, run like hell back here, and we'll take care of it."

"Of course, my queen," said the madman, sounding remarkably composed.

"I've got the north," Einar finally growled.

Jael could tell the giant wasn't happy with Dred's decision, but he was a loyal goon, incapable of defying her majesty's judgment. Which was good for Jael. His face went numb, then his whole head. It became a struggle to breathe. A slowing heartbeat warned him that he might not process the poison in time. *Odd. I can actually feel systems shutting down, one by one.* If anyone had asked, he'd tell them death from this poison felt an awful lot like sleep.

He lost control of his eyelids last. Then he couldn't see what was happening, only hear. He thought he recognized the distant noises of battle; this came and went as Jael lost any sense of time passing. The sounds blurred into an imprecise cacophony, like a busy market he'd once visited on

Gehenna, with all the voices speaking at once, languages fusing in nonsense syllables, impossible to separate from the roaring in his head. Madness gnawed at him from the inside out while a little voice whispered, *Let go.* And oh, he tried, but something tugged at him, relentless.

A pinch started as heat and ended in pain. He tried to strike out in protest, but his muscles still wouldn't answer. Anger boiled up, impotent as regret.

"He's unresponsive," the big man said. Those were the first words Jael had understood in some time. "We've killed three patrols, and you look like hell. We can't take a fourth. You're brave as hell, Dred, but I'm not letting you die for a no-hoper like him."

"Are you giving the orders now?" she asked in a deceptively soft tone.

Even from the verge of death, Jael could tell Einar had fragged up large. He would've taunted the enormous arse, except, well. *Right. Paralyzed and possibly dying.* The odd thing was, he'd beat it if he could. After turns of chasing oblivion, now that he had it on tap, he'd much rather live.

"No," Einar answered.

"Then return to your position and *stand your ground.*" He imagined her fierce look, the way she glared the bruiser into submission.

For me.

In that moment, Jael felt sure there had never been anybody who had fought so hard for his life for so little reason. She dropped down beside him; he heard it and felt her body heat as she moved toward him. Dred lifted one eyelid, then the other. Her face was very close, enough that he could see the pallor of her skin with the faint blue tracery at her temples, and minute nicks and scars from a life roughly lived. These glimpses came in twin bursts as she peered first into one eye, then the other.

"I wish I knew whether you're still in there. I was lucky . . . they had medicine to counteract the effects when I got hit. Blink if you understand me."

It took every last gram of determination, coupled with

pure willpower, but he managed a wink. Her breath huffed in surprise, but that was all he had left. His throat sealed, no air, and he could feel the burn of oxygen deprivation starting. His eyes closed, maybe for the last time. He couldn't help or resist when she laid him flat, lowering her lips to breathe for him. Thoughts became no more than a crackle of static, jumbled words cast up like confetti and coming down in desperate order.

dizzy, can't breathe, no air, dying
black
black
sunlight
fallow
why

"You don't have my permission to die," she said against his mouth. "I forbid it. I'm not *through* with you. You're *my* champion, and if you succumb to Grigor's poison like a little worm, it makes me look bad."

In his head, where everything was a black-and-red tangle, skipping images of violence and treachery, terrible things he'd done both by choice and necessity, laughter echoed. She was quick and inexorable as she pushed breath into his lungs; it went on long past what was sane or reasonable. He didn't know how she kept from passing out, but by the time she stopped, he sensed the poison wearing off. Little by little, the feeling came back to his body, then motor control. As with all of his miraculous recoveries, when his body's special services kicked in, they were efficient as hell.

"I can take it from here." His voice was a little raspy as he clambered to his feet.

Not bad for somebody who was just knocking at death's door. Sorry, Silence. I guess you'll have to wait.

"He's up," she called to Einar, who rumbled something less than enthusiastic in response.

"How long was I out?"

"Two hours, give or take."

"You look like shit." He wasn't kidding.

Her face was more than usually pale, almost fragile-looking, and her shoulders drooped beneath the weight of her chains. *Then there's all that blood . . .*

"Yeah, constant fighting will do that to you. I couldn't have them gutting your helpless body."

Jael didn't understand that at all. Nor did he recognize the feeling he had, something warm and rather awful. It made him want to touch her, so he curled a hand into a fist. He had manners enough to know he was in her debt.

So he spoke a quiet, "Thanks."

"Like I said, I haven't given you leave to cash out yet. I need you."

The words reverberated through him, likely in ways she never intended. Though she meant she needed him to suffer injuries that would fell a human, the way she looked now, the way she'd *fought* for his life like it was worth something, Jael would gladly bash his way through a hundred Peacemaker units, should he prove capable of it. He contented himself with a nod.

"I'm fit to move. Let me take point. I'll recover quick enough to fight on the move."

"Sounds good. Wills!"

The soothsayer came running, bloodstained and disheveled. His clothes were torn, filthier than usual—and that was saying something. He was also dragging one leg. As he neared, Wills stumbled against the walls, sending a resounding racket through the corridors. Jael realized the man was wounded.

"Did Wills fight?" he asked.

"He had no choice. This way. I don't want to run into another patrol here if we can help it. I bet they bring more this time." She was tense, jacked up on adrenaline but exhausted as hell. Not that it stopped her from pushing forward now that she had him moving again.

Damn. I've fought in squads that didn't have my back so well.

Jael jogged down toward the spot where Einar lay in wait.

"You're a tough bastard, I'll grant you that." The grudging respect in the big man's tone made nearly dying worthwhile.

Jael acknowledged the comment with a nod as he cut a course according to Dred's directions. In the distance, now and then, he heard Grigor's patrols searching for them, but his hearing was sharp. When he whispered, "You'd rather not engage?" to Dred, she jerked her chin in the affirmative.

Fair enough. I can guide us away. I'll save my best moves for the ship defenses.

At the next shaft, he headed down. Not into the ducts, though. A maintenance access ladder carried them down; it was close and tight like a damned barrel, and he wasn't delighted with having three people climbing down on top of him. Having Dred right behind him helped, though. By his count, they went down four decks.

Then she said, "Exit here."

With a quiet obedience that would've surprised a number of merc commanders, Jael did as she instructed. He whispered, "Wait, while I scout."

Dred shook her head, following him out into a grimy, poorly lit corridor. "This is no-man's-land, so we can move faster. But from here on out, it gets interesting."

"It wasn't before?" Jael felt stronger every moment, ready to drop some shock and awe.

Cocking his head, he could tell the environs had changed, just from the shift in altitude. It was obvious nobody claimed this area, not only from the lack of upkeep but from the absence of any signs of life—no scuffs, human scents, or territorial markings. Down here, he smelled rust, a hint of mold, the musky scent of animals, and a faint hint of machine life. Patrolling droids, probably, possibly gun turrets, though there was no cordite, so they hadn't been fired in a while.

"What're you doing?" Einar demanded.

"Getting the lay of the land." He completed his auditory and olfactory survey, then added, "There are no other humans nearby. But we're not alone."

"How can you be sure—" she started, but vibrations shook the floor.

He answered, "That's how."

Before anyone else could speak, he held up a hand, taking a few steps toward the origin of the noise. To their credit, they stilled and let him work. He heard the grinding of poorly maintained servos, along with the treads consistent with an old-school Peacemaker unit. That meant they were looking at heavy resistance and serious casualties unless he did what she wasn't paying him the big creds for.

"Verdict?" Dred asked eventually.

"Do you want the good news first or the bad?"

She gave a wry half smile. "Bad, always."

"There's a live Peacemaker unit down here between us and the salvage bay. How does your man Tam get around it?"

She shrugged. "He knows this ship unlike anybody else. Sometimes I swear he can all but make himself invisible."

"Well, that's not one of my tricks. Sorry."

"If that was the bad," Einar prompted, "then what's the good?"

Jael smiled and popped his knuckles, purely for show. "I'm pretty sure I can break it."

◀ 15 ▶

Now Featuring Killer Robots

Jael thinks he can break a Peacemaker unit? He's kidding. He has to be.

Without heavy weapons, their best shot at reaching the salvage bay in one piece was to avoid the bot altogether, but by the way Jael angled his steps, he seemed to be heading right for the Peacemaker. She tried to argue; he wasn't listening. His shorts were in a bunch, she supposed, because she'd seen him on the floor like a monkey with its ass hanging out. Now he had something to prove.

Jael paused as the movements rumbled closer. Dred could hear them now, not just feel the vibrations through the soles of her feet. *But how keen are his senses? He knew right where the Peacemaker was five minutes ago.*

"I'm trying to understand the layout of the ship," he said, looking thoughtful. "How can there be a salvage bay if you cons strip everything that's not bolted down?"

"I steal things that are," Wills mumbled. "It just takes longer."

Dred ignored that though it was true. This trip, the bone-roller was unusually lucid. She wondered if danger sharpened his mental focus—and if so, maybe she should send him on more missions. Because the longer they were at risk, the less loopy he seemed.

"The salvage bay is left over from when this was the Monsanto Mineral Refinery. Sometimes equipment broke down, and they needed somewhere to store it until they could get new parts delivered. Given the remote location, it took a while."

Jael nodded. "With you so far."

"When they retrofitted the place and turned it into a prison, they left certain defenses in place to keep us out of restricted areas where we might reroute systems or somehow jury-rig enough repairs to pull this tub out of orbit."

Jael seemed to consider. "Right. You never know when you'll incarcerate an evil genius. And if you get yourself killed trying to push past the turrets and the Peacemakers, it saves the Conglomerate credits in the end. So it's a win/win for them."

"Exactly. So that's why they didn't bother removing the old stored equipment in the salvage and repair bays. For turns, it's sat there like a lure, drawing us to our doom."

"Dramatic," Jael said.

"I don't mean to be. It's true. Other than Tam, who went in alone—and couldn't bring anything out—nobody's ever gotten inside."

"Then I expect we'll find bodies along the way. Let's count them." Jael started forward, toward the source of the thumps and rumbles.

She sighed, thinking that the impromptu lore class hadn't taught him anything. It would serve nobody's purpose if they exploded.

"Hold up," she said.

In answer, he made a shooing motion with graceful hands. "You three stay back. I can't watch out for you and draw fire, too."

"What do you expect to do?" Einar asked. "Pull it apart with your bare hands?"

"That's the plan." Jael sounded confident he could, actually.

And since he'd shaken off a lethal dose of Grigor's best poison, who was Dred to call it impossible? So she made a judgment call. "It's your show for now. Just understand that we can't stitch you back together like a torn shirt."

"You won't have to," he replied. "Just put the pieces of me close together. I'll do the rest."

Einar took a step back. "What the *hell*."

"He's the dark one," Wills stated.

This is just what I need. She imagined the garbled and superstitious report Wills would make about this journey. Lazarus, rising from the dead; by the time he got done mangling the account, there would be demons and hedge witches and a mass grave in the Warren. Actually, come to think of it, Wills *should* tell the story. That way, nobody would believe it.

"We've already wasted enough time." She speared Jael with a look. "When we get back, provided we survive, you and I are having a long talk."

He flashed her a cocky smile. "I hope it's about our feelings. I have at least two. Possibly three. Does hunger count?"

"*I* think so," Einar said with a touch of humor.

Dred couldn't decide whether she wanted to knock Jael on his ass or laugh. She went with the latter because it was rare enough that someone could work a smile out of the big man—and it was good to see them settling their differences without bloodshed. Odd, but good. She'd suspected for a minute that Einar had developed an authentic, irreversible distaste for Jael.

Good to be wrong.

With an impatient gesture, she said, "Get a move on, pretty lad. Go be a hero."

"You're seriously letting him take one of those on, alone?" Einar seemed startled or put out. Between his flat expression and the scars, it could be hard to tell.

"Did you want to help him?"

He scowled. "Sitting back makes me feel like a candy-ass."

"Mary forfend your ass should feel like anything but titanium." She pushed out a breath, then added, "If you're careful, you can be a hero, too. But you don't have my permission to die, either." Once Einar moved up, she glanced at Wills. "What about you?"

"I'm fine with you," he said.

More proof he's not as crazy as he seems.

Dred had no intention of getting in the line of fire, but she wanted to see the action, so she crept forward, keeping her movements slow and steady. Peacemaker units tracked humans two ways: via infrared and by sudden movement. She didn't think this one would disregard the two targets close by to come after her, though. So it should be fine.

She made it to the corner in time to see Jael run at the Peacemaker; it leveled its weapons on him. This thing had three of them—a rifle so powerful it was known as a Shredder, an actual cannon mounted on its chest, and an energy gun that could fry you like a side of meat. Though she'd seen him do some impossible shit, it seemed likely he'd only get himself—and Einar—killed. Projectile rounds slammed the ground and somewhere ahead of them, she heard defense mechanisms kick to life.

"Dammit."

"The turrets are live," Wills said. "And I suspect this part of the ship might be in lockdown."

"Force fields," she guessed. Then she offered the alleged madman a hard look. "It's all bullshit, isn't it? Your crazy act."

"Not always. But most of the time? Yes."

"Why?"

"It keeps me safe. People are superstitious about harming the infirm and insane, even in here."

"I try to keep people from knifing each other in Queensland," she said.

"That doesn't mean you know about everything that goes on in the dormitories or in the halls at night. Remember, this is still a prison."

Before she could reply, a boom called her attention back

to the fight. A smoking hole in the wall behind them testified to the strength of the laser on the Peacemaker's left limb. Jael was still moving, though, and so was Einar. The former had his shirt off for reasons incomprehensible to Dred. What they thought they could do when they got to the thing, though—Jael leapt, answering her question. He dropped his shirt over the Peacemaker's visual sensors, which would screw with its targeting.

"Help me with this," he said to Einar.

To her astonishment, they circled the bot, then took up a position to the side, at the wrong angle to be blasted, and snagged the Shredder. She could tell by the bulging of their arms that they were using all their strength; the Peacemaker caught on too slow and tried to spin, but she couldn't imagine it had been programmed for a couple of lunatics trying to pop its arm off. So the movement actually helped them, providing more leverage at the weakest point, against the soldered joint. With a shriek of grinding metal, the limb wrenched free.

"Get back!" he shouted at Einar.

Then he opened up on the Peacemaker, emptying the chambers at the thing's head. The first volley of ammo pinged off the bot's armor, but the next round dug in. The Peacemaker's chest opened and the cannon fired. The wall exploded. Beneath a smoldering shrapnel rain, Jael dove and rolled, coming up on one knee. He unloaded the rest of the ammo while Einar assaulted the thing from behind. The big man might be strong enough to break the laser, but she doubted it would fire, as it must be wired into the Peacemaker's power source.

Einar pulled and pulled at that arm, but he wasn't strong enough alone. "A little help?"

Jael dropped the Shredder, as it wasn't piercing through the bot's armor. He came in low and got behind the machine. With his added force and the Peacemaker fighting every inch they drew it back, it wasn't long before the laser bent until the next shot would probably make the thing explode.

"See if you can get it to cycle with the laser," she called.

Dred had no idea how, but Jael did. He snatched his shirt off the thing's head, so it could see its targets again. Since he and Einar were standing adjacent, the laser was the closest and most feasible weapon. Instinctively, she fell back around the corner, trying to avoid the fallout, and footsteps pounded in her direction. As Einar slid down beside her, she heard an incredible boom. When Jael staggered up, he had a hole in his chest, the skin blackened and charred. *That would've killed anyone else,* she thought. Dred could actually see inside his body, damage to his organs that should've been permanent and fatal. The hallway beyond smoldered.

"Why didn't you run?" she demanded, catching him as he collapsed.

"Just need a second. I'll be fine."

Dred cupped his shoulders. *"Why?"*

"Had to make sure it used the laser, so I stayed close. Otherwise, it might've shifted to the chest cannon and shot Einar."

"So you did it for me?" the big man asked.

"Don't take it the wrong way. It doesn't mean we're in love."

"I owe you," Einar said quietly.

Dred knew just how significant that statement was. Einar didn't offer his loyalty or a personal marker lightly. Whatever came next, Jael could expect the big man to watch his back. It took a lot to impress Einar, but Jael had gotten the job done. *They actually did it. They defeated a Peacemaker with their bare hands.* She'd never heard of such a thing. The armed units had a reputation for being unstoppable unless you had equal firepower.

As she held Jael, his internal damage resolved, new tissue replacing burned flesh, then the hole in his chest grew smaller. It was insane and hard to credit, but the process took less than fifteen minutes, eventually leaving no trace on his skin. Without thinking, she touched his chest, feeling like she was losing her mind.

She pulled him to his feet with a shake of her head. "What about blood loss? Are you weak for a while after you're injured?"

"My red blood cells reproduce at an accelerated rate. In an hour or so, a lab test wouldn't show any signs that I'd been shot."

"I don't even know what to say."

But Einar did. "Those were some smart-as-hell tactics out there. Where did you serve?"

It was a personal question, but Jael didn't seem to mind. "I've fought all over, but most recently, Nicu Tertius. I was one of March's Maniacs."

"Bullshit," Einar said. "That would make you at least a hundred turns."

Jael turned blue eyes to Dred. "How do you feel about May-December relationships?"

Part of her wanted to say she didn't believe him. Without access to Rejuvenex, there was no way he could look as he did, fight as he did, and claim such age. But she'd learned better when it came to him.

So she shrugged. "What does it matter?"

"See," he told Einar. "Age is only a number."

She ignored both of them, including Einar's grunt of laughter. "Wills, can you strip that thing, now that it's inert?"

"Of course, my queen."

The bone-reader was so unassuming when he wasn't acting crazy that it was easy to forget what he'd done out in the real world. It would be a mistake to get too comfortable with his sanity. She couldn't be sure he wouldn't suddenly decide *she* had to die because it was bound to happen at some point, according to his predictions. Dred watched his back warily as they moved.

When they approached, the unit was still active, but it lay in several chunks as a result of the misfire. The corridor was black nearly a meter around the unit, and even now, the heat was astonishing; Dred felt it through the soles of her feet.

I can't believe Jael survived this.

After donning protective gloves, Wills bent and popped out the power source, and the machine went still. Wills

studied the Peacemaker, then added, "I'll need help hauling it."

Dred held up a hand. "We'll leave the parts here and grab
them on the way out. Nobody will bother them in the time
it takes for us to get to the salvage bay and back."

"But you want them stripped now?" Wills asked.

"That way we don't stop long as we're leaving. I suspect
we'll be weighted down."

It seemed like the most logical suggestion to Dred, and
the other two men didn't argue, so she figured they agreed.
Beneath her watchful eye, Wills went to work with his ubiq-
uitous toolkit. Occasionally, he asked some help from Jael
or Einar with a stubborn piece, but soon enough, he had all
the usable gear laid in a neat pile.

"Ready?" she asked the three men. When she received
a trio of assenting nods, she added, "Then let's go loot some
gear."

TAM had been keeping an eye on Lecass for a third of a
turn. The maniac preferred things under Artan's rule, and
he had been pushed out of the new regime entirely. Men like
him didn't take kindly to loss of power. He was just surprised the brute hadn't made a move yet. But maybe he was
holding his grudge until the moment when it would do the
most damage.

Ike followed his gaze. They were sitting at a table, chopping vegetables for Cook, who was in no mood for nonsense.
Somebody had stolen some of his supplies—rare, dried
spices—that took forever to grow and process, and he was
demanding in his silent, furious way that Tam do something
about it. He had no time for small matters like this, but
things would escalate if he didn't step in, and Dred, who
had been gone for a long time, wouldn't thank him if she
returned to a bloodbath.

Muffling a sigh, he turned to Ike. "What do you think,
prank or serious theft?"

"Not sure. Lecass looks awfully amused."

"You think he's behind this? It doesn't seem like his style."

"He could be just enjoying the chaos," Ike suggested.

A new fish made the mistake of asking Cook what was for dinner, and the man replied by throwing a knife at his head. The man ducked just in time; the blade clanged against the metal wall all the way across the hall. Then Cook stalked over to fetch his weapon and resumed preparation of the next meal. Shoulders down, the fish slunk away, but it had become clear to Tam that he had to find those spices before somebody died over them.

"Property check," he shouted. "Somebody's got sticky fingers."

Tam sent guards to round up all the personal belongings that had been stored by men currently on patrol elsewhere. The Queenslanders moaned, but nobody protested. Since everybody got enough to eat, there was no excuse for pilfering from Cook. Plus, it was straight-up stupid, pissing off the man who made the food.

With Ike's help, he rummaged through all the packs and pouches until he found the missing items. Tam was honestly startled to unearth them in Lecass's bag. From the man's expression, he was, too. Lecass was an asshole with a lot of enemies, people he'd wronged under Artan's rule. The punishment for theft wasn't death; Dred couldn't afford to lose men over such a light offense. Which meant somebody wanted to see Lecass shamed and flogged.

Tam gave the spices back to Cook, then he turned to Lecass. "You know the punishment."

"I didn't take that shit," the larger man snarled.

"Evidence says otherwise." Though he disliked the sense that he was being manipulated, Tam couldn't see a way around the inevitable. Finding the spices in Lecass's pack was enough to convict him, and the other inmates didn't like him well enough to allow mercy.

"Touch me, and I break your neck."

Cook took exception to that. He laid down his spoon and

took up his two biggest knives, then he joined Tam quietly. Cook was a tall man, burly, without Einar's muscle mass, and Tam could remember every word he'd ever spoken in Tam's hearing.

So when he said, "Try," to Lecass, that made seven.

Being a spymaster hadn't equipped him for direct confrontation or keeping order. Tam would've been lying if he hadn't been grateful when Calypso appeared on his other side. The mistress of the ring didn't usually involve herself with mundane matters, but there was no doubt she was dangerous. None of Lecass's usual supporters came forward; they knew better than to intervene in an earned punishment. If they did, they'd earn a taste of the same, and while whippings weren't usually fatal, there was always a chance of infection setting in.

"The spices were among your things. That means you pay," Calypso said.

Other Queenslanders gathered around, eager for some drama. Tam would've thought that imminent invasion by Priest and Grigor, along with a terrifying alliance with Silence, should be enough to tide them over for a while, but apparently these men never grew glutted on bloodshed. He steeled himself to do what was required.

"You have a choice. I administer the lashes now . . . or we can confine you, so that the Dread Queen can punish you properly upon her return. What do you prefer?"

Hatred burned like dying stars in Lecass's eyes. "Get it over with, bitch queen's mongrel."

Cook and Calypso lashed Lecass to the metal frame where they had recently tortured a prisoner. To his credit, the man didn't struggle, though his limbs were rigid with fury. Tam said to Cook, "As the offended party, you decide how much he pays. How many strokes?"

Cook held up ten fingers. As floggings went, it was fairly light. Maybe he agreed with Tam, suspecting Lecass had been set up. That didn't mean they could pat him on the head on a hunch, however. Queensland ran on certain rules, and uniform application kept most of the mayhem in check.

"Take his shirt off," he said to Calypso.

The woman was careful with Lecass's clothing. In here, they couldn't afford to waste fabric. Ike delivered the whip; it was a ceremonial thing fashioned of leather made from rodent skin and tiny metal barbs. As one, the Queenslanders made room, forming a ring around the frame. Tam's stomach turned. It was one thing to orchestrate horrific deeds, another to perform them with his own hand.

"Count for me," he told the crowd.

One, they shouted as the flogger snapped.

Lecass jerked in his bonds but he didn't cry out. His eyes burned on, his mouth flattened into a white seam of rage and pain. Tam pretended he wasn't beating a human as he lifted his arm again and again, ignoring the cheers from the crowd. He registered it only when they shouted *ten,* and he delivered the last blow. Though he despised Lecass as a brute and a sadist, he took no pleasure in the man's pain.

A couple of Lecass's cohorts helped him down. Maybe they even liked him well enough to clean his wounds. The man shook them off with an enraged gesture, proud enough to walk away from the beating unaided. Tam scanned the crowd, seeking someone taking a little too much pleasure in the show, and he found Martine, wearing a satisfied smile.

"I fear the result of today's work," Tam said softly to Calypso.

The mistress of the ring nodded, her dark eyes inscrutable as a starry sky.

◄ 16 ►

Durasteel Heart

Before they left the Peacemaker, Jael grabbed the Shredder. With Wills's help, he popped the spare ammo out of the Peacemaker's chest, stowed neatly behind the cannon. The madman was fascinated by the internal loading mechanism, but Dred reminded him of the mission with a pointed clearing of her throat.

"Do the two of you need anything else before we go?" Her boot tapped against the metal floor, the only sign of her impatience.

"A kiss for luck?" Jael suggested easily.

Dred studied him as if considering the offer, then she shook her head. "We don't need luck with ability like yours."

It was the only rejection that had ever left him smiling. Jael moved out, pleased to have the Shredder as reinforcement to his mad skills. He led them along the route Dred indicated, based on what she'd learned from Tam. Eventually, the corridor came to a T with rough resistance at the crossing.

"Two turrets, live and tracking, dead ahead." Jael gave his report in low tones.

They shouldn't be difficult to take out.

"These don't have sophisticated programming," Einar added. "Just motion detectors."

"Then be still," Jael told him.

He crawled forward on his belly, remembering when he'd served as a sniper in various units. It had been a long damn time, however. In his last squad, they'd used him as a grunt, aiming him when they required a hole in the line. Hopefully, he hadn't lost any accuracy. Propping up, he peered down the barrel of the gun, sighted, then issued a warning.

"This whole area will be saturated in lead. I need you to fall back."

From the sharp look she gave him, Dred suspected he meant to take the hits. But hell, there was only an empty corridor. If he stayed still and didn't move much, the turrets would have some trouble tracking him. With luck, they'd shoot wide. If not, he could survive a few bullets in his back. The worst part would be digging them out before the wounds closed. Jael had a few pieces of metal in his body that didn't belong. Itchy as hell.

None of them argued, freeing him to do what he did best. He opened up, focusing on the connective wires that powered the turrets. It would be best if he didn't blow them all to hell. Then they could be transported as part of the salvage op. But if it came down to destroying the turrets so they could pass, Jael would get it done.

He slowed his breathing to further stymie the targeting, then he laid down heavy rain. Projectiles drummed the turret base, ricocheting until they dug into the wall behind. *Not enough.* The turrets fired back, both of them, but since he wasn't running toward them, they didn't have a clear map of where to aim. Jael held still and the bullets bit into the ground centimeters from his face. He was surprised by a cold wash of fear. He'd almost died once on this run, and he wasn't eager for an encore. *Enough bullets slam into my skull—and I'm done.*

So he didn't fire back until the turrets spent what they had in chambers, then they clicked and whirred, reloading from conduits in the floor. *That means there's more ammo underneath.* Jael saw his best chance and took it, though he didn't go full auto, as that would be a waste of rounds and too imprecise for the work he was attempting here. He shot through the knot of wires, and the turret on the left dropped, unresponsive. The right gun boomed to life, though, drenching the floor and walls with hot lead. He took two rounds, and in anyone else, it would've shattered the bone. But he had reinforcements, filaments in his skin, so his forearm took the damage and saved his arm from the break.

Still hurts like a bitch.

Two more exchanges like that, and the second turret went down. Jael stumbled to his feet, arm cradled against his chest. He felt his body fighting to heal the wounds already, but the presence of foreign material complicated matters. Einar clapped him on the back so hard, he almost fell down; Wills was more circumspect in his kudos, but clearly, the crazy little bastard was excited, too.

Dred came up beside him and checked the wounds. "Those need to come out."

Without hesitation, she drew out her shiv and took hold of his arm. It was lunacy the way she took command of him without asking, like she had a perfect right. For reasons unclear to him, Jael let her dig into his skin, though he'd cut people off at the knees for lesser offenses. He sucked a breath in but didn't turn away as she worked the bullets out of his flesh. One by one, they pinged the ground, leaving bloody droplets smeared on the floor.

"That's done it. Sorry if it hurt. I'd clean that for you, but—"

"No need. I'm not susceptible to infection." And even if it did fester, he wouldn't get gangrene. He'd just run hot for a bit while feeling like shit.

"I see why they sent you to us," Einar said quietly. "You'd be hell in the real world. Nothing stops you from taking what you want."

Jael flicked a look in Dred's direction, but she was talking in low tones with the soothsayer about how best to salvage the turrets and install them in her territory. Wills answered, "I'll need all the parts, plus the platform below. There must be ammunition nearby and a conduit for reloading."

"These can be set up for manual use," Einar said. The big man moved forward and indicated a switch at the base of the turrets.

"Good to know." Dred gave an approving nod. "Let's push on. I hope to hell we find some kind of dolly in the bay, though, or it will take us a month to get back to Queensland."

"We'd be jacked and killed before then," Wills predicted gloomily.

Jael laughed. "With all this gear? I don't think so. We did well enough with shivs."

"And we haven't slept or eaten since," the other man pointed out, as they pushed past the dead turrets and into a new set of hallways.

Yeah, that could be a problem.

"Can Ike and Tam keep things together? How well does Queensland run without you?" He aimed an inquiring look at Dred.

"It'll be fine," she predicted. "If I know Tam, he'll spin some story about how I'm meditating before the great battle to unearth a weakness in our enemies . . . and must not be disturbed."

"Seriously? And they'd believe it?" She was an exceptional woman, but she wasn't the messianic figure the Queenslanders painted her.

Einar answered, "Absolutely. Dred's got just enough Psi to inspire awe."

"Then if we can find a place to hole up, we should rest before we start back. There's no way I'm letting all this gear fall into enemy hands."

He didn't mind when the other two men glanced at the princess in chains for confirmation. Though it was his recommendation, she was in charge, no question.

She approved the suggestion with a nod. "I'm on my last legs. Anything we face, going forward, I won't be at my best. That's not fair to any of you."

She just admitted weakness again. In his experience, commanders didn't. They made excuses and blamed their men, knocked a few heads together and sometimes authorized some executions to teach the grunts to fight harder. Failure never came as a result of poor planning or insufficient leadership. Little by little, he was starting to understand why they idolized her.

Fortunately, there was no more combat. The turrets marked the last of the automated defenses, at least in this section. But the good luck didn't stretch further than that; instead of mounted guns or more Peacemaker units, an amber force field stood between them and the goal. Through the glimmering light, Jael saw all kinds of things they could use to shore up the defensive line, but there was no reaching them from here.

"Shit," he said. "We'll have to circle around."

Dred shook her head. "Then we'd trigger it from the other side. There has to be some way to shut it down."

"The controls are probably inside the bay," Wills said.

"That doesn't help us," Jael snapped.

Even as the smaller man recoiled, he knew it was unfair to take his rage out on Wills. He offered an apologetic half shrug and the other inmate made a dismissive gesture. They were all tired and surly, frustrated by this last obstacle. Dred stared at the force field as if she could dispel it with her mind, but it didn't seem like her powers ran in that direction. At last, she turned away with an angry snarl. She paced the way they'd come, then up to the force field, and back again.

"What—" he started to say.

"She's thinking," Einar interrupted. "Let her be."

They sat down while Dred paced, mumbling possibilities and discarding them. Her brainstorming might've gone on for minutes or hours, as Jael dozed off.

He woke to her saying, "I might have a solution. But it will require some backtracking, a lot of jury-rigging, a bit of luck, lot of daring, and some of your special genius, Wills."

"I'm in," the man said without hesitation. "Just tell me what to do."

By the time they hauled the Peacemaker's laser arm and the power source back to the force field, Jael was fragging tired in a way he hadn't been in turns. The snatched sleep had only made his head ache though he did better than most on reduced rest. He'd gotten soft sitting in the Bug prison, nothing to do all day but sleep, eat, and pace his cell. Furthermore, the other two men seemed to understand without being told what the princess in chains meant to do.

It pissed him off that *he* didn't.

Wills went to work wiring the laser directly to the power source. He'd stripped some components from the turrets in order to make the necessary connections, and Einar cheered when the gun powered up. Jael watched, frustrated, but determined not to ask for explanations. Next, Wills tinkered with the laser's settings, calibrating it somehow. From what Jael could tell he was attuning it to—*oh*. He got it, now.

"I think this should do it," Wills said, ten minutes later. "We're good to go. But if it works, it will only punch a hole for a few seconds."

"That'll be long enough."

Before Jael could protest that he was best suited to high-risk missions, she handed the gun to Einar, and said, "On my mark." After dropping the chains wrapped around her arms, she positioned herself in front of the force field, then called, "Now!"

The big man fired; two energy fields overlapped, and the amber light flickered, then shaded out. Dred took full advantage, diving through just as the field sealed up behind her. It caught one of her boots, which was smoking at the bottom when she flipped to her feet. With a huge grin, she held two thumbs up to show she was all right.

"Dammit," he growled. "She should've sent me."

Wills shrugged. "I suspect she thinks you've done enough. Dred's not one to rely on other people too much. Don't worry, she'll find the kill switch or control panel. We'll be inside soon enough. Hope there's something to eat, some leftover paste, maybe. That stuff keeps forever."

"But she left her chains," Jael protested. "She's in there with no weapons."

Einar flicked him a warning look. "Don't let her hear you talking like that about her. That woman hunted and executed forty men before they caught her. She may seem like she's decent, kind even, but she's a killer, just like you and me."

For some reason, that surprised him. Jael had known you didn't end up in Perdition for nonviolent crimes, but he'd almost expected her to be the exception. He wanted to know who she'd been killing—and why—because he felt sure she wouldn't do it without a good reason. Some people killed for fun, profit, or pleasure, but he sensed none of that from her. Her bio signs didn't accelerate when they fought, other than normal adrenaline. Junkie-rush killers always smelled . . . different.

"Maybe she pissed off the wrong person," he suggested to Einar.

But the big man shook his head. "Don't fool yourself, mate. I think the world of her, but deep down, she's got a durasteel heart."

Winning

Inside the salvage bay, Dred was cut off from the others. That didn't bother her much as she explored the enormous room; this was the closest she had been to the outside world in five turns. The walls were thick, true, but across the bay, she could see a docking door, where ships used to deliver parts or pick up machinery that couldn't be repaired on the refinery platform. It had been welded shut when the prison opened, but even if they could cut through the metal, there was still no way out.

No shuttle. No emergency pods.

People who were sent here had no possibility of parole. That had never been brought home more clearly than at this moment. Only a single door still functioned, the one where automated ships delivered new fish, more Peacemakers, and scant supplies, which were snagged by whatever faction found them first. If the looters were unlucky, they were killed and the goods stolen by a stronger group. Perdition had been designed so the prisoners could never leave.

The space was huge, bigger than the main hall, but it showed clearly just how old the Monsanto station had been before they outfitted it as a prison. Hulks of industrial devices lay unmoving at the far corners of the room, and the walls were lined with shelves groaning with various tools. *Wills should be excited to see that, if I can lower the force field to let him in.* A layer of grit covered everything, probably mineral dust left over from the mining days.

Cutting through the center of the room, there was a conveyor belt, though it wasn't moving. She had no idea what it was used for, but it split the room east to west and made Dred wonder what was on the other side of the salvage bay. *Nobody's been here in turns.* That was a strange feeling as she picked a path through rusted junk and discarded machines. A few of them might even be useful. Dred kept an eye out for other defenses—

She stilled. From the northeast section of the bay, she detected the unmistakable sound of movement. Her heartbeat accelerating, she crept toward the source of the noise. *Wish I hadn't left my chains.* Without them, she wasn't nearly as tough as Einar or Jael, so this might get ugly. On the plus side, if she died in here, the others would be all right. They could cart the turret and Peacemaker salvage back to Queensland and choose somebody else to sit on the scrap-metal throne.

She pushed forward, expecting combat, but instead of more defensive measures, she found a boxy little maintenance bot. The thing stood about a meter high, moving about on rusted treads, and it came over to inspect her when she stepped out from behind a pile of oxidized metal. The plates looked like they had been removed for reparation, but nobody ever got around to it. The bot scanned her shoes, then whirred back a few paces as if trying to decide whether she needed repair.

I definitely do.

"What's your designation?" she asked.

Some bots didn't have vocalizers, but this one did, probably to respond to voice commands. "Unit R-17."

"What's your primary function?"

"To collect defective articles on decks 47 through 52."

"What do you do with the stuff you collect?"

Lights blinked on top of the bot, and she heard the whirring as it searched. "Answer not found in unit database. Rephrase."

From the look of the bay, she could guess what the bot did with the articles anyway. Though it made her wonder what happened when it ran into a malfunctioning object too big for it to haul away.

"What deck is this?"

"Repair and Salvage Operations are located on deck 52. Please report to your supervisor. There is work to do." Somehow, the electronic voice managed to sound a bit pissy, as if she was inconveniencing Unit R-17.

"How many other salvage units are still functioning?"

"Answer not found in unit database. Rephrase."

Well, that's getting me nowhere. Since there was no threat from unit R-17, she returned to her original mission. She threaded past the tall piles of junk, reasoning that an office needed walls, and it would be easier to enclose it at the edges of the room. She found no rooms, but a ramp led up, so she climbed cautiously, listening for movement. No sounds reached her apart from the muted whir of R-17's servos.

Up the ramp, there was a second level to the salvage bay, a platform suspended by high-tension cables, and it swayed slightly with her steps. More parts and broken gear were stored up here; Dred moved through the salvage to a doorway she saw at the opposite end. The steel door was closed but not locked. When she opened it, the whole room sighed a little. It was just escaping air, but a shiver crept over her nonetheless.

Supervisor's office. Now let's find a kill switch.

After a couple of minutes of searching, she located a panel with various lights and buttons. They weren't clearly marked, so she pressed the wrong one first. The conveyor belt started, and she hurriedly hit it again. *How will I know if I get it right?* Sometimes when she pushed a button, something lit up on the panel, but nothing obvious happened. Those she didn't reset.

After she punched the button on the lower left, Jael called out, "You did it. We're in!"

Finally.

"All three of you?" She pitched her voice to carry.

"Present," Wills answered.

Einar added, "Me, too."

Then she brought the force field back up. With the defenses in pieces behind them, there was nothing to hinder anyone who might be following. No way would she give Grigor a chance to stroll right up their asses while they sorted the salvage. Dred came out of the office and peered over to find Wills gazing around in absolute awe.

"Do you think you can find parts to get our Kitchen-mate going again?"

"Definitely. I suspect there's enough broken tech here for me to design and *build* things." From his tone, she'd just delivered him to mecca.

"We're safe in here," Einar said decisively. "It's unlikely another group would have a laser or someone who knows how to jury-rig it to disperse the field."

"But we need to be careful when we leave," Jael pointed out. "They don't need to get in, as we have to come out at some point."

Dred nodded. "You're both right. I need to get some sleep. Once I feel sharper, we can decide what gear is worth hauling out right away."

She was concerned about leaving the force field disabled later so they could leave. *Not that we have a choice.* Sooner or later, somebody else would check out the area, realize the defenses had been breached, and the looting would begin. Before that happened, Queensland had to snatch the top-tier items.

Or maybe we can secure the bay somehow. Wills might have some ideas.

"Sounds good. I found some dorms this way if you're interested." Jael beckoned.

Her brows went up. She hadn't seen any doorways on the ground floor. Curious, she followed him through a warren of equipment, rusted metal, and scarred internal mechanisms. The place probably hadn't been so junked up during the Monsanto days, but now, with only one functioning bot to process everything, it was no wonder the place was overflowing. The system was breaking down; R-17 might go out on decks 47 to 52 and find stuff that needed to be repaired, but once he got it here, there was nobody to do the work. Wills needed to do something about that maintenance droid, or he might well be the straw that broke the camel's back. He needed to be programmed for more helpful services.

"The door's here." He nudged a heavy panel aside in order to open it, but inside, Jael was right.

This was a simple, functional dormitory, where the bay workers had doubtless slept. The design was typical of such a room, with twelve bunks set into the walls, stacked three high and four across. A musty scent hung in the air, but she was too tired to care. Dred rolled into the nearest bed.

"Dibs," she mumbled.

A few seconds later, she was asleep. For a while, she drifted, and there was nothing. Bliss. Then the dream came on as it always did when she was most exhausted, defenses down.

THE house is bright with sunlight, such a buttery yellow. It creates patterns on the white floor. I stare at my toes, listening to my parents argue in the next room. This has been going on since last night, and I'm angry, too. My father paces while my mother tries to calm him.

"Did you think she would stay here forever, Malcolm? This place is . . . nowhere. Dee wants to see the world. She's a lot like you."

"You know the risks," her father bites out.

"Enough," I call. "The freighter leaves in an hour. You can have breakfast with me or keep fighting. Either way, I'm leaving in forty minutes."

"Come on," my mother says gently.

When they join me in the kitchen, I see their concern and trepidation. I offer a cocky smile in return. "It'll be fine."

The meal stutter-skips, then I'm on the deck of the freighter along with a few other new crewmen while the captain lectures us about our responsibilities. I'm low dog on the roster, which means I'll get all the scut work until I prove myself. So long as it gets me off this rock, I don't mind. My parents have their reasons for hiding here, but there's nothing to keep me from the greater galaxy.

Then the first mate strides in. He's so handsome I can't stop staring at him. And he knows his effect on women, throwing me a cocky wink. But it doesn't hit me like he expects. The world trembles, even though the ship hasn't moved from dock yet. My eyesight goes, red washing everything. Inexplicably, the real world is replaced by a series of horrific, graphic images. I see the first mate, his face tight with lust and violence, throttling a woman while she thrashes beneath him. The pictures flash again, again, so many women, so many murders—

DRED woke in a cold sweat, Jael's hand on her shoulder. With utter self-control, she restrained the urge to lash out. "Time to get up?"

For a moment, she thought he would comment about the nightmare. Instead he just nodded. "The others have been up for a while. I thought you'd want to see what Wills has accomplished."

"Did he sleep at all?" she asked, rolling out of the bunk.

"Negative. He's like a kid on his birthday." Jael offered her chains.

She took them gratefully. *Feel naked without them.* "Let's go see what Perdition gave him." Before he pushed past her, she set a hand on his arm. "Thanks, by the way."

Jael seemed surprised. "For what?"

For waking me. For not asking. For restoring my identity.

Dred shrugged and kept walking. She suspected he knew; or maybe he wasn't susceptible to bad dreams. Either way, she'd said what was needful.

"I found some paste in the supervisor's office," Einar called. "Hungry?"

"Is there enough for everyone?"

The big man nodded. "The rest of us already ate . . . I found a full carton. Tastes like shit, but it'll keep us going until we get back."

"Any water to be had?"

"There's a sink in the lavatory," Wills offered. "Don't know if the filters and recyclers are still good, so I boiled some in the kitchenette."

"That's a yes," Einar added.

He handed her a drink, and she downed it in four swallows, then attacked the food packet. Using thumb and forefinger, she forced the paste down her throat; on freighters during long hauls, before her arrest, she'd found it was better to swallow without tasting. When she lowered the empty foil envelope, Jael was watching her with an odd expression. She raised a brow.

"Better?" he asked, obviously amused.

"Clearly. Now show me what you've found."

◀ 18 ▶

Hard Way Home

The maintenance bot proved unexpectedly useful after Wills reprogrammed it. The thing had engine codes for equipment Jael would've guessed didn't work at all. There were drilling rigs and bore bits and other bots with missing parts. Fortunately, that also included an air pallet, which was exactly what they needed to get all the gear back to Queensland. At the moment, he was helping Einar load the thing up. It had an impressive hauling capacity.

"I'm keeping him," Wills said to Dred, presumably about R-17.

"Specify my next task," the bot requested.

"In a minute."

"It's fine with me," she answered. "Just realize somebody may break him, even in our territory."

"I'll put the word out that 17's to be left alone," Einar offered.

She nodded. "Thanks." Then Dred turned to the unit herself. "The air pallet won't fit in the access shafts. Is there a working maintenance lift?"

It was a good question. From the look of the bot, he didn't

have the physical capability to go up and down ladders himself. So there must be another way if he serviced decks higher up.

"The lift is on the second level of Salvage and Operations, opposite the supervisor's office."

"Sweet Mary," Einar swore. "That's the best news we've had all day."

Wills frowned at the big man. "On the contrary. It was better when I reprogrammed R-17 and got him to follow new protocols. And we just received more exciting news still."

"What?" Dred demanded.

"I didn't like the idea of leaving the bay unsecured, but I couldn't figure out how to manage it. If we take the lift, directly from the bay, I can leave the force field on."

"Protecting our interests in here," Jael concluded.

Though he pretended to be crazy as a bag of rats back in Queensland, Wills was turning out to be smart as hell. Jael offered the other man a sincere salute, two fingers to the brow.

"Why don't we take the lifts more?" he asked.

Dred angled a look at him. "They don't work without an override key. And even if we had a key, in most cases, they're in such poor repair that we might fall, get trapped—"

"I take your point. This one's fine, though, because 17's been using it and keeping it up?"

"Yes," Wills answered. "It's also the only lift to which he has override codes, as he uses it to patrol and maintain his section of the ship."

Einar frowned. "I wish Tam was here. He knows Perdition better than anyone. I'm not sure where we'll come out, and I'd like to be ready."

"Just assume we'll have to cut a path back to Queensland," Jael advised.

"Probably not far off the mark. You feeling strong, mate?" The big man came over and slapped him on the shoulder.

His affection hurt, but it made a nice change from suspicion. The other convict didn't seem to care that his body did abnormal things, only that he could kick his share of ass and get up after being all but gutted. Jael didn't hold it against Einar that he'd wanted to leave him to rot. In his shoes, he'd do the same; that was just the way of the world.

Which makes it more inexplicable how she fought for you. Dred had claimed it was a matter of pride, but he wished her determination to save him meant something more. Jael put that out of his mind as he helped Einar guide the air pallet up the ramp toward the lift. Wills was already waiting up there with the maintenance bot. The princess in chains came last, after taking a last look at the force field. Amber light glimmered across the threshold, preventing anybody else from getting in here and ransacking the place.

"I love that this is our private stockpile," Jael said.

The big man nodded. "I want to figure out how to get to the spare rounds for the turrets, but we can do that another time."

"I found some in storage," Wills said.

Dred shot him an appreciative glance, which she extended to include the whole group. "Great work, all of you. I'm a little surprised we're still alive, but impressed as hell, too."

"Damn right," Einar said.

Since he'd done the programming, Wills commanded, "Enable lift access."

R-17 beamed codes to the device, and the doors swung open. Inside, it was more capacious than it looked from the outside, providing room for industrial machinery. Good thing, too, or the pallet wouldn't have fit. As it was, they stood in tight quarters, pressed up against the walls.

The maintenance unit showed no signs of following until Wills said, "Come with me, 17. Repairs are needed elsewhere."

"Supervisor override required."

"Damn, it looks like I missed some fail-safes in the code."

"Probably to prevent the unit from being stolen," Jael guessed.

"I just need a few minutes," the soothsayer said.

Jael studied Dred to see what she made of the delay, but she wasn't angry. The princess in chains merely leaned against the wall and watched Wills go to work. R-17 protested the intrusion to his inner workings, then the other man shut him down entirely. After the bot went limp, Wills finished the work-around swiftly, as he'd promised.

"Fire it up," Dred instructed. "See how you did."

This time, when Wills ordered the unit to accompany them, it beamed the deck 47 destination straight to the lift controls, and the thing lurched into motion. The movement made Jael queasy, reminding him of being stuck on the prison transport with so much foul and wretched humanity. He stumbled off the lift first, then turned to help Dred. Who didn't need a hand, apparently. She pushed past him with an abstracted expression.

Probably wondering where we are. I'd like to know, too. And what needs killing here.

Once everyone else disembarked, Einar maneuvered the air pallet with help from Jael. It took up the whole corridor, which would make it impossible to fight. Furthermore, the thing was piled so high with salvage and parts that it obscured vision for anyone shorter than the big man. Since Einar was already guiding it from behind, it made sense for him to stay there.

"You push, I'll pull. If it pleases her majesty, she can guard the rear."

In order for anyone to get to the front of the pallet, they had to climb up and over. Come to think of it, the thing served as a functional portable barricade. Its bulk also meant Jael was responsible for killing anybody who interfered with the convoy.

"Do you know this area?" the big man asked Dred. "How far are we from our border?"

She shook her head, obviously frustrated. "I've never been in these halls. And look." Dred indicated the floor.

From the undisturbed dust, Jael could tell nobody had been here in a long time. If R-17 had done any collecting on deck 47, enough time had passed for its tracks to settle. So getting back to Queensland might prove a problem even though they'd circumvented the ladders.

Wills tapped a finger on his chin, looking thoughtful. "Do you possess a copy of the station layout?" he asked the bot.

"Affirmative. Display on?"

"Yes." As soon as Wills said the word, a beam came out of the droid's head, projecting a 3-D holo model of the refinery.

Even at this scale, the place looked huge. Jael tried to pinpoint their location, but he had no luck. Navigation hadn't been his specialty in any combat unit. He was always on the front line, soaking heavy fire so the rest of his team didn't die behind him. Often they walked over his body and then vomited when they saw him stagger up despite horrific wounds, stumble after them with holes where no living creature should have them.

Wills frowned, then said, "Show our present location."

A glowing light appeared on the model. *Still not helpful,* he thought, *since we have no idea where Queensland is from here. And the bot doesn't know our names for things.*

"I can work this out," Dred said, bending closer. "Where's the central dormitory on deck 47?" Another dot appeared. Then she added, "Light a path as I go if you can, 17."

She traced a route from there to the access point where they'd gone down the ladders, then the corridors. Since a white line sprang up where she indicated, Jael guessed the bot had some interesting capabilities. Next she pinpointed the salvage bay and charted the course up the lift to their current location. By the time she was done, Jael knew exactly where they needed to go. Unfortunately, it was past a pair of blast doors that didn't open anymore.

Dred wheeled and booted a dent into the nearest wall, then spat a virulent curse. Just when he thought she might lose it, the princess in chains pulled herself together, took a breath, and looked to them for solutions. "Think the laser could cut us a path?"

Wills shrugged. "Not sure how much juice the power source has left. Wired into the Peacemaker, it had a self-charging system, but it's been out of the circuit for a while now."

Einar looked tired and pissed. "Can't hurt to try."

"The Shredder might do it," Jael suggested. "It would mean blowing through a lot of ammo, though."

She snarled a few more choice epithets, but she didn't flinch from making a choice. "Laser first. If it sputters or can't cut through, then we'll try the Shredder. Damned if I'm leaving this stuff and backtracking after we went to so much trouble to retrieve it."

"Is there anything to cut through a blast door in the salvage bay?" Wills asked R-17.

The bot searched its databases, then answered, "There is a grade two mining drill, but it requires repairs in order to be functional."

"How big is it?" Einar demanded.

Good question. If it's a huge piece of equipment, it won't fit in the lift anyway.

"Five meters by four," the bot replied.

"That's not a whole lot bigger than the pallet," Wills said.

"That's plan B." Dred gestured. "Get moving, all of you. We're marching all the way to those damned blast doors."

"R-17 might be helpful up front," Wills put in. "He can scan for movement."

Jael doubted there would be any living creatures, except maybe the rodents, but it would be good to know if they were about to run into another Peacemaker. "Do you detect any other droids active on this deck?" he asked the bot.

"Unknown. I am not configured for long-range surveys. Please refer to my counterpart, the RS-99, complete with upgraded sensors and scanning capacity."

Ah well. Worth a try.

Jael scrambled over the piles of gear on the pallet, nearly overbalancing, but it was so close to the wall that he caught himself easily, then leapt down in front. "Send him up."

What the hell. Maybe it'll draw fire away from me if we

run into trouble. Einar lifted the bot bodily and handed him over. Once on the ground, R-17 whirred into motion, checking the area for broken components. Since Wills hadn't told him not to, Jael let that go. They might end up with additional useful parts.

It wasn't far, and they encountered no trouble. *The fragging doors* are *the problem.* Jael stopped, giving himself room to maneuver, then turned to call, "Hand me the laser."

Dred brought it to him personally, graceful even as she clambered across the pallet. Between her chains and the weapon, she was overloaded, but she gave no sign of it. Her shoulders were square, eyes fierce with determination. Without asking for help, she jumped down beside him.

"Hell of a day, huh? And it's about to get louder."

"Damn right," he said, realizing he sounded an awful lot like Einar.

"You ready to make some noise?" she asked.

"Count on it," he said, taking the laser.

Dammit, he might even *like* this woman.

That never ended well.

◀ 19 ▶

And the Walls Come
Tumbling Down

Jael looked natural with a weapon in hand; to Dred's min[d] he handled the laser expertly. She backed up a few steps [at] his insistence, and he fired. That first shot slagged partwa[y] through the door, leaving another layer of durasteel betwee[n] them and Queensland. He rotated the power pack, bounce[d] it, while whispering to the gun in a coaxing tone.

"You think that'll help?" she asked, amused.

"Can't hurt. Treat a weapon like a lady, and she won't l[et] you down."

"Is that your experience with women, too?"

"Most women aren't ladies," he said.

"Would you *want* them to be?"

"Not in the slightest."

He threw a cocky wink over his shoulder, and for the fir[st] time in half a turn, Dred experienced a flicker of pure chem[i]cal attraction. She didn't enjoy it, but on another level, it wa[s] good this place hadn't broken her. Perdition had hardene[d] her, but it hadn't succeeded in destroying every human im[pulse. That was reassuring. His jiggering received n[o response from the laser, however. *Dead is dead, apparently. Unless it's Jael.*

The man in question called, "Einar, toss me the Shredder. I'm taking this door down even if I have to use your head as a battering ram."

Dred waited to see how that suggestion would be received. To her astonishment, the big man climbed on top of the air pallet and chucked the rifle. "Yeah, well, if you can lift my ass, I'll let you."

Jael laughed; it seemed their camaraderie was permanent. "Let's try something else first. Take cover. Some of these shots may not chew clean through."

In a metal corridor, that was sound advice. If a fragging door killed one of them, the rest would never live it down. She hauled herself onto the air pallet and hunkered down behind a pile of scrap metal. Then she checked behind her to make sure the other two had done the same.

"All set," Einar shouted.

The gun went full auto, and sparks flew, popping all over the hallway. Shots ricocheted until she felt sure crouching was the best idea ever. Rounds struck the panels where she was hiding and cut a peephole, so she could see how Jael was doing. He bled from several new wounds but the flow was sluggish, courtesy of freakishly fast coagulation. As for the hole, she could see light on the other side, but it wasn't big enough for a person to pass through. Yet.

Soon he ran out of ammo, though. With a muted curse, Jael dropped the Shredder. "It's safe."

The R-17 unit whirred forward to inspect the damage and lights flashed on what would be the bot's face if it were human. "The wall is damaged. It must be repaired."

"Frag, *no*," Jael protested. "It took all our firepower to accomplish this much—and it's not enough."

Wills came past Dred with clumsy urgency to stop the bot from deploying its hardware on the charred wall. From the bone-reader's expression, he had an idea. She hoped it was a good one, as they were fresh out of resources.

"This isn't a wall," Wills told the bot. "This is a door. And it's the *door* that's not working. Initiate stuck-door protocol."

The bot scanned the surface, then agreed, "Blast doors are fused. Solution may result in damage to organics. Please stand clear."

"Is this thing packing explosives?" Dred asked.

Wills shrugged. "I'd step back, just in case."

But instead of applying a putty charge, a thin wand extended from R-17's front chassis and a red beam carved between the doors but was too weak to open the way on its own, given that the durasteel had been soldered from both sides.

"Repair failed. Analysis: Desired result impossible within current parameters. Recommended solution: Dispatch complete technical team from Repair and Salvage Operations."

"If only," Dred muttered.

They didn't have a repair team to summon, but maybe Jael was on the right track when he mentioned a battering ram. She added, "The two of you managed to pull apart a Peacemaker unit. Until you did it, I'd have said it was impossible, too."

Einar caught on right away. "You want us to tag team the door, using the blast hole as a handle?"

Wills said, "It's possible you could bring enough pressure to bear to pull it apart . . . and if you create a gap, R-17 can run the minilaser again. It's not meant for heavy cutting, but it might be able to weaken the seal enough for you to break it."

"Best idea we've got," Jael said. "Let's do it."

The two took up positions on either side, braced to begin as soon as Wills gave the order to the bot. Dred counted it down, then the show started. Muscles straining, they hauled until their shoulders popped. Each man grunted and swore, pushing beyond human capacity, and still they didn't stop as the bot deployed the laser. The red line skimmed upward; and Dred was positive the door gave, just a little.

"One more time," she suggested.

"One hernia coming up," the big man mumbled. "Why the hell not?"

Jael didn't reply, just set his feet and nodded with a *bring-it-on* light in his blue eyes. Wills checked the power readings on R-17, then said, "If it doesn't work, we have to go back down for more gear. The bot's almost out of juice."

Dred inclined her head. "Noted. Now let's get this done."

It went off like clockwork between the crimson glow of the laser to the twin, straining biceps and thighs of the men to the left and right of the weld point. When the door gave, it sounded like the whole ship giving way. They were pulling so hard that both Jael and Einar fell, slamming hard into the corridor walls on either side. For a second, she wanted to go help Jael to his feet, but she froze the impulse and contented herself with an arched brow.

"You two all right?"

"I just need to cram my intestines back up inside," Einar said. "No problem at all."

"Did you really pop something? Shit." Sometimes that required surgical intervention. He could die—and what a way to go out, slow and ugly. If it came to it, she wouldn't let him suffer.

But to her relief, the big man smiled and shook his head. "Just screwing with you."

Dred pushed out a slow breath and glared. "Asshole. You did good work, both of you."

Never truer words. The doors stood open enough for the men to get inside and push them back. Since they were meant to retract into the walls, it was easy once the double-welded seam popped. When Jael turned back toward her, she noticed the red smeared all over his hands.

"What happened?"

He shrugged as if the sight of his own blood was nothing new. "I opened my palms on the burn hole I was using as a handle. It'll close up by tomorrow."

That doesn't mean you aren't hurting right now, you ass.

But she couldn't be soft with anyone, even if, contrarily,

he made her want to be because he was stoic to the point of insanity. She'd thought more than once that he wasn't human, but after this run, she needed to know exactly what she'd welcomed into her territory. They were all monsters and outcasts, but sometimes the shading mattered. More information was critical. But she pretended to accept his words at face value. The conversation she intended to have with him wouldn't occur in front of an audience, even part of her inner circle like Wills and Einar.

"Wrap it up. Queensland is doubtless full of bastards who have already given us up for dead and are taking wagers on who will replace me."

"Tam," Einar answered at once.

That gave her a twinge. "I offered, but he passed. Said the territory was mine."

"Heavy is the head that wears the crown," Wills said.

The big man corrected, "'Uneasy lies the head that wears a crown.' It's from an ancient play."

Wills nodded in apparent appreciation. "Yes, that's the line."

She mock-scowled as the bone-reader shifted the air pallet from stationary to mobile mode. "Either way, there isn't one. If I have to sit on that ass-ugly chair, I ought to get a scrap-metal tiara to go along with it."

Jael aimed a warm look her way, one that had doubtless melted hearts all across the galaxy. "I'll make you one, queenie."

"Then my life would be complete," she said dryly.

Such a handsome warrior was trouble on two legs, and, unfortunately, he knew exactly how attractive and charming he could be. Jael wore the attitude like armor, but Dred wondered just what lay beneath his determinedly bright exterior. He had no issue showing his physical peculiarities, but his emotions were completely armored. In a place like this, it was best not to show your underbelly to anyone . . . but she was still curious.

"Enough chatter," she added. "Moving out."

At Einar's insistence, she climbed on the pallet. Her extra

weight didn't slow the thing, which hovered so that Jael and the big man moved it along as they walked. She felt conspicuous up top, but so close to the Queensland border, such showmanship should be safe. When they turned a final corner before the checkpoint, she was perched atop their looted gear like a pirate queen. Recognizing her obligation, she lifted her arm in triumph, propped a booted foot on an ammo case, and let out a triumphant howl.

Dred recognized the men on duty. All four of them responded with victory cries of their own. They shifted the barricades, so the pallet could slide by, then replaced them, taking up fierce and ready postures behind the raid caravan. She'd prefer to hop down now, but it would be better for morale if she returned in theatrical fashion.

Mary, I've been listening to Tam too much.

By the time they reached the hall, their procession swelled to a huge mob, chanting, "Dread Queen! Dread Queen! Long may she reign!"

It was absurd, but she gave them the spirit to fight. But Dred wished it wasn't necessary and that it didn't require so much bullshit. She wasn't a dread anything, just a tired woman with a twisted and peculiar ability, who had let it drive her mad.

They cheered her for a full five minutes before Tam opened a path through the mob. "I was getting worried," he said in low tones. "Things got interesting while you were gone as well. I'll fill you in shortly. And I have some inquiries . . ."

She could answer his questions later. For now, he had to address the men. Tam intoned, "Let us congratulate our queen for the biggest raid in Queensland history."

War whoops erupted all over the hall, incoherent shouts of domination and glory. Tam motioned them to silence. "I'll be overseeing the allotment of gear. If you see something on the pallet that you know how to utilize, see me at once. Here, we believe in using everyone's talents. You all play a vital role in the territory." He paused, scanned the crowd, then added, "But if I see you take anything without permission, the queen's judgment will be swift and merciless. Let Lecass's recent punishment serve as a reminder to us all."

There was trouble with Lecass? Damn.

Nonetheless, Dred took the cue, as intended. She gazed coldly over the crowd, then nodded. Somehow, she managed to leap down from the pallet one last time, graceful and sure, when her muscles were stiff and sore. But everything in here was a game. With no future and no freedom, it was masques and feints, an endless game of Charm where everyone was a low card to be sacrificed on a whim.

Men surrounded Tam, all talking at once. They had ideas on how the new gear could be implemented, things to build, traps to lay, pieces to repair other things, and parts for the Kitchen-mate. Wills was muttering to himself, playing the madman again, now that there were witnesses. But she'd bet he would shortly find a way to recharge the laser's power source and the R-17.

Crazy like a fox, you are, Wills.

"Jael," she said softly, "I'll see you privately in my quarters. Now."

◄ 20 ►

Secrets and Lies

It took Tam nearly an hour to finish the work assignments. A haul like this one was unprecedented, so it was no wonder the men were eager. He sighed, but before he could decide what his next most pressing task might be, Martine approached him. She was a lean, dangerous woman with brown skin gone sallow from lack of sunshine, and her eyes reflected a ferocity that was unusual, even for Perdition.

"Yes?" he prompted, seeing her hesitation.

"Could I talk to you?"

"You already are."

Her dark eyes flashed, and Tam suppressed a smile. "In private, asshole."

"Certainly. My quarters are in use at the moment, but we can walk toward the hydroponics garden. Will that do?"

"Yeah."

He led the way, holding his peace until they were far enough from the hall that he judged there shouldn't be anyone in earshot. "What's this about?"

"I've heard some troubling rumors," Martine said. "Mostly from Lecass's people."

"I'm sure he's planning something." Tam expected there to be fallout from the flogging. It only remained to be seen how Lecass would handle his humiliation. So this wasn't precisely news, but then, he suspected it wasn't the whole reason Martine had sought this interlude, either.

"But that's not all," she went on.

The woman dug into her pocket and produced a scrap of cloth. It was dingy and ragged, of no moment—or so he thought, until she handed it to him. Someone had scrawled a message: *You lost your man. Want revenge? Come to the meeting. 2300. Corridor D.*

Tension rose, stiffening his shoulders, but Tam tried not to reveal it in his posture. "You think Lecass sent this?"

If so, then the man was more cunning than he'd expected.

Martine shrugged. "Dunno. Don't care. I just thought Dred's people should know. There's blood in the water, and the monsters are circling."

From Dred's perspective, this was the worst possible time to face internal strife. With Priest and the Great Bear gearing up for a full-scale war, they couldn't afford to lose a single warm body to Lecass's pride. If the Queenslanders lost, Dred would end up raped to death and probably skull-fucked for good measure while her men, himself included, would wind up murdered or enslaved. And that didn't even factor Silence into the equation.

Tam had to shut this rebellion down before it gathered momentum. He set a hand gently on Martine's shoulder. "Thanks. I'll remember your loyalty."

"See that you do," she muttered.

He let her return to the hall, counting to five hundred before he followed. For a few seconds, he stood in the shadows, watching the men, as if he could tell by looking who might join Lecass's rabble. But they were all acting like they normally did: gaming, drinking, scuffling. A few were arm wrestling, while others pierced things and created body art. There wasn't a lot to do in Perdition when you weren't on patrol, which was another reason the men had been so glad to get parts and supplies. Even repair work seemed better than another day of nothing.

Quietly, Tam joined Cook at the table where he was taking a break from his endless stirring. The man raised both brows in question. Tam didn't waste time; he whispered what he'd heard from Martine, then asked, "Do you know anything?"

Since Cook was so quiet, the men often acted like he was deaf, speaking within his earshot like he wasn't even there. Cook's gaze flickered to Lecass, who was sitting with a group of convicts huddled around him. They were his regular cohorts, nothing unusual about them scheming against Dred, but if they'd called a meeting, it must indicate some greater plan . . . and more men in accord with their aims.

Yes, them, Tam thought, *but are there others?*

Cook nodded. In subtle gestures, he identified five inmates, all being careful not to look at Lecass. Tam knew not to make his departure obvious, so he sat with Cook for a few moments more. The man wasn't much company, but he noticed things with an acuity to rival Tam's own.

Five wasn't such a large number, but that didn't mean the ones Cook knew about were the only conspirators. He pushed to his feet and sought Calypso, who was playing dice with a couple of women. She avoided males when she socialized though Tam didn't know her well enough to be sure if that was a sexual preference or a personal choice.

To be polite, he watched the game for a while, until the women came to a natural stopping point. Only then did he say, "Mind if I have a word?" to Calypso.

She measured him with a look. "Make it quick. I want to earn back what I just lost."

"You could use a break," the blonde mocked her. "Your mojo's gone."

Calypso made a rude gesture with two fingers and her tongue, then she rose in a sinuous motion, lithe as a snake. "Come, little man."

Some men might find that offensive, but Tam was used to such remarks. He stood just over 1.6 meters, so there was no arguing his lack of stature and no point in wasting energy in anger. Calypso towered over him as she led the way from the hall.

"Let me guess," she said. "Somebody told you about the meeting."

That irked him a little, not an easy feat. "Why didn't you?"

"I don't recall making any promises to you or the Dread Queen," Calypso answered. "At least regarding anything not pertaining to the games."

Tam was tired . . . and he *almost* lost his temper then. Somehow, he bit back his retort about how easy it would be to find someone more loyal to run the death matches. Calypso cared about nothing more than her status as Mistress of the Ring.

Her mouth curved with feline amusement. "I'd like you better if you blew off steam now and then, little man. One of these days, you're gonna go boom, and it won't be pretty."

"That's irrelevant," Tam said tightly. "I'd consider it a personal favor if you'd do something for me."

"What's that?"

Quietly, he outlined his plan.

"YOU don't know how long I've dreamed of getting you alone, queenie." After winding up in her quarters again, Jael reckoned it was best to open strong. Maybe if he annoyed her enough, she'd change her mind about this personal chat.

"None of that," she said flatly. "I have questions. You have answers."

"Many. But none of them will make you happy."

"As long as they're true."

"You want to know why I can heal like I do. Why there's almost not killing me."

"Clever lad."

"Not too much, or I wouldn't be locked up in here, would I?"

"Point. But you're changing the subject."

"I do that when I'm nervous."

She arched a brow, arranging her long body in the room's only chair. Her quarters were dim and dingy but better than anything he'd had in turns. His bed in the Bug prison had been a pile of filthy rags. With what he hoped was a cheeky smile, he perched on the edge of her bunk.

"You? I hardly think so. You're trying to disarm me, make me think twice about digging. Why don't I save you the trouble? I'm immune to your charms."

"But you admit I have them."

At that point, he had second thoughts about jerking her around. So far as he knew, she'd been straight with him from the jump, never promising what she didn't intend to deliver. Often, he could smell deceit in a person's sweat, a touch more acrid as it was often laced with fear, fear of failure, fear of discovery—and what he'd do if he learned of their treachery.

She smiled. "I'm immune, not blind."

"Carry on then." Jael folded his hands in his lap, suppressed a smile when she sighed.

"A while back, you made a joke about my father working on the Ideal Genome Project. I don't know what that is, but I'd be willing to bet it relates directly to why you are . . . as you are."

It was a kind, tactful way to put it. He'd heard other vernacular—fiend and monster, demon on the more primitive worlds. On some planets, they thought he was some undying beast come to drink their blood or their souls. Explanations were always messy . . . and exhausting.

But why not tell the story? One last time.

"You're uncanny," he said.

"So I've been told. Explain, please."

Where to begin?

"Before Farwan collapsed, their Science Corp had a number of experimental programs. The IGP was only one, an offshoot of a primary initiative."

"And you participated in it?" she asked.

Mary, he hated enlightening her, but the questions would

never cease until she knew the truth. And then, everything would change between them. It always did.

"No," he said softly. "I was created by it."

Her green eyes widened, but that was the only sign that he'd shocked her. *Good work, princess. Keep it up, and you'll convince me you don't think I'm an animal after all.*

"I think you have to start from the beginning. Tell me everything you know."

"Why? You have your answer. You're right . . . I'm not human. I'm Bred. Not even sentient according to the most recent legislation."

To his astonishment, she scowled at him. "I am *surrounded* by monsters, Jael. You're interesting, but not the worst I've run into inside Perdition. Now why don't you stop feeling sorry for yourself and answer my fragging question?"

Mary. She's . . . magnificent.

"The IGP sprang from a program that offered designer babies to wealthy citizens. Why end up with dumb, defective, or unattractive offspring when you can afford better, right?"

Her nod showed a hint of revulsion. "I read about that in my history coursework, I think, but they didn't name any of those gray programs. We didn't spend much time on Farwan or the Science Corp, either."

"I imagine not." That answer sent a pang through him. What he'd lived and suffered, it was *history* to her, and she didn't even remember the project name. Just another example how out of step he was, how he could never fit. "Naturally, once they started generating credits with the primary program, they saw other uses for the gene therapy and DNA shaping."

"Like what?"

"Military applications," he said, thinking she should know that.

But maybe she'd learned her combat skills inside. Surviving meant she was a quick study, not that she had professional training. Her father had been a scientist, as he recalled, a refugee from Farwan; he didn't think she'd mentioned anything about her mother. Odd he would remember a casual conversation with such clarity, or that she would remember the joke he'd made, days later.

Hm.

Determined to lay it out for her, Jael went on, "The Corp used the profits from creating these custom children to fund the Ideal Genome Project. Forget antiaging treatments— they intended to develop bodies that didn't decay or suffer from illness and required reduced amounts of rest."

"You don't sleep?" It was interesting that was what she focused on.

"I enjoy it, but I need it less than you do. I can get by with two hours a night though my reaction and regenerative abilities diminish the more exhausted I become." Jael shrugged. "This wasn't the first experiment along these lines. Governments have been trying to perfect the supersoldier for years."

"And that's you?" she asked quietly.

He tilted his head back, unable to summon the mocking laughter that would strip the question of its barbs. "Not even close."

"So you were created in a lab, then." Her neutral tone gave no sign as to what she thought about that, but he could guess. "There must have been others."

"Most subjects died before reaching maturity," he answered. "The Corp 'officially' shut the program down after religious outcry. But there are always hidden labs where the experiments continue, no matter what the public believes. See, the scientists needed to discover how strong we were and whether we were docile enough to be deployed in battle."

"You say 'we' . . . so you weren't alone?"

Jael's first memory came wrapped in pain: wires, tubes, translucent skin, floating in a glass vessel. Here and now, turns later, that genesis period remained vague; and it was for the best. Upon his "birth," he'd undergone an awful number of procedures and experiments to test his capacity for pain, healing, and recovery. A small pod of subjects, Jael included, received rudimentary combat training, education, and social interaction. The lab techs were . . . curious.

Why does JL489 survive when its sibling, created from an identical embryo, crashed and burned during the last phase of DNA shaping?

Jael had survived that first wave of experimentation. Eventually, most of his pod was designated as flawed and destroyed. In time, Farwan decreed the secret research too expensive to continue, and when Corp security personnel came to clean the labs of the remaining survivors, they'd fought and fled. The basic education he received from the Corp permitted him to get work as a merc, even though, emotionally, he was little more than a child.

The turns were not kind thereafter.

He broke from reverie to answer her question in a hoarse tone. "Yes, there were others. Twenty of us escaped. I don't know if any of them are still alive."

"You didn't stick together or remain in contact?"

Jael laughed quietly, though the sound contained an angry edge. "Does traveling as a collective freak show seem like the wisest way to stay out of enemy hands?"

"Probably not. And you wanted to forget where you came from, I imagine. Try to blend."

Truer than you know, princess.

"That's not an easy task when you're . . . like this."

"If you weren't *like this*, we wouldn't be prepping for war with the best gear Queensland's ever had. We'd be scared and hopeless with our backs to the wall, facing better weapons, more soldiers. I realize we're only a bunch of wretches and convicts, but you're the closest thing to a hero we've ever seen."

"As pep talks go, that was pathetic." But he was smiling; and he couldn't remember the last time it hadn't felt like cuts carved into his cheeks, wholly false, wholly for show. This time, he felt it. Knew his sincerity must show in his eyes. It alarmed him though he couldn't control it.

Dred lifted a shoulder, apparently unconcerned by his criticism. "It's the best I could do on short notice. This whole

Dread Queen business is all rubbish, as I'm sure you've guessed."

"You seem plenty tough to me. And the men believe in you. That's all that matters." He hesitated, then added, "If you win their hearts and minds, the bodies follow. They'll do impossible things because they believe in your legend and want to live up to it. You're the woman who can accomplish the impossible, raid unreachable locales, and read their minds."

"Careful," she said sharply. "You're being kind. We discussed my objection to that."

"I'm not, actually. I'm being honest. It's rare enough that I understand why you'd be confused, though." The fragile smile persisted; he couldn't kill it or drive it away.

Nothing had changed that he could detect. Not her expression or manner. Not her scent, as if she were secretly frightened of him. Then, inwardly he scoffed at the notion. Dred was as fierce and dangerous a woman as he'd encountered. And she didn't frighten easily.

"Thanks for the explanation." She folded to her feet, obviously ready to conclude the interview.

Jael found he didn't want to leave. That was a . . . unique development.

"Aren't you going to ask how I ended up in here?"

Dred shook her head. "I needed to understand why you're nearly fragging indestructible so I can best deploy that aptitude. Beyond that, it's your business."

"No curiosity?"

She read him like a book. "Look, if you *want* to tell me, if it'll put you at ease to treat me like a holy confessor, go for it."

"There's nothing holy about you, queenie, but you sure are divine."

The woman laughed, falling back into her chair with a graceful motion. "Were you expecting some particular payout with that line? You have my undivided attention. Explain how you ended up on the prison transport."

"Just to make you laugh," he said. "And look, it worked.

As for the how . . . it's fairly simple. I worked as a merc for turns. Killed a lot of people. I ended up in this oddball crew . . ." He trailed off, trying to decide how to explain his tenure with Sirantha Jax. It had been so long that the galaxy might've forgotten her by now. His need for vengeance had cooled, too.

For long turns in the Bug prison, he'd reflected on how he'd make her pay, should he ever catch up with her, but since ending up in Perdition, he'd decided not to waste turns chasing a pipe dream. Once he broke out of this hellhole, it was time to try something new. But Jael didn't kid himself it would be easy. He'd had a look at the ship's defenses now, and they had damn near cracked him in two.

"Odd how?"

"I dunno. Almost like a family, I guess."

"You didn't fit?"

"That's the thing," he said softly. "I could have, I think. But I was too quick to assume they'd sell me out, given the chance."

"So you shot first," she guessed.

"Yeah. It didn't end well. I did time on Ithiss-Tor. Then they extradited me in exchange for some Ithtorian POWs. The Science Corp snatched me up, ran another series of tests. They kept me under such heavy sedation, I didn't know shit until just before they put me down."

She sucked in a sharp breath, reaching toward him in an abortive moment, then her hands returned to her lap. "Clearly it didn't take."

"Pretty much. Imagine the morgue tech's surprise when I crawled out of the slot they put me in to await autopsy."

"What happened then?"

"I convinced them I was too valuable to destroy. They decided it was best to confine me here, where I'd be under complete lockdown, but within reach if they need me to run more experiments. And here I am. Charming story, right?"

"Unusual, definitely."

He had no idea what he sought from her, not expiation or forgiveness, something else. Understanding, maybe. He'd

never had that. Warmth trickled through him as he processed the fact that she absolutely wasn't afraid or revolted.
So far as he could tell, nothing had changed in her response
to him despite what she'd learned about his origins. It un-
hinged his tongue after decades of silence and secrecy.

Jael went on, "My name? It's the initials of the doctor
who made me. Jurgin Landau."

"It doesn't matter where you started," she said. "Or what
you've been through. That shit just means you're strong. In
here, if you're tough enough, you dub yourself whatever you
want. You think anybody called me Dread Queen before? I
made that happen. So can you . . . because from where I'm
sitting, you look pretty damn special, and not because of
the fast healing."

At her words, the warmth turned into longing too fierce
to deny. So he kissed her.

◄ 21 ►

Death Sends Word

It wasn't a hard kiss, more of a question. His lips were soft, tentative, as they moved over hers. The warmth felt unexpectedly good. Yet she sensed that Jael expected to be rebuffed, then he'd attribute the rejection to what she'd just learned about him. Since Dred knew what lurked beneath his charming exterior, she couldn't do it. The kiss bloomed into a soft and heated exchange, breaths shared, a glide of tongues and nibble of teeth. Her body flared to life as he settled her closer. He rocked against her, and the fit was *so* good. Dred flattened a palm on his chest to force some distance between them, feeling his heart race. He actually groaned from that light touch, his head tilted back. She had no idea why she didn't resist when he took her hand and slid it lower.

You should stop this. You can't afford distraction.

But his approach wasn't forceful or demanding. He wanted nothing of her but this, she suspected. Dred couldn't resist reading him, just a quick glimpse, but she saw only raw desire crackling keenly along the edges of old sorrow.

So she slid her fingers inside his trousers and watched his face as she touched him. "Yes?"

"Yes," he breathed.

Those were the only words they spoke during those odd, intimate moments. It didn't take long for him to arch and moan her name. She stepped back and gave him a moment to collect himself. Her breathing was unsteady as she washed her hands, but she was composed by the time she finished.

"Is that how you react to all such conversations?" she wondered aloud.

"There haven't been any like this. And if you hadn't touched another soul in thirty turns, you'd be easy, too." His lashes drifted up, blue eyes sharp with an ache she'd never seen in a human being. Jael collapsed on her bunk, looking rather ravaged.

It took all her self-control not to pounce. *So it's been that long.* Of all the strange and shocking things he'd shared, that one startled her the most.

"How *old* are you?"

He named a date. "That was when they started the IGP. I was created ten turns in."

After Dred did the math, she wondered if he was screwing with her. If not for his unusual physiology, she'd be sure he was. "You're saying you're over a hundred turns."

He shrugged. "I've aged well." His expression turned inscrutable, then he added, "I'm sorry, by the way. I shouldn't have started this with you. I promised myself I wouldn't."

She took the apology at face value though she wondered why. It also made her even more determined to level the ground between them. She didn't share confidence; she never had. Even Tam and Einar didn't know her story, but she'd closed her eyes while listening to him, and Jael's colors stayed steady. Generally, that meant he was telling the truth, and she felt like that bravery required something in return. Since she had no intention of investing in an actual relationship in here—that way lay madness and danger—she'd given him the honesty of a moment's physical contact. She had nothing else to offer.

Then she yielded to the impulse to give something back. She didn't want him walking out of this encounter feeling like half a person. "I'm from a small colony in the Outskirts."

Funny how just saying that brought her past to life. So easily she could picture the prefab corrugated metal buildings and the frontier feel. People went about their business with weapons on their hips because there were native beasts on that ball of rock that would eat you, given half a chance. There were other dangers, too. Pretty much everyone who ended up on Tehrann was hiding from something—or someone—one way or another. Dred hadn't let herself think of her parents in turns, not even to wonder whether they were still alive.

Jael sat up, visibly startled by the confidence, and part of her wanted to push him back and seek refuge in physicality instead. But it would be a lie, albeit an enjoyable one, and she . . . respected him too much for that. He deserved better than cowardice wrapped in sex, especially since she had no intention of letting him touch her heart. Her body was one thing; it had been used as a commodity so often that she wasn't sure she had it in her to offer more. Better to offer esteem and friendship.

So she went on, "I think I mentioned that my father was a scientist though that wasn't what he did on Tehrann. My mother was frightened all the time."

"Comes with the territory when Sci-Corp is hunting you."

"I hated it there. It was so isolated, so quiet. There were only four hundred people in our settlement, few of them children."

"You must've been lonely."

She was conscious of the irony, given what he'd suffered. Dred glossed over that with a shrug. "At eighteen I'd had enough. I found a freighter in dock that was down one hand. I signed on for board, minimal pay, and the chance to see the universe."

His mouth quirked in what wasn't a smile. "How did that work out for you?"

"It was . . . bad from the first." She swallowed the sick tide that accompanied the memories. "On Tehrann, there was nobody who set off my sensors. There, I was normal, more or less. But as soon as I came aboard the ship, I had an . . . episode."

"One of the crew?" he guessed.

"Yes. At the time I didn't understand what was happening. Everyone else seemed to like the man fine, but I found it hard to be in the same room with him. I ran every chance I got, which only piqued his interest more."

"It would. So what happened? Did you kill him?" By his tone, he hoped so.

"No. I wasn't that person, then. Instead I jumped ship as soon as I could, but it wasn't better in a larger port. More people got into my head and showed me their crimes."

"How did you stand it?"

She shrugged. "I didn't. I went a bit mad. Then I decided if I could see what they were doing, I could punish them, too. That worked fairly well for a while. Then they caught me."

"So that's how you ended up in here?"

Dred shook her head. "Not at first. But I wasn't . . . cooperative in the general prison where they sent me. There were . . . problems." That was all she intended to share at the moment.

"Then you were shipped here as the ultimate punishment."

"That's it. No daylight. No parole. I have eight lifetimes on my sentence."

Jael smiled. "I don't have one. A sentence, that is. This is just the warehouse where they decided to store me." Then he added, "If you don't mind, I'd like to use your sanshower."

For obvious reasons.

She nodded, and he slipped into the tiny cubicle set aside for hygiene. As she stood to leave, Tam strode into her quarters, looking purposeful. "The Speaker has arrived from Entropy. He has word from Silence."

Though she desperately craved a wash and hot meal, Dred nodded. "I'll be right there."

The spymaster nodded. "Be quick. I have no doubt he's making note of every detail to report to Silence when he returns."

That's all I need.

Tam led her to the center of the hall, where the Speaker waited. In this setting, away from the horror that was Entropy, he looked no less frightening. Despite the fact that it had been a hard fight for several of them to reach Silence, he stood there alone. Dred didn't know what to make of that; if it was a boast or a warning. She was inclined to take it as a bit of both.

"Speaker," she said, inclining her head.

Though she hadn't discussed protocol with Tam, she knew he wouldn't want her to bow. This wasn't Silence; therefore, he wasn't her equal. Or so the story went. For herself, she didn't care, but apparently the details made a difference, and it kept Queensland safe.

"Hungry?" she asked, hoping the man would admit to a human need so she could eat.

The Speaker shook his head. "I am here for but one reason—to impart Her words. She says, 'Make ready, for in one week, we will cleanse Perdition of the false god.'"

That must mean we're going after Priest.

"What's the battle plan?" Dred wished Silence had discussed it with her, instead of informing her like a lackey, but she needed the alliance and couldn't cavil at the delivery system.

"She anticipated that question." The Speaker set a sheaf of paper in her palm. "Read it. Follow your portion of the attack strategy to the letter. And there will be no survivors in Abaddon."

A chill ran through her. As Dred bent her head to read, the Speaker turned. She didn't attempt to call him back. The less she had to do with Silence's people, the better. Skimming the document led her to realize two things—Silence was, indeed, undeniably insane, but she was also an evil genius. Tam put out a hand when she finished, and she gave him the pages.

"Thoughts?" she prompted, once he finished.

"It's risky. And she's given us the lion's share of the open combat. The force that stands at the gate banging to get in will take the most casualties."

Dred nodded. "Can we trust her?"

If they committed their forces to a full, open assault on Abaddon, so many things could go wrong. It would leave Queensland vulnerable, so there might be nothing to return to, though the defensive measures they'd acquired down in the salvage bay would offset the risk. Executing this mad scheme required most of the manpower at Dred's disposal; only a skeleton crew would remain behind to guard their territory. If Silence was so inclined, she could tip off Grigor, and Dred would be done.

"I don't know," Tam said softly. "But I'm positive we can't trust Grigor and Priest. If we wait much longer, we'll have their combined might knocking at our figurative gates. I'd prefer an offensive where we control the numbers we're facing."

"Provided Silence doesn't sell us out."

"That's the key question," Tam agreed.

"Look, I'm not deciding anything on an empty stomach. Assemble the others." Tam would know she meant Einar, Ike, and Wills. "We'll have a meeting in my quarters in an hour. Bring food."

The spymaster bowed with ironic servility. "It will be as you command, my queen."

Jael joined her as Tam moved off. "I just realized he's taking the piss with pretty much everything he says to you."

"You thought he was truly in awe, believed he wasn't worthy to kiss the toe of my boot?" Dred raised a brow.

"Nuances sometimes escape me," he admitted. "But now I see that he likes and respects you, but there's nothing . . . humble about it."

"Not in the least," she agreed.

She turned then and headed for her quarters. A san-shower made her feel like a new woman though she was careful with the water. Two minutes later, she stepped out and dressed in her customary black leather pants and a thin shirt. The fabric was a dingy gray, worn from multiple washings. But at least it was clean.

Dred checked the time, then stretched out on her bunk, hands behind her head. A knot formed in her stomach as she considered the risk of Silence's plan. At base, it was simple; Queensland provided the distraction while Entropy came in from behind. The silent killers would execute many of Priest's people before they even realized security had been compromised, as they would be focused on dealing with the obvious threat Dred's people presented at the front.

So many things could go wrong.

◀ 22 ▶

Coordinations and Confidences

An hour later, Jael reported to Dred's quarters. Tam was already there, and he handed Jael a bowl with stewed vegetables in it as he came in. But there was protein, too, which meant Wills had already repaired the Kitchen-mate in the galley. Jael smiled at the soothsayer as he arranged himself on the floor. As the newest member of the crew, he figured it was best. Einar was the last to arrive, and, to Jael's surprise, the big man sat down beside him.

Einar nudged his shoulder. "Hell of a run, eh?"

He nodded as Dred filled the others in on everything they'd missed. Ike looked impressed when he heard they'd blown the blast doors open and that there was now a clear run down to the salvage bays. But Wills added, "We'll have to take 17 back with us, though. He has the lift codes."

"If there's a way to download them," Tam started, but Wills shook his head.

"I don't have a device to store them on."

Dred said, "We'll take care of the bot, but I recommend you upgrade him with self-defense capabilities if that's possible."

"I'll get on that, but I need to know what's priority here. R-17, installing the turrets, or repairing and optimizing the weapons we stripped from the Peacemaker?"

"All of it," Dred answered. "Since we can't go back for more gear without the bot, though, tackle him first. Turrets next. And then the weapons. If you need to go back down to the salvage bay for parts or ammo, take Einar with you."

"I can help out with some of the tech work," Ike volunteered.

Dred nodded. "Thanks. Any questions before we move on?"

Nobody spoke up. Jael was busy shoveling in his food, as the paste they'd swallowed hadn't been enough to keep him going, just enough to prevent him from digesting the lining of his stomach. Einar and Wills were eating with the same single-minded attention to their bowls, so with a wry smile, Dred called for a time-out while everyone ate. As Jael studied the assembled group, he wondered why there were no other females in her inner circle.

Figuring there was nothing to lose, he asked.

Tam answered him. "Artan had . . . a harem for want of a better word. When he died, a number of women in Queensland were unhappy with their change in circumstances."

Jael cut a look to Dred, who wore a conspicuously blank expression. He'd seen that look in his own mirror when he was most carefully showing the world how much he didn't give a frag what it thought of him. For the first time, he wondered about her relationship with Artan, but he didn't ask. If she wanted him to know, she would've told him.

"Then it's a matter of loyalty. They need more time to get used to the new regime."

Dred nodded. "In another half a turn, if none of them have tried to kill me again, I'll look at adding a female advisor. I'm not trying to keep them down, but the first month was . . . difficult."

"Again?" he repeated.

Einar raised the hem of his shirt to expose a nasty scar

on his abdomen. "Took that one for her. That's part of why she doesn't sleep alone anymore."

Maybe it wasn't, but that comment felt pointed, as if the big man suspected what had gone down in here an hour before. *Mary, I don't want to piss him off.* It made Jael feel like a leech; he'd never gotten between a man and woman before. There were enough free birds in the galaxy that he'd never been tempted. Locked up here in Perdition, though, there was a much more limited pool.

"Enough gossip," Dred muttered. "I didn't call you in here to talk about ancient history."

She produced some ragged papers and handed them to Tam, who read them aloud. Ike was rubbing his chin, brow furrowed, by the time the spymaster finished. Einar let out a burp as he leaned back against the bunk and crossed his legs at the ankles; clearly he wasn't present for his analytical abilities.

Wills broke the silence. "I can have Queensland upgraded in a week with Ike's help."

"That's not the question we're here to debate," Dred said softly. "It's whether we can trust Silence to keep up her end of the deal. I have . . . reservations about committing our forces fully to a frontal assault on Abaddon."

She didn't need to outline the reasons why. Jael saw awareness of all the ways it could turn sideways in everybody's faces. He tapped his fingers on his thighs, trying to imagine how Death's Handmaiden saw this playing out. The woman was crazy, no doubt, but she had regimented ideas about the way things functioned and regarding the role of Death. Did she see the reaper as honorable? That would be the best-case scenario for them. If she believed it was mercurial and unpredictable, then she might renege on their agreement without a second thought.

Finally, Tam said, "It's an all-or-nothing gamble right enough. But I don't see us weathering the conflict unless we take the risk."

Einar laughed. "If we're going to lose, we might as well

go out big. None of this holing up, dying in fives and tens, over a long, dreary turn."

"Do you care to discuss it more, or shall we put it to the vote?" Dred asked.

"No more talking," Wills begged. "My head aches."

"It's all the voices," the big man joked.

Dred scanned the room, her green eyes keen. "Right then. Hands in the air, all in favor of a suicide assault on Abaddon."

What the hell. Jael put his hand in the air.

Ike and Wills left theirs down. But Einar and Tam swung them up. The princess in chains considered for a few seconds, then lifted her own, though her vote hadn't been necessary for a majority.

She pushed to her feet in an obvious dismissal. "It's decided. We cast our lot in with Silence, Mary have mercy on our souls."

"Since when?" Einar muttered.

To Jael's surprise, the big man offered him a hand up. He took it and followed him out of Dred's quarters. They dropped their dishes in the galley, where a thin man glared at the addition to the washing-up pile. Jael wondered if they had even rudimentary housekeeping chores in other territories. From the look of Entropy, though, he guessed not. It was a wonder Silence's people didn't die of disease or food poisoning.

They probably do, and she calls it Death's lottery.

He felt odd, adrift, as if he needed to go talk to Dred, but she'd made it clear she was done with the lot of them. The big man slung an arm around his shoulders unexpectedly, which made Jael think he had been drinking, but Einar didn't smell of booze. But apparently that was his intention, as he dragged Jael over to the barman, who gave out liquor chits. Though it was impossible to prohibit drinking, Dred made sure not to send men out on patrol if they had been.

"We've earned a few rounds," Einar said.

Jael couldn't remember the last time he'd been in a proper

bar, so he sat down beside the big man and accepted a glass with amber liquid in it. "Does this come from the Kitchen-mate?"

"No. The men would riot if there was no grog when the thing breaks down."

"That's . . . impressive."

Einar laughed. "Dred knows how to keep her men happy."

The obvious truth of that rubbed him raw. To cover his misplaced anger, he downed the glass in one swallow. There was no point in mentioning that he was physically incapable of getting drunk. His metabolism was simply too efficient. If Jael imbibed enough to *poison* a normal man, it just left him mildly buzzed for half an hour or so. But he didn't plan on telling Einar that.

They drank steadily, companionably, for an hour. The big man grew ever more loquacious, and by the time he had six glasses in him, his arm was a permanent weight around Jael's shoulders, and he was calling everybody over who would listen to introduce them to his new best mate. The other Queenslanders were used to this, obviously. They indulged Einar even if they already knew Jael.

One convict looked like he wanted to start something with the big man worse for the drink, but Jael aimed a sharp look at him. "I've got his back. Sure you want this weight?"

Men almost never took him seriously. It was the damned pretty face, but in *here*, when you had no scars to speak of, it likely seemed scarier than Einar's ravaged mug. *You have to ask yourself, why can't anybody leave a mark on him?* Apparently deciding the answer was more frightening than he could deal with, the convict hurried off with a muttered excuse about being due on patrol.

Einar wasn't as drunk as he'd been pretending, though, as he watched the inmate go, thoughtful. "What is it about you, mate?"

"I don't know what you mean." That was a lie, the first of many, probably.

"You *do*. And you told Dred. I can tell by the way she watches you."

"I suppose she'll put the word out if she wants people to know."

"Do *you*?"

Jael shrugged. He didn't, really, but since when had anyone given a frag about his wishes? "If you want to swap stories, we can. You tell me yours, first."

"All right," the big man said unexpectedly. "What're you asking? About my pretty face, or what I did to get locked up in here?"

"Either. But mostly the latter," he was forced to admit.

Don't bond with him, a cautious inner voice ordered. *It'll be harder to sell him out if you need to. Not if. When.* But it didn't stop him from paying full attention when the man signaled for another glass and downed it in a single swallow, as if he needed liquid courage.

"I was a soldier, if you couldn't have guessed. Away a lot. I wasn't the best, or I wouldn't look like this." His self-deprecating tone made Jael want to dismiss the scars, but they weren't trivial, and the man had earned them. Whether they were pretty or not was beside the point. Einar went on, "I had a wife. And . . . I loved her, more than anything."

The man clenched the lip of the table, his knuckles turning white. Even the booze didn't seem to be enough to dull the memories. Comfort fell completely outside his purview, so he only raised a brow in silent expectation. *Damn, I knew any story that ends here has a painful trajectory.*

"One day, I came home from deployment to find my beloved wife six months pregnant." The brow bisected by a scar went up, and Einar's expression was ironic. "Problem was, I hadn't been home in nine months."

"Shit," Jael said.

"I'd always had a temper though I never laid hands on her until that day. I . . . ." The big man shrugged. "Lost my mind. There are no excuses. When I came back to myself, she was dead. I strangled her. Killed the unborn babe."

"Not to cast doubts on your story, but that doesn't seem extreme enough to land you in here."

The big man showed his teeth in what couldn't remotely be called a smile. "That's because I wasn't done. I found out who had been screwing my wife, and I killed him. He had friends. I killed them, too. Then his brothers came after me, and—"

"Now we're getting to the necessary body count. I get the gist."

"To revenge," Einar said, lifting his glass.

"I'll drink to that."

Jael wasn't ready to tell his own story to anyone but Dred, but fortunately, he didn't have to. A few minutes later, Einar passed out, his head on the table. The other men cast disbelieving looks, obviously comparing his size to the big man and wondering how he'd managed that. Jael just offered a cocky smile and strolled out of the hall. If he was lucky, he could put in a few hours in the hydroponics garden before the next emergency.

23

Feverish Preparations

"Hold the base still," Wills ordered.

Since it was just the two of them, Dred obeyed. She much preferred the bone-reader when he wasn't pretending to be crazy. Though sometimes episodes did genuinely overtake him, they weren't as frequent as he let on. She didn't begrudge him the fiction, though, as it kept other inmates from bothering him. Even in Perdition, there was a superstitious dread of harming a madman.

A day after their return, he was installing a turret at the east checkpoint. There was no ammo chamber built into the floor, so it had to be reloaded manually. All the men would need to be trained in that, but before it was necessary, they had to get the thing working. Wills had been trying for an hour before she came along, and he was in quite a testy mood, as it was rare for him to require this much effort to get something affixed to his liking.

"I need something to solder this in place," he muttered.

"Could your bot help?" She recalled the thin maintenance laser.

"Genius. Hold this, I'll be right back."

Dred nearly toppled backward as he released the full weight of the gun into her hands. Somehow she steadied it and kept it from toppling. *That could've been disastrous. Especially if it hit the firing mechanism on the way down.* Biting back a curse, she glanced over her shoulder to see one of the guards moving to help her. *Idiots.*

He didn't ask if she was all right, just took part of the weight for her. "These are motion-activated, right?"

"Yes, you won't need to fire it."

The convict grinned, showing rotten teeth. "Pity."

She donned her iciest look. "I've got it. Step back."

It didn't do to permit too much familiarity. Sometimes it was lonely, but better this way; she couldn't have the men remembering she had been Artan's preferred bedmate before she'd killed him. It might give them ideas about their place in Queensland. Tam had worked too hard to build her legend for her to screw with it now.

Fortunately, he obeyed, as how she would've forced the issue with her arms full of turret, she had no idea. Dred laid it down on its side, away from the firing mechanism and turned to look for Wills, who was on his way back with R-17. The work went faster with the bot's help, and two hours later, the first turret was installed.

"Why didn't you have 17 with you?" Given that the droid had accompanied Wills everywhere since they found the thing, she was surprised he hadn't been using it.

"Ike was finishing some upgrades."

"Like what?" she asked, as they headed back to the hall.

Wills glanced around as if to make sure there were no eavesdroppers, then whispered, "He's programmed it for self-defense."

"That's phenomenal news." It was a relief to know some drunken idiot wouldn't break R-17 in a fit of rage without realizing how critical the droid was. But she couldn't circulate the truth, or somebody would steal it. Even in Queensland—the least hellish of Perdition's territories—she couldn't alter the fundamental nature of the citizenry. "Great work."

"Ike did most of it. He's not much for general repairs, but he knows a lot about bots." The bone-reader offered a shrewd look, running a hand through his wild hair. "He's building something, by the way. I want to get back and see if I can help."

"Report," she demanded.

This was how Artan lost control. He lost touch, stopped paying attention to the details and thought only of his own pleasure. You need to keep your finger on the pulse.

"He's got spare parts, the scrap from the Peacemaker. I think he's trying to build a defense bot, like they have in Abaddon."

"It would relieve my mind if we had it up and running before we march."

"Me, too," Wills said soberly.

Dred remembered that he'd voted against trusting Silence. It bothered her that her two oldest advisors both thought it was a bad idea to commit to the assault. *But what're my choices? Wait for Priest and Grigor to join up and come to Queensland?* Death's Handmaiden seemed the lesser of the evils in this situation, not that she felt delighted with that conclusion.

Sometimes you just have to roll the dice.

"I'll want a reading before we move out," she said then. "But not today. Find Ike. Keep me posted."

"Yes, my queen."

Great, now Tam has Wills saying that, too. Only he didn't offer the same ironic edge as the spymaster, who knew full well that she wouldn't be sitting on the scrap-metal throne without his intel and machinations. *All I did was kill a man I hated. Tam did the rest.*

She lifted a hand in parting, then went to see Tam. He'd filled her in about how he'd crushed a budding rebellion, using Calypso to quietly spread the word that Dred's people knew about the meeting . . . and that anyone who attended would be executed. Not surprisingly, there was nobody at the appointed coordinates at 2300 hours.

After he thwarted Lecass, Tam had left last night to scou

Entropy to see if they showed signs of honoring their commitment. Dred needed to talk to him to see what he'd discovered, so she checked the hall first. She found him breaking his fast alone and joined him. As Dred hadn't eaten, she grabbed a bowl of mush, tasteless but filling.

"Do you have any idea why Einar didn't come to bed last night?" she asked.

The spymaster nodded. "He was drinking with the new fish. Think he's still passed out."

Dred didn't ask where Jael was; she refused to be curious. But with Einar on a bender and Tam out spying, she'd slept alone for the first time since Artan died. It was . . . strange. She hadn't gotten much rest, keeping an eye on the door in case someone took the opportunity to attempt assassination. From what Tam had told her, Lecass was looking for a way to get the job done. She suspected his patience would run out soon.

"What did you learn?"

Tam frowned. "Not as much as I wished. The angle was bad, and the lighting was worse. Silence doesn't speak, even when she believes nobody else is around."

"So you observed a signed exchange?"

"Exactly. And my vantage wasn't ideal; her throne room is set up to prevent surveillance."

"Don't keep me in suspense," she prompted.

"It was bits and pieces except this. 'We're nearly ready.' In context, I think it was a question for the Speaker."

"That, coupled with her adherence to her own code, gives me hope," she said softly.

The spymaster inclined his head. "If I'd caught her talking, it would make me doubt, too. But she seems fully invested in the Death's Handmaiden persona. It's my assessment that she couldn't betray us without losing face with her followers."

"Why would they care?" she asked.

"In her mythos, Death is unknowable, but even-handed. If he makes a bargain, he keeps it."

She said thoughtfully, "I remember some stories like that,

where Death comes for one person, but through cunning or negotiation, another soul is taken, or the reaping is deferred."

"Exactly. Death is inexorable but not treacherous."

Dred pushed out a breath. "I wish you had been able to get indisputable confirmation, but I imagine she must be wondering if we'll follow through on the frontal attack."

"The thing that troubles me," Tam said, "is that she wins even if *you* lose. You agreed to her demand for the new fish as payment if our stratagem fails."

Breakfast forgotten, she pushed to her feet and paced before the table. "I had to entice her somehow. What else did I have that she wanted?"

"I'm not saying it was a poor gambit, only that I can't fully trust allies who stand to gain from our defeat."

Dred muttered, "I suppose we have to wait and see what she wants more, additional space and resources or a single man. Even one like Jael."

"There is that. From her followers' perspective, annexing more territory would be the greater coup. And Silence cares about how she appears."

"Does she? I wouldn't have guessed."

"Oh, it's all studied. I don't think she's *entirely* mad."

"I know there will be casualties, but . . . do you truly think we're doing the right thing?" She spoke quietly, so the men nearby couldn't overhear her doubts.

"I do. There's no guarantee, of course, but I don't like our odds without this alliance. We had a chance against Priest on his own. Less likelihood of defeating Grigor. He has too many soldiers. Together? We were doomed."

Dred could always rely on Tam for the honest analysis even when it didn't paint a pretty picture. With his verdict, she squared away the last of her uncertainties. The Dread Queen couldn't permit anyone to see her waver even though she was largely a figment of Tam's imagination. Life had shaped Dred into a killer, not a leader.

But we make do.

She left Tam to finish his breakfast and made her rounds.

Unlike Artan, she made a point to circulate among the Queenslanders. It was impossible for her to know them all well personally, but she remembered names, at least. Dred called out greetings as she went, but Martine stopped her. The other woman had been angry since Priest's raid, but she didn't look hostile at the moment.

"What's up?" Dred asked.

"First, I'm apologizing for what I said the other day. I wouldn't have Artan back unless you were offering me his head on a stick."

Given that Martine had been instrumental in blocking Lecass, Dred's smile was sincere. "I hear some people feel that way."

Others missed him because he'd had his special pets, who didn't have to work or do anything but sleep with him.

There had been less organization, less attention to detail, under his regime. *And he made the mistake of ignoring Tam once too often.* The place was also filthier, smellier, and there had been a *lot* more drinking. She marveled that Grigor and Priest hadn't moved on the territory when that jackass ran it. *But maybe it took them this long to come to terms.* Wouldn't surprise her, as the two weren't the most reasonable of men.

"But that's not why I wanted to talk to you. This way."

Warily, Dred followed the other woman back to the dormitories. She'd *never* slept in here, as Artan had claimed her as part of his harem straight off the prison transport. He had found it amusing to encourage rivalry between his females, driving them to fight for his favors. At first, she refused to participate, only to discover that one didn't survive Artan's wrath more than once.

With some effort, she pushed those memories aside. Martine seemed oddly nervous, an expression at odds with her normally pugnacious demeanor. The other woman paced a few steps, before blurting, "I'd like more responsibility. Tam said my loyalty would be recognized, and I'm not sitting around, waiting for you to decide on a reward. I *take* what I want, right?"

That was such a turnaround from her rage a few days ago that Dred wondered if this was a setup. But surely if somebody wanted a cat's-paw, they'd pick a pawn more subtle than Martine. The woman didn't have a beguiling bone in her body; she was blunt to the point of rudeness, and her hair-trigger temper got her into as many fights as the men.

"What did you have in mind?" she asked.

"I want to be in charge of some worthless sons of bitches when the pain starts. I could get with giving orders."

That didn't sound like a bad idea to Dred, especially since it might raise her stock with the remnants of Artan's harem. It'd be nice if the women in Queensland didn't want to kill her. "Remind me before the assault on Abaddon, and I'll see what I can do."

"You won't be sorry."

"I owe you. And I'm sure I won't be. I can't wait to see you driving those convicts to push on and fight harder."

Martine offered a scary smile. "Me either."

24

Challenge Accepted

The mood was shaky the next day when Jael joined the rest of Queensland in the hall for breakfast. As he went through the food line, he listened to a lot of heated discussion, but he couldn't get a complete picture of the situation. Trying to be subtle, he took a seat with his plate nearby, listening to the conversation.

"Did you hear?" a man said, as another sat down.

"What?"

"We're aligned with Entropy for this attack." The first inmate gestured with his fork. "Don't you think it's stupid to put all our eggs in Silence's basket? That crazy bitch is probably just trying to get all of us killed."

"What do you recommend the queen do instead? She can't wait until the stars align, asshole. Priest and Grigor won't."

"You don't even have any proof they're coming. Maybe she just wants more territory, and she's telling people what she wants them to hear."

"Bullshit. I didn't imagine Priest's attack on this place.

They killed a mate of mine. Maybe you're just a fragging coward, eh?"

The second man whipped out a shiv and jammed it against the other's jugular. "Go on. Say it again."

Dred strode up before the conflict hit critical mass, thumping a fist between them. "If you have a grievance, then challenge him."

With an angry snarl, the inmate put away his blade and went back to his breakfast, but his face was dark. Whatever the rules, this wasn't over. Men like that didn't forget offenses, and he hadn't been locked up because he respected law and order. Jael ate, wondering how pervasive the fear was. They didn't *all* trust her leadership—that much was evident—but Jael hoped these idiots would pull together long enough to do their jobs.

Dred started to leave, but before she got two meters, a man stood up at another table. He was nearly as big as Einar, with small eyes and a heavy beard. He was grimy, like pretty much all Queenslanders, but that didn't diminish his menacing air. He had fresh lashes on his back, which meant this must be Lecass. Jael tensed, but the convict didn't rush her.

Instead, he took a few measured steps and addressed Dred. "Time to die, bitch. I bided my time and choked down your new rules. I let your lackey humble me, *but no more*. I was Artan's right-hand man, and I won't tolerate this shit for another second."

The words "death match" swept through the watchful crowd. Men who had been bored with their food became avid. This was unexpectedly good entertainment, better than the vegetable mush Cook had prepared. Jael pushed to his feet and stepped up beside Dred. He wasn't sure about the dynamics, but he did know he could kill this bastard for her.

"I'll fight as your champion," he offered.

Artan's former lieutenant shot him a killing stare. "Step off. This isn't a normal grudge match. If she wants to hold on to her throne, she has to fight me for it."

"He's right," Dred said quietly. "I have to answer this challenge."

"Which is more respect than you gave Artan." The bearded man spat at her feet.

Her jaw clenched. "Open combat's not the only way to power."

"It's the only one I respect."

Einar stomped up, big hands clenched into fists. "Why now, Lecass? You've had half a turn to speak your mind, issue a challenge. Why are you doing it right before a major offensive?"

"Tam," Lecass spat. "The little shit *whipped* me. Now I'll make him watch her die."

"Bullshit," a man called. "Maybe you're working for Priest or Grigor, trying to kill the Dread Queen before she has the chance to kick their asses."

Lecass snarled at the accusations. "I'll fight you next."

"You will not," Dred said softly. "You've issued a challenge to *me*, and you won't survive it. Let's have it done."

All around, the men scrambled to move the tables, creating a space in the center of the hall. Jael had seen the fights before, but he hadn't cared then. They were nameless thugs, and it didn't matter who walked away. This time, it did. The whole landscape of Queensland would change without her, and it infuriated him that despite naming him her champion, she didn't intend to make use of him.

This is what I was created for.

But at the same time, he understood that this was a personal challenge. If he won for her, it didn't demonstrate her strength. It only showed that she could order someone else to do her dirty work. In Perdition especially, delegation made the wrong point.

Einar threw himself into a seat beside Jael, scowling. "If he wins, I'll kill him myself."

Right. For a few seconds, he'd forgotten her complicated personal life. While he'd just met Dred, the big man slept with her . . . and he loved her, as much as anybody could in a place like this. Jael wondered if Dred knew his story: of how he'd strangled his faithless wife, killing her unborn child, then started a blood feud with the lover's family. He had no intention of telling her if she didn't; it wasn't like his hands were clean.

"You think that's a possibility?"

"I don't know. Artan used Lecass when he wanted to prove a point, but Dred's tougher than she looks."

Before he could respond, Tam sat down on his other side. "This is a hell of a mess."

"Didn't you see this coming?"

The spymaster nodded. "I couldn't prevent it. They're not looking for dignity, good judgment, or wisdom. Here, only the strong prevail."

Once the men finished clearing, they moved tables strategically to form a makeshift ring. Dred stood in the center of it, waiting. Lecass tapped a foot impatiently; and from the man's expression, he expected to finish her quickly. Jael had seen her in action with the chains, however, and he wondered if Lecass possessed an accurate estimation of her abilities.

Better if he doesn't.

Calypso stood just outside the ring, counting down from five. "Fight!"

Lecass held a blade in each hand. He leapt toward Dred, who was lashing her chains with customary fervor. But Lecass was big enough to take the lash on the shoulder, tough enough not to wince, and he barreled through her defenses. He slashed toward her throat; she spun low, dashing her chains on the ground to snag his ankle, but she didn't have the physical power to pull him off his feet. In such a tight space, she didn't have the advantage, either.

"Disarm him!" Einar shouted.

Dred blocked one knife, but Lecass was proficient with his left hand, too, and that one slashed down her rib cage. She gave no sign of the pain, however, merely danced back to regroup. Most Queenslanders cheered for her; some were taking bets as to how long she'd last. Blood streamed from her side as she changed her tactics. The Dread Queen wrapped her arms and knuckles with the chains, apparently deciding those tactics wouldn't work here. Jael agreed.

She made Lecass take the offensive, and the idiot bit. He charged like a bull with his knives at the ready; she waited until the last possible second so that Jael imagined she felt the scrape of steel on her skin, then she slammed him with two heavy blows as he went by. Dred followed with a kick to his kneecap, not strong enough to pop it, but her boots were bladed, so the spurs bit deep into his flesh. Lecass bit out a pained curse and wheeled on her in a move fast enough that Jael would've had trouble countering it even with his enhanced reflexes.

The right knife sank into her shoulder, and Lecass twisted it to maximize the damage. It took everything Jael had to stay in his chair. *This is* her *fight*. Beside him, the big man was pale, both hands clenched on his knees. Dred still didn't cry out. Despite the wounds she'd taken, she fought in silence. This time she fell back, and with her eyes on Lecass, she pulled the blade out of the wound and threw it out of the ring, where it spattered her blood onto the floor.

Lose something, asshole?

All around, convicts roared with approval at the deliberate challenge. The nonchalance of the gesture enraged her opponent; he snarled as he ran at her, the remaining knife in his right hand. She'd lost reaction speed, though, along with blood, so her spin this time was clumsy, and she didn't have complete range of motion in her injured shoulder.

Finish him, Jael urged silently.

Dred must've realized she didn't have a lot more fuel in the tank. She stepped up her game, unleashing a one-handed assault. The chains lent weight to her strikes; she pummeled Lecass until he was reeling, then she spun a kick, putting all her force behind it. He fell back enough to avoid the full impact. The move left her open to a counterstrike; his blade opened her stomach. Jael's heart surged into his throat.

That's it; she's done.

To his astonishment, she fought on. The pain staggered her visibly, but her resolve was apparent to everyone in the room. She wouldn't go down. Each move she made telegraphed her determination as if she were shouting it—*the only way I leave this ring is feetfirst.* A chill ran through him as someone started chanting:

"Dread Queen! Dread Queen!"

Lecass heard it as well, and he hesitated. Apparently it hadn't occurred to him that he wasn't the crowd favorite. She drew strength from her supporters and went at the bastard again. He slipped in her blood, stumbled back, and Dred slammed both fists into his head. He went down and she kept up the onslaught. By the time she raised her chained fists, they were bloody, and she was . . . well, dying. He could tell by the color of her skin, the clammy cast to her features. In all honesty, Jael had no idea how she was still on her feet.

"We have to get her out of there," Einar said.

Tam grabbed the big man's arm. "No. She has to make it out on her own. Otherwise, this challenge proves nothing."

Swaying, Dred took Lecass's knife and cut his throat. Then Calypso shouted, "Winner! The Dread Queen has defeated her challenger."

A ferocious cheer erupted from the crowd, and the men moved the tables to clear a path for her. Nobody touched her as she stepped out of the ring, each step a testament to her indomitable will. Jael surged to his feet, and Tam held him back.

"Let her finish this. We'll tend to her after."

Dred left a blood trail as she passed the men; the chanting continued until she left the hall. Only then did Tam release his grip, and the three of them sped after her. By the time they got to her quarters, she'd collapsed, and there was no rousing her. With wounds to her side, shoulder, and stomach, no surgeon on hand, no blood transfusions, there was only one way to save her, but he couldn't do it in front of Tam and Einar. He didn't trust either man fully. Hell, he didn't trust *anyone* fully. Jael only knew that after a fight like that one, he couldn't let her die.

"Mary curse it," Einar swore. "Lecass is dead, but she's not going to make it either."

Tam bent over her, checking her vitals. Then the spymaster shook his head, sorrow written clearly on his fine features. "It's just a matter of time now. I'll check in storage to see if we have any pain medication. That's all we can do."

"No," Jael said. The lie that came next was necessary. "I have some training, but I can't have either of you in the room while I work on her. If you want me to save her, leave now."

Both Tam and Einar vacated without another word.

◀ 25 ▶

Red Haze of Pain

"Do you think he can save her?" Einar demanded of Tam.

He lifted a shoulder, shrugging. "I hope so. Without her, I'm not sure if the alliance with Silence will hold."

"*That's* what you care about?" the big man snarled.

Tam sidestepped the punch, so that it slammed hard into the wall beside him. "I care about her, too. But it's pointless to yield to worry when there are more pressing concerns."

"You're an icy bastard."

Tam didn't deny the charge. He'd heard worse. "I know you won't budge until she's better, so pull up a chair. You can guard the door, send for anything Jael needs."

"You're leaving?"

"Queensland won't run itself in her absence," he said quietly. "There's work to be done to be sure there's a sector left to her when she's better."

"Thanks for saying 'when.'"

Tam slipped away without replying. He spoke to a number of people, assuring them that the Dread Queen would recover fully. He gave the story he wanted repeated, word for word, and soon enough, the news was making the rounds.

Men were drinking, toasting her victory. In fact, the din in the hall was deafening.

As he was trying to duck out, Calypso cornered him. "I saw that gaping wound in her gut. Tell me another story, little man. Like how she's *really* doing?"

"I believe she'll make a full recovery." Jael better be able to achieve the impossible; otherwise, all of Queensland would end up dead, chained in one of Priest's torture rooms or slaving for the Great Bear. In conflicts like this one, there could be no surrender, no merciful terms or treaties to sign. Anything but complete annihilation was unacceptable to their enemies.

Therefore, he had to finish what he'd started.

He was careful to lead anyone who might be trailing him on a wild-goose chase. It seemed as if Lecass's followers had been discouraged with his death. If not, then they were incredibly stupid, but it was best to take precautions nonetheless. His path carried him through the corridors in Queensland before he doubled back and entered the ducts at last.

From there, he went straight down to the bowels of the ship.

This part of Perdition held a musky smell, not unpleasant, but an interesting amalgam of odors, likely created by so many aliens living in close quarters. Though it didn't compare to Queensland for space or resources, Tam would judge the Warren the second-best accommodations on the vessel. As promised during his last visit, an envoy awaited him, the same creature he'd rescued not so long ago. Her name was Keelah, and she'd claimed to be . . . precious to the leader of the Warren. *That* had been a harrowing trip, as he feared the injured female would die before they reached her people. His arrival with her had caused tremendous commotion, ending in a grudging offer of hospitality, then the subsequent conversation had been . . . enlightening.

"How are you feeling?" he asked in universal, as she stepped forward.

She had a furry, rodentlike face, and there was a bald

patch on her torso from the wounds she'd taken at the hands of Priest's fanatics. "Better. Katur's waiting for you."

"Is he in a good mood?"

The alien female made a chittering noise he took for laughter. "The best *you* can expect, brown man."

"It would've been worse if I hadn't brought you back to him," he predicted.

At this, Keelah nodded. "This way, please. I hope you understand how privileged you are to walk among us. All other outsiders are killed the moment they set foot in our territory. For you to be permitted a return visit . . ."

"I understand the honor extended to me," Tam said.

He was eager to finish this and return to Dred's side. Despite his words to Einar, he was worried about her as well. But some courtesies couldn't be rushed or hurried. If he didn't present the offer just right, there would be no second chances. And if he offended Katur, his people would execute Tam without hesitation. In this endeavor, he was a long way from Queensland and completely on his own. Of course, that was part of the thrill.

With half an ear, he listened to Keelah's words and made polite responses. It was funny how much more civilized the aliens were than the rest of Perdition, most likely because so many had been sentenced, not for dire offenses, but because of their difference from humanity. New Terra had become insular and hostile to aliens, offering harsh punishments against those who were caught dirtside illegally. Which meant these folk might have been condemned to this hellhole for immigration offenses.

Damned Conglomerate bastards.

But Tam was past the point of being surprised by anything governments might do, after what he'd seen on Tarnus.

Keelah led him to a meeting room in what had probably been maintenance. Down here, the rooms were cramped and small, narrow corridors riddled with rust and heavy wear. He could still see signs of the old crew who had walked these halls in heavy boots coated in oil, impossible to eradicate all signs of the past, he supposed.

"I greet you in peace," Katur said, as they entered.

He resembled Keelah in that they appeared to be the same species, but his features were sharper, and the male's eyes were a keen amber, his fur a brindled brown where she was copper. They were a small and nimble species, from what Tam could tell, and he had insight as to why Katur had been chosen to lead when he didn't seem like an obvious choice, based purely on size and strength. That indicated he had intellectual qualities that made him powerful, enough that oversized species like the Rodeisians would still follow him.

"As do I," Tam answered.

Though it wasn't protocol, he bowed as if he were greeting royalty. Katur seemed to appreciate the courtesy. "Sit down. Now that my Keelah has recovered fully, I'm willing to listen to your ideas."

It went without saying that everything hinged on Tam's finding the right words. He revealed none of that pressure in his calm mien. "Thank you," he said. "This enterprise could be of great mutual benefit."

DRED awoke to incredible agony, unsure how long she'd been out. Her shoulder burned; her side throbbed; and the pain in her gut defied description. Worsening the situation, someone had stripped her naked and was kneeling over her on the bunk. She couldn't imagine Tam or Einar permitting one of Lecass's cronies to rape her corpse—plus she wasn't quite dead yet—so something terrible must've gone down after the challenge.

A riot, maybe?

She forced open her eyes and was astonished to see Jael crouched over her, a knife in hand. *I didn't see that coming.* Since he hadn't been around during Artan's regime, she hadn't expected him to side with Lecass. *But the bastard paid him to see it done, even if he lost.*

"I can't fight you," she croaked. "So I hope you'll be quick."

Instead of answering, he slashed his arm open; his blood trickled into the wound on her stomach. She couldn't see when he moved to the side, but she felt the hot liquid dripping onto her shoulder as well, then he repeated the process on her ribs. By the time he finished, he had slashes all over his arms.

The room was haloed in a corona of light. Everything seemed really far away, too. "I'm not sure where you went to medical school, but transfusions don't work like that."

He sat down on the bed beside her, studying her face. "That's not what I was doing."

"Enlighten me."

"You've seen me heal, right?" It was clearly a rhetorical question, but Dred nodded because he seemed to be measuring her ability to focus. "Well, the ability's conveyed in my blood, at least in a limited sense."

"So you're jump-starting my system. How long does it work?" It was a wonder somebody hadn't locked him up to use as a medical miracle.

"Once it's outside my system, I have no idea how long it retains its properties. But look, the shallow slice on your ribs is already starting to heal."

With trembling fingertips, she explored the bloody patch of skin and realized he was right. "You'll be in trouble in here if anyone else finds out."

"I know," he said quietly. "I would've been out there, too."

"You said they ran experiments on you. They didn't discover this?" If they had, there was no way they'd have stashed him here. Dred suspected he'd have been dissected and used to manufacture salves and ointments for fast healing.

"No. They were more interested in learning how much I could heal and trying to figure out how to reproduce me. I don't think it ever occurred to anyone to see if my abilities were transferable. And they're not," he added, as if worried she would consider eating him to absorb his talents. "At least not permanently. After a few minutes outside my system, the blood goes inert. I know it's foul, but I'll have to do this repeatedly through the night to keep you alive."

"Can you survive that much cutting?" she asked.

He laughed. "I've nearly been exsanguinated, love. If I lose too much, I slip into a coma until my cell counts get back to normal."

"Good to know. Then if you can live with the loss, I can deal with the blood."

"I can't have anyone else in here. As you pointed out, if anyone else knew—"

"Tam and Einar won't intrude if I ask them not to. You might wish to call them in to deliver water and paste, then post them outside to guard the door." Her head was getting foggy again, the moments of clarity hard-won.

The red haze of pain swallowed her up again.

Next time she roused, Jael looked considerably more haggard. His clothing was stained permanently red, and his skin had a deathly pallor. He sat on the floor beside the bed, his breath coming in shallow rasps. Alarm boiled through her.

"How much blood have you given me?" she demanded.

He couldn't even summon his usual charming smile. "Damn near all of it, I think."

Nobody had ever fought so hard for her life. "Why are you doing this?"

"I owe you," he said, his voice slurred. "Remember, I was poisoned. Dying, I think, and you didn't give up on me. If I can square things between us, I'll feel better about it."

Ah. So it wasn't personal. That made it better and worse, simultaneously.

"How am I doing?"

"It's been two days. The men think you're in a healing trance though some say you've crawled off to die. Tam and Einar are keeping things calm while Ike and Wills continue with preparations for the raid on Abaddon."

"That doesn't answer the question." She checked out her ribs. Healed. Her shoulder gave her a twinge, but it felt better, more like weeks of rest and recovery rather than days.

Her stomach? That still hurt with a raw, deep pulse that cradled fire in its depths. From her sweaty hair and hot skin, she guessed she was feverish. "An infection set in?"

"Your body's not like mine. Without my blood, you'd already be dead." From his flat tone, she guessed it had been a hard fight.

"Don't die over me. You don't owe me that much." She took a breath and was surprised at how much it hurt. Her whole abdomen felt swollen. Likely, she needed surgery to repair some internal damage, but that wasn't an option here. "Better you should work with Tam and Einar to run this place."

To her annoyance, he ignored most of what she said. "They've been in to check on you . . . but not during the procedure. They were most impressed with the way I've healed your other wounds. I don't see why I can't finish the job."

"Because you've practically bled yourself dry, and I'm still laid out?"

"You're not dying. I forbid it." Her own words came back at her.

"The universe orders itself to your liking, does it?" Dred raised a brow because that was all she could manage in the way of gentle scorn.

"Not often," he muttered.

"Is there water?"

"I've been spooning it into you, so yes. Let me get the cup." More tenderly than she would've guessed possible, he lifted her head and she managed three swallows.

That cool liquid felt good in her throat, but her stomach burned. She had no way to be sure whether her renal system was still functioning. The way she felt, probably not, which meant waste was backing up in her blood, and she didn't have too much longer. As deaths went, it should be peaceful.

"I feel like I owe you something for this," she said.

"Don't worry about it."

"You put yourself out there, showing me you could do

this. The easy course would've been to let me die. I don't know what I can do for you, but—"

"You already did it," Jael cut in.

"What?" she asked dizzily.

His reply was so soft, she might've imagined it. "You treat me like a person."

Jael . . . Pain had lowered her defenses, so the words arrowed right to her core. Somehow, she resisted the urge to reach for him as the world lost focus.

"If I don't wake again, thank you. And please don't fetch Tam and Einar. I'd rather they don't remember me like this."

He roared something at her, but the sound went out. Thereafter, everything was black and red, a rolling storm of impressions. Jael's face appeared again and again; and each time, he looked worse. She tried to tell him to stop— that it was pointless—but she couldn't speak. Heat blazed through her body in a killing wave until everything was pain, endless spasms of it. She would've vomited if she could have, but there was nothing in her torn stomach.

Two armies warred within her body, and Dred fell into a nightmare pit populated by regrets and memories. She shouted at people long dead and threatened others. The pain didn't diminish, and through it all, she heard him whispering to her. No making out the words but the intent was unmistakable. She wasn't allowed to die.

At last, she surfaced again. This time, her skin was cool and the bed was clean. *I'm completely naked, weak as a kitten, but there's no pain.* That was . . . surprising. Jael was unconscious beside her; she had no way to tell if he'd passed out in exhaustion or if he'd given her so much blood that he was now comatose. It didn't seem right to poke him awake to ask, if that was even possible.

Gently, she probed her stomach and found a fresh, ridged scar. "Dear Mary."

At that, Jael raised his head groggily. "You're awake."

"So are you, I see. Somewhat."

"How long's it been?" At this point, Dred had no sense of time.

"Four days, total."

"You look like hell." It was true. His face was beyond pale and into gray, his mouth white and bloodless. Deep purple circles shadowed his blue eyes, and his blond hair was dull, heavy with grease. The lines that slashed his arms filled her with guilt, a feeling she'd have said she was immune to.

Before her incarceration, she'd stalked so many murderers, hunted them like animals, and she hadn't cared if they had families who didn't know about their hidden proclivities. All that mattered was stopping them, so they couldn't hurt anyone else. That single-minded pursuit of prey had made her too much like her targets. So this resurgence of emotion surprised her.

It's the injuries. I'll be back to normal soon. I just have to ignore it and ride this out.

"I could use a bath," he admitted. "Do you mind?"

"Go ahead. And then you can help me. I can't stand myself another minute."

While he showered, she pulled herself upright. The room spun for a few seconds, but the head rush didn't end in another bout of unconsciousness. It was impossible that he'd healed her in four days. Doubtless the process had been torture for both of them—for different reasons—but she was grateful. It didn't sit well because the Dread Queen needed to be in a position of power . . . but Dred, the woman, didn't.

Maybe it's time I had somebody around who sees me otherwise.

That could be a dangerous game, but after the past days, she trusted Jael completely. If he wanted her dead, she would be. He'd suffered untold anguish to preserve her life, and the weight bothered her. She didn't like the sensation of being in his debt. Whatever he'd said about treating him like a person, that wasn't enough to balance the scales.

He was quick and efficient, returning wrapped in a length of cloth cut from some old mining uniforms. It draped around his hips as he moved. She noticed how thin he'd become just in a few days, though his build had never been overly muscular, which made his strength surprising. Dred hoped to Mary he never issued a challenge.

"I don't have any clean clothes in here," he said with a shrug. "And I'm not putting those back on. I think I might have them burned."

"My turn," she said.

There was no point in pretending he hadn't spent the last four days becoming intimately acquainted with her body. Modesty was for people who lived normal, quiet lives. She stumbled toward the lavatory with his hand at her back to help with her balance. By the time she'd made it to the doorway, she was exhausted, but she wouldn't admit it.

The men need to see me, if only a glimpse, for my victory to be complete.

She stepped into the tiny cubicle and Jael reached around her to turn on the water. The tepid trickle didn't feel as good as she wished, but it was better than nothing. With his help, she washed up quickly, conscious of the water she used. If the other territories were reckless with their use of it, the tanks might be dry for a while before it all passed through the recyclers and filters, then filled back up for use. The idea of a water shortage scared her as much as anything in this hellhole.

Dred rinsed quickly, then said, "You can step out. I'm pretty sure I can dress and dry off without hitting my head and dying."

"Forget it. I didn't spend all this time bringing you back from the dead for nothing."

"Fine." She accepted his help, bristling, but by the time he handed the shirt to her, she admitted she needed the aid. "Ask Tam for some pants, then let's go make a victory lap."

"You got it."

Outside, Einar stirred from a chair he'd hauled to the door. The big man's expression brightened, then he swept her into a bone-crushing hug. "I can't believe it. The last time I saw you, I was sure—"

"Just call me a miracle worker," Jael said dryly. "Put her down now, lug. She's breakable."

"I am not." Dred glared at them both and stalked toward the hall. When she reached her destination, the men rose as one and cheered in thunderous tones. They shouted for her as she marched around the hall, arms raised to demonstrate her strength.

She prayed nobody ever guessed how much each step cost her.

◀ 26 ▶

Zero Hour

Three days later, Queensland was as ready as it would ever be to march on Abaddon.

Jael still wasn't sure it was wise to put all their faith in Silence. Treachery from Death's Handmaiden would cost the territory everything. But Dred's crew had voted in favor of the strike, so they moved forward, laid in all possible preparations. Thanks to a couple of return trips down the lift and back again, they had a turret set up at two checkpoints and plenty of ammo. Wills had the maintenance bot running perimeter checks now, not looking for walls in need of repair but intruders. And Einar had crafted some really bad-ass armor out of the Peacemaker unit.

Jael had fifty men under his command. He had been concerned about the bottleneck leading into Abaddon, which was why they'd agreed to split their forces. He was leading one group, Einar another, Martine the third, and Dred the last. Wills and Ike remained behind to look after Queensland while Tam would be gathering intel quietly on his own, which was what he did best. It had been so many turns since Jael had fought in an actual battle—and he'd never led troops before. He was astonished she'd trusted him with the responsibility, yet life as a merc had prepared him for combat more than armed robbery, rape, or mass murder, the credentials other fish had to offer.

So maybe it's not that they trust you—only that they don't have anyone better.

That probability made him laugh softly as Dred strode into the hall. All eyes turned to her, and the men parted and fell quiet. She vaulted on top of one of the tables so they could see her from all corners of the room. That movement said she was strong and fit to lead, but only he knew how much it cost her. He read fierce pride and admiration in their collective faces; this woman could command armies in the real world. They would follow her, not for any cause, but through the sheer force of her will.

"This is phase one in the eradication of our enemies," she called in ringing tones. That received a howl of response, and she let them get it out of their systems before continuing. "By this time tomorrow, the hell Priest calls Abaddon will be a wasteland. If you're angry, show *them* your rage. Teach them what it means to be a Queenslander!"

Deafening cheers rang out. Jael couldn't believe it, but in half a turn, she had managed to unite these men into a nation. These criminals took *pride* in their homeland, such as it was, and he had no doubt it was because of her. The man she'd killed must have lacked similar magnetism, or there was no way she could've supplanted him so impressively. He'd worked for petty dictators who would've killed for her charisma.

Of course, they killed all the time, so that's not saying much.

"When you report to your commanders, remember that when you fight for them, you're fighting for me." Her gaze went somber, and she spun in a full circle as if making eye contact with everyone in the room. Jael noticed Martine propped against the far wall. Her men stood ready nearby, listening to the Dread Queen.

"Some of you won't return," Dred said then.

Damn. And she was doing so well, too.

But he had underestimated her. The room quieted again, and he glimpsed Tam pushing forward as if to rein Dred in. She ignored him and went on. "Once this is over, I'll have Wills carve your names on the wall. Your sacrifice will not be forgotten, nor will your bravery be in vain. The Conglomerate locked you away. They said you were too wicked to walk free. I say you're warriors, and I believe *all* of you possess the potential to be heroes."

"Damn right," Einar roared, and the crowd echoed it back.

She's got them back, right in the palms of her pretty hands. They'd die for her.

So would I, he realized a few seconds later, as she unwrapped her chains from her in an unmistakable sign she was ready to go to war. Dred swooped them over her head in a deadly arc, then slammed them down on the table. The echo reverberated around the room before she lifted her chains and twirled them; it seemed she would strangle herself or get tangled up in them, but her arms never slowed their graceful motion.

"What're you gonna do?" she called.

"Kill!"

"I can't hear you." She lashed again.

"Kill!" With his amplified hearing, the roar nearly blew out Jael's eardrums.

Fortunately, she took that as a sign that the men were sufficiently jacked up, and shouted, "Report to your commanders and don't let me see your faces until the enemy is dead."

Come home with your shield or on it. He couldn't recall where he'd heard that, but it echoed in his head as his men formed up around him. Though that wasn't strictly accurate, as several women were assigned to his company, including Calypso. He knew firsthand, however, how ferocious women could be—and if she'd been shipped to Perdition, then she could fight.

"We have the east corridor. Move out." He didn't wait to see if they followed him.

A few seconds later, footsteps assured him they had.

Dred would be approaching from the west and Einar from the south. Martine would be mopping up stragglers. He had no idea what back approach Silence intended to employ, but maybe her people knew hidden ways in the ducts, like Tam, or she could be coming up from underneath, through the Warren. Though Katur and his aliens wouldn't like it if they knew, Jael suspected that the silent killers could pass undetected.

His squad was large for the size of the corridors, however. Jael divided them up in pairs, so they formed a fairly long column. He chose Calypso to guard the rear, mostly because he thought she'd appreciate the responsibility. Retribution should feel sweet—and she would make sure their group wasn't ambushed on the way. From the gleam of her teeth as she accepted the assignment, she didn't want to miss out on the bloodbath to come.

Jael took point. It was an easy progress past the east checkpoint. The turret was looking good, and the man standing behind him couldn't have looked prouder as the troop marched by. *You'd think this was happening on a much larger scale.* But maybe it didn't matter. It was still important. Even though this wasn't a country or a planet, it was still their world.

It's all we have.

He realized it was human nature to make the best of all awful situations, even one as bad as this. The cream would always rise to the top. *And that's Dred.*

A few minutes later, Jael laughed when they ran into their first patrol. Men less fanatical would've fled. Priest's four guards ran at them with suicide in their eyes. Jael obliged two of them himself; he made it clean and quick, then he stepped back so the rest of the men could get their shot. It was a bloody, horrendous mess, and his soldiers laughed as they stepped over the mangled bodies. He'd served with chem-head mercs less bloodthirsty.

"Keep it up," he called.

"Maybe you should lead from the rear. You didn't leave much for the rest of us." He recognized Calypso's voice.

"Nobody will go home hungry, I promise you." He hoped they knew he meant sating their yen for violence. Someone had told him that people who ate their fallen enemies ended up in Munya—Mungo's domain—sooner or later, as they weren't welcome in other territories, not even Entropy.

"I'm holding you to that," someone said.

"I think we need some marching music. Anybody got a military background?"

A tall man near the back answered, "I served. Want me to lead the chant?"

He nodded. "Make some noise. We're not trying to sneak up anybody's ass."

With the former soldier leading the call and response, they rolled through four more patrols, and he made sure to stand clear, letting his men do the actual killing. The convicts shouted their appreciation and stomped the floor. Jael saluted and kept moving since there was a schedule to keep. Timing played a vital role in the plan Silence had offered. If the diversions didn't occur at precisely the same time, it would impact the effectiveness of her sneak attack. Likewise, if she betrayed them, and the attack didn't come, Dred's forces would be cut down by the automated defenses.

But he'd learned from the best and didn't let any of his doubts show. He pushed his squad forward though he could hear combat in the distance. Before long, they were hearing it, too.

"Are we late to the party?" Calypso yelled.

He answered, "Hope not. I'll be pissed if they started without us."

"No shit," she came back.

"Double-time! Let's move." Jael set a bruising pace, and most of the men kept up.

Their feet rang out against the floor, announcing their arrival, but something was already going down in Abaddon.

Dammit, I was keeping the count. This wasn't supposed to start for another five thousand ticks. Since they didn't have radios, they'd agreed to count down the action and begin as close to unison as they could.

His crew burst into the east corridor and were astonished to find Priest's people already engaging the enemy—but not Queenslanders. These were aliens, every last one of them. Some species he recognized, like the furry, larger-than-life Rodeisian, a stray Ithtorian, no Morgut, thank Mary, some humanoid, looking similar to humanity but half-baked— they probably came from adaptive colonies—and then there were creatures he'd never seen before. Ones with trunks and tentacles; others that looked like walking amphibians. And every one of them was fighting Priest's fanatics.

The battle raged just outside the range of Abaddon's turrets. The son of a bitch had more than one, too. Breaking them wouldn't be easy once he decided what the hell to do about this mess. Beyond the combat zone, he spotted a couple of Peacemakers, too. Mary only knew how Priest had managed to subvert them.

"What the hell," Calypso said, shoving to the front.

"My thoughts exactly."

"So what's the play?" she demanded.

"I'm thinking we wade in. I didn't come to this party to watch other people dance."

Calypso's smile lit up her hard face. "You're my kind of asshole."

"Thanks," he said, flashing her the standby charming smile. "I have no fragging idea what they're doing here, but they're not on our roster of asses to kick today. Understood?"

"No alien bashing today!" the men called back in unison.

He laughed because they were fairly cooperative for thugs and lowlifes. "Then why are you still standing here? For Queensland!"

◀ 27 ▶

Shut It Down

Dred had fifty men at her back. That wouldn't be so worri-
some if she felt 100 percent, but she was still weak from the
damage she'd taken in the challenge. Many Queenslanders
regarded her with awe, as they'd seen the severity of her
wounds when she staggered out of the hall. For her to be
back on her feet so soon? It seemed supernatural.

And it *was*, except she didn't deserve the credit. For obvious reasons, the miracle must remain between Jael and her;
it would cause trouble for him if anyone discovered the
healing properties of his blood. So Dred added it to the short
list of secrets she'd die to keep. Tam was ecstatic, as the men
were convinced she was half a step shy of immortality.

Ahead, she spied the first checkpoint. They hadn't hit the
automated defenses that Abaddon was rumored to possess
yet, but if Tam's intel was accurate, she could expect them
deeper into Priest's territory. Dred led the charge, as the
zealots had no missile weapons. She took one out with a
blow to the skull—and with the weight of her chains around
her fist, she cracked it. The guard hit the ground as
Queenslanders tore into the other three. In a close quarters

fight, with so many bodies around, she couldn't use her chains like she usually did, but numbers also meant she did less actual killing.

"Form up!" she called, to discourage mutilation.

While she had done her best to unify Artan's dregs, they were still criminals, and discipline wasn't their strong suit. A few of them grumbled and stomped the corpses as they went past, but they fell in behind her, two by two. With such superior numbers, they rolled through the next two checkpoints, but the noise of battle couldn't be concealed.

Zealots streamed down the hall toward them. They were moving so fast, Dred couldn't get a head count to see how many they faced, but they definitely belonged to Priest. The facial scars he carved on his loyal servants were unmistakable. *Dammit, we're bottlenecked.* She'd hoped to push farther before reinforcements rolled out. In a mob like this, it would be tough to avoid being knifed by her own men.

On the plus side, there was no room for fancy fighting. Around her, men grappled and punched. She caught an elbow and lashed out with a wrapped fist. The blow rocked the fanatic, and she pushed forward. Dred found room for a tight kick though not a high one. Still, a blow to the ankle was more effective than one usually suspected. Her target staggered back into two others. Their feet tangled and two of them went down.

Her men didn't hesitate. They ringed the fallen and kicked them until it was certain they weren't getting up. The corridor stank of blood and sweat until she couldn't breathe through her nose. Cries and snarls of pain added to the cacophony until it reminded her of the prison riots on New Terra. *Breathe. You didn't do this.*

Her focus wavered, but the Queenslanders were ferocious enough to compensate for her halfhearted swings. At this point, it was all she could do to push forward. Now and then she swung at a zealot who turned on her, but mostly, she shoved a path through the melee. Dred stepped out on the other side and realized she had the numbers advantage.

"Finish them," she shouted.

Outside the mob, she could breathe a little easier, and she waded in on the fringes. Her head felt dizzy and sick, but she couldn't show weakness, even if she had been dying five days ago. Weakness didn't keep a leader in power, and she'd gladly die before giving up what she'd stolen with Tam and Einar's help. She'd tried life as chattel. There would never be an encore.

Loathing overcame her, and Dred fought hard, living up to her rep as the Dread Queen. By the time the fight ended, ten of her men were on the ground, unmoving, but the enemy was dead, every last one of them.

She knelt beside casualties, hoping to recognize their faces. In some cases, they were so battered, she needed help from her squad to ID them. Once the names had been scratched on a scrap of paper, she tucked it into the top of her boot. At her nod, the men fell in again, grimmer this time. Maybe the march on Abaddon had started out glorious, but death had a way of killing the mood.

"We'll come back for their bodies," she promised. "I won't leave them here. I'll go with Einar to the chutes myself."

"We know," a thin man said quietly.

"The next part will be tricky if Priest has turrets and Peacemakers."

"How are we supposed to get past them?" a convict asked.

I have no fragging idea.

Without Jael and Einar, she didn't see a lot of them surviving. But this wasn't the time to tell them they had been given a suicide run. *Damn Silence anyway.* These men might be the dregs of the galaxy, but they listened when Dred spoke.

She hardened herself to their fate, and answered, "I have a plan." And then, surprisingly, she did; it came to her like a burst of light. "See Priest's corpses on the ground? Grab one. If you can, pick a meat shield that's bigger than you."

"Genius," one of the men breathed.

"If you're too big to hide or there aren't any bodies left,

then hang back. The rest of us will push forward and find a way to deactivate the turrets from the other side. There should be a manual override."

The Peacemakers would be another issue entirely. It had nearly killed them to deal with one on the way to the salvage bay; maybe Priest spread that story to discourage incursions. She hadn't gotten confirmation or denial from Tam, as even the spymaster couldn't penetrate that deep inside enemy lines.

Twenty-five Queenslanders found corpses to shield their bodies; the rest followed at a safe distance. Dred hadn't recovered sufficient fortitude to follow her own advice, so she stepped to the back—and remembered Wills's prediction, not so long ago. *Chaos comes. The dead will walk. He'll cost you everything.* Well, the bone-reader was two for three because the corpses were shuffling forward, as promised. But so far, Jael had *saved* her, not ruined Queensland. Dred knew better than to discount the visions entirely, however.

At the next corner, a turret slammed the floor, saturating the whole area. Her men pressed forward cautiously, testing to see if their meat shields would stand up to the onslaught. Four more went down, but a small, thin convict stumbled forward. The body he'd chosen was almost more than he could lift, and Dred watched his arms straining. He let the corpse fall as he passed the turret's target field.

"Turn it off," she called.

"Where?" On his knees, he peered at the thing, and the rest of the squad called out suggestions.

One man, however, sounded like he knew what he was doing, shouting above the others. "It's on the base. Tip it forward—no, not like that. There you go. Now move it to static mode."

The turret powered down, and cheers rang out from the surviving men. She shouted along with them because this was an incredible accomplishment, proving intellect and determination could win the day. In a place like this, that revelation felt an awful lot like hope.

"Nothing can stop us now!" a prisoner yelled.

"The Dread Queen's coming for you!" That came from the small man who had disabled the turret; he stomped his feet in triumph, then punched the air.

Mary, sometimes they're like children.

"Don't celebrate too soon," she cautioned. "If I know how Priest thinks, he's got the bulk of his men waiting for us inside. There's more room for an ambush, and these measures slowed us just enough to let him set it up."

Collectively, their eyes dropped, and the men nodded. Ruining their good mood was a necessary evil. She needed them to focus a little longer. The ones who survived could dance and chant, taunt their fallen foes, and drink themselves into a stupor. *But not just yet.*

She went on, "I need someone who can scout."

To her surprise, Tam slipped up from the back of the group. She hadn't known he was in the vicinity though that was the spymaster's specialty. Dred didn't ask when he'd arrived, best to appear omniscient. That advice, too, came from Tameron. It went against Dred's nature to take credit for his work, but Tam said he didn't want the attention as it would make his work more difficult in the future.

Tam offered, "I'll do it if you hold here for a few minutes."

"Please," she said, inviting him to check out the battle-field with a gesture.

Waiting was hard, but the death toll would be higher if they ran in without proper intel. Though she'd warned the men they wouldn't all come back, it didn't mean she was crazy as Priest or Silence—and without regard for those who lived in her territory. She didn't *like* most of them, but she didn't slaughter them for fun, either.

"What are our chances?" It was a good question.

And if she gave an honest answer, half of these men would run back to Queensland. So she paraphrased an ancient historical vid instead. "We will drive our enemies before us and hear the lamentations of their women."

The surviving Queenslanders whooped, stomped the

floor, and banged the walls. If they had been trying to sneak up on Priest, that would've put paid to the idea. But that wasn't the strategy, so their noise didn't affect the plan. If Silence was keeping her word, she'd be maneuvering her assassins into position while Priest worried about Dred's people. Between their combined forces, he would be crushed like a bug.

Well. That's the idea, anyway.

◄ 28 ►

A Priest Walks into a Knife

We are so doomed.

The assault had gone off as Tam had foreseen, but so far, Priest's people, who fought like madmen, woefully outnumbered them. Jael lashed out, slicing another throat. Of Silence's crew there was no sign. *Damn the bitch.* Katur's aliens were vicious despite their small number. The tentative alliance had held as they charged the main hall, only to be decimated by traps.

Since his crew was the first to hit the room, his people were decimated. Bodies hit the floor, severed at the torso, and the stench of blood overwhelmed him. Not just from the fight, either. This place was more of an abattoir than Entropy, where remains were preserved and stylized. Priest left bodies where they fell, evidence of his divinity and power. Some convicts lost their resolve when they saw what befell the men rushing ahead; Jael didn't blame them for running though what he was supposed to tell Dred about this, he didn't know.

I can't kill them all. Sooner or later, somebody will get lucky and take my head.

Still, he battled with the same determined ferocity that had carried him out of the labs, so long ago. He was down to his last ten men when Einar arrived with an impressive boom; the big man took out a wall in doing so, and Jael had never been so glad to see anyone in his life. He wondered where the hell Dred was, too; she had taken the direct route, the most difficult one, too, reinforced with turrets and Mary only knew what else.

"Glad you could make it," he shouted, as a fanatic slashed at him.

The blade whistled through the air as he dodged it, then Jael angled his palms and crushed the man's throat. He dropped clean; another took his place. The room was pure chaos—so much screaming, cries of pain mingled with the sucking sounds of open wounds and the stink of urine and visceral terror. In the confusion, he couldn't find the damned leader of Abaddon. Unlike Dred, he wasn't in the forefront shouting orders. Probably the bastard was hiding, cowering even.

Einar called back, "Sorry, had to do a little remodeling first."

"I saw."

No more time for more talk; Jael's position was overrun. If it had been a question of skill, he might've fought them off, but they charged and tackled as one, no dodging them all. He went down under five fanatics, one of whom seemed determined to cut out his heart and eat it. *Yeah, I won't survive that.* Jael rolled despite their weight, so he took the blade between the ribs instead of in his chest. He jerked an elbow free and knocked into somebody's face. Blood spurted from the broken nose, but pain only seemed to inspire them to greater violence.

What the hell.

He'd fought chem-junkies with more wisdom and a greater sense of self-preservation. Jael head-butted another and wrenched an arm out of its socket. The subsequent pop should've made a normal man scream. Priest's follower was so far gone that he *moaned*, like he'd had his pleasure circuits rewired or something. *Is that even possible? They get off on agony?* His sporadic education had informed him about certain antiquated cults that practiced self-flagellation, but he'd thought that was for chastisement, not enjoyment. This religion was all kinds of fragged up.

The floor was slippery with blood, and he used it to slide partway out of the grappling hold one of them had on his leg. He took another stab wound to the leg, but he cursed through the pain and snatched one by the ear, then slammed the man's head into the ground, hard enough to knock him out. He rolled and kicked, gouged with his fingers until they were slick and red; these men forced him to scrabble like an animal, and he loathed it. Even lifers shouldn't be reduced to this.

And they say I'm the inhuman one.

Einar reached him as he whittled the five men on him down to two. The big man grabbed one and chucked him into men fighting nearby. A Rodeisian turned, its furry face livid, and stomped the man into paste with his big feet. Quick as a snake, Jael snagged a fallen blade, wickedly curved, and opened the last man's throat. Grateful for the breathing space, he let Einar yank him to his feet.

"How many of yours are left?" he asked.

"Twenty or so. You?"

He skimmed the room, then answered, "Eight or so, I think. Have you seen Dred?"

"There she is." Einar pointed across the devastated hall. "Just in time, too."

She had more men than they did, but it wasn't enough to conquer all of Priest's territory. They would be hard-pressed to hold this room. Pure wrath rose in him. *If Silence set us up to fail, so she could get her hands on me, I'll strangle the crazy bitch with my bare hands.* Dred lifted an arm in a victory sign, but he could see by her pale, strained face that she was on her last legs. A lesser individual wouldn't have had the grit to get out of bed at all after the wounds he'd healed. Not that Jael felt the best, either. It took a while to regenerate that much blood. He'd be dizzy and light-headed for weeks.

Worth it.

For a few seconds, it looked like her men might be enough to turn the tide. He spun his knife and braced himself for another bloody round. Then more of Priest's men surged in, trapping them from all sides.

"What the hell," he said. "Ready to do some killing?"

Einar pulled out his axe, created from two soldered pieces of metal and some fabric braided around the haft for a makeshift grip. The thing was huge, like he could behead three people in a single swing. Jael took a wary step back. Though he believed he and the big man were on good terms, that thing could totally kill him. And as it turned out, he wasn't ready to go.

"If it ends here, it does," Einar said with a shrug. "I'll die with a blade in my hand. Could be worse."

"Could be better. Like on top of a pretty girl."

For some reason, the big man laughed so hard at that, he almost dropped his weapon. "Ask Dred about that, why don't you? Get her take on it. Provided we survive."

Before he could ask—and he wanted to—the next wave was on him. Dred's men weighed in, but they were just so damned outnumbered, even with the ferocity of Katur's small contingent. The aliens were furious about something, but he had no idea what. It wasn't like the Rodeisian was in the mood to chat as he dropped an enemy on his head. A tentacled thing was actually eating one of Priest's men, and that actually made a dent in the fanatics' stoic assault. A few of them stumbled backward, giving Jael the opening he needed.

He swept in, slicing hamstrings in a low roll, then he came up on the other side to spike knives into their chests. Neat placement, too. They died, but it wrenched the blades out of his hands when they fell. *That's the problem with elegance. Stop showing off.* There were just too many enemies to be particular about how they died.

Across the room, Dred swung her chains like a dervish, opening great gashes wherever they landed. Her men had the sense to give her plenty of room, and Priest's people were unable to penetrate her guard. But he could see as her gaze met his across the room that she knew—it was a lost cause, a hopeless fight, and yet she did not lay her weapons down as more of Priest's people poured in behind the others, a seemingly endless stream.

Nearby, Einar chopped off a man's head. It bounced across the floor, tripping another, and Jael kicked him in the chest as he went down. The blow was fierce enough to crush his sternum, not a clean death, so he found a shiv, poorly made, but good enough to take the zealot's life. He didn't watch the light leave the other man's eyes—too many other souls to serve.

He was tiring, though. *There are too many. We can't hold.*

Though he hadn't been here long, he understood there could be no surrender. No quarter asked or granted. Which was why the territories usually limited themselves to skirmishes, not full-scale raids. The potential for devastation and annihilation was too probable to make war a wise endeavor. But the alliance between Grigor and Priest was diabolical and inexorable.

Sometimes, with a desperate gamble, you lose.

Five Queenslanders dropped, thinning the numbers. More of Priest's men surrounded Dred, for now stymied by the brutal whirl of her chains. But she was weary, too; the fight to get this far had probably taken a lot out of her. Einar seemed to notice at the same time, and, with a nod, they fought toward her as one. For a few seconds during that quiet look, it was like he could read the big man's mind—and Einar wanted nothing more than to die at the Dread Queen's side.

At first, Jael was too busy fighting for his life . . . and carving a path toward Dred to notice the jaws of the trap had closed. *With us as bait.* He didn't see or hear them arrive—not surprising with the confusion of the battle and the constant cries—but Silence's killers were slicing the enemy from behind, as promised. They were quiet and brutal, and the Abaddon faithful had no hope. They fell between the desperation of the Dread Queen's men, and the quiet, lethal cuts driven by Silence's followers. He had never seen such efficient killing, as though these mute prisoners knew exactly where to place a blade, down to the millimeter.

The battle took mere moments after that. Even the faithful lost heart when they realized they were fighting on two fronts. Jael fought on alongside Einar, and by the time the last of Abaddon's defenders fell, he was standing beside the Dread Queen, with the big man on her other side. Neither of them reached to steady her.

She planted her feet and waited as the Speaker came toward her. "The compact has been honored. Now we will search this whole territory and find that cowardly Priest."

Dred nodded. "Please convey our compliments to Silence. Her plan worked."

Not without some heinous casualties from the Queenslanders. But Jael imagined that Death's Handmaiden wasn't overly concerned with body count. In fact, she might have planned in order to sacrifice more souls for her master's glory.

"I'll lead my own search party," Einar said then.

Dred nodded, but she didn't offer to go with the teams. Instead she propped herself against the wall, looking unconcerned by the carnage. He was supposed to believe she was stone-cold, unmoved by her losses or the gobbets of meat, the huge puddles of blood, and all the bodies. Tam would be proud of her iron face, but Jael recognized the truth of her. She wasn't the Dread Queen at her core.

An hour later, a short man with gray hair stumbled into the ruined hall, guided by Einar's palm on the back of his neck. He wore red robes that were stained nearly black in places, tattered at the hem. And his eyes, his eyes shone with pure madness, etched in evil. Jael had seen some crazy bad shit in his day, but this man? *Mary.*

"You cannot kill me," Priest was babbling. "I'm a god. I'm immortal. I will *rise*."

The big man glanced at the princess in chains for permission, hefting his axe suggestively. Jael expected her to nod and give him the go-ahead to serve as her executioner. Instead, she put out a hand and took the weapon from him. Her green eyes were like chips of jade in her pale, bloody countenance. *This* was the face of the Dread Queen.

"Kneel," she commanded, and the command had an inexorable weight.

Not only did Priest drop to his knees, so did other men in the vicinity; two belonged to Silence. The Speaker frowned at this.

In a single swing, she took her enemy's head. The crowd roared.

And Jael fell a little in love.

◄ 29 ►

The Spoils of War

It would take weeks of work to make this place habitable. Dred eyed the evidence of Priest's rituals with sheer disgust, then she turned back to the Speaker. He appeared unmoved by the carnage, but with the skull painted over his features, it was hard to tell. She beckoned him away from the others; to her surprise, he followed.

"Do we wait until the offensive is complete to begin dividing up gear and property?"

The Speaker shook his head. "You receive immediate possession of Priest's property and holdings. The Handmaiden will wait until Grigor has been conquered to claim her reward."

On the surface, that seemed like a generous offer, but Dred knew Grigor had more space in addition to having the largest standing army in Perdition. She wasn't clear on what defenses Grigor had, as nobody had ever pushed far enough past his borders to check them out. Earlier, she'd learned that the rumors about Priest's Peacemaker units had been nothing but bullshit, stories circulated to keep invaders away. It was a good tactic until somebody was brave—or stupid enough—to find out for himself. She had been so relieved when Tam came back to report there were a lot of enemies between her and the inner sanctum but no heavy weapons. Still, cutting so many men down took time, and she'd nearly been too late.

So was Silence. She left her sneak attack until the last possible moment.

But her expression gave away none of her thoughts as she replied, "That's satisfactory."

Then she turned to Tam, dismissing the Speaker. "Head back to the hall and check on things for me. Make sure Ike and Wills are holding down the fort."

Dred didn't tell him she was worried about an attack while their home front was so weak; she didn't need to. Tam only nodded and slipped out of Abaddon. *Queensland, now.* As usual, he went alone. If he spotted trouble, he would slip around it. She had never known anyone who moved like he did, the shadow of the wind.

As she turned, she caught a few concise gestures from the Speaker, aimed at Silence's quiet killers. As one, they formed up behind the skull-faced man and departed, leaving the mess for her to deal with. With so much blood, spilled entrails, and hacked-off limbs, it was impossible to judge the potential of this place. With a faint sigh, she went over to Einar.

"Take half the men back to Queensland. I'm putting you in charge of internal defense until I get back."

"You're supervising the inventory and cleanup?" the big man asked.

She nodded. "I can't imagine you're interested in such housework."

"I love you, but no."

She joked back, "So there are limits to your devotion."

"And you've found them."

Einar boomed out, "Sound off in ones and twos, you stupid gits! That's presuming you can count that high." Sometimes he sounded *so* military. The men complied, then he shouted, "Odd ducks, come with me. The rest of you stay with the Dread Queen. You get to haul off the corpses and spit-shine this place."

A chorus of groans met the announcement, but the even-numbered Queenslanders went over to Dred. The group included Jael; they clustered around her waiting for instructions as the rest of the men moved out. At this point, Katur's aliens decided they needed to move out, as they were definitely in the minority, and this cease-fire might not last. She also suspected they would carry word about the alliance between Queensland and Entropy, but as long as they stayed in the Warrens, Dred didn't care what they knew. They had served their purpose, just as Tam predicted; the man was positively Machiavellian. The day after her recovery, he'd told her about his scheme, a brainstorm resulting from a chance encounter in the ducts. Dred had to admit, it had paid off beautifully.

Smiling wearily, she gave concise orders, tasking the men to haul all the bodies to the chutes, then find cleaning supplies. Dred found a chair, not so much because she was above menial labor—though Tam would counsel her against it for the sake of appearances—but mostly because her knees felt like they were filled with water. Her head spun; hopefully, nobody could tell just how weak she was or how much the battle had taken out of her. The weight of her chains made her arms ache, the first time she could remember being conscious of them in that way.

A few minutes later, Jael joined her. She didn't chastise him for not participating in the work crew. He'd earned a place at her side as her champion. Dred inclined her head as he sat.

"You fight like a gladiator," she said.

"Tried that. I didn't much care for it. Too much depends on the emperor's whim."

She was never sure when this man was being facetious. "How're you feeling?"

"I ought to be asking you that, but I can tell by looking." His blue gaze swept her critically from head to toe.

"Do you think the others suspect?" The question slipped out before she could quell it.

"I doubt it. They don't look at you with appraising eyes. They're blinded by all the impossible things they believe you can do."

"It's the Dread Queen mythos," she said.

"That must be exhausting."

She pushed out a quiet sigh and leaned her head against the back of her chair, legs stretched out. The posture looked feline, relaxed, but the truth was, she lacked the energy to get up at the moment. "You have no idea."

"How do you feel about Einar?" That was the last question she expected to hear from Jael, mostly because it was so personal.

"He's steady, mostly. Reliable, though he's got a nasty temper. He can be a brute when he's properly riled."

From his expression, that wasn't the response he was looking for. But he didn't say anything more about it. Instead, he watched the men hauling the bodies. They were irreverent about it, forcing the dead into undignified poses, or dragging a body by its hair. Dred didn't chastise them; they were entitled to their small pleasures after such an impossible victory. For a few minutes, she'd thought this would be their last stand, the end of Queensland.

"I thought Grigor might hit Silence's people. Then we would've had a proper dustup."

A shiver ran through her, though Dred tried to conceal it. "We wouldn't be having this conversation. These tactics won't work a second time, and we don't have the numbers to mount a frontal assault on Grigor. Mary only knows how Silence thinks we'll defeat him."

"Don't worry about it," Jael said. "Enjoy the breathing room for now . . . and it might give him pause about coming at you, now that his alliance is defunct."

"We have to neutralize the threat." There was no way around the necessity, as she'd promised the Great Bear's territory to Silence in payment for her aid.

Jael probably knew as much. "Not today."

"This place will be very different with four of us in power. Lots more space."

"It can't be much longer before the supply ship arrives with fresh fish. Don't let Grigor bolster his numbers."

Dred had thought of that. "I'm aware."

It took several hours to clear away all the corpses. By that point, she was feeling stronger, so she put Calypso in charge of supervising the cleanup. She noticed how Jael watched the other woman, and when he turned back to her, she raised her brows.

"She's one of five survivors," he said quietly. "Of the fifty men sent with me."

"Damn." Regret cascaded through her.

He shrugged. "I've run ops where I was the only one who walked away. But it's harder when you're giving the orders."

"It speaks well of you that you feel that way. Some people have no trouble sending others to die on their behalf, and it doesn't bother them at all."

"I'm a prince, right enough. What's next on the agenda?" It seemed he had appointed himself the Dread Queen's bodyguard—or maybe he had instructions from Tam or Einar. That wouldn't surprise her at all.

"While they're scrubbing up from the battle, we need to walk through Abaddon and take stock of what we've gained."

"Ah, time to count our shiny new toys?"

Dred laughed. "Exactly."

Some of the rooms were beyond disgusting. The smell alone defied description, a combination of decaying flesh and rotting meat. She covered her mouth with one hand, trying to keep her breakfast down. Everyone had heard stories about Abaddon, but even the worst didn't do the atrocities justice. If she could have, she'd have chopped Priest's head off all over again.

"I was too quick," she said, coldly furious. "Too merciful."

When she turned to Jael, his mouth was pressed into a

tight, pale line. "Turns ago, I thought the Farwan labs were the worst place in the universe. I mean, it was hell . . . the things they did to us. But this . . . this is worse. Because however wrong I think they were, those scientists had a reason for the experiments. They were working with purpose."

"Whereas this is torture for its own sake."

There were four different places in Abaddon that seemed to have been devoted to torment and anguish. For the first time, Dred closed her eyes to see if the rooms had absorbed the pain and despair of those murdered within the walls. The area throbbed with red energy, echoes of madness. Stunned, she staggered back, and Jael steadied her with a hand in the small of her back.

"What?" he asked.

Softly, she told him.

He drew her away. "Have these rooms cleaned, then sealed. Give it time to fade." He hesitated, scanning her face. Whatever he saw made him add, "I'd keep the men out. I don't know how much I believe that atmosphere can drive people to do twisted things, but it just doesn't seem wise to tempt fate."

"I know what you mean. And Queenslanders are just as susceptible to violent impulses as anyone in Perdition. That's why we're *all* here."

To her relief, the rest of the inventory went smoother. She cracked open a case and gazed at Jael, eyes wide. "This is full of paste. I guess I know where all of the food supplies ended up."

Another carton yielded actual medicine. It made no sense that Priest would hoard such things, but maybe he'd had some insane religious justification for it. They also found a stockpile of ammo for the turret as well as rudimentary magnetic sensor bracelets. Jael snapped one on his wrist and beckoned her with a jerk of his chin.

She wasn't used to taking orders anymore, but Dred didn't make him explain. In some ways, it was a relief to spend time with someone who didn't expect her to be scary, awe-inspiring, and unknowable all the time. Tam and Einar offered a break from playing a constant role; and to a lesser degree, so did Ike and Wills. She didn't feel as close to them, however, possibly because of the power exchange she'd experienced with Jael.

First, he was helpless with me—and then vice versa. It . . . changes things.

Jael led her to one of the turrets, tilted it forward, and switched it to motion-sensing mode. Then, before she could protest, he dashed in front of it. The gun stayed quiet. Dred exhaled in nervous relief and tried not to show how worried she'd been.

It's just that he's useful. If he gets himself killed, I've lost a valuable asset.

"That was stupid," she commented. "What if you were wrong?"

"I almost never am." He flashed a cocky smile, but this time, she recognized the vulnerability; Jael only used that look when he expected nobody gave a damn.

Quickly, Dred checked. The corridor was deserted apart from them, as all of her men were clearing away the refuse in other parts of Abaddon. She took a couple steps toward him and tapped his chest lightly.

"We have a situation. You have a tendency to risk your life recklessly. I don't approve."

"And why is that, love?" For the first time, his use of that endearment didn't sound razor-sharp, laced with derision. Maybe he didn't mean for it to, but his voice softened, and his eyes burned with the blue found only at the heart of the hottest flames.

"I found you," she said softly. "I'm keeping you. Got a problem with that?"

◀ 30 ▶

Truth Hurts

Tam circulated among the Queenslanders immediately after the victory. The overall mood was elated, though a few weren't drinking away their ration cards. They had probably lost mates in the battle and didn't feel like celebrating. Since Cook was supervising the liquor allotment, nobody tried to take more than his share from the still.

Einar had settled down with Ike, who was favoring his left knee. Tam could always tell when it was paining the old man because he sat with it straightened before him. Once he finished his round, he made a cup of sweetleaf tea and joined his comrades. It was loud enough in the hall to cover any number of quiet conversations, so he didn't worry unduly about seeking privacy.

"Did anyone act suspicious while we were gone?" Tam asked Ike. He'd suspected the frontal assault on Priest might present an irresistible opportunity for a spy or saboteur to weaken Dred's holdings. Ike's word was the same as proof, so he'd have no qualms about disposing of a traitor who threatened Queensland.

Einar sat up at the question, planting both elbows on the

table. "I hope so. This would be the perfect time to make somebody disappear."

Unfortunately, Ike shook his head. "All the men who stayed behind went about their business. I didn't see anything that seemed out of the ordinary."

Hm. That struck a chord. What if the spy was subtle enough to disguise his work? "I'll be back. I need to take a look around."

It took Tam an hour to complete his assessment. The hydroponics garden was undamaged, and the barricades were all in place, but somebody had tampered with the Kitchen-mate that Wills had recently repaired. If he had ordered food without checking the chemical compositions programmed into the recipe databases, he mostly likely would've died. So would anyone else who used the machine. Men would start dying right and left in Queensland, and without adequate medical facilities, they'd think it was some unknown disease carrying off their number. Eventually, the superstitious bastards would blame Dred for not stopping the epidemic. As sabotage plans went, this one was elegant and insidious. And it sent a cold chill through him because it meant the enemy definitely had a man hidden among them; this wasn't something an outsider could accomplish. Even Tam, who had an unusual aptitude for stealth, would find it impossible to creep inside the Great Bear's lines and tamper with his Kitchen-mates. It required too much detailed knowledge of patrols and defenses for anyone but a Queenslander to have done this.

Calypso came in while he stood, studying the machine. "Is it broken again?"

"Yes," he said. "Would you mind getting Ike for me? He might be able to fix it."

"No problem, little man. Guess I'll be drinking my dinner again."

He managed a half smile. "Tired of Cook's goulash? Don't let him hear you say so."

The tall woman pretended to shiver. "I wouldn't dream of it. I like my fingers all precisely where they are."

She strode off, leaving Tam to guard the Kitchen-mate. A few minutes later, Ike limped in, his expression split evenly between annoyance and discomfort. He couldn't afford to let the old man's infirmities distract him, though if life was fair, Ike would be basking somewhere warm and sunny, not taking the blame for somebody else's scandal.

"What's wrong with it?" Ike grumbled.

Quietly, Tam told him.

Ike spent a full two minutes cursing. Then he said, "I don't know enough about programming to counter this. But I can power it down, then restore it to factory defaults when it starts up again."

"Do it," Tam said quietly. "How long will that take?"

"You're hoping we can get this done without the person responsible knowing we've neutralized the threat." The old man wore a shrewd expression.

He nodded. "We'll watch and see if anyone takes unusual interest in Kitchen-mate meals. He or she will probably also examine the machine when there are no poison victims."

"And we'll be ready," Ike guessed.

"That's the plan."

Ike got to work immediately, pressing the buttons to shut down the Kitchen-mate. "How can you be sure it wasn't me?"

Tam couldn't restrain a smile, despite the severity of the situation. "If *you're* the traitor, Ike, then I'm not the judge of character I believe myself to be. More to the point, so far as I know, you're the only innocent man in Perdition."

The old man shifted uncomfortably, pausing to aim a troubled gaze at Tam. "I was drunk when I told you that. Better if it's not repeated."

"Understood."

Men survived on reputations, here. The other Queenslanders thought Ike had butchered fifty people like livestock. If they learned he'd been pushed to a false confession, it would make life more difficult for him. A cold rage filled Tam when he considered what the bastards in law enforcement had done to Ike. His case had been riddled with

corruption until Ike was backed into a no-win situation.
Then the family of the real killer, in conjunction with high-
priced barristers, made Ike an offer he couldn't refuse. He
could take his chances and go to trial, where he would certainly be convicted, based on the false evidence, or he could
willingly confess. If he did so, his wife and children would
be compensated handsomely, and the true killer would be
confined for life in a posh asylum for the criminally insane
while his family avoided even a hint of scandal. Unsurpris-
ingly to anyone who knew Ike, he took the deal to provide
for his family. And he had been in Perdition ever since.

"I might've been lying," Ike said then.

"And I might be queen of Tarnus."

The old man grinned. "Only if she pisses standing up.
There, that's got it."

Lights flickered in the control panel, showing the
startup sequence. Ike pressed a series of buttons until a
menu came up. Tam was impressed at how adroit Ike was
with old technology. This was the first line of Kitchen-
mates, primitive compared to the new ones, which had
voice-activation modules. These, you still had to program
by hand.

"How's it coming?" Tam kept an eye on the door.

"Not long." Ike held his gaze for a few seconds. "Do you
plan to tell Dred about this?"

He considered, then shook his head. "Her poker face isn't
as good as she thinks it is. And the more people who know
about a trap, the more chances it will fail."

"I don't know if I agree, but I'm good at keeping secrets.
I won't say anything."

Tam fell quiet then. It would be disastrous if the saboteur
caught them, as it would return them to the beginning in
terms of laying a trap to catch the spy. Despite the danger,
however, this was just the sort of challenge Tam thrived on.
In the end, he'd come up on top. He always did, even when
winning meant life in prison. After all, his incarceration
signaled his greatest victory to date.

* * *

JAEL thought long and hard about his reply. In the end, he yielded to the impulse to flirt. "I suppose that depends on what you intend to do with me."

You know better. Don't be stupid, man. While three in a bed worked for some people, four was just asking for trouble. Yet he didn't step away or break eye contact. She gazed back from nearly at eye level; Dred was tall for a woman, just a few centimeters shy of his own height, and he measured a bit under two meters. He shouldn't cup the back of her head in his hand, but he did—and gave her ample opportunity to retreat.

This time, however, *she* kissed him. Dred gave him a little push, and he went with it, falling against the wall as her lips met his. She kissed like she fought: hard, demanding, and aggressive. The rasp of teeth on his lower lip made him groan, and she leaned into him, her hands framing his face. Such intimacy kindled a sharp ache. He couldn't remember wanting anything—anyone—more.

Trembling, he skimmed his palms down until they found her hips, and she still didn't back off. She moved against him, oddly tentative, as if she wasn't sure of his response—though that wasn't in question—or her own intentions. It had been a *long* time, but this felt like the precursor to sex.

Jael broke the kiss to ask, "Is that the answer to my question?"

"Part of it," she said softly.

He wanted to ask what this meant, if she was looking to add him to her stable of men, if he'd be rotated in and out of her bed. *Do Tam and Einar take turns or do they share?* But questioning her would imply he cared about her personal arrangements. If the other men didn't care if she slept with someone else, then he could deal with it, too.

"I'm not opposed."

"Then let's finish up here and get back to Queensland." That sounded like a promise.

He threw himself into the task of squaring Abaddon away, helping the others stack the supplies that would be transported immediately. A runner went back to their territory to fetch the air pallet, as some of the goods were too heavy to carry back by hand. Even so, the cleanup, salvage, and restoration efforts took hours.

She probably won't feel like making good on that implied offer by the time we get back.

It had been an incredibly long day with the promise of harder work to come. Now they had to protect their extended borders as well as figure out a way to defeat the Great Bear. Even to him, it sounded daunting. Dred proved that rack time was the last thing on her mind when she ordered him back to Queensland guarding the air pallet while she stayed on to continue working.

"You want me to return once we stow everything?"

She shook her head. "Help Tam and Einar. Make sure the place is in order."

Ah. He only nodded and departed along with five other men. Fortunately, they encountered no trouble on the way back, and it didn't take long to put away the supplies. Wills was delighted when he saw all the goodies Priest had stored up. Jael listened with only half an ear as the soothsayer went on about all the things he could do with such bounty.

"Do you need anything else?" he asked.

Wills shook his head. "Ike and I can take it from here."

The older man looked none too pleased to be volunteered for the task, but he set down his drink. "Fine. What do you need?"

Oddly discontent, Jael joined Tam and Einar, who held a mug of something alcoholic. From the cloudy look of their drinks, the liquor came from the still. Come to think of it, the rest of the men seemed to be living it up, too. It wasn't quite a victory party, probably because of the heavy losses, but given another hour or two, the wild celebration would be going, full swing.

"Do we have anybody sober and on watch?" he asked.

The big man scowled at him. "You think we're idiots? Of course."

"It's a low-risk opportunity for them to blow off steam," Tam added. "The odds of a retaliatory strike so soon are low, and the men need a break, especially when everything went off exactly as we planned."

Einar laughed. "And that's so unlikely, too. I can't believe your alien gambit worked."

Jael froze, not that the other two men noticed. With a drink in hand, even the spymaster had lost his customary wariness in the spirit of celebration. But clearly, they both knew why the aliens from the Warren had been attacking Priest at such a convenient moment whereas he'd heard nothing about the scheme.

"How did you get them to cooperate?" he asked.

Tam tapped a finger on his mug, then shrugged. "In my old line of work, I never got to boast when a plan came together. This is a nice change. I was afraid our numbers wouldn't stack up to the diversion Silence requested, so I took advantage of some . . . discord between Priest's people and the aliens in the Warren."

"Brilliant," Einar said, lifting his glass. "Priest's people killed some, and it's ugly stuff, dismemberment and evisceration, the markings and the blood painting left behind. The aliens keep to themselves, mostly, but they're quite vicious if you get them riled."

Jael registered the cold calculation in Tam's eyes. Often that look went unnoticed because the man moved silently and didn't draw attention with violent behavior. But it didn't mean he was a good man or better than the obvious brutes.

"Took advantage, how?"

"I performed a service for Katur. Between his anger at Priest and his gratitude, he was willing to fight." That was vague enough to be frustrating, but Jael suspected Tam wouldn't be offering full disclosure anytime soon.

To him, we're only numbers and probabilities. I doubt he has a single genuine emotion.

"It worked like a charm," Jael forced himself to say lightly.

In his gut, a hole opened up. Dred must have known about the plan yet she'd chosen not to tell him—when it was his squad that would've been annihilated if the aliens hadn't kept up their end of the deal. As it was, he'd lost all but five of his people. This meant she, too, saw him as a tool to be used: Sharpen the blade and keep it wet with blood. To make matters worse, she'd been perfectly willing to screw him as part of that arrangement, maybe even for the same reason she'd used her hand on him before—to keep him happy and compliant, asking no questions.

To his surprise, he wasn't content with scraps from her table. Never would be. In the hole where he'd languished for thirty turns, going quietly mad by millimeters, he'd come to the conclusion that he both wanted and deserved something better. He muttered about getting a drink, and neither Tam nor Einar watched him go, so apparently, he'd kept up a flat expression. Jael poured a mug of the strong liquor and took a seat at one of the other tables.

Since he wasn't paying much attention to his companions, he was surprised when Martine drew her chair over beside him. She clicked her drink against his. "Here's to surviving when the other bastards didn't."

"Cheers to that," he said.

"So what's up with you and the Dread Queen?" the woman asked.

Not shy, this one.

"Why?"

"You spent an awful lot of time holed up with her while she was recuperating. I thought there might be a reason."

There was, he thought. *I was saving her life.*

He shrugged. "I have some medical background. Tam and Einar thought it was best if I supervised her care."

"You did a good job, then. She's up and around faster than anyone expected." The woman's dark eyes twinkled, a contrast to her stark features and sharpened teeth. "I lost a week's liquor rations when she pulled through. You ought to make that up to me."

"I take it you have some suggestions, bright eyes?"

Her smile flashed; he could tell she liked the silly nickname. Some women had a partiality to it. Others fluffed up like irate cats, hissing and spitting until he convinced them he meant no disrespect. Oddly, it was impossible to tell which way they'd swing by their appearances. Sometimes women who looked like Martine were unexpectedly girlish.

"If you hadn't noticed, women are a minority here," she said bluntly. "I lost my man recently. I can take my pick because I'm honest, clean, and I don't have anything that'll make your dick fall off."

Jael laughed. "That's the most original proposition I've ever received."

"Chuckle now. Just wait 'til you develop a permanent callus on your wanking hand."

"I wasn't underestimating your value," he assured her. "I've no doubt you're a pearl beyond price."

"That nonsense won't fly with me. I'm not looking for pretty words or declarations of love. That's all bullshit anyway. Chemicals in your bloodstream make you think somebody matters more than they do."

Jael recalled speaking almost the same words to somebody else, turns ago. He wondered if she'd felt sorry for him then. His overall stance on romantic entanglements hadn't changed, but now it saddened him to believe people were incapable of constancy. Yet he'd seen too much pain and suffering to imagine human beings were innately good—and Perdition only underscored the capacity for wickedness.

"You were upset when they killed your man," he said, probing.

Martine practically snarled at him. "Because he was *mine*, not because I loved him. I counted on him for sex and company—and to have my back in a fight. If you're looking for more than that in here, you're crazier than Wills."

Since the soothsayer was currently holding an animated conversation with a maintenance bot of very limited programming, it was a compelling argument. Jael lifted one shoulder, forcing away the lingering sense of betrayal. "I'm not seeking anything in particular, bright eyes."

Except a way out of here.

But he'd had enough of people telling him that was impossible, so he didn't share his intention to escape. *Even if I have to pull this place apart, bolt by bolt, I'm not staying.* There was always a way if you fought hard enough, long enough. Sometimes, the ferocity of his resistance carved a new path. If that was what it took, so be it.

"Consider my offer," she said, downing the rest of her drink. "Not too long, mind. There've already been others asking if I want a new man in my bed."

He offered a wink. "None as pretty as me, I bet."

Martine tilted her head, inspecting him. By the time she finished, he suspected she knew exactly how he looked naked—and what he could do with his equipment. "That's true. But there are other considerations."

"Like what?" He raised a brow.

This should be enlightening.

"Some things, a man should figure out on his own. Another round?"

At his nod, she stood and refilled their mugs. The alcohol was strong as hell and tasted disgusting. There was no point in drinking except to blend in. So he downed a few mugs and laughed in the right places, trying to ignore the hot, red coal in his chest. *People can't be trusted.* No matter how many times he learned this lesson, he was like a dumb animal, just as they'd said in the labs. Always, someone managed to get under his skin and wound him again.

By the time the Dread Queen returned, Martine was perched on his knee, feeling no pain. It amused him to see such a dangerous woman laugh so hard over an improbable story related by a drunken convict. When she saw them, Dred stilled in the center of the hall, eyes intent. He wondered if he was supposed to set Martine aside, heel to her like a dog now that she'd returned at last. He met her gaze across the room, smiled, and lifted his glass in a silent toast.

Then, deliberately, he set his hand in the small of Martine's back and turned away.

◄ 31 ►

King of Infinite Space

I can't wait to get him alone.

Eagerness made Dred hurry; her boots rang on the metal floor as she strode into the hall, searching for him. Part of that anticipation sprang from human physiology. She wanted to celebrate their triumph in the most elemental way possible . . . and she'd chosen to celebrate with him because of the complex web that bound them. Sex would be different, more intense, with someone who had saved her life. *And I saved his, too.* Maybe those bonds should make her run even faster in the opposite direction, but she was curious—

Found him.

Jael's hand was elegant on the other woman's spine, a silent message. She turned away slow enough that no one would remark a reaction, spoke a few words to some nearby Queenslanders. Rightfully, they were celebrating the win with lots of liquor. She wished she had that same freedom.

Once she was sure her departure wouldn't be deemed strange or abrupt, Dred wheeled and went in search of other business. She was too proud to hole up in her quarters—and besides, she had work to do. The Dread Queen never rested. Fortunately, nobody knew that she'd planned to take Jael to her bed; and it would stay that way. If he preferred Martine, so be it.

She found Ike in a storage closet, a cramped space piled with junk they'd dragged back from the salvage bay and been unable to find immediate use for. With his long, iron gray hair and impressive beard, he resembled a pagan king of broken things. That unlikely thought in mind, she paused in the doorway.

"May I come in?"

He hesitated, as if there was something on his mind. Then he just answered, "Queensland belongs to you. Of course you can."

That wasn't entirely true. The power to rule came from the Queenslanders, and if she pissed off enough of them, they would find a way to remove her. She was always conscious of the line she walked and how fickle public opinion could be, especially when her constituents were hardened criminals. Voting wouldn't be anything so kind as chits of paper, either; instead, she would be impeached with a shiv in the throat or a weight upside her head. Constant caution made her paranoid though Tam would say it wasn't madness when the danger was real.

Dred joined him and closed the door; she didn't know how he spent long hours in here. "How close are you?" she asked.

The old man shrugged. He had been rebuilding the Peacemaker since they returned from the salvage-bay run. From what she could tell, he had the thing about half put together. It wasn't an original unit, however, more of a retrofit constructed of other materials. So it didn't look the same as it had before it was broken; there was probably a valuable metaphor in that. But more importantly, he had managed to get the weapons back in place. A Peacemaker without the Shredder and laser gun wouldn't serve much purpose.

"I'm having trouble with the programming," he said.

"And Wills keeps demanding that I help him with that stupid maintenance bot, or the turrets, and whatever else he's working on."

Dred smiled slightly. "You're allowed to tell him no, you understand. He's not authorized to give you orders."

"You know how he is. I can either help him out or listen to irrational ranting for an hour or watch him cursing the wall roundly. Then he starts in with his ritual of threes—"

"I'm starting to suspect he's not crazy at all, *ever*. That he slips in and out of it like a skin, when he wants something, needs a diversion or to make people look away."

Ike nodded at that. "Me, too. Can you hand me that—" She hovered her palm over a random pile of gears, metal bits, and wires. "Yes, that one."

"Is he helping you with the Peacemaker?" she asked, once he had the part.

"No, this is a project just for me. He's busy enough with his own work."

"You know an awful lot about bots." It was a borderline invasive question, as he hadn't given any indication he wanted to confide in her.

"Are you asking me what I did before I ended up in here?"

"If that's all right," she said quietly.

At the moment, she felt less the Dread Queen and more like Dresdemona Devos, who had worked on a freighter in the maintenance department before she made so many wrong turns. Consequently, she knew a little about repair work, but nothing compared with Ike and Wills. She watched for a few seconds, then at his signal, handed him another component.

"I worked for Pretty Robotics," he answered at length.

"I've heard of them. They manufacture those realistic androids?"

"Indeed."

The units came with human-looking bodies and advanced programming. A number of companies preferred them to flesh-and-blood employees as they didn't require benefits, never got sick, and took no vacation days. That created problems with the labor boards over their discriminatory practices, making it harder for organic workers to earn an honest living. She recalled studying the protests in her history courses, but growing up on remote Tehrann, she had never encountered a Pretty Robotics unit—or anyone who had designed them.

From his expression, she could tell Ike was waiting for her to ask how he went from working at a reputable company to a life sentence. She didn't. "That explains how you know so much about this sort of thing."

"Mmhm. So why are you hiding?"

Denying the charge would insult his intelligence. "I just needed a break. People won't look for me here like they would in my quarters. Tam and Einar come and go as they please."

"Then welcome to my kingdom," he said with gentle irony.

That put her in mind of a quote: "'I could be bounded in a nutshell, and count myself a king of infinite space, were it not that I have bad dreams.'"

"Do you?" he asked.

She dreamed of the life she'd left behind more than of the things she'd done, but knowing she'd never see her family again, never know what became of them? Those old memories took on the nuance of nightmare. "Sometimes. Doesn't everyone?"

"In here? I suspect so, though some would deny it; others have no conscience; and some simply can't remember. For them, sleep is more like dying."

"Is it possible to do the things we've done and keep one?" she wondered aloud.

"A conscience, you mean? Quite the philosophical inquiry."

"Never mind," she said. "I'm in an odd mood."

"It's all right to ask the tough questions now and then, just not when the questions become a way of avoiding or disavowing responsibility."

"Is that what I'm doing?"

"I never said so. As far as I'm concerned, you're just helping an old man chase an impossible dream." With that, Ike gave his blessing for her to stick around as his assistant; it was a welcome break.

"What's impossible about it?"

"Are you *looking* at this unit?"

At his incredulous tone, she tried to see the Peacemaker through his eyes. "It has less than half the original parts, and it's quite damaged. But somehow I don't think that's what you're talking about entirely."

"You're a perceptive woman. I also meant that if I can get it running, I won't feel as though I've outlived my usefulness—that I'm contributing to society again."

"Society," she repeated with a bitter laugh.

"It's strange and warped, but we have our own ways. You've changed things just enough since Artan died, made things better without taking away the promise of violence."

"That was Tam's idea," she admitted. "He said if we can limit grudges and grievances to the ring, there will be less random fighting."

"Tam's a clever one, full of intriguing notions." There was a coolness to Ike's tone.

"You don't care for him?"

"Hold this steady while I attach it." He wasn't avoiding the question, just delaying it while he fiddled with the Peacemaker. Dred did as he asked, then the old man answered, "Tam knows a great deal about manipulation. Look at the way he rules Queensland through you—all of the power and none of the accountability."

She'd never considered their relationship in those terms. Tam had been the one to find her, just after she killed Artan. Without his quick thinking and immediate intervention, things would've gone much differently. In truth, she hadn't been planning a coup or intending to steal the man's territory, it was only that she couldn't stand for him to breathe another second.

Dred framed defensive words like *He's only doing what's*

best for Queensland, but she had no evidence of it. She followed his counsel because he was smart and devious and had been at her side since she came to power, guiding her along the paths he chose. So far, his advice had built her an impressive legend and secure rule, but it didn't mean Tam would always play fair.

"You think I rely on him too much," she guessed.

"The others haven't noticed the way he pulls your strings, my queen, but the court fool always speaks his mind, even if the consequences could be dire."

"You're not my jester. And I hate that whole court nonsense." *Which was Tam's idea.* "As for the latter, don't talk rubbish. I'd never chop the head off the one honest man I know."

Ike laughed. "Glad to hear it. But so far as the rest of Queensland is concerned, I'm the fool, and I don't entirely mind. You've got Wills as the mad wizard, after all."

"You're saying circumstances could always be worse?"

The old man winked, leaving her to work out the meaning for herself. He changed the subject. "I've no evidence that Tam has nefarious intentions. I'd just like to see you think harder before you follow his advice, that's all."

"I will," she promised. Considering for a few seconds, she added, "Do me a favor. Don't tell anyone about this side project. If Wills was right about another spy in our midst, then I don't want him to have a full picture of our defensive capabilities."

Ike laughed softly, his pale blue eyes twinkling in the dim light. She wasn't sure what amused him so much, and when he asked, "Not even Tam?" she still didn't know.

"Nobody," she said firmly.

"Now you're thinking like a queen, tricksy as Tam on his best day." Ike frowned at the tangle of wires in the open chassis before him. "But right now, there's nothing to tell anyway. The damned thing won't even turn on, let alone function as intended."

"If you need any resources in particular to make it happen, let me know. A working Peacemaker would change everything in this territory."

"If Einar and Jael don't turn on you, then pull the thing apart for your enemies." The old man grinned.

"Wills told you about that, huh? It was . . . impressive as hell." She paused, tilted her head, then asked, "So why aren't you cautioning me about trusting *you*? Maybe you're working for Grigor, and you have instructions to use your subtle wit to drive a wedge between Tam and me. Without his good advice, my confidence will falter, the Queenslanders will notice, and it'll all be downhill from there."

To her surprise, Ike was nodding in apparent approval. "Those are the questions you need to ask, and only you can decide the answers. You might be right . . . I *could* be an agent provocateur. I'm relieved it occurred to you, frankly."

Groaning, she leaned her head back against the towering pile of parts lining the wall behind her. Dred drew her knees up and rested her chin on them. The chains that wrapped her boots rasped against the links twined around her arms. She closed her eyes, unsure how she would muster the drive necessary to destroy the Great Bear; there was no chance Grigor would back down, now that his alliance with Priest was done. She pictured him ranting to his soldiers, promising them glory, property, and additional living space.

"I have to kill him," she said quietly. "And it seems so impossible right now. We're better situated than before, but—"

"Stop there. No buts. You mustn't think of the insurmountable obstacles, only determine the way to get the job done. That's your role, making us believe in impossible things." Beneath his deft hands, something snicked into place, and the Peacemaker whirred to life briefly, the lights where its eyes would be burning bright as the sun, then it shuddered and powered down. Ike swore. "Just as mine is never to give up on this damned artificial beast."

"I'll leave you to it, then."

◀ 32 ▶

In the Garden

The room that housed the hydroponics garden was enormous, comparable to the great hall, only instead of drunken, smelly Queenslanders, this space was lush and green, every available surface covered with plants spilling out of specially formulated pods. Row upon row of tables supported the groaning weight of the garden, somewhat miraculous without soil. Not high-tech like a Kitchen-mate, but it *was* magnificent. Jael knew jack-all about nurturing anything; he was far better at killing, maiming, and setting things on fire. But some of his internal rawness drained away as he stood breathing in the cool, damp air. Special lights hung overhead, providing nutrients to the flora.

Beside him, Martine tapped a foot. "You wanted to stop in here. So?"

Two workers—a man and a woman—were doing something to the plants, not close enough to overhear their conversation, though. *Unless they have hearing like mine.* Martine grabbed his hand, tugging him toward the door. She wasn't as drunk as she had been, but Jael wouldn't call the woman sober.

"I think I'll stick around. See if they need a hand."

"Seriously?" She eyed him with disbelief edged in slow-dawning comprehension. "You're after the queen, aren't you? Talk about setting your sights high, new fish. But it makes no sense you let me on your lap if you wanted somebody else there."

Dred wasn't the kind of woman who perched on a man's knee; she was too prickly for that—or so he imagined. He figured he'd end up with a chain upside his head if he tried. He found himself muttering, "I was actually sending her a message."

"What, that you're an asshole?"

"She already knows that."

Martine gazed at him owlishly as she appeared to puzzle out his meaning. "So . . . you wanted her to think you're not interested in nailing her even though you are? What kind of stupid, fragged-up mess is that? In here, good sex is the best thing you can get."

"What makes you think I'd be any good?"

"Just a hunch." She shrugged. "Not like I'm about to find out, now. For the record, I'm not interested in your ass anymore. You're too stupid for me."

He laughed. "That so, bright eyes? I'm crushed to hear it."

"Don't come to me looking for help or advice again. I will *stab* you. But this once, here's a free tip. If a woman pisses you off, you talk to her. You don't grab somebody else's ass."

"I never—" he started. She gave him a look. "Maybe I did. A little."

"Damn right you did. Now frag off, new fish. I got bigger men to fry. Or something."

"Bigger maybe," he said. "But not better."

"Keep telling yourself that and wonder why you sleep alone." Martine sauntered out of the garden room.

It was a great exit line, but Martine's words made Jael realize that he'd let a lifetime of raw deals drive him to a number of assumptions. He'd leapt immediately to the conclusion that Dred didn't care whether he lived or died, as long as he served his purpose, but her behavior had run completely counter in every instance. For Mary's sake, she'd fought for his life against the odds when he was poisoned. Nobody had ever *done* that before.

With his behavior, he'd rewritten their tacit agreement without a word, reneging on the deal they'd made in the hallway with hands and mouths. At the moment, Dred was probably puzzled and pissed, so he'd give her some time to cool off before he explained why he'd used Martine as a defensive shield. That had always been his thing, showing people how much he didn't give a frag when they betrayed him. And maybe she wouldn't give a damn; that was likely, in fact.

In the meantime, he'd help out in the garden. Maybe he could be useful, if not wise. So he strode over to the two workers, bravado in place of skill. "I'm Jael. I don't know anything about gardening . . . but I have two hands."

"Vix," the woman said.

He didn't remember seeing her before. She had red hair that must be natural, as there were no salons or cosmeticians around to touch it up for her. A fine scar bisected her left cheek, pulling her eye sideways and cutting through her lower lip. The mark went all way the down her throat, a story, that, but he didn't ask. Beside her, the young man took Jael's measure; he was short and average-sized, not particularly muscular, but not soft, either. Brown hair, brown eyes, he was the sort the eyes slid away from, and people didn't remember his features when the authorities asked for his description later.

The perfect criminal. He was also the youngest person Jael had seen in Perdition, no more than twenty turns. But those brown eyes weren't innocent, not by a long shot; they radiated a bleak knowledge that the universe was a hellhole with no escape ladder.

What the hell happened to you, kid?

"I'm Zediah." He didn't offer his hand.

Jael received a territorial vibe from both of them and took a step back. *No handshake. Check.* Even after all these turns, he struggled with knowing how to relate to people. Mostly, he deployed the same cocky air, but it wasn't making anyone smile, here. Zediah offered the coldest look he'd received since arriving on this junk heap, and that included the initial inspection when Dred was playing the Dread Queen to the hilt. Even Einar hadn't looked this dead-eyed scary, which was saying something.

"If you prefer, I can go—" Since he craved some peace working in here, it wouldn't serve if he alienated the regular workers.

To his surprise, Vix shook her head at Zediah, as if warning him somehow. "If you're not picky, we could use your help moving some plants to larger pods."

"I'd be happy to, as long as you don't mind telling me exactly what to do."

"She doesn't mind that at all," Zediah said flatly.

Was that a joke? Sometimes it was troublesome being locked up with people who were likely insane and afflicted with any number of personality disorders. He settled on a half smile and was rewarded with a quirk of Zediah's lips in answer.

Yeah, he's testing me. Kid probably had to get hard and cold, fast.

The room really was amazing, especially the climbing plants. In a cunning design, the walls were dotted with holes permitting the creepers to twine around and through. Some must be herbs, as he didn't see fruits and vegetables, but others hung heavy with the produce that went into Cook's pot on a daily basis. This was a critical undertaking, and it occurred to him—

"Do we have a guard on this place?" As Queensland's primary food source, it was a natural target during times of war. Part of him thought that was a pretentious word for such a trivial skirmish, but the stakes were the same as in a larger-scale conflict. The losing side would be wiped out.

Across the room, Zediah nodded. "There's a checkpoint not far from here, and Dred keeps a double guard on it at all times. We've got the turret there now, too."

"Shot anybody?"

"Some of Grigor's people," Vix answered. "They're always testing our defenses, had been for months before he settled the alliance."

Jael lifted his face, feeling a cool, nearly imperceptible mist puff against his skin. The moisture came out of the ceiling, glimmering like jewels on the tender leaves. A lump formed in his throat; it had been *so long* since he'd seen any green and growing things. Entombed on Ithiss-Tor, he'd forgotten the freshness of new life in the lungs, the nutty burr of cut grain, and the melting sweetness of purple heather rolling over a hillside. Most of those memories were cut with pain and blood, however, like an infected wound stinging a healthy limb. He had no such recollections untainted by bitterness and battle rage. Maybe that made the memories all the more precious, because he knew with hard-won certainty that beauty could exist, alongside anguish, even in darkest night.

You're not a person. You're a thing. You will obey.

He could still hear the voice in his head, a persistent echo. The scientist had been dead for so many turns that he ought to have put that message aside; or possibly it should have faded like other experiences, some grim and some lovely. But he had been crafted too well; and the words were emblazoned in his brain like they had been soldered there. Of all the things he'd forgotten, that he never would.

Belatedly, he realized they were both watching him, then the two gardeners exchanged a speaking look. When he'd first entered, he was conscious only of the plants and the richness of the nutrient mixture, of how clean and wholesome this room smelled compared to the rest of the ship. Now, he discerned the warmth of her scent all over Zediah's skin . . . and vice versa. They shared an overall chemical aroma, a combination of sex and frequent contact.

Explains a lot. He saw me as a threat.

Then she said, "You really love it in here."

No harm in admitting as much. "It's beautiful. There are worse ways to spend your time."

"In a hydroponics garden on a prison ship?" Zediah raised a brow.

Jael laughed, feeling some of the weight slip from his shoulders. "Point taken. When I get out of here, I'll use my ill-gotten gains to plant a huge garden on my country estate."

"When?" Zediah asked, raising a brow.

"It's a dream. Don't you have one?"

"Not anymore," Vix said softly.

Everyone confined in Perdition accepted what they'd been told. *Escape is impossible; the prison is impregnable. You will die there.* Jael had that echo in his head, along with the scientists who had droned at him, repeatedly, *You're not a person. You're a thing. You will obey.*

And I didn't do that, either.

I refuse to die here.

But he didn't think these two would be interested—or persuaded by—his nascent escape plans. He had only just begun taking the measure of the ship. Once the smoke settled, he could explore more and put together a plan. Right now, it was impossible, with the Great Bear's soldiers watching and waiting, and with Silence playing her cards so close to her chest. He lacked Tam's skill for going unnoticed; stealth had never been a requirement in his line of work. Commanders looked to him for nearly indestructible infantry, a brutal killer, not a sneak thief. And most of them appreciated that his history didn't show on his skin.

"Anyway," Vix said. "This is how you do a proper transfer."

He didn't ask why they spent so much time in the garden. If he could, he'd move in here where he forgot that the rest of the station was rusted and pocked, that the parts had been stripped and stolen and reapportioned so often that it was a wonder primary systems like life support still functioned. Even the light felt brighter and cleaner; nothing seemed as desperate or awful in here.

For several hours, he worked in harmonious silence, which might surprise old acquaintances. He had been known for nervous energy and seeking ever more extreme entertainment. Here, he could just be. By the time he finished all the transplants that Vix asked of him, he felt calmer, more ready to tackle a discussion with Dred. He knew shit about dealing with women for more than one night; and while theirs didn't qualify as a relationship, she wasn't a woman he could sleep with, then never see again. Somehow, her respect had become important to him as well, and he imagined he'd lost it.

Still, I won't be twice the fool. I'll take Martine's advice.

"Thank you," he said to Zediah and Vix as he headed for the door. "I needed this."

She nodded, a smile creasing her sharp cheeks. Surprisingly, the woman had a dimple, and Zediah gazed at it like it was the greatest wonder of his life. Jael felt something twist inside him, a sharp sideways shift.

Zediah added, "You're welcome here anytime. You're a good worker."

How fragging sad—that might be the nicest thing anyone had ever said to him.

◄ 33 ►

Sweeter Than Honey

Dred had just stepped out of the san-shower when the door to her quarters swished open. It was a little early for Tam and Einar, so she stepped out of the lavatory with an inquiring look. When she saw Jael, the curiosity curled into a hard, cold emotion, a kernel of anger burning in her belly. She'd call it wounded vanity; the Dread Queen wasn't used to being refused.

Deep down, it wasn't the Dread Queen who minded, though.

"You can go," she said. "We have no business."

His blue eyes were more open than she'd ever seen them, a shift she didn't expect. "If you still feel that way after I've said my piece, I'll agree. Will you give me a chance to explain?"

Unable to restrain the impulse, she slipped into second sight, eyes closed, to read his current state of mind. Once, she hadn't been able to do this. Her empathy was born in violence, but she'd strengthened the ability through repeated use. Sorrow lingered in pockets of deep blue, but mostly, she read the deep green of remorse. For a few seconds, she wondered if he could shield his emotions or project what he wanted her to see. Ike had her doubting everything these days. Then she released that question into the wild.

For the sake of privacy, she secured the door.

"Go on," she said with deliberate detachment.

"I don't know if this will matter—and perhaps it shouldn't—but there was a reason I didn't finish what we started in the corridor. When I learned that you and Tam involved the aliens in the Warren, without telling me, it . . . bothered me." Two distinct emotions flickered across his face: hurt and anger. "I thought I'd proven myself. Then I learned I was a weapon to you . . . and that you apparently didn't care if my people and I survived the attack. It's not that I haven't been treated like that before . . . just that I didn't expect it from you." There was a bleak, leaden quality to his words, as if he'd resigned himself to nothing better.

"So you let me know I was only a warm body to *you*, and one's as good as another."

"Not subtle," he admitted, "or particularly admirable, but yes."

She sank down on the bed, giving him the height advantage. It was a choice, as Tam had taught her far too much about body language over the past half turn for her to do any such thing without full cognition of what it portended. Dred waited a few seconds for that to register.

Then she said, "I haven't been an actual person in a long time, since before I left Tehrann. Everything changed when I stepped foot on that freighter. *I* changed. Soon enough, I was just a killer of killers, devoid of anything but my mission." Those had been empty turns, but also darkly euphoric. There had been pleasure and satisfaction in terminating a threat nobody else could see. "Then they arrested me, and I was a prisoner, just one-note, too. I was . . . angry, and I made sure everyone else in the facility was, too. It wasn't difficult."

He nodded. "That's how you ended up here. I remember."

"After I ended up here, I was a new fish, fighting to

survive, and it was doubly difficult because I'm a woman. Most don't last long."

"Females don't seem to get sentenced here as often, but when the rare one arrives, the men probably react like predators with blood in the water."

As if though a dark glass, she glimpsed a memory of the circling and the feeding frenzy before Artan claimed her. "That's not far off the mark. So after being a new fish, then I belonged to Artan. He didn't leave room for me to be a person, either."

So much I'm not saying, there. There were horrors that dug into the throat like shards of glass wrapped in barbed wire, and speaking of them would end in a fountain of blood. Dred wasn't sure she could survive it, even now. He was watching her from across the room, unmoving, with those blue eyes focused like twin lasers.

"Then you killed him . . . and Tam turned you into the Dread Queen."

"Exactly. My point is, it never occurred to me how you'd feel about being left out of Tam's scheming. I don't consider you a weapon, though, Jael. To be honest, I'm not used to thinking of anyone else at all."

"So it wasn't a purposeful exclusion?"

She shook her head. "No more than Tam's usual caution. Half the time he has plots percolating that I don't know about until he unveils them."

"And you're all right with that?" In his quiet expression, she read reservations and skepticism, which echoed Ike's warnings.

"Until recently. I've been advised that it might not be wise to put so much faith in him."

"You probably shouldn't put much in me, either."

"Now there's a novel approach. Get me to trust you by telling me not to, thereby making me assume you have nothing to hide."

"Is it working?"

"I think I'll leave your curiosity unsated."

"I didn't tell you this because I have any expectation of

picking up where we left off earlier. I just wanted you to know that, though I was an arse, I had a reason. You might not agree it was a good one, but—"

She held up a hand to staunch his unexpected, nervous rambling. "Stop. I'd have been pissed, too. Don't know that I'd have shagged someone else to make the point, but men are led by their pricks, or so I'm told."

"I didn't," he told her. "What you saw in the hall, that's all there was."

"But you left with her." *And were gone for hours.* But she didn't say that part out loud because it would seem like she'd been watching for him.

"I was in the hydroponics garden, working with Vix and Zediah. You said I could take a shift in there, but so far, you haven't assigned me any time. They didn't mind the help."

In the midst of all this chaos, she'd forgotten his request. "I'm sorry."

"I can see you're juggling land mines."

Just then, the door chimed. Tam's voice followed the sound. "What's wrong, Dred? You never lock your door."

True. Instead, she had trusted Tam and Einar to keep her safe; she'd known how easy it was to work around technical solutions. "I'm fine. Jael is with me. It's best if you and Einar find other quarters for the night."

"Are you sure?" the big man asked.

"I'm certain. There's no coercion."

Jael made a face at that, and he had a point. He wasn't a cretin who required a shiv at a woman's throat to secure her attention.

Tam only said, "Understood. We'll be around if you need us."

She felt guilty about dismissing them, but it was only one night. They could evaluate things after she squared things away with Jael. Though she wasn't sure where it was going, this conversation wasn't over.

"Will that cause you problems later?" Jael asked.

"I don't think so. There's plenty of space in the dormitories after the losses we've taken."

He came over to her then, perched beside her on the bunk. "What's the worst thing you've ever done?"

Odd question, she thought, but for him, she answered.

"Two turns into my vigilante work, I ran into a man who had a thing for carving people up. He had a fetish for dismemberment . . . there's a name for it. Anyway, I hunted him, learned his habits. That took weeks. I planned his execution down to the last second. I would make him suffer for the ghastly pleasures he craved."

"Sounds like he deserved it."

"Definitely," she said. "But here's the thing. My plan went wrong. That afternoon, he deviated from his routine. I found him in the park with two little girls, his daughters, instead of hunting his next victim."

"What happened?" he asked quietly.

"I killed him anyway. I'd already booked my passage off world. I planned such things down to the second, and I wasn't prepared to accommodate a change in his behavior. So I told myself they'd be better off. They were playing a few feet away when I shot him. They didn't know anything about his dark side, or the awful things he'd done. To them, I was just the woman who murdered their father for no reason."

That was the critical mistake that led to her capture. Those two fatherless girls created so much sympathy for her victims that the authorities started hunting her in earnest. A turn later, they caught her though she'd ended a lot more killers by then. They estimated her death toll was close to a hundred, but the number was close to twice that. There were articles in scientific journals about her, as she was one of the most famous female serial killers who ever lived. They'd interviewed her and picked apart her brain to figure out how a woman could go so wrong.

"Why did you tell me that?"

"Why did you ask me?"

"Because I wanted to know."

"That's why for me, too." A cloud of puzzlement furrowed his brow, so she clarified, "I chose for you to have the answer. Now I'll pose you the same question."

Confusion shifted to quiet dread; she had seen that expression in her own eyes enough to recognize it. "I should be careful of asking you anything. It's always an even exchange."

"Clever of you to notice."

He slid backward on the bunk as if to put some distance between them, but when he put his back to the wall, she realized he just wanted something solid behind him. The story shook him that much. For a few seconds, she was sorry she'd asked, but his recounting and reaction to it would tell her a great deal about the kind of man he was now, as well as the one he'd been. She already knew he had been a traitor, but with a history like his, she understood it. When people had sold you out enough, it became natural self-preservation to strike first.

"I was working in a merc unit on Nicu Tertius, nothing glamorous. The noble who employed us was a shit-eating lummox, an imperial hopeful who had about as much chance as my left bollock at winning the purple robes."

"Sounds like a real charmer."

Jael flashed her a wry half smile. "Oh, he was. Prince of a fellow, and his commander was worse, a bundle of filthy rags where his brain ought to be."

"Why were you working for them, then?"

"Clearly you've never been homeless or hungry, love. I fought for them because they'd have me, no questions asked. It might've been a terrible place, but . . . it was mine."

She understood that, better than he might imagine. "Right. Go on."

"There was a remote village, and the lord wanted it cleared. The property was in dispute. He said it belonged to him . . . his neighbor disagreed. This had been going on for turns while the people went about their lives unconcerned. My employer got the bright idea to turn us on the peasants. If there was no income potential, then his rival might lose interest. It wasn't the first time he'd aimed us at petty matters, diverting us from his Imperial campaign, just the worst conceived use for a full merc unit."

She didn't have to prompt him. Jael closed his eyes and finished the story though she already knew how it ended. "I followed orders. The universe is full of quietly terrible men who blame their sins on other people, on the necessity of following orders. So we wiped that village off the map. Everything burned, and there was this awful naphtha smell in the air, hanging, along with the stink of charred flesh. I can still hear the women screaming, the children crying." When his lashes fluttered up, she swore she saw flames crackling in them.

Hell is our own memories, our bad choices.

Dred wasn't sure what she'd craved in this information exchange, but she'd learned he wasn't a man who could do something so terrible and feel unmoved. That meant he was better than Artan, at least. He'd known no remorse for any of his atrocities and taken pleasure in pain, as if it were sweeter than honey.

"Come to bed," she said then.

◀ 34 ▶

Darkness Falls

"Don't take this the wrong way, love, but I'm not in the mood." Jael tried on a smile, but he couldn't quite fasten the thing properly.

His teeth clicked in more of a snarl with the sickness of that old wrong simmering in his head. He couldn't even believe he'd answered her, just because she'd asked. She must have some kind of insane power over men because otherwise he'd never have emptied himself all over her bunk, as if he were pissing on an alley wall. Jael just . . . he never did this; it was too far below skin level, down close to the bone.

"Me either. So my invitation's not for that. Just . . . stay, if you want."

Mary, why would he want to be in a woman's bed if *not* for that? He had no precedent, but her power over him didn't diminish. If anything, he was more of a puppet than ever as he settled beside her in the bunk. It was just large enough for two, but only if they turned on their sides. He had no idea how it functioned with both Tam and Einar in here, but he shunted those questions aside. For tonight, if only for tonight, she'd chosen him. Jael would deal with the fallout from that later.

"What do you want from me?" he asked, hearing the raw confusion in his own voice.

"I'm using you as a magical talisman tonight."

"Against what?"

"Everything else."

She wrapped an arm around him, and he had no idea what to do. He'd never lain with a woman like this. There were bedroom tussles; he was good at those, but always, he rolled away with a smile or an exchange of credits afterward. By degrees, he relaxed against her and curled her closer to him. Her leg twined with his. Before long, her breathing leveled off. It was always hard for him to fall asleep, either a product of his accelerated physiology or a result of his precarious lifestyle. This time, however, it took only minutes instead of hours for his brain to power down.

Later, he woke in confusion, his face nuzzled into the softness of a shoulder. Recollection came quickly. His first instinct was to shove her away and run. This seemed much weightier than her fingers, briskly bringing him off. Jael couldn't make his muscles respond; he only wanted to pull her tighter. His whole body ached in that sleepy, needing way.

She pressed closer, drowsy and delicious with it. Half-awake, she kissed him, her lips soft and warm on his throat, and his heart stuttered. *Not like this. I won't survive if the first time is like this.* Everything was too raw, too real, and he'd had no chance to erect any defenses.

No, but plenty of time for other erections.

"I sense you changed your mind." Her voice was husky.

She moved against him, a thigh cradling his hip. Nothing coherent emerged from his mouth in response. There were so many reasons this was the wrong time, but he was beyond control for just as many. Jael told himself it was because it had been so many turns since he'd felt a woman like this—any man would react the same.

Then she kissed him, sweet and deep, all heat and luxurious languor. If anything, her dreamy slowness increased his fever. He made a sound against her mouth, one hand digging into her hip. He wasn't like this. *Oh, please. Please, just—*

And then she did, thank Mary. It was just right, exquisite, and he moved with her in short, frantic lunges. He was only barely aware that the thing was only half-done, that their clothing was still in the way, but he was mad enough not to care. He watched her eyes with hungry intensity and saw the moment she fell into it. That was all it took. They clung together, shivering, then reality set in.

"I highly suspect you're a witch," he said, falling back with a groan. "I don't usually forget to take my pants off."

She was smiling down at him, propped on an elbow. "I didn't mind. There's something to be said for efficiency."

"Stop. I'll die of shame."

"I don't think that's possible, especially for you. And even if you do, you'll get better."

From anyone else, the joke about his otherness would bother him, though he'd feign a laugh and act like it didn't matter. With her, it was all right because she knew the worst things about him and accepted him. It was better, somehow, that she could tease him.

You're not a person. You're a thing.

No, he told the scientist who raged in his brain. *I am not.*

"Awful creature. You've stolen my dignity." But he was smiling when he said it.

"I doubt you'll miss it," she answered.

"Possibly not, if it means more mornings like this one." Before he could say anything further, the door tone sounded.

"The Speaker is here, my queen. Silence commands your presence to discuss the next leg of your joint offensive." Tam's voice sounded like usual, as if he couldn't care less what had gone on in here overnight.

He's got ice in his veins. If this woman sent me out of her bed in favor of another, I'd break the place apart with my bare hands.

"I'll be there shortly. Offer him a drink."

"Or whatever Skullfaces eat," Jael said, as she switched off the intercom.

"I doubt we have anything he would find tempting. I'll take the first san-shower. I want you to come to Entropy with me, so you'll need to be quick."

"I've made do with a cupful of water and a chunk of pumice. I won't keep you waiting."

She smiled, and the brightness of her eyes wrapped a fist around his heart. There was an actual pinch as she turned away. The feeling scared the hell out of him. Jael ran his fingers through his hair once she disappeared from view.

What the hell.

Every instinct told him to get the frag away from her. She'd destroy him when she turned, as everyone did. *Don't hope. Just focus on finding a way out of this hellhole.* He clutched fast that voice of reason and pushed to his feet. He was poised to leave when she emerged, damp and lovely. It would seem odd if he retreated, so Jael pretended visceral terror didn't have him by the throat as he slid past her to take a lightning shower. As he washed up, he was haunted by the visual of water droplets beading on her skin, sliding down her shoulder, over the ridge of her collarbone, and—

Stop.

He shut that part of himself down by focusing on the meeting Silence had requested—commanded, rather. In Dred's shoes, he would shut down that peremptory behavior straightaway. To his surprise, she had left him in her quarters unattended; though she didn't have many personal belongings, she'd left them all in his care. The punishment for transgressions against the Dread Queen would be swift and fierce, no doubt, but maybe this was a taste. *Or maybe she trusts you.* Whatever the reason, Jael touched nothing of hers as he rinsed out his skivvies, then put them back on damp. From life on the march, he knew he'd soon get a fungus if he carried on that way, but maybe if he charmed the right person later, he could acquire a spare set of togs.

When he stepped out of her quarters, he found Dred arguing with Tam and Einar—but not about what he expected.

Neither man looked particularly put out at his appearance. In their shoes, he would've started the conversation with a ferocious punch. *They've been in here too long. Hm. But you were locked up for turns, too. If Bug solitary didn't make you grateful for every snippet of attention, nothing will.* In truth, that loneliness broke and reshaped him, and he was still figuring out where all the pieces went. Sometimes he fancied he could hear them jangling around his innards.

Tam was saying, "That's imprudent. I counsel against it."

"I don't care," Dred answered flatly.

Well, that's plain enough.

He propped himself against a wall to listen as Einar put in, "Seems to me, she's right, Tam. I know I don't have your brain for murky business, but if she constantly comes to heel like a bitch, then Silence will treat her like one."

Ah, so that's it.

He asked, "So you're refusing to go see Death's Handmaiden, then?"

"That's the size of it. She can pass the message along through her Speaker, or she can bloody well come to me herself." At this moment, the woman he'd spent the night with was nowhere in evidence. She was 100 percent the Dread Queen.

Her boots rang with imperious intent as she strode toward the hall. Unwilling to miss a moment, Jael followed her, and he knew the precise moment Tam realized he'd lost this argument. He wondered if it was the first one. A look over his shoulder caught Einar grinning, as if he found it entertaining to see the spymaster thwarted. Jael reckoned it didn't happen often, as the man was good at making others dance to his tune.

"I greet you, Speaker."

"You have kept me waiting. I am the Handmaiden's—"

"And *I* am the Dread Queen. In my presence, you will take a knee or lose your head."

The Skullface spluttered but under the glittering ferocity of her green eyes, he gave the demanded obeisance and stayed low. He quieted, seeming to realize her tenure as a supplicant was done. Jael enjoyed the hell out of the show, as did the rest of Queensland. The men rumbled with quiet pride, seeing the Speaker humbled.

When the hall quieted, she went on, "Pass a message to the Handmaiden. She may convey her desires through you, or come personally. No longer will I leap to her summons when there is so much preparation at hand. Does she mean to help me crush the Great Bear or not?"

"That is what she wished to discuss with you, my queen." The courtesy sounded as if it choked the Speaker, but he finally seemed to remember with whom he was dealing.

"The Handmaiden discusses nothing, as you well know. She conveys her wishes through you. If she has not done so, you may return when she has. Or do you have a message for me, after all, other than, *You must come to Entropy*."

A clash of wills followed, and Jael wasn't surprised when the Speaker dropped his eyes first. "I do. But it is for your ears only."

Jael's gaze swept the crowded hall and decided that was a wise precaution. Only a fool of a general revealed his whole battle strategy to every grunt in the army. Generally, it was best to parcel information out on a need-to-know basis, keeping the enemy from making use of spies and traitors.

Dred offered a regal nod. "Rise and whisper to me, Speaker. None but my most trusted advisors will be apprised." As she said that, her eyes met Jael's, and the intensity of the connection felt like a silent, secret message.

This time, I won't leave you in the dark.

Or maybe that was wishful thinking. She could be thinking about sex or food, and he happened to be standing in her line of sight. He'd never been as good at reading cues as he wished; sometimes he saw treachery where there was none, and at others, he failed to miss all the signs of imminent betrayal.

The hall fell quiet as the Speaker rose and whispered in her ear. Jael sensed the thundering hearts, the anticipation, because each man knew this scheme signified a change to everything inside Perdition. If the Dread Queen took down the Great Bear, Queensland would rise—in strength, prestige, and territory. Dred listened with a flat expression for long seconds.

Then she inclined her head. "It shall be done."

◀ 35 ▶

Water Damage

Tam cornered Ike after the meeting with Silence's emissary. He found the old man in one of the back corridors, carrying a box of tools. "Is there something you're not telling me?"

"Many things, I expect."

"This is the first time she's chosen to ignore my advice. I wonder why." He didn't know if he was angry or alarmed. It would be more difficult to ensure that his schemes and stratagems played out smoothly if he couldn't count on Dred's reactions anymore.

"I might've mentioned it would be better if she did her own thinking. That's all."

"Are you *trying* to undermine me? You know what's at stake here."

The old man smiled. "You don't know as much as you think you do. There are currents in motion that even you can't measure."

To his dismay, Tam had no idea what that meant. "Are you attempting to irritate me?"

"Is it working?"

In the end, Tam ended the conversation without learning

what Ike knew. He had no doubt it was something, as he'd learned to recognize the twinkle of secrecy in the other man's eyes. Yet it was no exaggerated claim when Ike said he was good at keeping information close. Which meant Tam wouldn't learn anything further, and persistence was pointless. Since he despised wasted effort, he nodded at Ike, quietly alarmed, and slipped away.

Thinking back, he decided things had changed when they recruited Jael. At some point, Tam had lost influence with Dred. He didn't know that the new fish was directly responsible, but that was the only change that he could identify. The calculating thing to do would be to discredit the other man somehow, making Dred think he wasn't to be trusted. After a few seconds of consideration, he discarded the notion. Ultimately, such discord would only hurt Queensland; better that he lost a little personal power than to create conflict where none was necessary. They already had enough to contend with, as he still hadn't spotted anyone paying undue attention to the Kitchen-mate.

The spy's smart, whoever it is.

He felt pleased that they'd thwarted the Great Bear's plan to attack on two fronts; Grigor must be frothing at the mouth by now. But the work wasn't over, not by a long shot. Their numbers wouldn't stand up to a straight fight this time. *Time to head behind enemy lines and see what I can learn.* Tam dodged the checkpoint and pulled himself into the ducts.

He was more careful than he ever had been. The stakes were higher this time, and detection meant more than his own death. At the halfway mark, he avoided a trap one of Grigor's men had left in the vents. If triggered, it would've drawn down multiple patrols. After he disarmed it, he regulated his breathing, refusing to let nerves get the best of him. Though he thrived on such challenges, that didn't make him devoid of fear.

If I die, I'll never finish what I've started.

The rest of Perdition would be astonished if they learned his ultimate goal . . . and then they'd laugh. But with the completion of each stage of his plan, he drew a little closer.

Dred's new independence might complicate matters, but he could work around it. The important thing was to assemble the personnel capable of pulling off the greatest trick in the history of the universe. *One step at a time.*

Tam paused. His nerves prickled in the darkness, dust stirring to coat his cheeks. There was a faint tang to the air, unfamiliar and unwelcome. It wasn't blood but . . . sweat. Which meant he wasn't alone up here. In perfect silence, he drew out a garrote he'd fashioned of old wire; he had affixed rudimentary metal handles on either side, so he didn't injure his palms. He lacked the strength for open combat, and he preferred maneuvering other people into doing his dirty work, but sometimes killing was necessary and unavoidable.

Tam clenched the weapon between his teeth and followed his nose. Grigor's sentry sprawled directly above the access vent, and by the smell of him, he'd been there long enough to grow complacent. *He must be watching the corridor below as well as the hidden access up here.* For a brute like Grigor, it was a surprisingly subtle countermeasure, but it wouldn't prevent Tam from accomplishing his aim; he'd be in and out of the Great Bear's territory before Grigor realized his guard was dead.

The angle wasn't ideal, as the victim was sitting sideways from Tam's current position. In the best scenario, he could approach from behind, leaving the target no chance to resist. But he'd make do. In these close quarters, his foe would be limited in how much he could fight back; there was little advantage to size and strength in here. Tam crept forward by millimeters, letting the other man's lethargy work to his advantage. He was almost on him when the enemy turned his head, so Tam lunged and got his garrote around the bastard's neck.

They wrestled for a few seconds, then Tam slammed the guard's head against the metal wall. That was a calculated risk. If there was anyone else posted nearby, he might hear the thump and come to investigate. *I'll deal with that when the time comes.* The impact dazed his target enough for him to close the loop, then he crossed the handles, applying all his upper-body strength to crushing the larynx. He ducked the flailing limbs, as asphyxiation wasn't a peaceful way to die, but gradually, the target's resistance slowed, then stilled entirely. Tam didn't let up for another minute, just in case it was a ruse. He checked the pulse, then pocketed his weapon.

Nobody's come to check. He must be the only guard.

Soon, that theory proved to be correct as he navigated the rest of the turns until he reached the best place to spy on the Great Bear. The stench was remarkable.

Angry voices echoed from below, making it difficult to sort specific words from the clamor. Eventually, Grigor boomed out, "Shut up, all of you."

His men weren't fool enough to argue, so they quieted. "We can't afford to wait," the man with the deep voice said.

"True," the Great Bear agreed. "With Priest gone and Abaddon fallen, we must take Queensland. If we give the bitch a chance to treat her wounded and strengthen her defenses, it will cost us."

"He who hesitates is lost," another man said. "If she's allowed to conclude the arrangement with Silence, we'll be annihilated and used in the Handmaiden's mad rituals."

"That sounds like cowardice," Grigor snarled. "We fight for glory, not from fear."

It bespoke wisdom and caution to Tam, but by the thumps and screams, the speaker received a beating anyway. Apparently it didn't pay to offer the Great Bear honesty. The punishment continued for a while, then the discussion resumed.

"How long before the weapons are ready?" Grigor demanded.

"Two days," the deep voice answered.

"Then that's when we strike."

Tam listened a little longer, but it was clear he wouldn't learn anything more pertinent, as they showed signs of arguing strategy for hours. If he delayed here too long, he risked someone's coming to relieve the dead sentry and sounding the alarm. *Time to go.* He had news to carry and work to do, before they surprised the Great Bear in the worst possible way.

ONCE Dred located her inner circle, she called an emergency meeting, but finding everyone took some time. Tam had disappeared, Ike was working on the Peacemaker unit, and Wills was obsessed with the maintenance bot. Only Jael and Einar were easy to locate, as they were talking in the hall—about what, she had no idea.

Not my concern, she told herself, though she hoped Jael wasn't bragging. *If he is, Einar will make him eat his fist.*

Dred found Tam returning from outside their territory boundaries, so she tapped a foot, waiting for his report. She remembered what Ike had said, and, for the first time, she wondered if she'd given the spymaster too much autonomy. Those thoughts fled when she heard his report.

"Two days. We have to work fast."

Tam nodded. "I'll round up the others."

"The meeting with the Speaker went better than I expected," Tam admitted, once everyone was assembled in Dred's quarters.

They weren't quite words of praise, yet Dred still knew a moment of sheer satisfaction. Since Tam had found her shaking, covered in blood in Artan's quarters, none of their conversations ever ended with his acknowledging she might know better than he did. Yet he didn't chide her over the stand she'd taken with the Speaker.

A good thing, too. He might've invented the Dread Queen, but I am her now, and I won't be manipulated, even by the man who made me.

The others seemed to be waiting for some conflict, but Tam only murmured, "I have some ideas on how to improve Silence's scheme."

Then he outlined them while Jael, Einar, and Ike listened.

She nodded in approval. "Genius. How soon can we be ready to move?"

"As soon as I get with Wills and check some schematics he downloaded from the maintenance bot."

R-17 had proven unexpectedly useful. He had tidbits of information not readily available about the station, information about hidden resources, and byways that had been sealed off. But with sufficient effort, they might be able to reclaim said passages for exclusive use by Queensland. That would give her so much leverage.

"Yes, we don't want to warn them that we're coming."

"You don't have to do this personally," Einar said. "I'm sure Tam and I could take some men, get the job done."

Unsure if she could explain, Dred tried nonetheless. "No, I need to be there. It's more meaningful, more insulting, if I lead the team. The Great Bear thinks women are weak, and—"

"I get it," Jael said. "It's a personal challenge and an articulation of your abilities."

She nodded. "Exactly."

Tam added, "We also need you present in order to claim full satisfaction of the compact with Silence. Death is all about the details."

"I hadn't thought of that," the big man said, visibly crestfallen.

His support against Tam earlier had meant a lot to her. She touched his arm and smiled. The small gesture lit him up like a laser beam; and when she turned, Jael's mouth was a flat, white line. She thought she understood why.

"You'll be on the squad," she assured him.

"I'm so pleased, queenie." He hadn't called her that in such a tone for quite a while.

So he's not worried about being left out. Though it seemed unlikely, maybe she'd pissed him off by touching Einar. She wouldn't have guessed that Jael was the territorial type, but . . . *Maybe he's jealous?* They hadn't talked about what sex meant between them, if it was a one-time stress release, never to be repeated, or something more. But currently she had more pressing concerns, like keeping Queensland from being annihilated and her men decimated and enslaved.

So she made a peace offering as a stopgap measure, until they had time to talk. "I've put you on the roster for the garden, by the way. You have a shift later today."

His gaze softened. "Thanks. I'd prefer that to patrolling if you can spare me."

"Not a problem." She turned to the other two men. "If possible, I'd like to set out first thing tomorrow. Is that possible?"

"Anything's possible," Tam answered. "Some things aren't probable."

She narrowed her eyes at him. "Don't do that."

The spymaster permitted himself a faint smile. "Yes, I think I can have everything in order by then."

I can't wait.

Tam was right; it was a brilliant plan, conceived by an evil genius. Dred shivered to think of going up against Silence in earnest. *Maybe it won't come to that.* A faint hope—the Handmaiden likely wouldn't rest until she owned the whole prison, until Entropy had swallowed everything else. That was the nature of death. What Grigor did for conquest, Silence did in the name of reverence and glorification. In the end, the results were about the same.

The rest of the day passed in preparation for the mission. That night, Jael didn't ask for a reprise, so Tam and Einar took their places in her quarters, as usual. In the morning, she was ready early and waiting at the checkpoint before any of the men arrived. They came one by one, and Dred took some satisfaction in that as Einar arrived last.

"You took too long with your hair, big man. You're late to the party."

"Worth waiting for, though." Einar ran his fingers through said locks.

"Definitely," she agreed.

The big man's axe was slung over his shoulder. Given their objective, she hoped he wouldn't need it. With Priest out of the way, travel was easier. Still, it was best to be safe, which was why she wore her chains. They moved with caution; Dred expected to see Grigor's soldiers out in force, but

Tam had mapped a good route, using remote corridors. That made the path circuitous, exactly what they needed. This plan depended on secrecy.

Tam fell into step with her. "I owe you an apology."

That surprised her. "Do you?"

"Yes. I've been treating you as if you haven't grown into your role. In the beginning, you were . . ." He hesitated. "Less than prepared."

"I was a mess," she said wryly. "You and Einar kept me together."

The spymaster shook his head. "You bore up, grace under pressure. From this point on, you have my word. I'll behave as an advisor, not your handler."

"You say that as if you have some experience with both," she noted.

He ignored that remark, as he did most personal matters. "Moving on. There may be defensive measures here. If Grigor has a brain, there will be."

"Guards?" If so, that could be a problem. If the men went missing, somebody would come to investigate and discover their handiwork soon enough to prevent the emergency she was trying to instigate.

"I don't know, but I'll scout before the rest of you get there." So saying, Tam set off ahead. His footsteps were near silent against the metal floor, overwritten by the ambient noises of the ship. Dred had gotten used to the low hum, so she didn't notice it except when she was listening hard. *Like now.*

She checked over one shoulder, seeing nothing amiss in the guttering lights or the pocked walls. A cascade of wires tumbled from a missing wall panel, and a number had been cut or stripped. *Jael's right. The ship can't go on indefinitely like this.* Which meant the Conglomerate had authorized a slow execution. Realizations like that made everything seem futile.

"How does it look?" she asked when Tam returned.

By her calculations, they were more than halfway to the target.

So far, so good.

The spymaster seemed elated. "No guards that I saw. No security immediately visible."

Immediately, she wondered why. "Would he not have identified this as a viable target?"

"It's possible he hasn't," Tam allowed. "Some men consider only the frontal assault. They lack the subtlety to envision the other ways the enemy can hurt them."

Dred called to the others, "Let's get this done quickly, in and out."

As she approached the ladder, she said, "There's a reason we need four people to make this work. Each of us must toggle the reset levers at the same time, then Tam will race to complete the programming."

Which will include bad code for Grigor's recyclers.

Dred climbed down as fast as the shaft allowed, then moved aside to make room for the others. She'd never been down to the recycling and sanitation chambers before. It was hotter down here, vents puffing steam into the room, so it felt damp on her skin. Much of the equipment was rusted, barely functional. Nobody had salvaged these rooms or stripped components; either they hadn't thought of it, or it was much too difficult to reach with Priest's fanatics butchering people in the corridors above.

But not anymore.

The computer that controlled the allotment of water was down here, protected by a number of fail-safes. Tam had a work-around for all of them, starting with the initial reset. She spotted the reset levers in each corner of the large room, impossible for less than four people to decide to work on the system. When it was a mining refinery, there had been that many people working down here easily, and a reset wouldn't have been undertaken lightly.

"Get to your corners. I'll count it down." Dred jogged to the northeast side of the room. "Everyone in position? On one." She checked and saw Tam, Einar, and Jael with hands on the power switches. "Five. Four. Three. Two. One!"

In sync, they clicked the levers down, and the computer

powered down. This would result in a minor hiccup in the power above; hopefully, the others would think it was a docking supply ship and head to Shantytown, or they'd blame it on Perdition's aging systems. Tam called out the count to thirty, then they powered the machine back on. As it ran through diagnostics, the spymaster sprinted for the console. He flipped the input pad out of the wall and went to work, fingers flying against the keys. Chains of code skimmed down the screen, errors flashing, then Tam swore, trying again.

"How we doing?" Einar asked.

Dred counted in her head, fifteen seconds left. Tam had no brain cells to spare for questions since he was racing the clock. If he didn't get the commands accepted by the time the computer completed the restart, system defaults would kick in. *Five seconds.* The screen flashed red again, and the spymaster spat something so filthy that the big man looked impressed. Just when she thought they'd be locked out, the screen gleamed blue, and new words appeared: NEW PROGRAM ACCEPTED. She cheered along with everyone else, then loped over to congratulate Tam on his amazing work.

"I couldn't cut off their water entirely," Tam said. "So I programmed the system to apportion rations suitable for a much smaller population. And I turned off their filters, so when they use it—"

"It doesn't get recycled. Comes back dirty." That was clever and revolting, she thought.

"They'll be sick as dogs before long," Jael predicted.

Dred pushed out a relieved breath. "That's the point. Grigor just has so many men . . . we have to weaken them before we take them on."

"Hyena tactics," he said.

She raised a brow. "You disapprove?"

"I support doing whatever's necessary to win. But will it occur to them to check the system?"

Tam nodded. "Yes, they'll come looking eventually. And Dred has a plan for dealing with them."

She grinned at that. It was rare that she could honestly

take credit for the ideas that created havoc for their enemies. But this was her brainchild, and she intended to make the most of it. "I think it will work."

"Definitely," Tam agreed. "Even if her plan fails, and they identify the problem, then reset the system, I doubt any of Grigor's men have the skill to change my command parameters."

"He tends to recruit brawn, not brain," Einar agreed.

Dred asked the big man, "Then how did you end up in Queensland?"

"The Great Bear took one look at Einar and kept walking. I suspect he was afraid the big man wouldn't be content to follow his orders." Tam beckoned as he headed for the door.

She laughed. "He doesn't follow *any* he doesn't like. As long as you can work around that, it's fine."

"I'm *right* here," Einar said in an aggrieved tone. He hefted his axe, following Tam out into the corridor.

Dred hurried after them. "Mission accomplished."

Jael was the last to leave, and she wondered at his scrutiny of the console. Before she could quicken her step to catch up to the other two, he put a hand on her arm. "How do you know he changed the programming in the way he claims?"

First Ike, now Jael.

She pitched her voice low. "I don't. But things have been a lot better for Tam since I removed Artan from power. People listen to him, and they treat him like he's important, these days. Why would he jeopardize that, particularly in such a visible way? I mean, if *we* end up with a shortage or people get sick from drinking tainted water, I'll know exactly who to blame, and Einar will cut his head off."

"You make a compelling argument." The flickering lights rendered his expression diabolical, slanting sparks across his skin.

She met his gaze. "Something's bothering you about all this."

"Yes. I just can't put my finger on what. Silence has all

these brilliant schemes, and she's just handing them to you. Doesn't that trouble you?"

"Yes," she admitted. "I suspect there's a knife hidden behind her back, but I have to play along until the game ends and hope I can dodge her final gambit."

"Hope's a bitch. Better to be prepared."

Dred completely agreed.

Guerilla Warfare

Jael wasn't sure if he was supposed to be pleased by this assignment. Two days ago, when Dred said she had a plan, Jael hadn't realized *he* would be executing it. Maybe it was a little flattering, but mostly, it was boring as hell, hunkered down in a side corridor near the recycling center with Einar and thirteen other Queenslanders, along with water bottles and packets of paste.

He'd been a little jealous at seeing her touch Einar, but she was sensitive to it, at least. This sharing business really wouldn't work if she was a bitch who got off on pitting her men against each other. Normally, he'd run at top speed in the other direction, faced with the prospect of sharing a woman, but Perdition had a way of eating into your resolve, making you willing to accept things you wouldn't otherwise.

Which is why I've got to get out of here.

He cocked his head, listening, then whispered to the big man, "We've got a group of four, incoming. Don't scare them off with your stench."

Einar growled back, "I smell like angels at sunrise."

"Dead ones," a small man cracked.

The rest of them snickered and nudged each other. These guys were about like the mercs he'd served with, not a psychotic break among them. Other territories were full of face-eating maniacs, so far as he'd seen, so he reckoned the reading she'd given him helped weed out the worst of the new fish.

Someone was asking, "How does he know how man—" when another inmate silenced him by clamping a hand over his mouth.

Jael settled to wait. As their footsteps drew closer, he leaned out to get the first glimpse of the incoming patrol. *Einar wasn't kidding when he said Grigor went for brawn.* These four men all stood taller than two meters, each as broad through chest and shoulders as the big man. Most had scars but few so colorful as the ones Einar possessed. Jael signaled to his team, but at least half of them looked totally blank regarding the hand signals. Fortunately, Einar understood, and he was confident the two of them could take these four, no matter how big they were, so long as the rest of his squad didn't actively get in their way.

A deep voice said, "I thought I saw something move."

"You're imagining things."

"Might've been a rodent," another said.

"I hate those fraggin' things. They—"

But he didn't get to finish his thought because Jael was on him. He went with a knife hand to the throat, followed by a clean takedown. Once he had the soldier on the ground, he rammed an elbow in his face. The blood from his smashed nose would disorient him. He took a couple of wild swings—and they were strong hits—but he'd been hurt much worse for much longer. He shook them off and finished the piker with a half-closed fist to the temple.

Einar had the sense not to swing his axe. Instead, he had a jagged blade in his hand, punching it rapidly into the smaller man's sternum. The two closest Queenslanders laid into the remaining men and took them out; they were messy deaths, full of mob killing, with shoving and stomping and shivs slashing wildly. The corridor was a bloody smear by the time Grigor's soldiers stopped moving.

"I'll get this hauled away," the big man said.

Jael turned to the others. "Head down to the recycling center, see if you can find a mop and bucket. We don't want to leave any evidence for the next group."

"How many more patrols will he send?" someone asked.

He shrugged. "Hard to say. I suspect one or two smaller groups, tops, before Grigor deploys a larger squad to wipe out whoever's picking off his men. Hope you lot like paste because we'll be here awhile."

There was a collective groan, but most of the Queenslanders didn't look too displeased with the mission. They got to lie in wait, and there was the chance of constant, queen-sanctioned violence. To men who had been locked up for being unable to control their base natures, that was a good day. As for him, if you swapped out this rusty, grim-lit corridor for a rocky hillside or a muddy field, he'd done this job countless times before.

While the men cleaned up the signs from the battle as best they could, he helped Einar lug away the corpses. Jael bent and slung a body over his shoulder, marveling at the deadweight. Corpses always felt heavier than any other burden, he thought, of the same relative size and weight. Then he grabbed another, before realizing he'd surprised the other Queenslanders. A few men whispered, as he didn't *look* this strong. Ignoring them, Jael followed Einar, who always seemed to know where all the chutes were located.

"Keep this up, and I'll start calling you the undertaker," he joked.

"I could do worse."

They dumped the bodies in front of the chute, then the big man stuffed them down. A pneumatic whir carried them away, one by one, leaving only a red smear on the floor. Einar rubbed at it with his boots until it was more grungy than distinct. Jael lifted his chin to indicate he thought it was enough.

"They're not likely to be skilled investigators," he observed on the return.

"They're brain-dead shit birds."

"You've a poetic nature, you know that? I rather like you, undertaker. Didn't think I would . . . but here we are."

"You're not a complete wart on a toad's arse, either," the big man muttered.

"I feel a hug coming on. Should we?"

"I'd rather let you cut my face off with this axe." Einar hefted the weapon hanging over his shoulder.

"Could do that, too, I suppose. That couldn't make it worse." He gestured to indicate the whole extreme ugliness Einar had going on.

Jael could've dodged the punch, but he reckoned he deserved it. So the hit landed on his ribs and rearranged some bones. They snapped back into place; sometimes there was a deep internal itch when the healing started. He stopped to let the work complete, then realized the other men were gaping at him.

"What?" he demanded.

"Nobody roughhouses with Einar, unless they're looking for a broken neck."

"I'm tougher than I look," he said coldly. "There's a reason the Dread Queen made me her champion."

"No doubt," another Queenslander said hastily.

He dragged the other man off to call him names in private, but Jael heard every word. "There's something off about that one. Try not to be stupider than you can help, all right? I don't want to find somebody else to watch my back while I'm asleep. Keep mouthing off to the queen's man, though, and I'll have to, won't I?"

"Sorry, wasn't thinking."

That small exchange put a damper on everyone's mood, so the team sat in silence while they waited for Grigor to realize there was a problem. Hours turned into watches, as the men wearied. Jael took the first shift; frankly, he would prefer *not* to sleep with so many inmates all around him.

Somebody might take a mind to stick a knife between his ribs, and then, well. Best not to tempt fate.

By his calculations, it was ten hours before they sent a second party to figure out where the first group had gone. They must be thirsty up in Grigor's territory, too. This time, there were eight soldiers, all big bruisers, like the first four. He counted their footfalls to calculate how far away they were, then he whispered the ETA to Einar.

"Ready for some action?" the big man asked the team.

"More than. I sit here any longer, my ass will be rooted to the floor."

"Pair up," Jael said. "I need you fighting together, no mob rules this time. Pick a target, take him down together."

"But we outnumber them," a Queenslander protested.

"They're bigger. Don't ever underestimate your opponent. That gives him the advantage from the jump, and it doesn't always matter how many people you've got."

Einar said, "Agreed. Look sharp. We have incoming in thirty seconds or so."

Jael eyed the other man with surprised approval. When he'd given him the estimate, he didn't realize he was still counting down. Soon, the rest of the men could hear the approaching combatants. They were moving fast, too, all but running, so their treads came in heavy thumps. He swung out fast enough to surprise the leader, landing a kick in the enemy's chest.

This one had some combat experience, as he checked two of Jael's blows, but he glimpsed the flash of pain that came on impact. He was strong enough that even a block delivered enough damage to fracture a forearm. Jael speeded up his strikes, hands becoming a blur as he went at the leader. The other man couldn't keep up; and Jael snared his wrist. Pop and twist—the bone snapped clean in two as he wrenched it behind the brute's back. He combined the move with another kick; this one rocked the other man's legs out from under him. Jael ended the fight with a boot to the throat, crushing his enemy's larynx. He was trying to avoid a bloody mess, but around him, other men didn't share the same concern.

A Queenslander dropped, taking a knife in the kidneys; he wasn't dead yet, but he might as well be. *No recovering from that.* Despite his orders, the men weren't fighting in an organized or unified fashion. Not their fault, really; they'd never drilled. *These are prisoners, not soldiers. They're used to mixing it up in riots, not orchestrating strategy.* Still, that lack was costing them.

Another Queenslander fell, and Einar pushed forward to fill the gap. Jael shoved forward beside him, scowling as blood spattered on him from someone else's knife. He curled his fingers around his blade and punched forward, shoving the knife through his foe's sternum. In an efficient motion, he pulled it back, kicked the man out of his way, and went for the next victim. He raked the blade across the man's eyes, then stabbed him up through the chin.

"Wish I had room to move my axe," Einar bitched, as he hauled back to deliver a killing blow. The weight of his fist crushed the man's lip, more blood spewed out, along with a mess of teeth. Fortunately, he wouldn't live to suffer the loss.

When the last body fell, they were down three men, better than Grigor's men should've done, frankly. "This is a hell of a mess. Clean it up."

"Why should we?"

His jaw clenched. "Because I'll kill you if you say another word. Try me."

"Sorry. I was just asking," the man muttered.

Einar's quick nod said he understood the point of sending them to dispose of their fellows; if shoving corpses down the chute didn't make the idiots more cautious in the next engagement, then they were dumb enough to deserve to die.

"How long will we be here?" one of the men asked.

He glanced at Einar, wondering if he knew. "Until the Dread Queen calls us back."

"What if she never does?" the man persisted.

Jael snapped, "Then we fight here until we die."

"Until we're overrun," the big man agreed. "It's not for us to question."

He suspected it wouldn't be much longer. If Dred was right, Grigor's men would soon be too drunk or too dehydrated to find their way down to the recycling center. Rebellion would begin within his territory, and then—only then—would the Dread Queen strike. All told, it was a cunning plan, well crafted and layered. He looked forward to executing it, step by step, and seeing Dred's enemies brought low. At some point, this damned microwar had become more important to him than scouting possible escape routes.

In time, he told himself.

"I always wanted to hunt a Great Bear," he told Einar conversationally.

◄ 37 ►

Tooth and Claw

Using Tam as a messenger, Dred recalled the men from their post outside the recycling center. They looked grubby as hell when they returned, and they'd lost five men. The posting took a full day, but fortunately, it didn't take long for dehydration to set in. Three days without water entirely would kill the Great Bear and all his men, but the ship couldn't be programmed to kill. So dirty water would weaken them, then the lights would go out, step two in the plan to diminish and demoralize the enemy.

Her heart didn't settle until she found Jael and Einar in the crowd, then she despised herself for feeling relieved. Attachments didn't prosper in a place like this.

"How many did you kill?" she asked, as they reached her.

"Close to fifty," the big man answered.

"Good work."

"The last batch were ill," Jael added. "It was mercy to put them down."

"Then the plan's working." It also meant she needed to set a permanent guard down there, as somebody else might be capable of duplicating Tam's success. "That's all for now. Go find some real food and get some rest."

Some would undoubtedly call it superstitious, but after she finished with Einar and Jael, she went in search of Wills, who was fiddling with R-17. He scowled at her interruption. "What do you want?"

"I'd like you to do a reading for me, regarding the outcome of the battle against Grigor."

Wills sobered at once. "Of course. I've had troubling dreams, my queen."

Under her watchful eye, he drew out his bones and rolled them in his palms to warm them, then he sliced his arms to lubricate them in his own blood. Not for the first time, Dred wondered how he had come to his precise ritual. She didn't look away, even when he spat on the mixture, then slicked it over the surface of the bones until they looked like writhing maggots. Blinking hard, she looked again; and they were just bones rattling together.

He tossed them to the floor and squatted over them. Though she could discern no pattern in the mess, he paled, the salt-and-pepper bristles on his jaw standing out in contrast. "Victory requires a life for a life, my queen, and there remains one disloyal to you in his heart, watching and waiting."

Her fingers curled into fists. "Does that mean for every one of theirs we kill, someone here will die? And can you tell me the name of this traitor?"

Hoping to glean more, Dred slipped into second sight, but as ever, Wills burned a sickly yellow all the way through, no shades or striations. It was always the same when he read for her, though his colors returned to normal once the foretelling died away. She opened her eyes to see him shaking his head.

"Names and faces are not given for me to know."

"That would be too easy," she muttered.

"Have a care," he warned. "I saw long ago . . . this may cost more than you care to pay."

Dred nodded. "Thanks, Wills. I'll keep it in mind."

She could tell by his expression that he realized she wouldn't alter course. Even if the body count was insanely high, she couldn't back off, not when she was one or two moves away from clearing the board and claiming the Great Bear's assets. With Silence's teeth on her neck, there was no other path open to her. Unsettled, she left the bone-reader to tidy up the mess and return to tinkering with the maintenance bot.

"Did you learn anything useful?" Tam asked, as she joined the meal queue.

"You know how his predictions go. He prognosticates doom, as usual."

"I'd hoped he might sing a different tune. Things are proceeding exactly as we planned."

She accepted a bowl of food, then followed the spymaster to a table. Tam ate as efficiently as he did everything else, but with better manners than most men. He didn't do the prison yard hunch, either, with his arms framed around his tray and his body tensed to stab anyone who reached for his bowl.

"You're an enigma," she said. "I wonder how you ended up here."

"Are you asking, my queen, or demanding?" His voice was wooden, like an old staircase that led down into darkness, and about as safe.

"Neither." She ate a few bites in speculative silence.

Tam's face was cold and hard in profile. "If it matters, I don't regret a single thing I did that landed me here. And I'd do it all again."

"You don't have normal prison manners."

"This was my first stop once I was taken into custody."

That surprised her. Dred put down her spoon, eyeing him with pure curiosity. "No preliminary holding facility? No trial?"

"That's correct."

"Is that even legal?"

"Not entirely, but it was part of a larger agreement. I'm satisfied." By his abortive gesture, she guessed he was done talking about the past.

"Will you tell me the story someday?"

"It's not mine to share." His dark eyes went distant.

"I understand." And it wasn't a Dread Queen inquiry, either.

The queen cared only for the state of her territory, nothing for the feelings of those who dwelled within it. In Perdition, the greatest monsters clawed their way to the top of the heap. She wasn't sure what it said about her that she'd let Tam plant her on the scrap-metal throne. Dred slanted a look at the horrific thing, squatting at the far end of the hall. There had been an inmate who Artan kept chained at the bottom of it like a dog. He'd eaten, slept, and defecated, right there, until he ceased to be amusing, then he died slowly.

"How long has it been since you slept?" he asked.

She started, covering a guilty look. "How did you know?"

"You think I don't know when someone's pretending?"

Dred hated the thought of his listening to her toss and turn. They never talked once they went to bed; it was a peculiar and functional relationship. Tam was like obsidian, utterly impenetrable; and he kept his own counsel, except as pertained to the campaign. That was safest, but at the moment, she wanted more from him, if only to disprove the doubts Ike had planted. She wanted to believe Tam valued their association, superficial though it might be, but he wasn't the sort of man to offer a centimeter more than he must.

"I can't remember," she admitted. "It's been days, though, I think. It's hard for me to unwind with everything—"

"Go. Get some rest, or you'll be useless later." It was a practical suggestion, not an order, so she didn't bristle.

Sighing, she pushed away from the table. "Very well. Einar will probably be crashed out, too, so at least I'll have company."

"There is that." Tam nodded in farewell.

She turned and strode toward the corridor leading to the dormitories. Queensland would become difficult to hold, too much territory and not enough bodies to guard it, unless something shifted between now and the end of the conflict with Grigor. *Maybe the supply ship will return soon. I could bolster our numbers that way.* But unlike Artan, she didn't recruit en masse, taking everyone capable of stumbling after her. If a man didn't hold up to close scrutiny, she let him be; it made Queensland easier to govern. Slowly, she had been weeding out Artan's original recruits, subtly encouraging them to challenge one another during the blood-sport matches.

Between Priest and Grigor, we haven't needed them lately to keep the men in check.

She was deep in thought as she rounded the corner toward her quarters. Consequently, her reflexes were slow—and the bastard nearly sank his knife into her spine. She wheeled on the traitor, livid, as his blade skimmed sideways over her ribs. Blood welled, but she could tell it was a shallow cut, just another scar for the collection. There was no time to unlash her chains, but even with a knife in his hands, she thought she was a match for him.

Evidently, he agreed because he turned to run. Dred came at his back, snapping a kick that rocked him forward onto his knees. Then she slammed a spiked boot into the back of his thigh, effectively crippling him. She backhanded him across the face, and while he was still dazed, she dragged him back to the hall, leaving a blood trail behind. It was impossible that she didn't even know this man's name, but he was a relative newcomer to her territory, fresh off the ship just before Jael's arrival.

"Who knows this scum?" she called in furious tones.

Tentatively, a young man came forward. It took her a few seconds, but she placed him. Zediah, who worked as much as possible in the gardens. "His name's Niles, my queen."

"Well, Niles just tried to assassinate me."

"Dumb shit," someone muttered.

Another shook his head. "Imagine, trying to take the Dread Queen on your own."

"On your knees," she bit out.

The scrape across her back was burning like mad. *If the cowardly piece of shit poisoned me*—She cut the thought. Regardless, he had to die in spectacular fashion, and this time, she didn't look for Tam. She'd killed enough men to know how to make a show of it.

"Shall we see what a traitor's blood looks like?" she asked the Queenslanders.

"Aye!" they roared back.

Taking the man's knife, she bent, held him by the hair like an animal to be slaughtered, and gutted him, so a red pool spread beneath. The men howled their approval as the body fell. By the time Tam made his way over to her, she had dropped the weapon.

"Einar didn't wake?"

"I wasn't close enough to the dormitories for him to hear. Though Niles was a cowardly dog, he chose a good, isolated spot to strike."

Wills joined them a few moments later. "You ferreted him out, my queen. Well done."

Relief spread through her. *The traitor he's been predicting all along, unmasked at last.* Part of her had feared it would be Jael.

"I did little enough. He simply wasn't as skilled as he thought."

"Still," Tam said, "it means we can proceed with no impediments."

She nodded. "Time to finish this."

◄ 38 ►

Dying of the Light

"You positive you know where we're going?" Jael asked Tam.

"Reasonably sure."

They were trying a two-pronged attack—tainted water and full darkness—against Grigor. Jael's team was heading down into the bowels of the ship for some prelim work; he hoped they didn't run afoul of Katur's aliens. The last thing Queensland needed was another conflict, just before this one was to be settled. Tam seemed to think as long as they were respectful, there should be no problems.

"Why are we taking such a small party?"

"Because we're not staying to kill. Once we accomplish our task down below, we're regrouping to join Dred for the final assault."

Ah, got it.

Their goal was quiet efficiency, not mass slaughter. Once they cut the power, the mayhem would begin. Jael followed as the others went to the shafts and headed down. Tam and Martine, along with Jael, made up the team. The other two were quiet as they climbed, none of Martine's usual wit. The enemy had to be feeling the pressure of constant watches, constant patrols, by now, and the Great Bear wouldn't take such strikes lying down; if he could muster any soldiers fit to fight, they'd soon be knocking at Queensland's figurative gates.

"Tam, why did she pick us for this?" Martine wanted to know.

"Because we have the best chance of surviving it."

Now that's reassuring.

The other man went on, "And you apparently told her you want more responsibility."

Jael laughed at that. "That'll teach you to volunteer, bright eyes."

"Shut up," Martine muttered.

The rest of the way, they skulked in the shadows, cautious not to engage other patrols. Tam was an expert at finding places to hide, then barely seeming to breathe while enemies tromped past. Martine wasn't bad either, which made Jael curious. She cut him a look over one shoulder that she wasn't interested in conversation.

Just as well, stick to business.

He heard the sibilant sounds of an alien tongue long before they stepped into normal auditory range. From what he could tell, a group from the Warren was headed this way. Jael glanced at Tam, whispering, "How do you want to handle it?"

"This way," the spymaster said.

They had just dodged around the corner and stepped into a storage closet when he detected the sound of pursuit. Martine cocked her head. "They're saying they can smell us."

"You speak the language?" he asked, impressed.

"Enough to get by. It's helpful when you travel a lot . . . though not so much lately."

Jael lifted his chin and smiled to indicate he thought that was funny. So many inmates had let incarceration steal their senses of humor—or maybe they just never had one. Tam raised a hand, quieting them, and he stilled in response, head tilted to catch any movements nearby. *Surely Dred didn't want us to delay the mission inevitably.* But the spymaster wouldn't permit them to kill a single soul down in the Warren, which made traversing it difficult.

At that point, Tam apparently decided it was smarter to acknowledge the aliens. He stepped out with both hands visible, and said, "Katur has given me permission to pass through his territory. Feel free to send word . . . I'm the one who saved Keelah."

The scouting party discussed among themselves while Martine translated. "They're saying all humans look alike, but that they think they've smelled Tam before. Now they're trying to decide what to do about us."

"This isn't a hostile incursion," Tam said quietly. "We're passing through to strike at the Great Bear, and his defeat will make life a great deal safer for your people."

Jael knew that much to be true, as Grigor's men hunted aliens for sport. His heart was actually pounding, not because he feared they couldn't defeat these creatures, but in anticipation of disobeying the Dread Queen. She wouldn't like doing so, but protocol demanded punishment for failure, if they had to kill counter to her orders. and he couldn't submit while she delivered it. Just . . . it was so much better, all around, if this ended without bloodshed.

Finally, the alien scout leader said in universal, "You have ten minutes. If you aren't gone by then, we'll hunt you down."

"Thank you. Give my best to Katur and Keelah." Tam's tone was almost courtly.

Once the aliens moved off, Martine asked, "Will that be long enough?"

"Hope so. We're going down here." Tam stepped over to the nearest hatch and started his descent. This was lower than even the normal maintenance shafts.

What the hell is below the Warren?

Soon, Jael had his answer.

This was the sheer guts of the ship, a tangle of sparking wires and metal pylons. It formed the framework for everything else, attaching to the walls that supported the upper levels. Martine looked fascinated; she started forward, but Tam checked her.

"Careful. Things are in bad repair down here. Those are live wires, ungrounded."

"I'm starting to see why you need me," Jael said.

Tam flicked him a look of veiled perplexity. "I wish *I* did. Over there, that section of the grid keeps the power on in Grigor's territory. If you unplug them, they drop into the dark. But to get there, you have to cross that—"

"And a normal man would die before he reached the panel since the charged metal floor would fry anyone else." He didn't realize he'd spoken so freely of his ability until Martine aimed a speculative look at him.

Oops. Guess she knows I don't consider myself normal. Or a man, by most definitions.

"You think you can live through that?" she asked.

Jael didn't bother replying. He hated electricity; it screwed with his coordination and his ability to think clearly, plus it made him smell like roasting meat. The scientists had tried to train him with electroshocks as well as dream therapy. Neither proved useful in modifying his behavior. They'd stamped his file with a big red REJ, citing the fact that he was ungovernable. It was clearly that he must be damaged, or he wouldn't be considering this task.

"If you wait, I can try to move the wires," Tam said. "When I scouted earlier, they weren't touching the floor. They must've shifted."

He nodded. Tremors weren't uncommon. Sometimes the ship ran into debris that had fallen off the ship over the turns in orbit. If prisoners didn't have so much to worry about inside, they might fret about a potential hull breach. For now, he'd focus on getting this done for Dred. It must be important if she'd pulled him off the front lines.

"If I fall," he said to Tam, "don't come after me."

"*I* didn't plan to," Martine muttered.

The spymaster nodded. "Noted. Are you clear on which wires to disconnect?"

"You pointed out the section. But how many?"

"All of them within that white square, outlined in red. Try not to rip them, however, or it will be difficult to get the power back on. Silence won't be happy if we deliver her new territory, complete with permanent blackout."

"You sure?" the woman asked. "Death might enjoy the dark."

Tam seemed amused. "I'd rather not deal with an invasion straightaway. We need time to work out the best way to defend the additional ground we've gained, how best to use it, too."

Martine shrugged. "That's for you to worry about, not me. I'm here to guard the door, right? And listen to what the aliens are saying as they approach."

"Exactly."

"Hope you're fast," she said. "I get the feeling Katur's people won't be generous in their countdown."

She was likely right about that. So no more talk, no more fragging around.

Bracing himself, Jael ignored the other two and leapt toward the panel on the far wall. *Damn.* There wasn't enough space for him to get a running start, so he landed square in the shock field. It didn't matter how much he prepared mentally, though; the fierce, white-hot lightning zinging through his body made him dizzy—and it hurt *so bad*. The pain was constant, shooting up through the soles of his boots, along his calves, and into his knees. His legs wobbled as his whole body heated. He pressed forward with steps so careful they were clumsy.

Wonder how I look to them, if I'm glowing or sparking.

As if from a distance, he heard Tam say, "You're doing great, nearly there."

His eyes felt queer, melted, and he couldn't see very well anymore. Smoke poured off the top of his head. He stepped off the live wires in front of the panel, staggered against the wall. That hurt, too, as his palms were bright red, cracked, and peeling. His arms showed black in spots, and he could only imagine how his feet looked.

"Dear Mary," Martine breathed. "How's he still moving?"

He would've made a joke but his lips were fused. *The things I do for a pretty girl.* Tam didn't say anything about hurrying, probably because he understood Jael lacked the coordination to finish the job just yet. His body kicked in then, attacking the damage with efficient ferocity. Martine gasped, rubbing her eyes like she might be hallucinating. By the time his hands regenerated enough for him to finish the job, she was pestering Tam for more information. To his credit, the spymaster said nothing though that would be because he didn't know.

Jael had no idea why he was so sure, but he believed that Dred hadn't told Tam a damned thing. She'd kept his secret, even from her two closest confidantes. Jael unplugged the wires one by one, careful not to tear them and leaving the metal connectors in place for future use. At last he turned, still a white-hot ball of agony. Burns took a long time to heal, relative to other injuries, and now he had to face it again.

"You two go on ahead," he said thickly. "I need some time."

Tam shook his head, looking skeptical. "My orders are to stay with you."

No wonder he looks doubtful. I must look like death itself.

"It's going to take me longer than they gave for me to recover enough to get out of here." Technically, they were under the Warren, not in Katur's territory, so maybe as long as they stayed down here, the aliens wouldn't attack. *Mary, this hurts.*

The other man made himself comfortable. "Recover? I'll believe that when I see it."

Martine stared at him. "If you think I'm going anywhere without some answers, you're as crazy as you are pretty."

Since he was a crisped monster right then, Jael appreciated her pretense at flirtation. But he suspected the other two didn't understand. "If I try to cross now, I'll be incapacitated. I have to heal enough to make it back across. It could be hours."

"Then settle in," Tam said. "Take however long you need. We're not leaving."

"Why?"

Martine answered, "Dred's orders. But look, even without them, I wouldn't bail. You need me to kick some alien ass if they venture down here looking for us."

That was a stupid argument. "They couldn't get to me without frying."

"They have missile weapons," Tam pointed out. "It's my hope, however, that they will check in with Katur and that he'll grant his blessing to our expedition."

Shit. Jael gave up trying to get them to abandon him, an odd feeling. People had never proven reluctant to cut him loose before—and they were usually *more* eager to get away, once they learned how inhuman he was. He should be troubled about Martine's knowing the truth, as she had little reason to wish him well. It made no sense that he'd encounter loyalty like this inside Perdition, where the worst of humanity was imprisoned.

But maybe there are a few of the best, too.

◄ 39 ►

Beyond Madness

The lights went out on schedule.

Dred commanded all able-bodied men for this final run at Grigor. Between the water and the lack of light, his men should be weak and disoriented. Add in her forces and the ones led by Silence—the Handmaiden was on hand with garrotes and knives, ready to deal some death—and the Great Bear's days were numbered. With no power, it was eerily silent in the Korolévstvo, not even the low hum that meant the ship was functioning.

"Lights up," she ordered.

Nearby, Silence gave the same command to her men.

As one, they donned the mining helmets they'd salvaged from Priest's hoard. That would make it possible to finish this without decimating the Queensland or Entropy populations. Not that she'd weep overmuch if some of her men stabbed Silence's people; and Dred imagined the Handmaiden felt the same way. Talk about a precarious alliance.

With hundreds of thin beams of light at her back, she led the march on the Great Bear. The first checkpoint was deserted, which spoke well of Tam's plan with the water. It was cruel and underhanded, not a warrior's strategy at all. But she couldn't afford to fight fair, not when Grigor had so many more soldiers. As she pushed closer to the Korolévstvo, the stench swelled to awful proportions, mingling feces and urine with the stale sweat of sickness and the sweet stink of decay. Dred covered her nose with one hand and pressed on. They crossed two more abandoned checkpoints, and she started to wonder just how bad it had gotten. Closer to the hub of the territory, she found the first corpses. Dred bent to examine them, shining her light across the cold, pallid skin.

"Head wound," Einar said. "Bled like a stuck animal before he died."

The Speaker stepped up beside her, translating for Silence. "This is a good omen . . . Death strides before us, clearing our path."

That was an impressive, overflowing bucket of crazy, so she just inclined her head and stepped over the corpses. "Stay sharp. I doubt they're all dead."

"We couldn't be so lucky," Einar said.

They'd left Wills and Ike to man the automated defenses, along with a minimal defense crew. Those who had stayed behind had no taste for personal violence; they were killers of another stripe, who preferred long-distance weapons or poisons. As she moved into the heart of darkness, she wondered where Jael and Tam were. They had orders to regroup with the main force as soon as they finished down below. It seemed like they ought to be here by now.

Before curiosity could blossom into concern, she stepped into what must be Grigor's great hall. She skimmed her light around the room with countless men at her back doing the same; the result was disconcerting, multiple streams of light crisscrossing the darkness and giving staccato impressions. Immediately, she readied her chains.

"Give me room," she said, starting forward.

A brawl was ongoing across the way, draped in darkness. Tam had said cutting the lights qualified as a psychological weapon to terrorize and demoralize their foes. She hadn't been sure it would work that way, but these men had already been pushed to the breaking point by the dirty water and unexpected illness. Now they had no reason to try to restrain their savage natures. Fragments of argument reached her, along with the muffled thump of fists on palms, panting breaths, and moans of pain. From this distance, in the broken light, it was impossible to count how many there were, but they were oblivious, drowning in anger.

The Speaker said, "These are the dregs he left behind. We will not find Grigor here."

"Then we cut through them," she answered grimly. "For Queensland!"

The men rushed in a roar, wading into the brawl with an enthusiasm that nearly deafened her. Since her chains hurt her own people as much as the enemy when she fought in a tight cluster, Dred stood away from the melee, catching the enemies who tried to flee. One of Grigor's soldiers broke from the scrum and stumbled toward her; she planted her feet and lashed her chains, hooking them around his knees. One tug, and he went flying. She finished him with twin, artistic lashes, but it was nothing to be proud of—the man was thin and sick, sclera showing yellow in the thin beam from her helmet.

The whole room was a blur of misery and violence. *This was probably what the Conglomerate had in mind, but I suspect they imagined it would happen sooner.* There was an awful beauty in Einar scything through his enemies. He gave no quarter, and the broad swing of his deadly axe demanded the broad clearance his allies offered. Nobody fought near him; they didn't dare. Even among Grigor's brutes, he towered head and shoulders above the rest. He was a juggernaut of wrath, dealing destruction to the enemies who rushed him from all sides.

Dred picked off another coward, this time breaking his neck with a skilled twirl of her chains. His body flew forward, then dropped, and a few Queenslanders cheered. They didn't need to see her dive into the melee to believe she could hold her own. She'd carried them to this point, but sometimes a queen had to step back and open her hands. When they won the day, the Queenslanders would've earned their revels, and they'd appreciate the victory more, feel more invested in the new territory. These lessons, she'd absorbed from Tam without realizing he had been teaching her statecraft.

Who the hell are you, spymaster? More to the point, where *the hell are you?*

Dred glanced over her shoulder and was unnerved to find the Speaker standing just behind her, just outside her peripheral vision. Trying not to be obvious about it, she angled her stance. If he thought he'd murder her during the battle and blame the enemy, well. She put her back to the wall, just in case. Silence fought like a shadow, slipping from victim to victim with her garrote. It shouldn't be possible to execute men with such surgical precision in such a mess, but the Handmaiden was like Death itself, hardly visible between the moving lattice of lights. Only her long gray hair showed when she moved, like the dingy shroud on a corpse come back from the netherworld to reap men's souls.

Shaking her head at the thought, she looked for Einar again, then realized he was in trouble. Her heart in her throat, she pushed forward, but there were too many bodies between him and her, too many allies. She lashed out with her chains, but if she killed a bunch of her own men while striving to reach the big man, she'd face a rebellion, so her movements were abortive, fruitless. Still, she shoved and jabbed with a small blade, driving deeper into the mob. Einar had come too deep alone, and the remaining enemies backed him toward the wall. There were eight of them, at least, focused on taking down the most obvious threat.

"Come at me!" she shouted. "Think how pleased Grigor will be when you bring him the Dread Queen's head."

Four of his foes turned, started pushing toward her. *That's right. This way.* It might be tough to take out four men in such close quarters, with Queenslanders jostling her from all sides, fighting, grunting, spitting, and bleeding. *I'll manage. I have to.*

"No," the big man roared.

Like a berserker, he wheeled into the fight, leaving himself open to knives and fists and shards of metal. The idea that she'd take the blows for him clearly maddened him, drove all ideas of caution and self-preservation out of his head. All around her, the scrum tightened so that she could hardly move her shoulders, let alone breathe. More bodies surged between them; she couldn't even see Einar anymore.

"Help Einar," she ordered.

But her words were lost in the chaos of the fight, in whirling darkness. A few men tried to find him, but they couldn't spot him, either. Bodies surged, a flurry of blows and the unearthly screams of men dying in agony. Reckless, she lashed at anyone who got in her way, whether they were wearing a light helmet or not, and the crowd parted. The big man took two blades in the stomach as she watched, helpless, only three meters away. Two more sank into him, then Grigor's men frenzied, stabbing, kicking, punching. Einar dropped to his knees. She spun her chains and yanked one of them away, snapped them free and stunned another.

"To me!" she shouted.

The Queenslanders rallied, fighting the enemies who had focused on the big man. One by one, they died, and the tide turned. That broke the enemy's will, so that Silence's people surged in and executed them, little resistance left. She pushed forward and knelt beside the big man, whose breathing sounded awful and liquid. *Blood in his lungs. Blood everywhere.* In the dark, it gleamed nearly black on his skin, and he was covered in it. She put her hands over his wounds—or she tried—but there were too many.

"Get me some bandages."

Einar fell back onto his elbows, too weak to kneel. His eyes reflected like winter ice, set in an incredibly ugly face. Somehow, he mustered the strength to cover her hands with his own. "Bandages won't help, and there's no surgeon to patch me up. Do the right thing, my queen."

Tears knotted her throat, burned in the back of her eyes, but the Dread Queen wouldn't let them fall. Dred wished she had the freedom to weep, but all eyes were on her, and she still had to finish this with the Great Bear. She couldn't afford to show weakness.

"If you prefer," she said quietly.

Einar managed a quick nod. "Better to have it done swiftly . . . and by your hands. It's impossible for me to imagine a better end than this."

"Picture the last beautiful thing you saw," she whispered.

The big man closed his eyes, blood trickling past his lips as he said, "I am."

"Good-bye, my friend."

As she sank her blade into his chest, he opened his pale blue eyes for the last time and whispered, "It's you. It's always been you."

He closed his eyes and saw my face? Her heart twisted. Deep down, she'd suspected how he felt about her, but she hadn't pursued it. First, she was too broken, mad with pain inflicted by Artan, and then Jael arrived. If he hadn't, she might've eventually invited Einar into her bed instead of letting him sleep beneath it. He'd done terrible things before being shipped to Perdition . . . *But so have we all.*

With grief eating a hole in her heart, she closed his eyes with bloody fingertips. "I'll miss you, big man."

Then she pushed to her feet in a silent rage. *The Great Bear will die for this.*

◀ 40 ▶

Never Dead to Us

This is my fault.

The room was awash in blood, bodies everywhere. Long before his palace days, he had worked in a slaughterhouse, butchering meat when he was scarcely big enough to hold the tools. That place had been clean and orderly in comparison to this. There had been more of a sense of respect for life and for the value of the animals being processed for consumption.

This . . . this is monstrous.

Though he had willingly signed the deal that landed him here, for the first time, hate swelled in him—for his fellow man, for the people who had put him here. For a few seconds, he even hated the queen of Tarnus, for whom he had given up everything. *She's the rightful ruler,* he told himself. *And though it took fifteen turns to finish that game, it ended as it always must—with her on the throne and me in exile.*

They always need someone to blame.

Staring at the body of the man who had been the closest thing Tam had to a friend in this hellhole, pain swelled in his skull until his temples felt like they might burst. If he'd listened to Jael when he'd pressed them to leave, he might have reached Einar before it was too late. Instead, he'd gone against all experience, chosen mercy instead of expedience. *And look where it got me.*

Though open battle wasn't his forte, he could've stabbed multiple enemies in the back before they noticed him, enough to turn the tide. *Jael would've been fine. He said he would be, but I didn't believe him. I thought he was lying, choosing an honorable death, and Dred would've been furious if we left him to die alone. I thought he was the sacrifice to the cause. Not Einar.* Tam dropped to his knees.

"You can't blame yourself," Dred murmured. "I'm doing that."

His face felt too frozen to smile. "Do we have time to take care of him?"

She nodded. "Doesn't matter. We won't leave him here."

Words of gratitude got stuck in his throat. "I'm sorry we didn't get here sooner."

"I'll ask why you didn't later."

Dred doesn't know about the electrified floor or how long it took Jael to recover. More reason he should've disregarded her orders to stay; she'd given them without a full understanding of the situation. When circumstances changed, he ought to have adapted his mission parameters. *Yet the first battle was hard fought, more than I expected. I didn't know it was so urgent or that our presence would've made a difference.* Queensland was spread thin, taking losses it couldn't afford. It was an awful realization, but the way Tam felt, he'd chosen the new fish over Einar, like a life for a life was required to pass this point. He didn't realize he'd said it aloud until Dred touched his shoulder.

"*What* did you say?" All the blood drained out of her face. Confused, Tam repeated his thought, and Dred shivered. "That was the last reading Wills did for me. He said, 'Victory requires a life for a life, my queen.'"

If Einar's death ensures the Great Bear's defeat, I think he's glad, wherever he is.

A Queenslander overheard her and shouted it for the rest.

"That means we're guaranteed to triumph. The madman said so, and Einar's given his life to make it so."

Tam didn't know if foretellings worked like that, but it seemed to be improving morale. As the rest gathered close, his humble posture drew attention from other Queenslanders, probably damaging his reputation for having ice in his veins, too, but he couldn't lock it down. A few men patted his shoulder as he knelt beside his friend. There were no calculations to reduce the loss, only the immutable truth that Einar had died beneath Dred's blade, a mercy killing. Tam glanced up, studying her face. She was pale but composed, green eyes dry and determined; her resolve bolstered his own.

Dred offered him a hand, and Tam took it. She pulled him to his feet while the rest of the men shuffled among the dead. Grigor's men were larger than the Queenslanders, so it was easy to tell enemy from fallen comrade.

An inmate whose name Tam didn't recall offered his hand, and said, "He went out well."

Another added, "Yeah. Never figured the big man would die before me."

"He was a good mate. Remember the time—"

Tam listened as they shared stories, mostly about wild risks Einar had taken when he was drinking. He'd loved to brawl, and he never backed down from a challenge. Part of him knew they didn't have time to reminisce, not here, not now. Yet it felt like disrespect to his friend's memory to stop them. So he said nothing when the men continued, paying homage in their way.

"I thought Einar'd be the one to take out the Great Bear," somebody said.

Dred squared her shoulders. "He died saving me. I'll never forget that."

"Hell of a place to become a hero," Jael muttered.

Tam glanced over at the new fish; his skin was pink and new, some spots still raddled with burned tissue. The men hadn't noticed the damage yet, but they would soon. It was difficult not to take note when scars vanished before the naked eye. He had no idea what kind of creature Jael was, but he definitely wasn't human. The electrified floor had been an unwelcome surprise, one for which Jael could compensate. He suspected that was why Dred had assigned the man to the team—in case something unexpected occurred.

But why didn't she tell me?

"What happened?" Tam asked eventually.

She paced, the trinkets in her braids clicking a mournful tune. "He took on too many. I couldn't reach him."

Tam curled his hands into fists. "We owe him absolute victory."

The Queenslanders shouted their agreement.

JAEL waited for Dred to acknowledge him. He figured she and Tam had a right to some privacy; they had lost a friend. When she turned his way, he glimpsed a question in her eyes, *Where were you?* Guilt swamped him, and he bit back the vilest curse. If he'd recovered faster, he might've saved Einar. Jael didn't relish draining his veins again—and in truth, he wasn't sure he had enough blood left to do the job. But still, he would've tried.

And killed yourself in the process. There's a reason it took you so long to recover from those burns. You're not at full strength.

"We'll come back for the dead," she said to the Queenslanders when Jael didn't speak.

He couldn't.

The other men chorused, "Yes, my queen."

He touched her on the shoulder. "A private word? If you can spare the time."

"Of course." She followed him, stepping over corpses along the way. Dred seemed to take a closer look at him when she stopped. The scars were red, some purple, where the burns had been worst. "Are you all right? What happened? Tam said it would be a straightforward run, just some wires to unplug."

"This is my fault," the spymaster said from behind them. "When I scouted the site, the ungrounded wires weren't touching the floor. Given the altered conditions, it would've been impossible to turn the lights off if Jael hadn't been willing to suffer the most grievous injuries. After, he told me to go, but I chose to stay. I wasn't sure he'd recover, and . . ."

Oh, Mother Mary of Anabolic Grace. You didn't want me to die alone.

While Jael reeled at that realization, Dred touched Tam lightly on the shoulder. "You were following my orders. I'll take the weight for Einar's death."

"No," the smaller man began, but Dred shook her head. "This is mine. And I'll carry it."

This is friendship. How strange that I'd understand it for the first time in here.

Heartsore, Jael watched the Queenslanders rolling the Great Bear's fallen men, stealing their trinkets and treasures. He felt odd and awful, unfamiliar emotions coursing though him. It was one of those things, where events conflated in the worst possible way, but Jael felt sure that if he'd been fighting with the big man, he'd be standing here alive and smiling, that huge axe slung over his shoulder.

Tam inclined his head, his expression inscrutable. For his part, Jael saw the huge, swamping sorrow in the other man's dark eyes. The other man crossed the room and sat down beside Einar, keeping vigil. Once they were alone, or relatively speaking, Dred put a hand on his arm. He tensed at the contact since his skin was still raw.

Apparently she felt the flinch and drew back. "I wish you'd stopped when you saw how dangerous it was. I would've accepted that the goal had become untenable. Please know, I'd never assume you're willing to suffer for Queensland's sake."

"Queensland can go sit on a spike," he said quietly. "But for you, I'd do a whole lot worse. I'm sorry I wasn't here—"

"It's not your fault. I couldn't get to him, either. They backed him into a corner . . . so many of them, too." She slammed a palm against the wall; and he could tell she wanted to scream or rage, but the Dread Queen couldn't. In public, she was all regal composure, limned in icy wrath.

"They did it on purpose, I'm sure. Probably had orders from Grigor. It's no secret that Einar was your man."

One of them, anyway.

"He was all warrior," she said softly. "I told the men I'd come back for the dead, but I can't leave him here. What if Silence's people—" She broke off, likely unable to articulate the grotesqueries that awaited him in Entropy.

Jael beckoned. "Let's take care of him. The men can hold this room long enough for us to find the nearest chute."

Tam glanced up when they crossed the dark room, regret etched on his countenance as if with knives. "Hubris. I thought I knew everything, saw everything. Could weigh all the factors and make the best decisions."

"Nobody fits that profile," Dred said. "Pick somebody to take charge for a few."

Tam stood. "Martine, you're in command while we're gone. We'll be back shortly."

"And if reinforcements show up while you're gone?" the woman asked.

"Queenslanders?" Dred prompted.

"We kill the bastards for Einar!"

Jael watched as Dred strode over to Silence. "I must offer my lieutenant honor before we press on. You'd do the same for your Speaker."

The gray-haired hag signed.

Skullface interpreted, "Death respects ritual. It is well with us."

Then Dred said to Jael, "I know you can take him, but we should do it together."

A sigh escaped the spymaster, likely at the prospect of such a permanent farewell. It wouldn't be much of a service, but the fallen giant would get more than a shove; somebody would say a few words at least. Together, they hoisted the big man and carried him out of the hall. Dred's mining helmet gave off little illumination, but enough to keep Jael from tripping over his own feet.

The three of them walked quietly in proper funereal procession, according to Tam's directions. A few minutes later, they turned down the hallway with the chute at the end. He hurt physically as he lifted his share of Einar's weight—and not because his skin was still tender. Though he hadn't known the man long, he'd miss him.

I wonder if I have the right to say he was a friend.

Men didn't hang such emotional labels on things, generally. There were drinking buddies and people you trusted not to punch you in the face, those who might not sell you out at the first offer. Einar, well, he hadn't known him well enough to draw those lines. Jael wished he had.

"You were strong and fierce," Dred said softly, "and you never once let me down."

I could do worse for a eulogy.

"You were like a brother to me," Tam added. "We came in on the supply ship together. Joined up with Artan together, not knowing what to expect or what he was like. You won his approval with your fists, your refusal to back down, and with that giant axe. And more often than not, you kept him from killing me when I didn't know when to hold my peace."

Feeling like an interloper, Jael murmured, "You'll be missed, big man." A fragment of a quote knocked at the back of his brain, so he offered that, too: "'Our dead are never dead to us, until we have forgotten them.'"

Dred gave a jerky, approving nod. There were no tears as they lifted him and sent his body down. He waited to see if he could hear the fallen giant hit bottom, but only silence came back, bleak and unknowable as the grave. Then Dred set out with no further commentary; and Tam fell in behind her, his steps small and meek, a man weighed down by his humanity and capacity to err. But if he thought choosing mercy, choosing not to let Jael die alone, was a bad thing, then Jael would argue with him on that point. As she strode toward the hall, Jael watched Dred construct the Dread Queen's armor, scale by scale.

By the time they arrived, she was magnificent in her determination. "We have not come this far, only to let the final prey elude us. The Great Bear's hiding somewhere in this territory. Divide into scouting parties, each eight strong. Find him." Queensland forces howled in anticipation, but she held up a hand to quiet them. "Do not engage. Grigor belongs to me, and I'll have his blood in recompense before the day's done."

The Skullface watched Silence's response to the queen's words, then pronounced, "Your loss is greater than ours. We approve your blood vow." Death's Handmaiden etched a final symbol in the air, spoken by her painted mouthpiece. "So must it be."

◄ 41 ►

Death's Dominion

Dred appointed Tam and Jael to lead other squads. It was a risky maneuver, dividing up her men, but Grigor had a lot of space to hide. Maybe he thought if he vacated his throne room and went to ground, she'd forget about his alliance with the now-dead Priest, ignore his offensive against Queensland.

Not bloody likely.

If it hadn't been personal, with Einar's loss it became so. Dred wouldn't rest until she took the Great Bear's life. And she suspected Jael felt the same. Certainly Tam did. The spymaster was taking it hard, though she didn't know for certain that it would've mattered if he'd brought Martine to the battle sooner and left Jael alone in the bowels of the ship. She liked the man better now because he'd finally shown a hint of human kindness.

"I'll take the low ground. Tam, search the upper levels. Jael, see if he's hiding in his quarters nearby."

Orders given, she took Martine in her group, along with six others. On the surface, this was less a glorious final battle than a manhunt. But it wasn't surprising, given the nature of her foe. There was no point in seeking honor here; expecting treachery was the best way to keep your guts inside.

"We need to backtrack a bit," she said to Martine. "Shaft access isn't technically part of his territory, but he has some lower levels."

The other woman nodded. "Let's find this bastard and kill him. My feet hurt."

It was such a prosaic complaint that she smiled. "Mine, too. And everything else."

"You're not half-bad when you pull that stick out of your ass." The men laughed. Tam might've advised her to admonish Martine for the familiarity, but she let it slide.

"I need it to keep me upright. Come on."

Her team combed the whole lower level and found only a handful of terrified deserters. Dred played to her squad, letting them choose thumbs-up or thumbs-down on each man's survival. *Damn,* she thought, after the last body fell. *They're a bloodthirsty lot.* That wasn't exactly a secret, however.

When she met up with Tam, he shook his head. "Nothing on the upper tiers, either."

She swore. "Then let's hope Jael found something. If he didn't, we might have to scour the entire ship for Grigor."

And there were so many nooks and crannies, so many places where a desperate man might hide. He could've taken it into his head to conscript reinforcements in Shantytown. They were waiting in the ravaged throne room when Jael returned. He was down a man, and by the bloody state of his clothing, he'd found something.

"Report," she demanded.

"I located him. The men we killed here don't approach the numbers he's got guarding him. Grigor's holed up in the engineering department, lots of gadgets to turn into traps. We nipped at the first wave of defenders, but there were too many. We have to hit him en masse."

She nodded, then called for the Speaker. "Did you hear?"

"I did, my queen. Death stands ready."

Silence's people hadn't helped with the search, but now

that it was time to fight, they clambered quietly to their feet. Their empty eyes were unnerving, but she needed the bodies and blades. With a gesture, she told Jael he should lead the way. The trek carried them past the rooms Grigor's men squatted in, no dormitories in this part of the ship.

"There's a long hallway," Jael said. "At the end, we come to a choke point. There are at least forty men guarding it, and they won't go down easy. They're a little drunk, a bit dehydrated, a lot desperate, and completely devoted to the Great Bear."

If anything, his warning only riled the Queenslanders up further. The men snarled, surging from behind her to charge. She went with a blade, chains wrapped around her arms both for protection and to lend weight to her blows. It was hard to fight under these conditions, between the dark and the press of the crowd. There was no elegance in the mob, only anger and ferocity. She was buffeted from behind, men pushing to break the Great Bear's line.

With her slim knife, she slashed at a soldier, whose face gleamed with hatred in her mining light. "You'll never get to him, bitch! Never."

"I'll dance on your corpse," she answered.

Each centimeter took forever to gain because of the sheer volume of bodies surging in the small space. The Queenslanders wore mining helmets and Silence's people appeared behind the enemy a few seconds before they jammed a blade into the enemy's back. It was all a blur of shadows and flickering lights, skimming off bloodstained walls as they surged closer to the front, where the Great Bear's surviving forces tried to hold the line. Men dropped beneath Dred's boots and sometimes she couldn't tell who was dying.

She stepped over the corpses, then slammed into the wall as one of Grigor's men lunged at her. He was an enormous brute with arms the size of her head. There was no room to swing her chains, hardly room to breathe at all, with her own men pressing from behind, Silence's killers worming toward the front, while the Great Bear's soldiers pushed back. She'd never been in a mob fight like this one, where she might as easily take a random knife from somebody who was supposed to be on her side. Dred lashed out with a tight kick and broke the brute's ankle, but the bodies were slammed so close together in the corridor that there was no room for him to fall. She slashed outward then, gasping for air. Her knife carved some room and she shoved forward, stomping over his bloodstained body. Five centimeters closer to the end of the hallway.

Mary. I'll be trampled if I go down.

Somebody's helmet went flying, light bouncing down toward their goal. For a few seconds, prisoners scrambled for it, looking for an advantage in the melee. Dred took advantage of the confusion to shove forward farther. *Something has to give.*

Just when she thought she couldn't take it a moment longer, Silence broke the standoff. When she appeared at the back of the throng, gray hair swirling, looking like a shade from legend, Grigor's men took a reflexive step back—and that was all they needed. Dred pushed with all her might, and once she had space, she went to work with her blade. Four men wheeled on her, but she didn't let them surround her. She dove and rolled past them and came up to her feet; before they could charge, she unleashed her chains.

All the rage she'd suppressed over Einar's death went into the first lash. The beam from her mining helmet showed her the bloody gash that opened on the enemy's face, but she had too much rage, too much pain, to stop even though he fell back. Her chains twirled until she could hear only them whipping around her, drowning the cries and heavy thumps of bodies dropping around her. With full strength, she slammed the links downward, then wrenched her wrist forward. The man's neck snapped.

Artan taught me that move. He thought it was funny to show me such things, like I was a pet capable of learning a clever trick.

Two more rushed in to fill the breach, but in the half-light, they didn't look so confident anymore. With the choke point breached, they had lost their advantage. She ravaged one with a flurry of strikes to his torso; and when he dropped, she kicked him in the face. The barbs on her boots bit into his skin, so he was screaming in pain when he died of the final cut, a kindness with her knife. She looked up to catch Silence's eye; the other woman smiled. Then the Handmaiden's garrote bit deep into her victim's neck. His struggles slowed, slowed, as his air ran out. With her arms around him, Silence made death look almost like a lover's embrace, and Dred turned away with a shudder.

More Queenslanders surrounded her, driving the enemy away from her. They laid in with shivs and fists, and didn't stop until every last defender was on the ground. Some of them were still alive, just grievously wounded. The Speaker strode over to her, a great carrion bird of a man, and goose bumps formed on the nape of her neck when he loomed before her, the skull paint highlighted by the beam from her helmet.

"Do we have your permission to reap these souls?"

"Give me one to question," she answered. "Take the rest."

Tam and Jael appeared beside her, but the spymaster didn't interfere, as she pulled a soldier to his feet. He was bleeding profusely from multiple stab wounds, and she didn't think he had long. That was fine; she only needed to know two things.

"How many men does Grigor have left in the engineering bay?"

The prisoner spat at her. "I'm not telling you shit."

"Pity. Then I guess I'll have to tend your wounds." Her expression was flat and cold, her eyes full of murder, as she jammed her fingers into the slice that had opened his belly.

He screamed, startling the Queenslanders nearby. A few pushed closer to see how far their queen would go. *Good. Watch this and mark it well.* By the time she curled her fingers, the captive was pleading for mercy. It only took a few seconds to break him. Her hand was wet with blood when she pulled it free.

If not for Tam and Jael holding him, the inmate would've collapsed. "No more than fifty inside, my queen."

"And are there automated defenses?"

"They're broken. Or out of ammo. I'm not sure. Grigor was trying to fix them, but I don't think he got it done before the water dried up, and the power went out."

"What about Peacemakers?" If Priest had one, the Great Bear might, too.

"We never had one. And Grigor thinks it's a coward's solution anyway. He prefers to kill his enemies personally." The last word devolved into a moan as they let him fall.

"That's all I needed to know." She stepped back and gave Jael permission with a nod.

He cut the man's throat neatly, but with none of the distressing pleasure or intimacy she'd witnessed from Silence. The other woman took so much pleasure in death that it was practically sexual. Grim and nauseated, Dred wiped her palm on her trousers, then beckoned to the rest of the Queenslanders. Tam was quiet, letting her do all the talking, all the planning. She suspected his confidence had been shaken by how badly he'd miscalculated earlier.

"One more push, lads. Do you have it in you?"

"All the way, my queen, until the Korolévstvo is yours!"

"Ours," she corrected with a look at Silence.

Death stared back from the woman's impenetrable eyes. In the faint light, she could almost see the smoky arm curled around Silence's shoulders, a bony hand cupping her shoulder. Dred shivered and shook herself. *You're just tired. Been too long since you slept. And you're letting imagination get the best of you.*

Then she went on, "For every cut they delivered to our man, Einar, let's give them ten. For every wound we've taken, every insult offered, we strike them down a hundred times over. Are you with me, men?"

"Yes, my queen!" they answered as one.

"There's nowhere he can hide," Jael growled. "I promise you that. That bastard will pay for what happened to Einar."

She swept her arm forward in a commanding motion. "Well said. Let's end this."

◄ 42 ►

The Great Bear

It was like stepping back into the Dark Ages. With the power still out, the Great Bear had resorted to torches; oily rags wrapped metal shards and sent a wreath of smelly smoke into the air ducts. Jael had fought as a merc on a few planets nearly this primitive; those weren't fond memories. *Wonder if the antifire system's still working.* Apparently not, as the ship took no measures to extinguish the flames burning in the room. He listened, counting heartbeats.

"There are forty-seven men just past these doors," Jael warned Dred.

She slapped a palm against her thigh. "Grigor better be among them."

Dred broke away from the pack and strode toward the entry to the engineering bay. She was two meters away when it blew off the hinges, showering her in shrapnel. His world shrunk to the sight of her body on the floor, and before anyone else could even take a step, he was there beside her, checking her over.

"How bad's the damage?"

"My ribs hurt," she managed. "Son of a bitch. I didn't ask that asshole about traps."

"Can you stand?"

"I have to." The set to her jaw told him she didn't care if getting up killed her or crippled her for life. He'd never known a woman so impressively stubborn. He braced and pulled her up, moving so the others couldn't see her flinch as she found her footing. Jael didn't let go until she gave a quick nod.

Without looking back, she stormed through the gaping doors, a small army at her back. Jael sprinted after her, grateful his speed let him catch up, then pass. He could probably see better in the flickering torchlight, too, despite the smoky miasma and the mechanical smells, like spilled oil and more acrid scents. This was where all the work on the ship used to take place, but now it was just an empty shell, full of metal scrap and piles of broken machinery.

"Show yourself!" Dred shouted. "Or is the Great Bear afraid of a woman?"

"I fear no one!" a deep voice thundered in reply—the sound came from above, echoing in the rafters.

Jael spun, trying to figure out where the forty-seven men were hiding. There might be others, but they had already broken and fled, not a factor in the final confrontation. *There.* They stood to the back of the chamber, along the far wall. He imagined Grigor had some spectacle in mind, where his men rushed in an unbreakable wall, overwhelming the enemy, but tactics like that only worked in vids, especially with such an undisciplined fighting force.

A man scaled down from the upper level on a set of pulleys and chains. At last Jael got his first glimpse of the Great Bear. He stood two and a quarter meters tall, with arms and shoulders that made Einar look small. His leather armor looked as if it might be human skin and was stained with grease, food, and darker smears, likely blood. Wild brown hair stood upright on his head, defying gravity in a bush so wild that small mammals could live in it. His beard grew nearly up to his eyes and far down his neck, so he seemed more animal than man.

"Finally you face me," he roared, "after all your coward's tricks. You knew you couldn't defeat me in open combat."

Dred leveled her coldest look on him, one that impressed even Jael. "You must've felt the same way, weakling, or you wouldn't have allied with Priest against me. The Great Bear, brought low by two females?" She gestured at Silence, who flashed her yellow teeth in a terrifying smile while she created terrible patterns with her garrote, wrapping it around and around her fingers until they showed purple.

Skullface intoned, "We come for your soul, Grigor of the Korolévstvo. Death knows no mercy, only judgment. The scales *will* balance."

At those ominous words, Jael heard a stirring from the soldiers at the back of the room. Heartbeats increased, and terror sweat spiked. *They're that frightened of Silence?* Her ghastly air might be enough to send them all screaming into the dark.

A Queenslander muttered "Enough chatter. Let's gut 'em all and go home."

Grigor's surviving soldiers reacted even more to that; actual whispers reached his ears. *We can't win. They outnumber us now. Do you see, Death's come for us all.* The Great Bear appeared to hear none of this as he drew his weapon.

"To me, men!"

But apparently they feared his retaliation more than oblivion because they shuffled forward, knives drawn. These men had a taut look, a little unsteady; they'd been drinking liquor instead of water for the past few days, but with some men, it imbued them with greater ferocity and false courage. He reckoned it would still be a battle, but they had the advantage; Jael was calculating probable casualties when Dred held up a hand.

"There's no need. You want my territory? Come and take it. I challenge you before these witnesses, winner take all. Unless you're a craven bastard, you'll take up the gauntlet."

What the hell. She's injured. Why's she doing this? We can win.

Given the size of her opponent and how much she'd already suffered, Jael wouldn't put credits on her to win this. The watchful crowd rumbled as if in agreement with his judgment. The Great Bear's men relaxed a bit, pulses slowing now that they had an option that didn't end in total annihilation. But Grigor's hairy face broke into a smile, revealing black and broken teeth.

"I accept. Your pride will be the death of you." He brought up his weapon, a primitive bardiche that could be mistaken for a scythe.

One hit from that thing would cleave her in two. Jael wanted to volunteer to fight in her place, but she'd repudiated him once before. So though it required sinking his teeth into his tongue, he held his silence as she said, "Build a ring."

The Queenslanders leapt to do her bidding; and soon, they piled enough metal to form a barricade to prevent anyone from interfering with the fight. Dred stepped into the center, head high, as if she couldn't hear the whispered speculation. And maybe she couldn't—best that way—occasionally when he fought, everything got still and quiet, so he could focus completely on his foe. But he had advanced senses for that, their pulse giving cues, their sweat, even muscle tics telegraphed their movements, so he could be there before they executed the planned strike.

In a cocky move, Grigor vaulted the stacked metal panels, then spun in the circle as if inviting applause. His men cheered, then he whirled to face Dred, faster than a man his size should move. She stood her ground with chains lashing hand to hand. The bay got quiet, just the sounds of her clanking and Grigor's footsteps as he rushed her. She dodged his charge and landed a strike, but the pain only enraged him. He let out an awful roar and went at her again. This time she wasn't quite fast enough and the bardiche sliced into her thigh. Tam muttered beside him, low imprecations that ended with the Great Bear choking on his own vomit.

Damn you, Dred.

She danced back, but her gait was off, and everyone in the room likely thought she was done for. And Jael was the only one who knew the severity of the damage to her ribs. *She can't take much more.* Incredibly, she was smiling. She slammed her chains toward the Great Bear, twirling them around his weapon, then she hauled with all her might. On another man, the move might've yanked the huge blade away from him, but instead, Grigor used his haft as a lever to haul the Dread Queen to him to drop the finishing blow. As the bardiche sank toward her skull, a slim knife stabbed upward through Grigor's chin, all the way into his brain. The giant staggered back—and the audience sucked in a collective, disbelieving breath. That was when Jael realized she'd dropped the chains a few seconds before; and when Grigor thought he was spinning her helplessly toward him, in fact, that dance of death was Dred's, and the measure ended with the clever spike of her hidden blade, the one she kept in her boot.

You didn't need to be stronger. Or better. Because you're smarter. Oh, well-played, love. Even I doubted that you had a plan. Shouldn't have. I'll know better now.

The Great Bear frothed at the mouth, blood pouring out, as he tried to remove the knife. It was madness that the beast wasn't already dead. *Also says something about how much he uses his brain.* Dred snagged her chains and slashed Grigor's feet out from under him, then she put out an imperious hand.

"Tam! Einar's axe. Now."

In a single, sweeping stroke, she chopped through the Great Bear's neck—just as she had with Priest—and for a few seconds, the silence was absolute.

43

Complete Submission

Dred fought the urge to drop to her knees. She had never been so exhausted; it felt like days since she'd slept. *Might have been for all I know.* Instead, she lashed her chains, giving the impression she could take on the rest of the Great Bear's army. Grigor's hairy head tumbled to a stop at her feet. All around her, the men fell silent.

Then the first dropped to his knees. Others followed one by one, prostrate before her. She wanted to tell them not to bow, but it was an affectation Grigor had required from his soldiers, and she couldn't afford to show a flicker of weakness in this moment. Gradually, she slowed the chains and wrapped them around her forearms. She didn't look around for Jael; she could feel him behind her, a low hum of connectivity. That was a disturbing and unexpected development—one she'd deal with later. For now, she had two empires to carve up.

"You have three choices," she called out. "Serve me, serve Silence, or embrace death."

Options two and three were essentially the same, and by their gaunt, weary faces and hopeless eyes, Grigor's soldiers knew as much. One lifted his head to speak for the others. "We are your men."

The others agreed with hesitant nods. Between the Great Bear's mad confidence and his overweening ambition, they hadn't expected to lose. *Now you're at the Dread Queen's mercy.* Fortunately for them, she needed bodies to replace those lost in the conflict. Since she recruited the best of the worst, her population had never been among the highest. Yet at this point, she couldn't afford to be choosy, and these men should be grateful for their lives.

She studied the new recruits, then said, "Row by row, deliver your weapons to Tam, all shivs, blades, clubs, everything. You won't be armed for the first turn. Until then, expect to take on the shit jobs and earn my favor."

They did as she demanded with a flattering alacrity. Tam stared at the growing pile before him. She kept her feet until they finished, then she turned to Martine, standing behind and to her left. "Can you supervise them in getting this place set to rights? It looks as if a truck drove through here."

"You know I can," she answered, looking pleased with the responsibility. "Leave a few men with me in case anyone gets truculent."

"Certainly." She signaled ten Queenslanders to stay for backup.

She summoned her remaining strength to stride from the hall, past the sentries. It was a measure of her exhaustion that she left all the details to subordinates, but all the fighting, Einar's death, and the final duel with Grigor had taken its toll. All her instincts told Dred she was a few paces from collapse, and she couldn't let anyone see it.

How far am I from Queensland?

Counting steps, she had to take frequent breaks. The wounds on her back, on her thigh, on her shoulder, burned like fire. Just when she thought she couldn't go farther, Jael caught up to her. He had the good judgment not to speak; he merely put an arm around her and helped her the rest of the way. They cheered Dred and Jael at the checkpoints, but she didn't stop to chat or give information. Tam would be along presently to do that, anyway.

My quarters. Finally.

Dred reeled against the wall as the door swished open for her. With Jael's help, she stumbled inside. Her fingers were clumsy as she peeled the chains off her arms; she lacked the endurance to manage her boots. She fell into the nearest chair more than made the decision to sit down, then she leaned her head back.

"You should let me clean your wounds," he said.

"I can't move," she admitted. "If you've been waiting for a chance to strike, this is it."

"The men won't follow me." Jael came toward her and knelt, not in obeisance, but to roll the thin leather of her boot downward.

The slice was long but not deep, lateral across her thigh. It burned, but it wasn't bleeding; during the long battle, the cut had clotted and sealed. She stared down at pale skin and the red scab, unable to believe her eyes. It hadn't been long enough for the slash to be pink and puffy, or for red rays to be crawling up her leg. If she died of a putrid wound after surviving so much, that was incontrovertible proof that the universe had a sense of humor.

"Is that normal?"

Dred rubbed her eyes, confused. *The wound shouldn't look like this.*

"For me, the healing is." He touched the streaks. "This definitely isn't."

"I thought the effects from your blood were temporary," she said, puzzled.

"So did I. But I gave you an awful lot of it. We'll be parsecs away from Perdition by the time I regenerate it all."

She laughed. "Still singing that tune? You should've given it up as hopeless by now."

"I don't accept that. We've been a little busy of late, but I'll get around to it. I'm not dying in here, and neither are you."

"You seem so sure. Sometimes certainty can sound an awful lot like madness."

"Then run amok with me."

"Why not? I've tried everything else." She offered a crooked smile, mouth pulled sideways by the pain lancing through her as he took hold of her leg.

"This will hurt," he warned.

"Don't go soft on me. You've been so admirably implacable up 'til now."

"As you wish, love." He handed her a strip of leather. "You know what to do."

Dred closed her eyes, biting down on the skin as he sliced her thigh. Pressure and pain followed, then the most white-hot agony imaginable as he cleaned it. More pressure as he worked the poison out of the wound. Teeth clenched, she panted around the leather, sweat beading on her brow, and by the time he finished, she was fighting the urge to vomit.

"It doesn't need stitches if you keep it covered. Let me see your ribs."

She didn't have the strength to help or to fight him as he raised her shirt. "How bad?"

"A couple of them might be fractured. Let me . . ." He leaned in, touching her gently, but she wasn't sure what the point was, until he said, "Yes, broken."

"You could hear the difference?" Dred opened her eyes, gazing down at him.

"I'm a handy freak to have around."

"Stop it. Anyone who thinks less of you because of how you came to be, well"—she donned her most ferocious expression—"I guess I have to kill them."

"For me?" He seemed . . . astonished.

Which was strange. He'd seen how she treated her most trusted men. Jael had earned his place among them. He'd proven himself and he'd faced near impossible odds at her side.

"For you," she agreed. "You're my champion, but if you need me to fight for you, I will. I *am* the Dread Queen, after all. You say kill, I kill."

A shudder worked through him, then he swallowed hard. For a few seconds, he lost his mocking edge, the keep-away charm—and sheer intensity shone from his blue eyes. His gaze held hers as he twined his hands in her braids. When he kissed her, there were no questions asked, only the same mad certainty he brought to their proposed escape. He didn't draw her close, yet the kiss was so sweet and fierce that she didn't care if he did, no matter how it hurt.

Pleasure and pain, sides of the same coin. Jael ran graceful palms upward to cup her hips. She wished he'd touch her more. "So I say I'll kill for you . . . and *that's* what you can't resist?"

"I'm a violent man," he said lightly. "Look, love, you've got me aching for you."

Dred took that as an invitation to verify, so she closed her eyes. The field of snow had thawed, giving way to sparks of red and gold, shimmers of purple around the edges. He wasn't lying; right now, he only wanted sex. There was no sorrow, no cold. Just desire.

"You want it bad," she said.

"You've no idea. But I'm not sharing. I want my own night."

She arched a brow. "Excuse me?"

"You heard me."

"Let me guess. Ike told you that I never sleep without Tam and . . . Einar." But the big man was gone, so he wouldn't be a factor, going forward. Her chest tightened, grief and pleasure twisted up into a Gordian knot.

He paused, as if trying to recall what the old man had said. "That sounds right."

"But did he ever mention sex?" Dred sighed, knowing how Ike loved screwing with new fish. In a place like Perdition, the little things got you through.

"I don't think so."

"It was for my protection, after the coup. Artan had a few loyal men, and they were afraid somebody might come after me. I got used to having them in here." She shrugged, not having cared until now what anyone thought about the arrangement.

"So the Dread Queen's without a man in her bed? They must all be neutered."

"I wasn't in the mood," she said. "I had a lot on my mind."

"And now?"

"I have broken ribs and a slashed thigh. What do you think?"

He stroked her knee, her hip, her shoulder. "I can be gentle."

"That's the last thing I want. Swap seats with me?"

For once, he didn't argue or offer a clever retort. If he had, she might've changed her mind. She *wanted*, but there were ghosts and echoes, demons in her head; it was different the last time because he'd caught her fresh from sleep, defenses down. He only helped her to her feet and sank back. As she unlaced her pants, she said, "Get ready."

"I've been ready since the first time I saw you." And his fingers shook as he unfastened.

There were no pretty words or preliminaries. Her leg burned when she sank down on him, and it wasn't smooth. She was too tense to be fully engaged, but he sensed it and kissed her, his mouth clever and hot, hands working down her hips. She found a rhythm, and by the sound he made into her mouth, it felt good. His hands cupped, tightened, dragging her down harder. The movement jolted her ribs, sending a sharp wave of agony through her, and she went taut.

"Dear Mary," he whispered into her mouth. "Tell me you like it, or I might just die."

"I thought you couldn't," she taunted softly.

"Little deaths, all the time, every second I'm alive."

"But some deaths are good ones."

He gasped in answer, head thrown back, and his obvious pleasure did what touch couldn't when she was wide-awake. She lost herself in him, sensation blazing through her in whorls of amber light. Some ached; some glowed; and she melted into him, kissing deep into his mouth as he arched, as she bowed.

Afterward, his arms came around her. "I hope you still respect me."

Before, she might've offered a cutting comment in reply, maybe about how she never had. Instead, Dred kissed him on the brow. "Absolutely. Bind up my ribs?"

"You'll make me feel guilty for taking advantage of a wounded woman."

"Who's on top of whom?" she asked with an arch of a brow.

"You make a good point. Get off me, love, unless you want to go again."

44

The Sound of Silence

"Not just now, I think. There's work to do." Her response might've been painful for someone else, but Jael took it as reassurance.

Though he wouldn't call what they had a relationship, he trusted Dred. Since the moment he'd stepped off the prison transport, she'd proven that she wouldn't turn on him, wouldn't offer him up for *any* payout, and she'd fought for his life like it mattered. And now, he felt the same. That was further than anyone had gotten with him in fifty turns.

"Damn," he said, feigning disappointment. "And here I could sleep for a week."

"You can sleep when you're dead."

"Promises, promises." Despite his lazy words, the black core at the bottom of him had gone; he no longer courted death like the one woman who would never love him.

She didn't reply, then the san-shower kicked in. Jael lounged on her bunk waiting for his turn. No point in getting dressed since she didn't seem to mind sharing her facilities with him. There were perks to being part of the Dread Queen's inner circle. He contemplated the revelation that she wasn't shagging Tam and vowed to get even with Ike. *Rotten old bastard.* It was Jael's fault, however, for not asking pointed questions, but he'd been unwilling to display that much interest. *Maybe if you cared less about the look of the thing, you'd have been in her bed sooner.* Once she finished cleaning up, he took his turn, then they joined the spymaster in the main hall.

"Are you two ready?" Tam asked.

Dred nodded. "Let's go finalize our arrangement with Silence."

Ike caught up to her in a rush, then handed her something. She exchanged a long look with the old man, who simply nodded. Then she stuck whatever it was into a pocket. Jael tried to ask her what that was about, but she shook her head. He took that to mean there was no time to talk, but he didn't take it personally.

The mood was much different than the first time they'd made this trek—and they didn't use the ducts. They marched boldly through what had been Grigor's territory. Silence's people paused in their cleaning and watched them pass, but they didn't take action. Jael wondered if the alliance would hold, now that the initial agreement had been executed.

The Speaker met them at the border and escorted them to Silence personally. Silence's man wasn't much for conversation, so it was a quiet walk. Dred fell in beside Jael naturally, Tam walked ahead with the emissary, and Jael took quiet pride in her choice. His title as champion felt more vital, now that she'd chosen him on a personal level, too.

Death's Handmaiden was waiting on her grisly throne when they arrived, and Dred strode toward her, one queen to another. In that moment, Jael knew a flicker of unexpected pride, as if he had the right to take credit for anything the princess in chains did. He mocked himself quietly as he folded his arms.

Silence signed rapidly to Skullface, then he turned to interpret. "The truce between us is formally at an end. This is the last time you will be welcome in Death's territory.

Should you or any of your people trespass, you will be ushered into His kingdom."

That's plain enough. No more alliance.

"I understand." Dred didn't bow, but she did dip her head.

Then she led the way back as they'd come. Nobody spoke because of Skullface dogging their heels, but once they passed the final checkpoint, and the Speaker retreated, Jael glanced at Tam to take the spymaster's temperature on their current situation. The alliance with Silence had bolstered their defenses, no question, but now Queensland stood alone again.

To his surprise, Tam looked visibly worried. "She cut us loose too fast with no further demands, no references to her desire to get her hands on you." He jerked his head at Jael.

Yeah, something's off.

Dred increased her pace until she was nearly running. "We need to get back ASAP."

"My thoughts exactly," Tam agreed.

Though he wasn't sure what they were worried about, Jael caught the mood. "Wouldn't it have been easier to attack on her home ground? There were only three of us against her collective might."

Tam nodded. "Easier, yes. But remember, she has a sense of rightness and ritual."

Dammit.

"And she's devious," Dred added grimly.

She glanced over her shoulder as she ran. Jael didn't think whatever Silence had planned would hit before they got back. Maybe he was giving Silence too much credit, but after the way she'd planned and executed the assault on Abaddon, then the decimation of Grigor's forces, he could almost believe she served Death itself with ruthless efficiency and raw cunning. He didn't know what experience Dred had in planning actual campaigns; from what he'd seen, she took a lot of advice from Tam, but the man wasn't infallible, and he couldn't see in all directions. He'd proven that—at great cost. Jael listened for the distant whisper of careful feet, scented for a stray smell that reeked of death, but nothing drew his notice.

"They're not following," he said.

That didn't mean he thought they should slow down. Instead, Dred quickened the pace further; she didn't stop until they sprinted past the first checkpoint into Queensland. The four sentries on duty gaped when they blew past, but nobody wasted time on explanations.

A guard called after them, "Trouble incoming?"

"Maybe," she yelled back. "Stay sharp, keep the turrets hot."

"Already done."

In the hall, Jael skimmed the scene with a measuring eye. Nothing appeared out of the ordinary. The men who weren't patrolling, as usual, were playing cards, drinking, gambling, or talking shit. At the far end, two men exchanged a flurry of blows, but since nobody was bleeding, it couldn't be a serious altercation. *Probably just sparring to keep in shape.* Dred's territory was big enough now that a man could actually go for a run for exercise if he wanted.

Provided she can hold the new ground.

And that was the question that had everyone on edge. Things weren't nearly settled yet. Patrols hadn't been established in a routine fashion, and defenses hadn't dug in. *If I intended to attack, it would be now, while we're settling in.* Beside him, Dred vibrated with tension. Part of him wanted to take her hand, but the rest of him scorned the gesture. She would give him that icy look if he tried—and for good reason. The Dread Queen required comfort from no man.

"Everything seems to be in order," Tam finally said.

"Find Ike and Wills," she answered, ignoring the comment.

Tam nodded and jogged off. The two men were likely to be together, working on some invention. Wills had been especially feverish since they got a share of Grigor's gear, which was more generous than Silence had to be, and he insisted on Ike's participation. The old man pretended to loathe the extra work, but Jael could tell he liked being appreciated.

We all want to be more than we seem.

Just as he was starting to relax, Tam returned with Ike; and the old man had a huge knot on the back of his head, slowly seeping blood. A cold chill washed through him as he hurried toward them with Dred close behind.

"What happened?" she demanded.

"I was working when somebody jumped me. Lucky I didn't end up with a knife in my ribs, I guess."

"They got Wills?" Tam asked.

Ike lifted a shoulder, his face pained. "I haven't seen him since I woke up."

Dred curled her hand into a fist. "How long ago was that?"

"Not sure," the old man said helplessly.

Tam wanted to know, "Were there any signs of a struggle? Blood trail to follow?"

Ike shook his head as if to clear it. "Come with me and we'll check. I wasn't thinking straight when Tam found me."

It wasn't like the spymaster to overlook such a critical detail. Then he answered, "I didn't see one. If they took Wills unharmed, then there's no injury to follow. The man's a genius but not much of a fighter."

Jael silently agreed. When they had made the run to the salvage bay together, anytime there looked to be direct combat, Wills had run and hid. He couldn't imagine the man fighting a party of armed men even on his home ground. He'd predict a swift surrender, followed by as much crazy talk as the man could generate, likely in hope of being judged worthless and incompetent and discarded by a gullible enemy.

"We don't have much time," she said. "Split up. Check the ducts, the side corridors, all checkpoints. Tam, if that's too much ground to cover, recruit some help."

The spymaster nodded.

"They're not in the main hallway. I would've heard them." Jael didn't explain to the others, but Dred nodded.

"Get moving, people!"

Jael headed for the east corridor and he jogged all the way down to the checkpoint. Everything seemed quiet; the men were at their posts, unharmed, and they looked as alert as Queenslanders on duty ever did. One of them frowned at him.

"Did she send you to check up on us?"

He ignored the question. "Have you seen or heard anything unusual today?"

The man shook his head. "Not so far. Why? Is there something I should know?"

"Just be wary."

"I always am." That was pure cockiness, but Jael didn't have the time to chew the guard out properly.

Instead, he backtracked, checking other corridors, other guard posts. Everything was quiet until he heard a shout from Dred. Jael doubted anyone else could've heard it, but he pinpointed her location and ran, his heart pounding in his throat. Before he realized he'd done it, he had two blades in hand, sharp and lovely ones that he'd pried out of Grigor's dead hands.

That's surely a good omen.

When he found her, Dred was facing down a hunting party on her own; there had to be a hundred men here. Somehow, they'd gotten past all the checkpoints without alerting the guards or setting off any turrets. At that moment, Silence's mute slayers were poised to attack—and Wills stood at the head of the column. The man wasn't injured that Jael could see, nor did the enemy beside him hold a weapon to his throat. Unease itched at the back of his head.

The throne room in Entropy was too empty. Silence had already deployed her troops.

"That's why she didn't attack us earlier," he realized aloud. "To satisfy the letter of the law, she needed us to dissolve the alliance first—"

"And she already had a way in," Dred finished in a tight voice. Her green eyes glittered as Silence's men glanced at Wills for their orders. The soothsayer doubtless felt confident—only two of them against a hundred and one killers.

Even I can't beat those odds.

Dred demanded, "Why? I thought you were loyal."

"I *am*. But examine my history," Wills said coldly. "Ultimately, whom do I serve?"

Jael remembered the story Einar had told him about how Wills blew up an office building with five hundred people inside because it was going to happen anyway. He ran recent events in his head, and every move Wills had made led to more dead bodies, more corpses for the pile. A shudder worked through him.

"Death. You serve Death."

"You're a clever one despite such a pretty face. I have *always* belonged to Silence. Who do you think suggested the alliance to Tam?" Wills laughed then; and it was a raucous, awful sound, like the call of carrion-eating birds.

Dred squared her shoulders, but Jael glimpsed the despair in her eyes. "You set up all our defenses. You know all the codes."

"That was a master stroke, I must admit. I'm a little surprised you didn't work it out sooner, my queen." His tone became ironic. "I did warn you with my reading, some time ago."

"You said, 'He'll cost you everything.' I thought you were talking about Jael, then we found Niles . . ." That was the man who'd tried to assassinate Dred.

That made us think we'd rooted out the last traitor.

Jael wondered if his former crewmates had felt like this when he betrayed them. *Not fond of the flip side of this. Now come on, love. We've come too far. Produce the trick up your sleeve.*

Yet she only stood, clicking something in her palm, a nervous gesture. That was when he got worried. "Run. I'll hold them off."

She flashed him a cryptic look, smiled, and shook her head.

◀ 45 ▶

All Fall Down

Dred wished she could explain since Jael looked like he was ready to fight a hundred men to give her a chance to get away. She had the remote Ike had given her earlier, just in case Silence betrayed them; it made sense to have a backup plan . . . and to expect the worst. Despite the cold tightness in her chest, she wanted to smile. *I called for help sixty seconds ago.* Hopefully, the cavalry would arrive before Wills lost patience. Then she heard it.

Finally.

The thumping tread and whir of gears behind them made Silence's death squad whirl as one. Wills froze, apparently recognizing the unit without even looking. The feeling that came over her was a cross between jubilation and triumph. Somehow, she schooled her expression to one more suitable to the Dread Queen.

Dred gestured with a mocking smile. "Don't you want to turn around?"

She enjoyed the moment more than she had any in a long time. Satisfaction exploded like a heavy missile, filling her head with color. She savored the despair that flickered across his face when Wills realized he was beaten. Then he snarled, both hands clenching into fists.

"How?" he demanded.

"Peacemaker unit 1574 reporting to distress call. Please state your emergency."

She ignored his question and spoke the first command. "Hostiles in Queensland territory. Neutralize threat immediately."

The Peacemaker unit intoned, "Acknowledged. Noncombatants please stand clear."

Wills tried to run as the rounds tore through Silence's killers like so much meat. Their skills lay in slitting throats, the silent blade in the back. Against such a mechanical juggernaut, they were all but helpless. Gamely, they charged the machine, but without Einar's raw strength—now lost forever—and Jael's resilience, they had no hope of damaging it. Her former bone-reader crawled underneath a corpse and didn't move, though if he thought escape from *her* judgment would be so simple, he was entirely mistaken. Her stomach turned at the raw carnage, but as the Dread Queen, she couldn't look away. Drawn by the din, her men gathered at her back, cheering the bot on. She couldn't waver, couldn't show how weary she was, or how disgusted with the waste, with death itself.

It's endless. It won't stop as long as I live.

She watched until the last of Silence's assassination squad dropped. Then she gestured Jael forward. "Pull him out of the pile."

Wills looked like a ghoul when her champion hauled him out from under the bodies, so covered in blood that the whites of his eyes gleamed in comparison. His whole bearing radiated thwarted malice. As Jael dragged him forward, he spat at Dred's feet. She backhanded him with calm brutality, earning a cheer from the assembled audience at her back.

"You've succeeded in weakening Silence considerably. Thank you for that."

A cunning light entered the bone-reader's eyes. "Yes, that was all part of my plan. I knew you would foresee—"

"Kill him," she told Jael.

"With pleasure." Most likely in honor of Einar's execution style, he snapped the traitor's neck and dumped him in the pile with the rest, then kicked it for good measure.

Queenslanders howled in vicious approval behind her. Maybe she should have made the execution more entertaining, but she lacked the heart to make an arena spectacle out of a traitor's death. That was more attention than Wills deserved. *That bastard thought he was so clever, taunting me with false readings with real warnings layered in.* She thought about kicking his corpse but decided it went against the ice-cold persona Tam had created for her, one that felt more real than her own soul at this point.

I would give so much, she thought, *just to feel the sun again.* But it took a special kind of insanity—Jael's brand— to believe that was possible. Dred was pretty sure she would die here.

"Now get a cleaning crew going. We have a lot of material to be recycled." Speaking of the corpses so impersonally didn't help with the stink or the knowledge that she'd nurtured a viper in her bosom. For a bit longer, she watched Tam organize the men, then she turned to the Peacemaker, now standing like a giant armored paperweight.

"Resume patrol pattern Alpha Zeta 24."

"Acknowledged."

The only way we'll be safe is if we kill everyone who doesn't swear to Queensland. Though the idea of being the supreme leader of Perdition held no appeal, Dred understood that she'd changed things irrevocably. With Grigor and Priest's territories annexed and Silence weakened so drastically, it wouldn't be long before Mungo responded. *Nature abhors a vacuum.* With any luck, he'd go after Death's Handmaiden, smelling an easy kill. There was no doubt Queensland was as strong as it had ever been, though she wasn't sure if she could count on the men she'd acquired from Grigor.

Yet another worry.

Pausing in his cleanup efforts, the spymaster studied her

face for a few seconds, then he shouted, "Make way for the Dread Queen!"

Like the sea in the old stories, the bodies shifted aside. Men stared at her with awe and admiration as she passed; a few patted her daringly on the shoulders in congratulations. To their minds, she had laid waste to their enemies in a way nobody could've ever predicted. Dred offered regal nods to one and all, conscious of the weight of her chains on her arms, slowing each step with the way they twined around her boots. She'd never been more aware of the burden of her role, more desperate to shake the pretense for a private hour. Her whole body ached.

The past weeks had taken their toll. She made it all the way to her quarters before a hand snagged her shoulder, spinning her around. There was only one man who dared touch her with such confident demand. Unsurprised, she faced Jael, whose beauty was only heightened when he was in a passion. Sex rendered him exquisite, but wrath suited him just as well.

By the fierce press of his fingers, he was even angrier than she'd suspected he might be. "How did you know? You never let on."

"Not here," she said. "Inside."

A muscle twitched in his jaw, but he followed her and waited until she locked the door. She didn't want anybody overhearing the conversation for a number of reasons, not least of which was, if people believed Jael was important to her, they would find reasons to hurt him. The next traitor could also use a personal attachment as leverage; she didn't kid herself that Wills would be the last. In this place, allegiances shifted like the tide on water planets.

He said quietly, "Back there, I was ready to die so you could get away. More fool me, right, love?"

Though the man pretended he had a black hole where his heart should be, he still had feelings. *And I hurt them.* In a place like this, it was an odd thing to consider. *But maybe it's all that keeps me from becoming just like Grigor, Silence, and the rest.* Dred walked a thin line, verging on losing herself to the role she played, until everything inside froze, and only the Dread Queen remained.

"That was . . ." Words failed her, for it had been brave, stupid, and gallant, everything she'd learned never to expect in Perdition. "Heroic. Unexpected. Don't think I'm ungrateful, but . . . I had the situation in hand."

He pushed out a furious sigh, raking a hand through his messy hair. That dishevelment rendered him even more appealing. "Obviously. How long have you known?"

She shook her head, disclaiming the credit. "Ike warned me yesterday. Working with Wills so closely, Ike noticed him adding extra kill switches and shutdown codes."

The light dawned quickly in Jael's blue eyes, attesting to his keen wit. "Which he'd only do if he wanted Queensland vulnerable."

"Exactly. Ike has been rebuilding the Peacemaker from parts we brought back from various raids. I asked him not to demonstrate it . . . or boast when he got it up and running. At the time, I was just being cautious, but—"

"Why didn't you tell *me*?" he cut in.

That was a tougher question. "Nobody knew but Ike and me. It seemed safer that way."

Yet he only seemed taken aback. "You didn't even tell Tam and Einar?"

"For the right offer, they might've turned. Not Einar, of course. Not now." *And not ever,* she suspected. "And word has a way of getting out, the more people are in on a secret. I didn't want the men talking, spreading gossip. Once Ike warned me, I knew I was right to keep it quiet. It's best not to show how many shots you've yet to fire."

Jael nodded. "And Wills was clever about hearing things he wasn't supposed to, pretending to be mad."

More than once, Queenslanders talked about private matters in front of Wills while he was ranting. They'd imagined he was deaf, dumb, and blind, then he'd reported what he overheard back to Dred. *Probably, he carried word to Silence, too.* Of all the men who had served Artan before she took over, Dred never would've guessed that Wills had the spine to be a spy. *He always seemed so frightened . . .*

"He gave us just enough information to keep my faith in him," she said quietly. "But never enough for me to guess the truth."

"And he didn't seem to be lying when you read him?"

"He was always the same, a wash of confusion and fear. Did you want to interrogate me further?" she asked dryly.

Some of his outrage had faded, replaced with an enigmatic smile. "I'm good for now."

"Glad to hear it." Without waiting for a reply, she stripped out of her chains and set them on the floor. There, they coiled like a pile of mechanical snakes.

She rolled her shoulders and sank down on her bunk, wishing she saw light at the end of this endless tunnel. But in the bleak future, Dred glimpsed only more killing, more mayhem, until she made a fatal mistake, or until her own people decided they'd had enough and wanted a new legend to admire. Then somebody would poison her food or jam a shiv in her spine.

I ought to be happy now, or at least relieved. But there's no room for hope in here. The nightmare never ends.

"Now there's a dire look," Jael observed.

Tentative, he perched beside her, as if wondering whether he ought to leave. For the first time since she'd taken on this role, she didn't prefer to spend her private time alone, however. Dred set a hand on his thigh; and he responded by winding an arm around her shoulders. It felt, oddly, more intimate than sex. That was a physiological reaction, but this? Something else. She was afraid to name it for fear the exotic emotion would hiss and vanish in the light.

"I'm just reflecting on how pointless it all is."

To her astonishment, he leaned in and kissed her. She'd touched him, worked him to a quick conclusion, had sleepy sex with him, then, much later, ridden him until they were both satisfactorily exhausted. But this was a different sort of kiss, less about lips and tongues and more about everything else. There was a raw honesty to it, an emotional hunger that he hadn't offered before. Her stony heart cracked.

He broke away and leaned his brow against hers. "The thing is, love, you're looking at this wrong. You're imagining a life in here."

"What else is there?" she asked.

Jael brushed another kiss over the corner of her lips. "The whole universe."

It was so ridiculous, she laughed. "Let me know when the shuttle arrives. I could do with a vacation."

He cupped her face in his hands, eyes as serious as she'd ever seen them. "Nothing's impossible, remember? Look at everything we've accomplished. The only question is, how bad do you want it?"

He's not kidding. The idea of leaving Perdition finally took root, and madly, she believed he might work out a way, achieve the impossible. There were so many obstacles, but they'd deposed two petty dictators, found supplies deemed lost forever, and set up turrets at all the checkpoints. From a struggling territory, in a few short weeks Queensland had become a territory to be reckoned with. Her breath hauled hard in her lungs, both from his proximity and the winged creature fighting for freedom in her chest. *Hope.*

"Bad," she whispered. "More than anything."

He flashed the cocky smile that once annoyed her, but this time, she saw the solemn promise behind it. "Then we're out of here. Just give me some time to work it out."

From *USA Today* Bestselling Author
ANN AGUIRRE

The Sirantha Jax Series

GRIMSPACE

WANDERLUST

DOUBLEBLIND

KILLBOX

AFTERMATH

ENDGAME

Praise for the Sirantha Jax series

annaguirre.com
facebook.com/Ann.Aguirre
facebook.com/AceRocBooks
penguin.com

M1208AS1112

"Aguirre has a gift for creating strong characters who
keep her readers coming back for more."
—*Publishers Weekly*

From *USA Today* bestselling author
ANN AGUIRRE

The Corine Solomon Series

Corine Solomon is a handler. When she touches an
object, she instantly knows its history and sometimes
its future. Using her ability, she can find the missing,
which is why people never stop trying to find her....

Blue Diablo
Hell Fire
Shady Lady
Devil's Punch
Agave Kiss

"Outstanding and delicious."
—#1 *New York Times* bestselling author Patricia Briggs

"An authentic Southwestern-flavored feast,
filled with magic, revenge, and romance."
—*New York Times* bestselling author Rachel Caine

annaguirre.com • facebook.com/Ann.Aguirre
facebook.com/AceRocBooks • penguin.com

M1160G0712